BEYOND ASIMIOS

BOOK 1 OF THE BEYOND ASIMIOS SERIES

MARTIN FOSSUM

Three
Lights
Press

Copyright © 2021 by Martin Fossum
ISBN 978-1-7361423-0-1
Ebook 978-1-7361423-1-8

Published by Three Lights Press
Minneapolis, Minnesota
www.martinfossum.com

Cover art by Curtis Square-Briggs.
Book design by Annie Pearson.

First Edition
1 2 3 4 5 6 7 8 9 10

For Mike Marshall

BEYOND ASIMIOS

1 – Asimios Station

DR. AVERY GRAF, Asimios Station Manager, glanced at the messages on his VI, the visual interface displayed on the retina of his left eye. He cringed. This was a conversation he didn't want to have.

ASST-01:37:22 Wolfe–ESCOM> Dr. Graf, I want to say…

ASST-01:42:52 Wolfe–ESCOM> Dr. Graf, please…

ASST-01:43:27 Wolfe–ESCOM> Graf, I know you've been…

ASST-01:58:01 Wolfe–ESCOM> Avery, I feel that you…

ASST-02:02:36 Wolfe–ESCOM> Avery, goddammit…

ASST-02:12:12 Wolfe–ESCOM>…

Graf took a slug from his flask of whiskey. With a swipe of his hand, he cleared his embedded VI display. He gazed out his cabin window for the last time, looking beyond the station's solar-array field to the horizon, where a black carpet strewn with stars stretched up into the night sky. In that tapestry of stars, half a million kilometers away, lay the invisible wormhole that connected Asimios's star system with Earth's.

Now ESCOM, the company that funded Asimios's terraforming project, had sent the *Rosario* and the frigate *Guemes* for final-stage evacuation, with orders to destroy the station after evacuation was complete.

But Graf had made himself a promise: He'd be dead before he ever left Asimios.

After another slug of whiskey, he screwed on the cap and tucked the flask into his coat's inside pocket. He smoothed what hair remained on his bald head and raked a few chubby fingers through the salt-and-pepper beard that swept the top of his barrel chest.

Time to face the music.

Outside his cabin, Graf ran into an ESCOM demolition crew, all dressed in tight-fitting combat synthskins with holstered sidearms. They pushed carts stacked with metal boxes labeled DANGER—EXPLOSIVES in bold, red text. A pair of hovering sentry bots, basketball-sized security droids of burnished gray plasteel, floated like tethered balloons behind the crew, their single roaming eyes scanning for threats. When the crew turned a corner, Graf removed his flask and extracted another dose. It burned like lava on its way down his throat.

He growled and spat on the floor.

From around the corner, one of the sentry bots reappeared. It had disengaged from its demo crew. It glided up to Graf.

"For Christ's sake," Graf shouted. "Get away from me!"

The bot followed Graf as he stomped through the station. Through the central marketplace and the eerily silent children's school. Through the theater district, where the lights were darkened. Past the entrance to the bio-dome wing. Through the gangways and silent recreation halls and empty conference rooms with tables and chairs in various states of disarray.

Graf marched past more ESCOM demo crews, who ignored him as they bustled here and there. Groups of higher-level ESCOM officials huddled in conversation. Graf drew up his VI.

Dr. Graf, you have 12 unopened packets.

At the edge of the mess hall, Graf felt a tug at his arm. He found himself face to face with ESCOM Security Officer, Preston Wolfe.

"Avery." Wolfe looked up at the taller Dr. Graf. "What a surprise. You've been ignoring me, haven't you? I wish this didn't have to be so difficult."

People lingering in the mess stopped what they were doing to watch the confrontation.

Wolfe had short hair with a trendy wave to his platinum bangs, dull green eyes, plus small scar above the left corner of his mouth, giving it a sanctimonious slant. He was in his mid-sixties, like Graf, or perhaps slightly older, depending on one's interpretation of life-extension therapies. Wolfe said, "I need you in my office for a final debrief in one hour. Understood?"

Graf planted his hand on Wolfe's shoulder.

"My dear Preston," he said, making sure Wolfe got a whiff of the whiskey coursing through his blood, "I shall meet for debriefing, but I must take care of certain things first, things to be included in my report!" Graf jabbed an index finger skyward for emphasis. "I've done everything in my power to accommodate you and your band of corporate wastrels. The last thing I need right now, in my final moments on the planet I call home, is to stand here and be berated by a company hoodlum. Yes, I mean you! Now, call off your metallic pitbull..."

Graf swatted at the sentry bot hovering behind him. The bot swooped up and activated a blue defense shield while a nasty-looking aperture opened from its side. He thrust a finger at the bot.

"And get off my back!"

He shoved past Wolfe and made for the door across the mess. The sentry bot dropped its defense shield and fell away.

"You've been drinking, Avery!" Wolfe shouted.

"Yes, I have."

"One hour. In my office!"

"I'll be there in two!"

When Graf entered the atrium, he encountered another ESCOM demo crew huddling at one section of the tall, cylindrical room. Graf pulled out his flask and took a slug. He wiped his sleeve across his mouth, returned the flask's cap, and slipped the bottle back into his pocket. Then he passed through the airlock that led to one of the ground transport hangars. Two doors down the hall, he tapped an entry icon to open the door. He stepped inside, and the door slid shut.

The room smelled of solder, acetylene, and penetrating oil. It looked like a gargantuan machine had imploded, its innards scattered in disarray. Nuts, bolts, and strands of wire, solenoids, hydraulic rams, and relays littered the floor and pushed out from under heaps of titanium-fiber atmosphere tiles, plasteel wheels, and strips of crawler fuselage. A small barrel was stuffed with droid heads, the sundry eyes frozen open as if in morbid surprise. Graf kicked a head that lay on the floor. It made a few oblique rotations before wedging itself under a slab of polymer matting.

A snap and buzz of activity sounded, and a light quivered in the back of the room.

"Paul, you in here?" Graf called. He squeezed through a narrow canyon cut through the debris until he emerged in a clearing, where Paul Ness was pressed against a work bench.

Paul was lanky, with disheveled curly hair. His big nose close to a magnifying display, he was working on some kind of module or motherboard. Several robotic arms scissored at blurring speed beneath the magnifying display. Micro-welds sparked and spat.

"Hello, Avery," Ness said, eyes glued to his work.

"Hi, Paul. Am I interrupting?"

The robotic arms came to a stop, and Ness looked up. His eyes were pools of black that had been tinted for protection. With a few blinks they rinsed back to their natural green.

"Of course not." Ness stroked his thick mustache, which was discolored by chemicals and metallic dust. "I've been expecting you. Take off your coat."

That request struck Graf as odd. "I'll keep this on, if you don't mind." He dug into his pocket to remove the flask.

"I insist. Miranda will take your coat. Miranda!" Ness called over his shoulder. "Miranda, could you please take Dr. Graf's coat?"

A droid appeared from out of the shadows. Slightly taller than Graf, she had the logarithmic feature placement of a standard marketing-agency face, with requisite turquoise eyes and widely spaced cheekbones, which Graf found both attractive and repulsive. Her bare body was a frame of dull plasteel and glistening blue and green alloycord, so she seemed unfinished, an incomplete project. She tilted her pretty face just so and extended her arm. Graf was drawn to the grace of that motion, the economy of that simple action. Her biomechanics represented a higher design.

Speechless, Graf surrendered his coat.

"Thank you, Dr. Graf." Miranda's voice had the sonorous timbre of a cello, from the higher strings. She retreated into the shadows.

"Jesus, Paul. I've never seen a droid like that."

"She's the product of many years of work."

Graf unscrewed the cap on his flask and took a slug, then offered Ness a taste.

Ness waved it off.

"Why didn't you show her to me before now?"

"One must often shelter a child," Ness said. "Keep her away from corrupting influences."

"Is she going home with you?" Graf said. "Can they fit her on the *Rosario*?"

"No. She won't be going."

Graf grated his teeth. Another loss. One more example of hard work thrown to the trash heap. He ran his hand over his smooth head. Moistness formed in his eyes. Must be the booze.

He said, "Don't suppose you want to tell me anything before this shit hole turns into a puddle of plasteel? Anything sentimental or heartfelt?"

Ness coughed, more like a wheezing sneeze, and returned to his magnified display.

"Well," Graf went on, "it's been a pleasure. I can say that much."

Ness turned to Graf and frowned.

"What are you working on?" Graf asked as his eyes travelled over the table. Ness's fingers moved swiftly over an intricate circuit board and shuttled among trays of electrical components.

"You know those sentry bots that came here with the ESCOM crews?"

Graf gave a nod, keeping his disdain for ESCOM security bots to himself.

"I'm doing a little exploratory surgery on one of them. Wanted to see what made it tick." Paul smoothed his mustache with his thumb and forefinger.

"Please don't tell me you stole a sentry bot."

"Borrowed it," Paul said. "And I'm a little disappointed in ESCOM's quantum magnetics work. Although they've finally developed a stable gravitational buoyancy system, they're still a long way from where they should be. Mainly pre-wormhole tech here." He waggled a finger at the contents of his work bench. "Should be a decent bot when I'm done with it."

"If they find out, they'll throw you in a meat locker for your trip back to Earth."

Paul grinned. "They won't know. Probably time you got going though, don't you think?"

"Guess you're right. I should be going."

"Miranda!" Ness called.

Miranda stepped back out of the shadows and handed Graf his coat. He felt through the pockets and found a small box. He removed it and nodded to Miranda. She smiled politely, helped him put on his jacket, and retreated again.

"Thank you," Graf said to Ness. "Everything in order, I take it?" He tapped the box a couple of times with his finger through the cloth of his coat.

"Yes," Ness said. "They'd definitely throw me in the meat locker if they learned I made that for you."

"But they'll never know, will they?"

Graf took another slug from his flask and planted it on Ness's desk. "Guess this is it, Paul."

"This is it, I guess," Ness said.

"'Once more unto the breach, dear friend.'" Graf turned to leave. "Do good things, Paul Ness, and remember me."

"Your drink," Ness said. "You're forgetting your drink."

"Do with it what you will. It has served its purpose!"

—

Leaving Ness's office, Graf started for the Asimios Station medical clinic, where he had one more appointment before his final showdown with Wolfe. The ESCOM demo crews were gone from the atrium. They'd left a cordoned-off area with a holo text that warned:

DO NOT ENTER—ALARM WILL SOUND

Graf steered clear and made his way to the infirmary. He punched the entry icon to the clinic door. When it slid open, he stepped inside, where it was cool, bright, and scrubbed clean. The middle of the room held four empty medical chairs and a dormant medical mech assistant, a gangly tower of surgical arms and light booms. Against the far wall was an array of readouts and displays. Dr. Brit Fredriks turned from the displays.

"Come in, Avery." She spoke in lilt, a remnant of her childhood in South Africa, speech that drew out its vowels and softened them before they rested on the ear. "Come, sit here." She crossed to the nearest medic chair and patted it softly with her hand.

"We're on schedule, I assume?" Graf took the small box from his pocket and handed it to her. He hung his coat on the wall near the door.

Dr. Fredriks wore a white medical bodysuit, its badge displaying her First Medical Officer rank. Her charcoal hair, streaked with gray, was done in a ponytail that fell over her shoulder. Under the clinic's lights, her eyes were two bright caramel discs.

She showed Graf to a chair, and he sat.

"You smell like a distillery," she said.

"That was my intention."

"Why don't we get started?" She motioned for Graf to lie back. "You know that only ten years ago this procedure took over two hours, with a success rate of 93 percent. Now it takes sixteen minutes, with a 99.7 percent success rate."

Graf's heart rate increased. His palms grew wet. "Ah, the joys of modern medicine."

Dr. Fredriks directed the mech assistant into place next to the chair. An arm extended from the droid, and a bright lamp blinded Graf. She redirected the beam and moved closer.

"I always like VI procedures. You get to see a living optical nerve. It's rather extraordinary."

"Too much information." Graf spoke through clenched teeth.

Dr. Fredriks leaned into the light. "I'm about to administer a sedative. Lie still."

He felt a sting in his arm, closed his eyes, and waited for departure.

—

Dr. Fredriks's calming voice informed him that she was removing his suture skin. Graf gripped the armrests as she peeled away the bandage. He was bathed in gauzy light and felt an awkward relief to be alive.

"The new VI Paul made for you is installed," Dr. Fredriks said. "The swelling will go down over time. You might experience pain or discomfort for a day or two, but that's the least of your problems, I'm sure."

Graf said, "Yes, I know. Saying goodbye to this place won't be easy."

Dr. Fredriks waved a metal wand over Graf's old VI, which she held in her hand. It looked like a bloody, oversized nerve cell with stringy tendrils at one end.

"I've just looped your bio data," she said. "This old VI will stay with me till the *Rosario* is far away from Asimios. It will be as if you are right there with me. No one will know." She placed the VI in the box Graf had brought with him, and she shut it tight.

She handed Graf a tissue. He blotted tears on his cheek. When he gestured to actuate his new VI, a time stamp appeared with a pair of initialization instructions.

"From what Paul told me, your new VI is a base unit," Dr. Fredriks said. "Standard functions, nothing fancy."

Graf squinted, looking at the fuzzy contours of Dr. Fredriks's face.

"Otherwise, good as new," she said.

Graf stood from the chair, woozy. He struggled to find his balance. "Can you do me a favor, Brit? Can you help me get to my office, er...I mean, Wolfe's office? I'm expected there in about..." He searched for the time stamp again on his VI. "I'm expected there ten minutes ago. Can you help me get there?"

"It'd be an honor," she said.

Dr. Fredriks grasped Graf's arm and helped him put on his coat. Together they started toward the central tower and the main administrative offices.

"Nine years on Asimios," Dr. Fredriks said as she guided Graf down the hall. "A good part of one's life. It's hard to see it come to an end."

"Eleven, for me, if you include two years of project planning."

"There's one thing I won't miss about Asimios, though," she said.

"Don't tell me. The food."

"I won't miss the food, that's true. The thing I'll miss least of all—and this stays between you and me—is being the Band-Aid and aspirin distributor. Playing mother figure to a bunch of cry-babies, present company excluded."

"You were the best of Band-Aid appliers," Graf said. "And yes, there's been plenty of cry-babies here, myself included. But 'we shed our tears for thee,' knowing full well we'd be taken good care of."

"What did happen to Preston, by the way?" Dr. Fredriks asked. "I used to like him, but he seems to have changed."

"He flew too close to the sun," Graf said. "He was always partial to power. It's his mortal flaw."

"But we all aspire to power, more or less."

"More or less," Graf said. "But Preston has always tended toward the *more* end of the spectrum."

"I'll say one thing, Avery."

"Yes?"

"I hold your leadership in high esteem. You've been an exemplary station manager. No one else could have achieved what you've done here."

"Save your praise."

"I will not save my praise for you," Dr. Fredriks said. "I admire your courage. You've handled difficult decisions well. You've won broad respect."

Graf frowned. "I'll tell you a little truth, Brit. It's never about courage. It's about concealing cowardice."

"You had us fooled."

"Other topics, please."

They stopped outside the elevator to Wolfe's office.

"You know," Graf said, "I envy you."

"Oh, and how is that?" Dr. Fredriks said.

"I envy that you will return to Earth. There are two things I'll particularly miss about Earth."

"And they are?"

"Walking outside, through an atmosphere without a pressure skin. Seeing the ocean. I wish I could see an Earth ocean again, in all its polluted and degraded splendor."

Dr. Fredriks pulled affectionately on Graf's arm. "Ah yes, both wonderful things."

They took the elevator to the third floor and were soon in front of Wolfe's office. Two ESCOM guards stood further down the hall, cooling their heels. Dr. Fredriks stood on her toes and kissed him, right on his lips. She hugged him, then let her arms fall away.

"I never could get over Julie," Graf said, daring to say his lost wife's name aloud. "I'm sorry."

"I know."

"That kept getting in our way. I don't know how else to describe it."

"It's okay. I understand." Dr. Fredriks wrapped him in her arms. "I love you, Avery. You will always be in my heart." She let him go, then walked away.

Graf searched his pockets for his flask, but couldn't find it. Julie was the reason he was staying behind, of course. He had buried her remains as she had requested, under a cairn out by the Rift almost two years ago. Along with his commitment to the success of Asimios Station, Julie had been everything to him. To abandon Asimios, and to leave Julie here alone, was something he couldn't bring himself to do.

Graf tugged at his beard, then punched the security icon next to the door of his old office. The door didn't open, so he pounded on it. Finally, the door opened. He took a deep breath and stepped inside.

—

"Hello, Avery." Preston Wolfe sat behind Graf's old desk. "Please, I'll only be a minute."

Seeming to be focused on a stream over his VI, Wolfe leaned back in Graf's old chair, fondling a small totem pole that Graf had left behind on his desk. Wolfe was bare headed and wore his space tacticals, a dull brown-gray body suit with red epaulettes.

Graf dropped into the chair opposite Wolfe and made his eyes into slits.

Wolfe set the totem pole on the desk. "One of our sentry bots has gone missing. Do you know anything about this?"

When prevaricating, Graf habitually ran his fingers through his beard and rolled his eyes. Hence, his fingers combed through his beard; his eyes travelled their arcs. Then Graf leveled his gaze at Wolfe. "Is this important, Preston? Because if not, fuck you."

Wolfe ran his tongue over his teeth. "What happened to your eye, Avery? Did you piss somebody off?"

Graf leaned forward. "Had a run-in with a door. Why didn't you tell us that ESCOM was going to torch the station? Why didn't you consult me, Preston?"

"I learned about it only a few days ago. When I got the news, I was as surprised as you were. I didn't have the heart to tell you. That's the truth." Wolfe stood and rounded the silver asimite slab that was Graf's old desk. "The higher-ups gave the directive. They called it 'Assertive Disengagement.'"

Graf labored to his feet and leaned in close. He was two inches taller than Wolfe, and he took advantage of it.

"You might not be able to do anything about it," Graf said, "but that doesn't make it right. Do you realize the extent of research and work going on here? Do you recognize the human capital this station represents?" He leaned closer. "What people gave, personally and professionally, to make this place an alternative to the hell back on Earth? The dreams and ambitions that made this place possible?"

"Off the record, Avery," Wolfe lowered his voice as if someone might overhear. "ESCOM has a hunch that Excelsior Capital intends to start nosing around here once we pull out. Torching the station is a preventative action."

"For goodness sake," Graf said. "What would they find here, a heap of abandoned terraforming tech? That's what you're worried about?"

"We're taking out the wormhole, too," Wolfe continued.

"What?"

"We have a disruptor onboard the *Guemes*. On our way out, we'll detonate it right in the middle of the wormhole. It's our insurance policy. If that fails, and the wormhole isn't snuffed out by the blast, at least we've left Ex-Cap with nothing."

"You're going to blow up the wormhole?"

"Call it energy reallocation," Wolfe said.

"You're going to destroy one of the most incredible pieces of science since...since Leachian quantum magnetism?"

"It's not about that, Avery," Wolfe said.

"It isn't? Lay it on me, old friend. What is it about?"

"We've had pressure from high up the ladder to seal the wormhole."

Graf threw his hands in the air, feeling beyond helpless.

"Earth may be in danger," Wolfe said.

"Danger? From what?"

Wolfe went back around the desk and sat down. "It's classified. You'll have to trust me."

Graf jutted his chin skyward and rubbed his temples with his thumbs. "Trust you? You must be joking."

"I'm sorry, Avery."

Graf wrung his hands. "We were close to self-sustainability. It was only a matter of time."

"Without an ESCOM supply chain, this station was dead in the water. You know that."

"You're an asshole, Preston."

"I think we're done here. Get your things and prepare your staff for evac in one hour." Wolfe turned away, riffling through his VI. "Goodbye, Avery."

The office door opened. The two ESCOM guards came in.

Graf shook his head, laughing, though nothing was funny. "Why didn't you include me in the discussion, Preston? What a waste. What an incomprehensible waste."

"This meeting is over," Wolfe said. "Guards, remove this gentleman from my office."

The guards started toward Graf, who raised his arms in submission and left of his own accord, only a slight wobble to his step.

–

The further Graf got from Wolfe's office, the more his rage grew. He wanted nothing to do with the turncoat, nor with ESCOM or the authoritarian mandates that oozed from the soulless cult of its ignorant and ill-considered board members.

Graf made his way to the bio-dome, bizarre fantasies clouding his thoughts. Hungry, he became fixed on the idea of dining on tenderloin synthsteak and asparagus, paired with a foamy mug of Asimios ale. He also craved a viewing of *The Last Man on Mars,* Abdel Perkovsky's classic dark comedy about one man's fantasy of staying behind on Mars when everyone had been called back to Earth. Couple that with a bag of potato chips and another glass of ale.

Keep focused, keep focused!

Graf pushed through the bio-dome doors and was met by a wall of hot, sticky air smelling of soil and flowering plants. The clear night and the Asimios half-moon gave enough light to navigate the pathways through the vegetation. The entire bio-dome was alive, of course, with small mammals, plants, and bacterial concentrations. Birds fluttered and flapped when they were disturbed from their slumbers. Small rodents rustled in the brush.

He cut over to the spring that steamed from a volcanic source beneath the station. Its oily surface opened before him, hot to the touch, but not scalding. He felt the ground near the pool and under bushes until he found what he sought: a stashed bag with a pressure skin.

He removed the pressure skin from the bag and gave it a shake. He took off his coat, balled it up, and tossed it aside. Then he stripped to his skivvies and stepped into the pressure skin leggings, tugging the fabric over his thick legs and stout gut, until he had the suit pulled tight over his arms and neck. He pulled the hood over his head and drew down the mask to seal his face.

The suit generated oxygen through recirculation, environmental leaching, and a body-contoured chemical generator that padded the area of the lower back. The generator, if resorted to, could produce two hours of breathable air. Pressurization was achieved through capillary action, and body temperature maintained through metabolic feedback tech. The suit was rated for up to twenty minutes at zero atmospheres and from 90 degrees Celsius down to −100. It was more than enough to keep him safe while he bided his time submerged in this natural hot tub.

To protect against infrared and organic scanners, Graf slipped his ample body into the water, like a seal slipping off a rock into the drink. He held his breath until he had no choice but to trust the suit's closed respiration. He watched through the dome's ceiling for the landers that were to be sent down from the *Rosario*. It was just a matter of lying in wait, lying in this hot bath until the coast was clear.

—

Two hours later, Graf got a visual of the first lander's pulse engines firing. He'd passed his subsurface time by thinking about tenderloin synth-steak, potato chips, and the scene breakdown of Abdel's film, and by dozing intermittently once he became comfortable.

The bio-dome flared blue when each lander lifted from the surface of Asimios. After what seemed like an eternity, Graf saw the blue flash of the final lander's pulse engines as it shot toward its mother ship. That was his cue.

Let's do it!

Graf emerged from the water. He crawled up the side of the spring, then stood on solid ground and pulled back his mask. He made for the path, picking up his pace. His goal was the maintenance hangar where he could commandeer a crawler and try to outrun the detonations. Klaxon horns sounded. The station throbbed in pulses of red and black warning lights. Graf stumbled forward, navigating the twisting, turning halls by memory as he careened ahead.

He jogged through the empty marketplace, through the theater district, and past the silent school. He wasn't sure when the charges would go off. Could be anytime. But he knew the risks in the deadly game he was playing.

At the central atrium, he froze. A sentry bot hovered in the middle of the large room, its ruby topographic-laser sweeping the area for movement. Graf's heart raced, and the BIOmeter on his VI touched red. He spied the open door on the opposite side of the room. He grabbed a discarded chair, testing its weight, then abandoned it to grab a small fire extinguisher from the wall. When he threw the extinguisher across the atrium floor, the sentry bot lit up its blue defense shield and painted the extinguisher with its laser.

Graf made a run for it. Twenty years ago, it might have been a sprint, but now it was an awkward waddle. When the laser brushed his shoulder, Graf was across the atrium and through the door. He landed hard on his side, but not before he hit the close button. The door slid shut behind him. Breathing heavily, his hip howling in pain, Graf stood, then lumbered down the hall, past Paul's lab and toward the hangar's door.

He slapped the entry icon.

The airlock didn't budge.

Graf heard heavy thumping through the ground that shook the floors and walls.

Detonations.

Was this as far as he'd get?

He pounded on the icon, then threw his weight against the airlock. No luck. The door at the other end of the hallway was now melting into a pool of glowing goo. The sentry bot emerged through a cloud of smoke and gas. Graf closed his eyes. He prayed it would be quick. Then, instead of dark oblivion and death, Graf's VI was lit like a Christmas tree. Paul Ness's face appeared in a lower corner.

"Hello, Avery," Ness said. "I hope this finds you well. If you're receiving this message, then you've encountered my bot, who's called Jeg. Not to worry. He's on your side. But I'm sure you're in a hurry, so let us dispense with formalities."

Graf's eyes grow moist with tears.

A datasquirt appeared.

Dr. Graf, my name is Jeg, and I will be assisting you. The door to the hangar behind you is closed. You will not be able to unlock it. Please find a safe distance behind me. I will open it.

Graf moved to the other end of the hall. Then the bot directed a pulse round at the hangar door. An explosion left Graf's ears feeling as if they'd been jammed with cotton.

"Thanks for the warning!" Graf said out loud, though it was unlikely that a bot understood sarcasm.

When the smoke cleared, the door was gone. The hangar pulsed red on the other side. Jeg sent another squirt.

Dr. Graf, please follow me. Miranda has selected a crawler and is waiting for you.

"Lead the way!" Graf called out.

The security bot surged forward. Graf stepped over the threshold and stumbled into the hangar. Alarms sounded, low-frequency sirens howled with misery and loneliness. From the middle of the large room, a six-wheeled crawler lurched into motion, stopping in front of Graf and Jeg. The vehicle's utility door slid open.

Please enter the crawler, Dr. Graf.

"You got it!"

Graf stepped into the crawler. Jeg was right behind him.

"It's good to see you, Dr. Graf," Miranda said out loud. She was sitting in the driver's seat, her hands grasping the control sticks. The door slid shut, and the crawler lurched into gear. "Please sit up front next to me, Dr. Graf. And please fasten your body restraints."

Graf complied. He sat in the seat next to Miranda and reached behind him to draw down the restraining belts. "It's good to see you, Miranda. I don't know how much time we have, but we sure are giving ESCOM a run for its money."

The hangar's outside door began to open, dust swirling as it rose. Miranda pointed the crawler in its direction. There was a flash and the crawler shook. The hangar door stopped suddenly mid-motion.

"Hold on, Dr. Graf." Miranda opened the throttle and accelerated the crawler.

Graf drove his fingers into his armrests.

With a jolt, the crawler shot under the disabled door, taking with it plasteel and carbon cord. When he opened his eyes, Graf saw they'd cleared the hangar and were barreling eastward along Asimios Station's main road. The station was ablaze, and a wall of conflagration moved swiftly in their direction.

"If we can reach Mount Washington, we might find shelter from the concussions," Miranda said in her cello-calm voice.

She steered the crawler off-road, toward the squat hill that served as a station reference point for anyone leaving the northeast hangar. Graf glanced out the window. The wall of flame was closing in.

They were hit as they approached the hill. The crawler lifted off the ground and turned upside down, landing on its roof. Screeching and grinding, the crawler slid and spun for a hundred meters, as it scraped the ground until it struck an obstacle and came to a stop.

Plumes of black smoke swirled and streamed. Fire flickered and licked. Graf hung in his seat, blood rushing to his injured head. He could barely see.

He made out her form, though.

She came for him at the end.

Graf smiled with relief as he reached to take Julie's hand. Then he drew a sharp breath. Such a cold hand. She had such a cold hand.

Δ

PRESTON WOLFE STOOD beside Captain Puck on the *Rosario's* bridge. Along with five operations officers and a helmsperson, they observed the displays as explosions raked over Asimios Station. The demolition concluded in less than ten minutes. A short time later, the cloud dispersed to reveal a black scar where the station once stood.

Satisfied, Wolfe turned his attention to his next objective: disabling the wormhole that connected Earth's star system with Asimios's. After the *Rosario* was in position on Earth's side of the wormhole, the escort frigate *Guemes* would release a disruptor charge in the middle of the portal. Then the *Guemes* would join the *Rosario* a safe distance away and detonate the bomb.

ESCOM physicists had agreed that a massive explosion was the most likely tactic to guarantee the destruction of this type of space aberration. The charge was the astrophysical equivalent to swiping a hand through the whirlpool as the water drained in a tub. Once the disruptor was detonated, no more wormhole. Or so the physicists' theory asserted.

It took an hour to reach the wormhole and another half hour to reach the separation distance of 10,000 kilometers. Once the *Rosario* was in place, Wolfe gave the go-ahead for the *Guemes* to deploy the payload. After the disruptor was deployed, the *Guemes* reached separation distance alongside the *Rosario*.

Wolfe gave the signal to light.

A flash flooded their displays. A few minutes after the blast, com officers on both ships reported no communications with the other side of the wormhole. The link was down. Other scans were run: infrared, radio, quantum, visual light. All came back negative. By all metrics, the wormhole had been decommissioned.

Under Wolfe's orders, the *Rosario* and *Guemes* set course for Phobos, the Martian moon. Then Wolfe called Asimios Station officers to convene in a muster room for a final debrief. Everyone showed up, except for Dr. Graf. When Wolfe checked for Graf's VI signature, the scan put Graf in Dr. Fredrick's quarters.

Wolfe said, "Dr. Fredriks, get him down here. If he's sleeping off a hangover, administer a coherence drug. He's had plenty of time to feel sorry for himself."

"I can't, sir," she said. "It's not possible."

Wolfe rubbed the back of his neck. "What do you mean, 'it's not possible'?"

"Dr. Graf isn't in my quarters. He's not on the ship."

"You're testing my patience. Of course, he's here. Everyone has an active security certificate. Roster shows Avery Graf on this ship."

"Your scans are picking his VI, which is in a suitcase in my quarters."

"Please, Brit, I don't have time for games."

Dr. Fredriks shook her head. "Avery stayed on Asimios."

"Impossible."

Wolfe ordered a search of Dr. Fredriks's quarters. A pair of ESCOM security personnel returned with a small box containing Graf's VI. The tendril-like implant was connected to a power cell and active.

"I'm sorry, Preston," Dr. Fredriks said. "It was his plan all along. He was determined never to leave."

Wolfe had Dr. Fredriks arrested and confined to her quarters. After completing a debriefing of the remaining Asimios staff, Wolfe returned to the bridge to get a systems summary and to confer with Captain Puck on course and timetables.

Avery Graf, you old dog.

Wolfe stared into the bridge's bow display at the blackness of space surrounding the ship.

Sorry it had to end this way.

2 – Zeltstadt 483

MICHAEL CLUTCHED NAVA'S hand, and she, his.

For two hours in the dark, the taxi driver had steered his car through a rainstorm, passing only one or two other cars traveling in the opposite direction. Occasionally, in the rake of the car's headlights, a tree emerged on the side of the road, the wind shaking its remaining leaves, the lightning illuminating its skeletal branches.

After the New Liberation Army (NLA) protests in Hamburg three days ago, word came that Excelsior Capital had put out a Red Notice for organizers of the event, and Nava and Michael were on that list. They had escaped their Hamburg safe house with nothing but forged e-passes and a paycard with a few thousand credits. Because of Nava's medical condition, NLA contacts had directed them to go to Zeltstadt 483, a refugee camp, to find Dr. Jafari, a physician sympathetic to their cause.

Nava had pulled her headscarf back and lowered her veil. Michael caught a glimpse of her face each time lightning lit up the world. Her dark eyes, smoldering with a ferocious intelligence, searched the darkness beyond the car window. Her lips, thin and pensive even in the fullness of her pregnancy, bore the mark of grave concentration, the willingness to speak, and the courage to be heard. A line of boyishly short hair traced her soft ears. Dark bangs floated above her furrowed forehead, as if a painter had taken a large stiff brush but then gave up, leaving a dark messy stroke across the subject's forehead.

Michael loved her right now, probably more than ever. They had been through so much in such a short time, and the fact that she was ready to deliver their child compounded the uncertainties and amplified his emotions for her.

They'd agreed that they wouldn't name the baby. It wasn't something they felt was in their right. They'd agreed to hand over the small thing to Helena, their Swiss friend and NLA contact who'd offered to take the child and give it a good home until Nava and Michael found themselves in a safer situation. How could they attach themselves to this new child right now? They might be imprisoned. They might be killed! No, to hand over this baby into hands that could care for it was the right thing to do.

A row of floodlights cut through the darkness. The driver glanced over his shoulder and nodded to Michael and Nava in the back seat. The driver followed the pylons to a guard post. Two giant enforcer droids stood idle next to the gate, rivulets of water streaming over their faceless and tarnished bodies. They were like giant golems, totems of the oppressor class, extensions of the cruelty and indifference that Excelsior Capital had exerted over Europe.

A guard rapped at the window with the blunt end of a glowlight. A beam of light swept over the back seat. Nava pulled up her headscarf and adjusted her veil. Michael extended his hand to shield her. When the driver lowered the passenger window, the guard emerged from the rain and leaned in. With eyes red as fire, her expression was crooked, disfigured by past injury. She was jacked on rocket or chemstim to stay awake. She pointed her scanner at the databar on the car's dash, and the unit flashed green. She smiled at Michael and Nava. Her teeth were carious. She turned back to the driver and spat on him. She laughed and pulled her head out of the car, drew a hood over her head, and returned to the guardhouse.

The gate was raised, a long inert arm that delineated fate.

"*Shukraan!* Bitch!" the driver cried as he fiercely wiped the spit from his cheek. He pulled the car forward a hundred meters and parked under the floodlights. Michael pushed his paycard at the driver, but the driver pushed it away. He said, "No. It's enough. Out, now."

Stuffing the card into his jacket pocket, Michael pulled his hood over his head and ran around to help Nava. She had the door open when he got there, her feet already on the ground. When they were both free of the car, the driver jammed his foot on the accelerator and the car bolted away, gravel spitting under its tires as sped down the road from which they'd come.

Michael helped Nava toward an entrance next to the tall chain gate. He pounded on the door while attempting to shelter Nava from the rain. A window slid open and a nose protruded. Chubby cheeks. A trimmed gray mustache. "*Was gibst?*" the nose said. "*Was wollen Sie?*" The shadow of a body cut in and out of a rectangle of light.

"*Sprichst du Englisch?*" Michael said. "It was arranged that we could be let in. This is my wife. Please, you must have heard."

"No arrivals scheduled tonight," the man said. "Show papers or send e-stamp to the receiving office. They will check you in the morning." The rectangle slid shut.

"We are here to see Dr. Jafari." Michael pounded the heel of his fist against the steel door.

Nava collapsed, crumpling to the ground.

"Please!" Michael shouted. "Please help, my wife! She is about to give birth!"

He pounded again. The rectangle slipped open again, and the nose and its face peered out at Nava, where he must have seen her condition, even in the poor light.

"Oh, good grief!" the man said. The door opened, and light poured out onto the wet gravel where Nava had fallen. "Bring her inside."

"I need help!" Michael cried. He tried to lift Nava.

The bald man stepped out on the gravel and got an arm under Nava's arm. Together they helped Nava to her feet. Inside, the old man secured the door behind them, then returned to take one of Nava's arms. They helped Nava through another door into a larger, brightly lit room for migrant and refugee intakes, with cordoned lines and stations for screenings and inspections.

The place was empty of people except for a uniformed official who was watching a newsfeed on a big display on one of the empty walls. On the table in front of the official was a backgammon board in the middle of play. When the official saw them, he cut out the feed on his nexpad and stood from a table. He started toward them. The old man shouted in what must have been Arabic. The official, who seemed to be called Rafiq, shouted back.

Nava collapsed again, slipping from under the arms that held her.

"Help me!" Michael called. "She needs something to drink."

"*Warten Sie hier,*" the bald man said. "I come back."

Michael, his arm under Nava's shoulder, attempted to raise her again. The official came over to assist.

"I'm sorry," Nava said. "I need to lie down. I think I'm getting close."

That should have taken all of Michael's attention, but now that he stood in proximity to the official, he was transfixed. The man, who wore a blue shirt with an insignia, was an inch shorter than Michael and had a thicker beard and longer, darker brown hair. Yet Michael felt as if he were staring into a mirror, seeing his doppelgänger in the official's face, from his straight black brow to the mole on his cheek.

How could this official not be affected by this discovery?

It struck Michael just then that he'd applied synthskin patches to foil facial scans. The official could not know he was in the presence of his twin.

Once Nava was resting on a short couch, the official removed a sensor wand from his belt and waved it over Michael and Nava, past their ears in search of any VI signatures, and along their bodies and clothing in search of contraband or weapons. When done, he holstered his sensor wand and pulled two white plasteel bands from a pouch on his belt. He secured these wrist bands, one each, to Michael's and Nava's wrists.

"What do we do now?" Michael said.

"You remain here till morning," the official said in English.

"Are you joking?"

"I could lock you up in a cell. Would you like that?"

Michael lowered himself on the couch next to Nava. She rested her head on his shoulder.

The official went back over to his desk and sat down. He picked up a nexpad from the table, and the newsfeed came up on the wall again. It was a propaganda broadcast, which told everyone everything they were supposed to know about the world. "You can watch this. It's been the same story all day."

The stiff German-speaking announcer was decrying the latest Hamburg riots, declaiming that Ex-Cap would soon find the radical agitators who'd caused the death of two policemen. They showed video of the protest with throngs of people in the streets, then cut to a video of one of the protesters who they said had provoked the crowd. It was a woman, standing on a makeshift platform. She was speaking in English, and when she spoke, she was repeatedly interrupted by cheers and shouts.

The revolution continues with both progress and setbacks. We continue to suffer, but for a higher purpose.

This blood, the blood of our families, will fill the cup of justice and remain a symbol of the reasons why we started this together.

We continue the fight for Mother Earth and Sister Mars.

For freedom. For a halt to endless war.

For open borders, and free education.

For freedom from genetic tyranny.

For transparent democratic governments, and for an end to the totalitarianism of the transnationals.

The serpent has encircled the world and has begun to devour itself. And we stand in eternal solidarity until we have won our rights.

It was Nava on the platform, showing a will and strength that betrayed her right now. The official crossed his arms, studying the two newcomers while the footage of the protest continued. Nava pulled her veil tighter to her face. Then the bald man returned. He had a bottle of water in his hand. Michael took it, unscrewed the cap, and handed it to Nava.

The official turned the volume down on the feed and said something in Arabic.

"No, Rafiq," the bald man said, then he answered in Arabic. Rafiq, the official, looked mildly surprised. He stood and came back over to look at Nava. He stepped back when he saw her swollen belly.

"She is pregnant?" the official said.

"Yes," hissed Nava.

"Impossible," he said. "You can't stay here. Tonight, you go to the doctor. Report to this office tomorrow, or when you can. Good luck."

The official returned to his table, where he sat down and lit a cigarette. He picked up a nexpad again, and started scrolling through other broadcast channels that were projected on the wall.

"I am Sargon," the bald man said, "I know where you can find Dr. Jafari." He helped Michael to get Nava on her feet.

"We sent a message that we were coming," Michael said. "But that was a couple days ago. We were held up."

"Yes, yes," Sargon said. "Always delays. Always a change of plans."

"We do thank you for your help, Sargon," Nava whispered in his ear. She was back to herself for the moment. Her discomfort seemed to have temporarily passed.

"It's not a problem." Sargon pushed open a door that led to the outside. "Welcome to Zeltstadt 483, where dreams come true. If you have any left."

—

It was dark, cold, and raining as Michael helped Nava to step out onto the main street of the refugee camp. A dirt road stretched from the gates at the guard post clear down to the lighted gate at the far end of the camp. Canvas tents rose at each side of the road, structures pitched with wooden ground stakes, their awnings tied tight with ropes. The rain had turned the road surface to a muddy paste, and the cool air carried smells of wet canvas, stale food, and sewage.

"Once you get used to the smell of shit, it's not so bad." Sargon pulled a square of plastic from inside his vest and draped it over his head. "A ten-minute walk, that's all. I hope she can make it."

They followed Sargon along the dimly lit road, taking careful steps but slipping as they went. At one point, Sargon lost his footing. His legs shot out from under him and he fell to the ground. He was up immediately without complaint, wiping his mud-soaked pants with his hand, shaking the dirty sheet of plastic before placing it back over his head. He didn't say a word, just marched on, drenched and covered in mud.

"He's fine," Michael whispered in Nava's ear. "He wasn't hurt."

"It's coming," Nava said. She let out a groan, and Michael braced against her weight.

They turned off the main street into a muddied alley. Sargon led them to a sheltered porch lit by a small lantern that glowed warmly against the dark.

"Hello, hello!" Sargon called. He pulled the canvas door aside and ushered Nava and Michael through to a small entry with rugs laid over the board floor and a thermacone set out for warmth. A statue of a rotund Buddha smiled gently where it sat against a wall, his hand raised with index and pinky straight. Two saffron candles flickered on either side of it.

A woman came through a draped door, a dark shawl wrapped around her head and neck. "Hallo?" she said, her voice low, husky. "*Brauchst du Hilfe?*" She possessed warm brown eyes and a thin, gold nose ring that glinted in the candlelight. The blush on her cheeks must have been applied earlier in the day. Sargon spoke in Arabic. The woman narrowed her eyes, then stepped back and let the cloth door fall into place.

Sargon shrugged. "She's Dr. Jafari's assistant. She's consulting the doctor. It might be a moment."

Michael pointed to a small stool near the door. Nava stumbled as she tried to sit and rest her back against the soft wall, but she caught herself. A moment later the assistant emerged again from the cloth door. "This is she?" the assistant said with a nod in Nava's direction. Sargon nodded. Michael nodded. The assistant approached Nava.

"I am Nava." She looked up at the woman, then dropped her head again.

The assistant placed a hand on Nava's cheek and on the exposed part of Nava's neck. She kneeled and placed her hand on Nava's belly. She stood and said, "Please come with me. There is nothing to worry about. You will be fine. Dr. Jafari will see you now."

The assistant took Nava's hand helped her stand. Michael stepped forward to help, but the assistant prevented him from coming through the door.

"It's okay," the assistant said. "We can take her now. She will be safe."

"Please, Michael," Nava said. "This is right."

"Nava, should I..."

"Please, sir." The assistant glanced back at Michael. "Your work is done for now. Ours begins."

"I love you," Michael called. Nava and the woman disappeared behind the curtain. Something in the assistant's eyes obliterated Michael's anxiety. He felt a sense of release from a tension that had been building for months. He took a breath and surrendered.

"She is in good hands." Sargon took Michael gently by the arm. "You come with me. We aren't far away."

Michael hesitated, but his feet turned to follow Sargon, as if his mind had shut down and his body was making the decisions. They pushed through the canvas flap and went back to the street. The rain had let up. Lightning flickered and thunder sounded, but it was distant. The storm had passed. Drops of runoff struck surfaces, raising a gentle symphony in tones and rattles and thumps. The street was slick, but there was a solemnity to the night.

Δ

NAVA WAS LED to a small room with a comfortable couch. The assistant removed Nava's coat and then motioned for her to sit down on the couch. With some help, she was seated.

"I come right back with water and tea," the assistant said. She hung Nava's coat on a hook and pushed through a door flap opposite from the one they'd come through.

"Thank you," Nava managed.

There was a thermacone in a corner, which kept the place warm. A pair of lamps at the ceiling cast a bright light over the room. Against one wall was a tall, folded cot, and against another stood a white cabinet with a glass door that revealed an assortment of medical equipment, like bandages and bottles of antiseptics and medicines. Beneath the cabinet was a short desk with three metal drawers. A stool was tucked under the desk. Beside the desk, a basket was stacked high with laundered towels and linens.

There was a strange smell to the room: part medical, part wild. Perhaps the woven rug under her feet was producing the earthy smell? There was a large tapestry that hung on one wall: a fortress with a single minaret on the side of a mountain. A river wound its way through a distant plain.

Nava felt a sharp pain in her belly just as the assistant returned with a tray of tea and a couple bottles of water. She poured a glass of tea and handed it to Nava, who sniffed the liquid and looked at the assistant.

"Peppermint!" the assistant said. She pulled back her headscarf and exposed her graying hair. "Don't worry. All the women come here to birth. And the men pace outside, and they kick up dust." She laughed a short laugh. "You will be fine."

Nava craved Michael just then. She needed him. She wondered how he could have so easily abandoned her. In the next moment, she felt relief. It was good to be rid of him. He'd been hovering over her night and day for weeks. She couldn't move without his constant nursing and observation. She was pregnant, and she needed to consider her and the baby's health, but the constant attention had been maddening.

"Drink the tea," said the assistant. "I am Anya."

"Thank you, Anya."

Nava drank. The tea was soothing. The movement in her belly was coming in spasms, the pain increasing in frequency.

"Dr. Jafari will be here in a moment," Anya said. She went to the cloth door again and disappeared through it.

—

If everything proceeded as anticipated, Nava was to be a mother. So strange and fascinating this situation. How happy it would make her own mother, Esther, to know she would soon be a grandmother. But there was much to settle first. So much to get through.

Her father was a different matter.

Nava hadn't spoken with him for close to ten years, and there was scarcely a chance she would soon. He'd abandoned her long ago. He was part of a much larger problem, the problem which she had devoted her life to defeat.

How had they been torn apart?

She'd attended prep school in Seattle, growing up in the company of world elites. She knew what wealth was. She received a lavish twentieth birthday party and spent weeks visiting all the great capitals of the world, dining at five-star restaurants, dancing in the most fashionable clubs. Nava took horsemanship lessons at an Austrian riding club, and she spent a semester studying art in Milan. Her mother showered her with love and affection, her father with money and expectation. She suffered what most children of wealthy parents suffer: a belief that the world was good, that anything was possible, and that the universe revolved around her.

Then one summer everything changed.

She fell in love.

During a semester at Oxford, she'd left her college dinner club one evening to drink in the sunset. Alone, with glass of wine, she made her way along the river. Before long, she encountered an exhausted young man waist-deep in the slow-moving water. He was handsome, with playful eyes. A biologist, he was taking samples of the river bed, and he'd managed to get himself stuck in the muck. He couldn't move, he told her frankly. He needed help.

She debated whether to notify the school porter or simply to leave the poor fellow to his own fate. Instead, she tipped the bottom of her glass to the sky, found a sturdy stick, and extended the limb.

The stick broke, and in she went.

Michael Valeros was the young man's name: an Englishman with a passion for life that Nava had never experienced. He took Nava home to his cottage that night. The place was rustic—cold and damp and dark. He fired up a thermacone, and the place warmed up quickly. He made a dinner of pasta and mushrooms while they waited for her clothes to dry, and everything fell into place.

They spent that summer together, inseparable. He introduced her to his friends, and she experienced for the first time what it meant to be among people who didn't care what clothes she wore or what she looked like. They weren't interested in where she came from, but rather what she thought about—what she believed in. These friends of Michael's had made it to Oxford through exam scores and hard work, not through high-ranking company contacts. They were real people, and had real stakes in reinventing the system, a system that had failed the people it claimed to serve.

The people in Nava's new circle were dangerous; they drank in subterranean pubs and plotted the downfall of regimes. They listened to one another and spoke with candor and openness. They cared little for outside opinion and even less for those who judged them. They argued passionately, drank beer, overturned tables, and broke plates.

It was in this scene, among these people, that Nava found her voice. She was quickly regarded as someone to respect. She was a natural speaker and had a talent for telling a story, a story that resonated with an audience hungry for a restructuring of the way the world was failing them.

By the end of that summer, Michael and Nava had invested in one another an unwavering loyalty and love. She decided to stay in Oxford past that summer, to take classes and wait until Michael finished his coursework. After that, she followed him back to his northern English town, and there began the new arc of her life.

And here she was...waiting for a doctor in refugee camp in the middle of Germany, waiting to give birth to a child. She was waiting for this arrival, waiting, in a sense, for a new beginning, for a new stage in their fight against the companies. She was waiting, preparing, plotting for the next assault against everything her father represented.

Δ

MICHAEL FELT FATIGUE beginning to overtake him. He followed Sargon, step by step by step, over the muddy streets. They made a turn and continued along another dirt street.

"This way," Sargon said. "It is not far." A moment later: "Just to prepare you," Sargon continued. "My wife...she can be, how you say, persistent. But don't let that color your impression of her. She's smart and wise, but she can be a bit dramatic. She will be very interested in you, understand. But don't let her bully you. Only tell her what you wish. Her intensions are good, that is certain. But again, reveal too much, and that's when she has you."

Michael caught Sargon's shining eyes for a moment and nodded.

They passed several tents, some with figures out front who squatted under the dripping awnings, the red ends of their cigarettes tracing arcs, the glow of vape apparatuses illuminating the sharp contours of their faces. Smoke and vape filled the air. These smokers observed but said nothing as Michael and Sargon passed. The quarter moon broke through the clouds. A right turn, another right, and then Sargon approached a tent and tapped several times on a canvas door.

"Hallo." Sargon moved through the opening. "Hallo, Zahra. I have company. Zahra, are you awake?" Sargon held out his hand through the door, motioning Michael to wait. There was whispering inside. An exchange, but not angry. Sargon came back out the flap. He put his hand on Michael's shoulder. "Give her one minute. I hate to do this to her, but she understands. She's just tidying up a bit. She's embarrassed. But don't tell her this."

Michael was tired. Wasted. All he wanted was to find a place where he could collapse. If that didn't come, he'd settle for any flat surface, even the mud beneath him. Before long, Sargon tugged the flap away and pulled Michael inside.

"Hallo, Zahra," Sargon said. "We're here. Hallo!"

They entered a small room lit by a single lantern that hung from a low ceiling. The room was no more than six meters long and about four meters wide. A faded Persian rug covered a dirt floor. A short couch was pushed against the opposite wall, and another wall had a bookcase, its three shelves stuffed with papers and old books competing for space. A picture hung on the canvas wall above the bookcase, a complex mosaic of tiles or bricks that lent the room a sense of order and calm.

The kitchenette, if that's what it could be called, consisted of a small counter with a thermaburner and a kettle above and a refrigerator the size of a suitcase beneath it. There was a table just large enough for two chairs. It held a tray of spices, a cup filled with cutlery, and a small brass vase that lacked fresh flowers. A tangle of wires sprung from an outlet that hung on the wall above the thermaburner.

Michael was leaning down to take off his shoes, setting the muddy things to the side, when a woman pushed through a door near the kitchenette, seeming surprised to see them.

"Zahra," Sargon said. "This is...this is..."

Michael stood from undoing his shoelaces. "I'm Michael." He gave a bow.

"You are a mess," Zahra said to Sargon. "What has happened to you? You should change your clothes. At once."

Sargon nodded. "I won't be long, Michael. This is Zahra, my dear wife." He pushed his way into the back room, from where Zahra had just emerged.

Zahra wore a tan-and-green bodywrap. Her head was covered in a turquoise shawl, and her eyebrows were dark, almost black. Zahra pointed to a chair at the table. "Please, sit."

Michael sat.

With Sargon gone, Zahra turned on the thermaburner, tested the weight of her kettle, and then added water from a from a canteen stashed under the counter.

"Sargon says you've just arrived." She set three cups on the table and placed a bag of tea in each. "He thinks you're in trouble."

Michael frowned, clamping his mouth closed.

Zahra said, "That's not our business, of course. Please, dry off. Rest. You are our guest." She tested the kettle and pushed forward a small ceramic bowl with packets of sugar and powdered creamer.

"My wife is having a baby," Michael said. "That's why we're here."

The water boiling, Zahra lifted the kettle and filled the three cups. She sat opposite him.

"We knew about Dr. Jafari," Michael went on. "She came recommended, and we were close." He removed the tea bag, then took a packet of sugar from the bowl, ripped off the paper end, and poured the contents into his tea.

"Dr. Jafari is well known," Zahra said. "She is an expert with childbirth." Zahra leaned in closer. "But why are you really here? You're not refugees. You are English. Sargon said your woman friend might be American. You're hiding something."

Michael looked up at Zahra. Her dark eyes were merciless, they nailed him in the heart.

She leaned in and whispered. "Be honest with me. It may save your life."

"We're on the run," Michael whispered as he stared into his cup of tea. "We've been running for days, and I haven't slept in that long."

"Who are you running from? Eh! Don't answer that. It may be best."

"I just want the best care for her, but there's really nothing I can do. Our fates have been in other's hands."

"She is your wife?"

"Not officially."

Zahra held Michael in the vice grip of her gaze.

"She's so stubborn," Michael went on. "It doesn't matter what I say anymore. We've been involved in some of the protests, but just when we seem to get the attention we seek, she needs to take it a step further. It's like her sole nourishment is this vision of hers, and that has become the only thing that matters."

"NLA?" Zahra whispered.

Michael was about to speak when Zahra put her finger on his lips. "Speak softly…the walls have ears."

"But I wonder if I can take it anymore?" Michael said. "I'm so tired. Years of fighting, years of constant movement and the fear of arrest and torture. One wrong step and it's all over. Some days I just want to run away and leave the struggle to the others. Everything seems so pointless. One step forward, two steps back. I'm afraid for Nava and us. I'm afraid for our future child. I'm afraid that nothing ultimately matters."

"Don't give up," Zahra whispered. "You may still find what you seek. Only god controls our fate."

Michael sipped at his tea. It was soothing.

"You are lucky to have found us," Zahra said with a wink. "You could have fallen in the hands of Kareem and Suliman. They wouldn't be so accommodating. I don't mean to frighten you. I speak truthfully. Such is it in this city of tents. If one is not careful, one's luck can quickly turn."

Michael nodded and took another sip from his tea.

There was a rustling from the other room. Sargon had returned.

"Please, listen," whispered Zahra. "Forgive Sargon, if you can. He can be nosey. But he can't help himself. He likes to put things together, like a puzzle. He has a natural curiosity, and this often gets him into trouble. But he is a good man, and I say this as his wife. But don't allow him to string you along in one scheme or other. Draw the line before you are reeled in. Believe me, I know this."

Sargon pushed the cloth door aside. Now dressed in a clean pair of pants and long-sleeved shirt, he brought a chair from the other room and wedged it next to the table beside Zahra. He took his cup and stirred his tea. He said, "I am sorry we have no supper for you, Michael. The food tents open in the morning. These are humble accommodations. We are out of biscuits, and it might be a week before we see them."

"You are generous," Michael said. "I want you to know how grateful I am."

Michael's eyes were heavy, ready to close. He fought to keep them open, not to offend his hosts. He thought of Nava.

"I apologize." Zahra rose. She pulled a cloth towel from a shelf near the refrigerator and handed it to Michael. "Take this to the bath and wash your face. Sargon will show you."

Sargon grumbled as he stood.

"You can sleep there on the couch," Zahra said to Michael. "It might not look comfortable, but it really isn't so bad."

Sargon produced his own towel, then he found sandals and motioned for Michael to follow when he pushed outside the canvas door. Michael slipped into his muddy shoes and followed.

—

The bath was spartan, with two sinks and abused steel mirrors above them. Sargon took one sink, Michael the other. Sargon offered Michael a glob of toothpaste, which Michael took on his finger and rubbed over his teeth. Then Michael peeled off his synthskin patches. As if seeking approval, he looked over at Sargon, who was nipping at the ends of his mustache with a small scissors. Sargon glanced at Michael and nodded. Once the synthskin was off, Michael rolled the wad into a ball and stuffed it in his pocket.

"What's security like here?" Michael said. "Do I need to wear this stuff in the morning?"

"There's no security here. Only informants." Sargon continued snipping at his mustache with his scissors. "Getting into the zeltstadt is easy. Getting out is difficult."

"I recognized the Arabic when we arrived," Michael said. "But you are Persian."

"All refugees of the water wars," Sargon said as he snapped his scissors in the air. "There are a good many Persians here. Africans and some Pakistanis and Indians, too, but mostly Arabs. I call it the great melting pot. Eventually, everyone gets cooked."

Michael went to a toilet to piss. When he came back, Sargon was splashing water over his face and then combing his mustache.

Back at Sargon's tent, a pillow and blanket had been set on the couch. Sargon said, "I told the doctor to send word to us if there's any news. I suggest you sleep while you can. After your baby is born, you'll never sleep again." Then he turned the lantern down, pushed aside the cloth door to the other room, and disappeared.

Michael felt around for the blanket and pillow, then stretched out on the couch and took a long breath. He heard muffled voices as Sargon and Zahra, the soft, round fricatives of the Farsi, the sound of blowing leaves, whispered on the other side of the thin wall. Their bed must be right next to him. Zahra laughed, then Sargon laughed. Then they grew quiet.

The night descended with all its weight, and in a chorus, risen from the nocturn stage, came the snoring, the coughing, the growling, the distant shouting, hacking, the weeping, the clearing of throats, and the sneezing. Thousands of sounds rose above the zeltstadt and swirled around the small cosmos like little bug stars and galaxies and traces of meteors.

At some point Michael woke, or so he thought. There was a rustling and a sound of voices. A voice (Sargon's?) told him to go to Dr. Jafari's tent. It was important. Michael left the tent and stumbled through the darkness of the zeltstadt, through twisting dirt streets to Dr. Jafari's tent.

Once there, he entered and found a diminutive Dr. Jafari sitting at her desk. She seemed annoyed that he had come. Reluctantly she rose and showed him to Nava, who was sitting up in a bed, pillows raising her up. She was holding a small package wrapped in dark cloth. Michael stepped forward, but he was disturbed that Nava did not remove her veil.

"It's me, Nava. Can't you see that?"

The baby cooed and gurgled as Nava handed it to him. Carefully he parted the cloth so he could see the child's face, but he could not find it. He unfolded more of the clothing, then unfolded more and more until he began to panic.

He could not find their child!

He clawed at the cloth, grabbing the material, tossing it in the air, shaking it free to reveal the baby. But nothing was there.

"What is this?"

He demanded that Nava tell him what had happened. But smoke filled the room. Somewhere the baby wailed. Michael searched, but he could not find Nava or the baby. The smoke was so thick, he found it hard to breath. He clutched at his throat, gasping, frantic to find help. Frantic to find Nava and their little baby.

—

A light lit up the small room. A rustle of footsteps. Michael turned away, tried to fight his way back to sleep. A hand shook his shoulder.

"What is it?" Michael said. "What's happening?"

"You should get up," Sargon said, his sleep-creased face producing a fractured smile. "We have word. We visit the mother of your baby."

Michael sat up straight. He scrambled to get his clothes together, to get his shirt and pants on, and to pull on his old socks. "She's okay?" he asked. "Nava's okay?"

"Yes," Zahra said. Her eyes half-closed, she stood at the therma-burner, her long gray hair uncovered and in a thick braid that fell down her back. She stirred two cups of instacoffee and handed them to Michael and Sargon. "She's okay. You're a father now. A lucky father of a splendid baby girl. Drink this and go to her."

A low peach glow traced the sky to the east, and the air was crisp as they headed to Dr. Jafari's tent. When they arrived, the assistant greeted them. She was tired, it was clear, but she took Michael's hand and led him to a warm room where Nava lay on a large couch. She was wrapped in sheets and warm blankets. She looked up at him, smiling but clearly depleted, then stared at the small creature cradled in her arms.

"Can you believe it?" Nava said.

Michael sat next to her. She passed the bundle of white cloth to him. Out from the oval opening emerged a small wrinkled face, a gurgling pink larva. Its lips were pursed and demanding, and it flopped around a tiny larva-pink hand.

"Congratulations," Nava said. "You're a father."

Michael shook his head as he stared at the mite. "More importantly, you are a mother. Congratulations to you."

Tears rolled down his cheek and slipped from his chin into the soft swaddling cloth. The baby curled the fingers of its little mitt around Michael's pinky. Michael looked over at Nava. Her eyes were closed and she breathed heavily, a wan smile indelible on her tired, beautiful face.

3 – The Rift

MIRANDA LAID THE unconscious Graf over a long seat at the rear of the crawler. She wrapped a bandage over the injury near his left eye and placed a splintpack over what might be a fractured left arm. She sat next to him on the seat, near his head, and applied a strip of medical cloth to the saliva that ran through his soiled and bloodied beard.

Jeg floated just above Graf's feet, short-range datasquirts darting between Miranda and the security bot: updates on pulse rates, blood pressure, and skin conductivity that Miranda obtained by applying the sensors on her fingertips to the skin on Graf's wrist.

The human needed to repair itself.

"We just have to wait," she said.

Jeg began to drift, soon settling into a pattern of tight figure eights.

"Perhaps you should survey the station wreckage again," Miranda said aloud to the bot. "Your movements are repetitious."

"I have already completed a thorough scan of the base." Jeg spoke in a reedy voice that came through its invisible transducer.

"Perhaps you missed something. Perhaps you should make a more extensive survey."

The bot swung its sensor eye in Miranda's direction. "What is it that you seek?"

"I am not sure. Can you widen your survey to include a perimeter beyond your initial scan?"

"Yes."

Miranda waited.

The sentry bot hovered in place.

"Why are you not going?" she said.

"Father Paul's instructions."

"We discussed this earlier, before you went on your initial survey."

"Father Paul said that I should remain with Dr. Graf at all times," Jeg said. "If I leave, I am concerned that I will be disobeying Father Paul and putting Dr. Graf in danger."

"But I am here to protect him," Miranda said.

"Will I be disobeying Father Paul if I go?"

"As discussed, you will not be disobeying Father Paul. By studying the base, you will be collecting data that may serve to help Dr. Graf. That is not disobeying Father Paul. Sometimes one must depart from the letter of a directive in order to better obey its spirit."

"How do you know this?"

"Father Paul gave me this wisdom."

The sentry bot seemed to consider this for a moment, then drifted toward the crawler's rear hatch, waiting until Miranda threw down the handle and the hatch swung out. The cabin depressurized as the thin, not quite human-friendly Asimios atmosphere pushed its way into the crawler. The spheroid sailed into a bath of sunlight.

Miranda punched instructions on a wall-mounted read-out, and the hatch closed and the crawler gradually re-pressurized. Returning to Graf, she sat down and adjusted the position of his splinted arm. Then she examined the tension on the bandages covering his head and eye.

It was likely that he'd live. A short time ago, she'd been uncertain of this, but his condition had stabilized. With adequate rest, he'd regain consciousness and continue to recover.

Miranda felt a twinge in her leg where she'd suffered an injury during the crash. Her core temperature climbed just over half a degree in what she determined was a physiological reaction to the memory of pain. Was it pain? Her internal fluid pressures had risen slightly. This was good. Her design called for fluctuation in vascular pressure. Rather like the human, she was also in the process of healing.

Δ

"I SMELL PEANUT butter," Graf said as he regained consciousness. He felt extremely uncomfortable and in pain. "Where the hell am I? Oh, for God's sake, what happened?"

"Hello, Dr. Graf." Miranda sat next to him on the seat.

Graf looked up at Miranda with his right eye, his left eye hidden under bandage. "Oh, no," he said. "Oh, no, no, no."

Miranda held a water tube to Graf's mouth. He drew several sips, then leaned back on the thermal blanket.

"Miranda?" he said, "Is that you, Miranda?"

"It is I."

"Miranda, if it is indeed you, can you explain why my eye is bandaged and why my left arm feels as if it's being crushed in a vice?"

He coughed, then choked from coughing. He jutted out his chin and clenched his teeth.

"You have been injured, Dr. Graf," Miranda said. "We were riding in the crawler when the station was destroyed. The force of the explosion overturned the vehicle."

"How long ago?"

"Eleven hours, forty-seven minutes, and eighteen seconds."

"Is that why I'm hungry?"

"Quite likely. You have not eaten since the event."

"Is that why I'm thinking about peanut butter?" He raised an eyebrow when he asked this. "Oh, how I miss peanut butter right now."

"We were apprehensive about feeding you while you were unconscious," Miranda said. "There was debate about the potential for asphyxiation."

"Debate?"

"The debate between myself and Jeg." As if hearing its name, Jeg broke away from the figure eights and moved to hover, once again, above the doctor's feet. "Jeg's knowledge of human physiology is limited, but I made allowance for the bot's input, nonetheless."

Graf squinted to see around him, then fell back on his pillow. "Oh, for Christ's sake. Asimios Station is gone, right? ESCOM's blown it to oblivion."

"Correct," Miranda said. "Asimios Station has been destroyed."

"And the *Rosario* and *Guemes* have flown away. They've left us? We're stranded here?"

"Correct, Dr. Graf," Miranda said.

Graf winced, reeling from his pain. When Miranda offered him the water tube again, he struggled to find the straw with his lips.

"Have you made contact with Paul?" Graf said.

"No, we have not," Miranda said.

"Have you attempted to contact Paul?"

"We have not attempted to contact Paul Ness."

"Why not?"

"We were not instructed to."

"How about food? Is there any food in this place? A jar of peanut butter, perhaps?"

"There are two packages of S-rations in the storage locker," Miranda said. "Would you like me to bring one to you?"

"That'd be nice of you, Miranda. It's only an S-ration, but at least it's something."

Miranda crossed the crawler to the opposite wall. Jeg moved to let her pass. She opened a locker and removed a ration pack, then returned to Graf's makeshift cot. Graf sat up without assistance and took the pack from Miranda. He set the large envelope-sized parcel on his lap, rolled it loosely into the shape of a cylinder, then unrolled it. He struggled to open the corner of the pack one-handed, but was able to pull the corner out. Steam rose from the flexible tray.

"Curry," Graf said. "Vegetable."

"Do you like this?" Miranda said.

"I doubt it. I'd prefer a broiled synthsteak or roasted chicken."

Miranda moved away from Graf. She seemed confused about why Graf wasn't eating.

"One thing about humans," Graf said.

Miranda cocked her head. "Yes?"

"Their skin burns easily. They can't hold hot things in their hands."

"Yes," Miranda said. "Human skin is susceptible to damage from excessive heat."

"Consequently, they can't eat hot food without assistance."

"Oh." Miranda leaned down and scooped food from the tray with her fingers. She raised the food to Graf's mouth.

Graf laughed and pushed her hand away. "I was hoping for something more like a fork."

"I am sorry. I think I understand." Miranda lowered the food back to the tray and let it slip off her fingers. She went back to the supply locker and returned with a package containing an eating implement, packets of salt and pepper, and a napkin.

"Thank you, Miranda," Graf said. "This should do."

Miranda smiled. Graf carefully took out the fork, removed the napkin, and proceeded to eagerly consume his food. When he was done, he wiped his mouth and tried to belch. Instead, the entire contents of the S-ration shot up from his stomach and onto the floor at his feet. Stunned and embarrassed, Graf made his way to the side hatch, where he pulled frantically at the lever to open it.

"Your breather, Dr. Graf," Miranda said.

Graf opened a small locker near the hatch. He removed a breather mask and struggled to put it on, with his left hand mostly useless and the bandage on his head complicating the process. Finally, he deployed it.

Miranda said, "You have a breach in your pressure skin, both on your head and on your arm. Extended exposure may be lethal."

"Thank you, Miranda."

"You are welcome."

When he managed to open the door, Graf pushed through the hatch and stepped down to the ground. After several seconds, the door auto-closed behind him.

—

Graf watched as Miranda and Jeg peered out at him from the crawler windows. He tried to find a place out of sight, a place where he could vomit and piss and shit in peace. But the cold crept quickly into his body where his pressure suit was torn. Eventually, he punched the icon on the crawler door and went back inside.

Once he was back in the crawler, he waited for pressure to return before removing his breather, then he cleaned his face and hands with sterile wipes from the medikit.

Miranda continued to just stand by, and Jeg continued to hover, both watching Graf as if waiting for instruction.

Graf threw the thermal blanket he'd been using as a pillow over the vomit-covered floor. He sat down on his cot and looked at Miranda, then leveled his one-eyed gaze at the sentry bot's large oculus. He picked up a water tube and sucked down a long drink, then ran his fingers through his blood-caked beard.

"So, what's the story, my metal-minded friends?" he said.

There was no response.

"There's one more S-ration and half a tube of water," Graf said. "What do you suggest we do?"

Still no response. Miranda looked at the doctor patiently.

"Well?"

"We will do as asked," Miranda said.

"This crawler isn't going anywhere," Graf said. "I got a look at it when I was outside. The whole front end is folded up like an accordion."

"Most control systems were destroyed," Miranda said. "Two rear axles are broken. The transmission has been damaged."

"You pulled me out of the front seat, didn't you?" Graf said.

"Yes."

"And you pulled me into the back here, put my arm in this splint, and bandaged me up."

Miranda nodded. "I turned the crawler over, too," she added. "It seemed the simplest solution. You were trapped, your arm was pinched. Having the position of the crawler corrected improved your chance of survival."

"You lifted a five-ton crawler on your own," Graf said. "I suppose I should thank you."

Miranda said nothing.

"Now what?" Graf said.

Miranda blinked again. The bot returned to tracing figure eights.

Graf gazed out one of the rectangular windows on the side hatch. It was getting dark. The temperature was dropping. No lights emanated from the station. There was no station, nobody to call. Nobody to meet and talk with about some project or other. No one remained. Yet here he was.

In many respects, this was exactly how he'd anticipated his last hours on Asimios: a slowly depleting oxygen supply, a gradual temperature drop, a peaceful descent into unconsciousness, and a final walk down a hallway toward a warm and inviting light.

Graf sat on his cot.

"So, what's the story here?" he said to Miranda. "What did Paul tell you to do with me? I mean, there's nothing left for me. This is it. This is the conclusion, you understand."

Miranda said, "Father Paul said that we are here to help you fulfill your objective. That is our only instruction."

"I see. That makes sense. If you want to stick around for the show, you're welcome to. But my objective is to die here on Asimios."

"Then we shall help you to do so," Miranda said.

"I don't know how reassuring that sounds," Graf said. He ran his hand over the fabric of the cot, tugged at his beard. "How much oxygen is left in the crawler?"

"Under current consumption settings, the crawler will lose power in three to four hours. One battery cell was damaged. After that, artificial climate will rapidly decline."

"Should I just go outside and start walking?"

"Where would you go?" Miranda said.

"I don't know. South? South sounds good to me."

"What will you look for in the south?" Miranda asked.

Graf shrugged. "Nothing. There's nothing I'd be looking for. I'm going to die, and I need to figure out how to do it. Get it? My initial idea was to drive this crawler out to Camp Heyerdahl, take a few days to reflect on things, then make my exit. But without a crawler, that isn't an option."

"No, it isn't an option," Miranda said.

"Is there a mirror in this piece of shit? I'm wondering how cut up my movie-star face has become."

Miranda opened a locker and pointed to a small square mirror on the inside of the door, and Graf leaned in to get a look at himself. With his good eye, Graf saw that his face was pale and gray, drained of blood. His good eye was watery and strained, with blood on the bandage above his left eye. His beard was filthy, caked with a sticky red syrup. He looked like a pirate who'd barely survived a siege. With teeth clenched, Graf unwound the gauze of the bandage around his head, and the closer he came to the wound, the more soaked with fluid and blood the bandage was.

When the bandage was off, Graf examined the laceration that stretched along his forehead to his left ear. Part of the pressure skin hood had been cut away by Miranda. The wound wasn't bleeding, but the cut was deep, crimson, and dark with clots. His left eye was swollen shut.

"That's going to leave a nasty scar." Graf started to laugh, but pain hit him in the stomach like a club. "Can we get a new dressing on this, Miranda? A new bandage?"

Miranda helped him find sterile gauze from the medikit. When she finished applying the new bandage, Graf went back to the back of the crawler and lay on the cot.

"I can't see out of my left eye," he said.

"It is unresponsive," Miranda said.

"Dr. Fredriks just put a new VI implant in that eye," Graf said. "But I can't see a damned thing with it now."

"Is it possible that the visual interface has been damaged?" Miranda said.

"It's possible."

"It may be that your vision is permanently impaired," Miranda said.

"That may be true, Miranda."

"Or it may only be temporarily impaired."

"That may also be true, Miranda."

Graf closed his eye. He could hear the purring of the bot's hover-drive as it approached and receded, approached and receded, in its endless loops of figure eights. The soft noise was hypnotizing, and it synchronized with the throbbing in his head. He considered whether sleep might be the easiest thing to do. *To sleep no more.* To fade out, let the crawler's battery drain away and let that be the end of the story. *The rest is silence.*

"If you'd like to travel to Camp Heyerdahl," the sentry bot said in its reedy voice, "why not use the other crawler?"

"What other crawler?" Graf propped himself on his elbow and gazed at the bot's sensor eye. "Weren't they all melted down with the station?"

"Many were, but not all," the bot intoned. "While conducting my area scans, I found an abandoned crawler on the southeast side of Cascade Ridge. Identification number M72-895AS"

"No shit?" Graf rubbed his good eye with his thumb. "I'll be damned. I ordered a team to leave a crawler behind a few days before evac. Night project—faulty headlights, perhaps—and it didn't seem to make sense to bring it in. That's eight to ten clicks from here. Let me think...that'd be about a ninety-minute hike."

"Will you walk there?" the bot intoned.

"Sure! Why the hell not?"

"It'd be dangerous for you to walk so far," Miranda said.

"Oh, you think so?" Graf said, looking over at Miranda with a loll of his head.

"You should know," Miranda said, "that it is soon night, and temperatures have begun to fall. There are no reserve pressure skins on this vehicle. It is reasonable to assume that if you attempt to reach the crawler on foot, you will suffer hypothermia and frostbite."

Graf's eye was wide. "You'd rather that I stay here? You think I should stick around and wait for the power to go out instead of making a run for that crawler? Is that what you're saying?"

"I am stating that it would be dangerous for you to try to reach the crawler by foot," Miranda said.

"I'm going to die," Graf said. "I might as well die doing something, don't you think?"

"You do not have to walk there, Dr. Graf," Jeg intoned as it came closer.

"Explain what you mean," Graf said, shooing off the bot with a wave of his good arm. "This is frustrating. In fact, I'm starting to wonder if having you two around is helping my situation."

"I can retrieve the crawler, Dr. Graf," Miranda said.

Graf looked at her. "You can retrieve the crawler?"

Miranda nodded. "I can move quickly over the terrain. I can power it up and return here in approximately forty-three minutes, if that is what you wish."

"Now, that's what I like to hear!" Graf shouted, doing his best not to hurt himself when he jumped up from the cot. "What are you waiting for? Go get that crawler. Then I'll stop complaining."

—

After Miranda left and the hatch was secured, Graf looked out the window that faced Cascade Ridge. He wanted to get a look at her out there, but the angle of view was poor. Miranda's ghost-like figure disappeared quickly toward the ridge, and that's all he saw. Outside, Asimios's small moon, in gibbous phase, had crested the horizon. It cast a silver tint over the station grounds and the roads crisscrossing Asimios's rough surface.

Graf lay back on the cot. His head throbbed. He felt an acute discomfort in his injured arm. He was hungry, but didn't dare touch another S-ration. The sentry bot kept its dark disc-eye on him. Hoping that little bastard didn't start asking him stupid questions, Graf turned away and stared at the wall.

After a few minutes, the bot floated over to Graf. "Pleasant evening, is it not, Dr. Graf?"

"What do you want from me?" Graf said.

"What do I want?"

"Go away."

"I am sorry." The bot turned away and searched out a new starting point for its figure eights.

"Why the hell do you have to do that?"

The bot halted. It came back to Graf. "Do what, sir?"

"Fly in that incessant pattern. Can't you just hover in one place? Or can't you park yourself on a shelf and turn yourself off? That might be good."

"Sorry for bothering you, doctor." The bot moved to the far corner of the crawler and turned its sensor eye away from Graf. It hovered there, quietly.

Graf leaned back in his cot and closed his eye. He was on the verge of unconsciousness, when he felt Jeg come near.

"Dr. Graf," Jeg honked. It hovered in front of the doctor, its sensor eye wide and searching.

"What?" Graf cried.

"Miranda has reached the crawler. She is returning to our position."

"Hallelujah!" Graf called out from out of his near sleep. "Camp Heyerdahl, here we come!"

—

Graf sat beside Miranda, laced snuggly in his safety belts, as she plunged the crawler into the darkness, traveling the unlit road at a hungry pace. He was uneasy at first, since a crawler moving at fifty-plus kilometers per hour without any headlights seemed reckless. But over time he grew to trust Miranda's skill at the wheel and to appreciate the wide-spectrum vision Paul had equipped her with.

It'd take them four hours to reach the fork in Asimios Road. To go east at that point would be to travel to the giant fluorocarbon generator plants, one hundred and twenty-two colossal cloud-giants that would continue unabated to churn out the greenhouse gasses intended to thicken the Asimios atmosphere. To head west would take one to the albedo-reduction fields in Death Valley, where crushed obsidian and black sand had been sown over tens of thousands of square kilometers to absorb solar radiation, essential to planetary warming and key to spurring bacteria, fungus, and lichen growth, the experiments which Graf's wife, Julie, had overseen. To the south of the fork, fifteen minutes down what could barely be considered a road, lay Camp Heyerdahl.

Graf felt a sense of liberation as the burnt-out hulk of Asimios Station receded behind them. There were no depressurization emergencies to worry about, no fights in the casino lounge to police. There were no emergency station epidemics, nor were there anxieties about when the next supply freighter would arrive or whether ESCOM would deliver on this or that promise. Graf had no responsibilities. No planning committees to attend, no maintenance reports to review. No one was looking to him for direction.

Except for Miranda and Jeg.

"Would you like me to wake you when we arrive at the crossroad?" Miranda asked.

"I'm not asleep," Graf said.

"You will soon be, I predict."

"I'm just relaxing."

"You may lie down in the back of the crawler if you wish."

"I don't think so. This is too much fun. Asimios is so empty. So quiet. It's beautiful. Can I tell you a story?"

Miranda said, "Yes. I'd like to hear a story."

"Camp Heyerdahl was neglected for years," Graf said. "It was a recharging depot initially, and a hostel for equipment crews heading to the greenhouse stacks or the heat farms. Once those installations were completed, the camp was abandoned. When Julie and I got married three years ago, we had members of the terraforming team go there and give the camp a scrub down. I told them to stock it with a bunch of nice things, such as nonperishables, books, candles. Anything that'd charm up the place. We spent our honeymoon there, Julie and I. Ever since, many people have used it as a secret retreat. A romantic getaway, if you will."

"I see," Miranda said. "This is where you wish to go?"

"Yes."

Miranda kept her eyes on the road. They drove through the night, Miranda piloting the crawler while Graf, chin tucked tight to his chest, slept.

—

Graf stirred and shook off his sleep as Miranda drew the crawler to a halt. It was early morning and still dark when they'd arrived at the crossroads. If there'd been power to the old streetlamps at the fork, as in former times, one would have seen the signs fastened crudely to a tall post:

ASIMIOS STATION: 204 KM

FC GENERATOR BASE: 343 KM

NEW YORK: 503,000,004 KM

Just past the fork, in the locus of old worker shacks and material depots, the place was bleak and empty of people. A series of low-roofed warehouses huddled on one side. Across the road ahead of them stood a fueling station with large bulbous gas tanks, ten set side by side. A short distance to the east were abandoned housing units on both sides of the road. There were no lights, of course. Everything was cold and lifeless. A ghost town.

Miranda asked, "What would you like to do?"

"Take a right, off the road, and drive due west for about 75 meters, then turn south when I tell you to. There should be an opening in the shoulder and then an old road that snakes past the refueling depot."

Miranda turned the crawler west. They soon came to the road and began the short trip south to Camp Heyerdahl. The road was poor, the ride bumpy. Yet not too long after making the turn south, Miranda pulled the crawler in front of the camp building and parked. It was still dark. Graf could make out only the rough outlines of the old shelter.

"Would you like me to try to gain access, doctor?" Miranda asked.

"I suppose that'd be a good idea," Graf said. "There's a door right there." He pointed to an airlock obscured in the darkness. "It has an external lock. Break it."

"Yes, doctor." Miranda left the crawler.

Graf shivered in a blast of cold air as the droid opened and then shut the crawler door. She dropped to the ground and moved to the building. Graf watched as she paused briefly before finding a way to open the door. Once she was inside, the airlock closed behind her.

Next, a floodlight lit the landing outside the building. A red light on the roof antenna came on, and the oval windows around the building began to glow. Graf deployed his breather mask, careful not to disturb the new bandage, and clambered out of the crawler, Jeg close behind him. A moment later, Graf and Jeg reached the door, and Graf pushed quickly through it.

There was a considerable chill inside the camp. Miranda had booted the generator cells, but it'd take time for them to catalyze. It'd also be a while before temperature and O2 levels were stable. To Graf's delight, the camp was intact. Nobody had ransacked it. The kitchen was tidy, books were on the shelves. The beds were clean and bare.

Graf pulled a sleeping bag and a pair of pillows from a closet and heaved them onto one of the empty mattresses. He went inside the latrine and closed the door. When he came out, he dug around in the kitchen to find a water tube. He took a long drink. He didn't bother to remove his pressure skin. He didn't attempt to wash his face of the blood and grime from the crawler accident.

He didn't care to sit and share words of camaraderie with his companions. Instead, he shook out the sleeping bag and fluffed the pillows and prepared to sleep.

"Goodnight," Graf said from his puffed womb.

"Goodnight," his fellow outcasts replied.

Miranda found a chair and sat down.

The ESCOM bot found an open space to hover.

Everyone seemed to spend the night in comfortable deep-cycle.

—

"I'm not such a pleasant person before my morning coffee," Graf said. He stumbled around the kitchen in search of his fix. To his disappointment, ESCOM instant was the only coffee he could find. He chuckled. "Then again, maybe I'm not so pleasant after my morning coffee either."

Graf flash-heated a water tube, threw in a coffee pellet, and stirred. The atmosphere indicator on the wall had turned green while he'd slept, which indicated that he no longer needed his breather. It was also warm inside, almost too warm in fact, and Graf stripped to his skivvies. He toyed with an on-site comm device mounted on one of the desks, trying to pick up a signal. But other than one of the low-orbit Asimios satellites automatically broadcasting Asimios Station Standard Time (ASST), weather data, radiation levels, and classical music, there was nothing to be found.

Leaving the music playing, Graf explored the outpost's supplies while he considered his next course of action. In one closet he found a treasure: an intact jar of Victor Nguyen's home-made hootch, or as Victor liked to call it, Asimios aqua vitae. Ethanol with extract of bio-dome mint. Graf unfastened the lid, took a whiff, and shuddered. He put the lid back on the jar and tucked it into its hiding place.

After a dry chem-bath and brushing his teeth with a withered toothbrush from the bathroom cabinet, he made a meal of dehydrated insta-bread, speggs, and desiccated soystrips. He succeeded in keeping the meal in his stomach.

Miranda re-wrapped the bandage on his head, allowing for the exposure of his left eye, which remained swollen. He found three intact pressure skins in one of the closets. By providence, one of them was an XXL. He applied a local anesthetic to his arm before stepping into the suit. When the pressure skin was on, Miranda applied a new medisplint to his arm.

"What do you wish to do now, doctor?" Miranda asked.

"The Rift. I want to visit the Rift. I want to see how Julie is doing."

"Julie?"

"Yes. Julie," he said. "My wife. Would you mind driving?"

"Not at all," Miranda said.

—

Washed of color under the stark Asimios sun, the hollow arroyos, loose shale, and tall mineral spikes showed what a hostile environment Asimios still was. When the crawler came to the edge of the Rift, the view was sudden and spectacular: an enormous gash cut through the silver Asimios crust, hundreds of kilometers wide, the result of catastrophic glacial melt millions of years ago. The drop to the canyon floor was several kilometers at places. On the horizon, above the far canyon wall, the thin atmosphere shivered and danced behind a curtain of refraction and haze.

Graf asked Miranda to steer the crawler to a specific location not far from the Rift. She stopped on Graf's cue before a man-made structure, a tall collection of stones that resembled a cairn, like other mineral spikes dotting the landscape.

"You guys stay here."

Graf deployed a breather, released the hatch, and dropped to the ground. He glanced back at the crawler. Miranda and Jeg peered out of the windshield. Although obnoxious and meddlesome, they weren't so bad. They were even good company, in a way. And without their help, Graf wouldn't have made it here.

He walked to the monument and placed his gloved hands on the collection of stones. He muttered a prayer worthy of that moment's solemnity. Then said what had been first in his mind.

Hello, Julie. I've missed you.

She'd been buried here, entombed at the base of the cairn.

After a few moments of contemplation, Graf left the cairn and stepped over to the canyon wall, where he considered the view. He threw up his arms, then dropped them to his side. He'd stayed behind on Asimios to give Julie a final farewell. He'd done that. So, now what? Call it quits?

Submit a final resignation letter and leave those two metalheads behind?

Just jump into the Rift right now?

Yet, to toss his flabby flesh into the Rift would be to desecrate it. Blemish this holy site.

He felt good, not perfect, but good. His arm already felt better. Although he still had no sight in one eye, he was managing well, with Miranda's help.

Why not think this over before making that last leap of faith?

Graf stepped back from the rim of the Rift and made his way back to the crawler.

—

Back at camp, Graf dug out the jar of aqua vitae, removed the lid, and took a good drink. The liquid warmed his stomach. He sat on his mattress and leaned against the wall.

"I suppose you two are wondering why I didn't end my life back there? Why I didn't jump and finish myself off? That's why I stayed behind, after all. I signed up for a suicide mission."

"I was going to ask." Miranda sat next to Graf on the cot. The sentinel bot hovered nearby.

"The more I consider the philosophical implications of taking my own life," Graf said, "the more difficult the act becomes. The will to live is inexorable. The concept of killing oneself is primordially dissonant, you see. If a human isn't depressed, suffering mental illness, bound by an irrational honor code, or in a drug-induced state of euphoria or hallucination, the idea of taking one's life is counter to every expression of every cell in one's body. I now find myself in that odd boat, caught between the will to live and the rational necessity of death."

Miranda tilted her head. Jeg hovered close, its sensor eye level with Graf's.

"Don't get me wrong," Graf continued. "I will kill myself. But there's this business of screwing up the courage to do it. Then there's the question of how to do it. Expire slowly from hunger or thirst? Alter my environment by removing oxygen from the camp?"

"Would that be painful for you?" Jeg asked in its reedy voice.

"You could run me over with the crawler," Graf said to Miranda, "but that might be messy. And if it didn't work the first time, I'd hate to be run over twice."

"My programming wouldn't permit it," Miranda said.

"Another option," Graf said, "would be for me to strip down and just go out for a walk at night. That might be the best solution. Hypothermia and hypoxia are great bedfellows, and by many accounts, a pleasant way to go."

Miranda and Jeg remained silent.

"But all of this has nothing to do with you," Graf said. "You are simply spectators in this sordid mess. You're lucky not to have to deal with these kinds of human dilemmas." Graf stood. He wobbled as he crossed the floor. "Why don't we take a walk? Have ourselves a picnic, perhaps? There's a spot close by with an excellent view of the Rift. It might be nice."

Graf foraged around the camp for a few things, protecting his arm in the splint. He found more soystrips, water, and a couple of thermacones, plus a pair of folding chairs stashed in a supply closet. He enlisted Miranda's help in carrying the thermacones and chairs, while Graf took charge of Nguyen's aqua vitae, a few bottles of water, and food.

The three of them left the camp, Graf leading the way, until they reached an overlook at the Rift's edge. It was late afternoon, with ambient temperature in the mid-twenties Celsius, but it'd fall quickly below freezing once the sun set.

At the site, Graf kicked around stones and dust until a suitable clearing was made. He instructed Miranda where to set the chairs so they faced southwest, where the evening sun was brushing against the distant mountains. Graf retracted the thermacone's feet, found the igniter switch, and soon it radiated warmth.

"Please sit," Graf said. The micro-transmitter in his breather synched frequencies with Miranda and the bot. He gestured for Miranda to sit in the free chair. "I want you to enjoy this sunset with me. It may be my last."

They observed Stelos Proxima, the Asimios sun, as it slowly succumbed to the advancing horizon. The thin Asimios atmosphere produced no breeze. A sky of stars gradually unfolded above them, a deep velvet and yellow tapestry, remote and calm. Graf lifted his breather and took a sip from the jar. He shivered and coughed.

"Maybe this is the part of the story where I tell you about Julie," Graf said.

Miranda nodded. The droid seemed awkward sitting on a folding chair, but she was being a good sport.

"Julie Singh joined our staff about three years after the station came online," Graf said. "That'd be six years ago. She was a botanist, a damned good one. She became integral in implementing fungus and bacterial injection processes for early-stage terraforming, and she fell in quickly with the station's terraforming team."

"This is your wife you are describing?" Miranda said. "The human buried under the stones?"

Graf nodded. He took a sip from the jar. "Julie was an infectious optimist who could get anybody to do anything. This made her an appreciated member of the team. She was a ranked chess player with interplanetary credentials, and a menace at poker too. And she was irresistible."

Graf paused. His eyes turned west. The light had suddenly shifted. The mountains had finally claimed the sun.

"She cut her straight dark hair at her shoulders," Graf went on. "She had a way of sizing up a situation quickly, be it social or scientific. She had an instinct for politics and a brilliant analytical brain. We were quite different, she and I. Where I was large and bear-like, she was petite and delicate. Where I was loud and outspoken, she was reserved and circumspect. This disparity worked for us. We were married, with a handful of friends attending the ceremony, atop Mt. Utrecht, Asimios's sixteenth tallest peak."

"That must have been amenable," Miranda said. She seemed to be trying to get comfortable in her chair.

Jeg had glided back to where they conversed, but remained quiet.

"We became famous, as you might have heard." Graf took another sip of Nguyen's potion. "We were the first couple to marry on Asimios, so Nexus and the Earth media ate it up. Once the initial buzz fizzled, though, we got back to work. Things were booming at the station. People were getting comfortable traveling through the wormhole. More people came with each transport ship, and more demands were placed on us. Asimios was billed as the next Mars, the next Eden. Everything was looking up."

Graf took another sip from the jar. He adjusted his breather and moved his chair closer to the thermacone.

"Although prospects for the station were in ascendence," he said, "things weren't going great among the admin ranks. People have a hard time when a couple is prominent in decision-making positions. Accusations of bias and favoritism percolate. Of course, Julie knew that her connection to the boss—me—might be perceived as a threat to others. Tensions arose. Divisions formed on the terraforming team. Rumors circulated that Julie might be influencing, or benefiting, from my leadership."

Graf took another sip from the jar.

"Egos were bruised," he said. "Some scientists resigned and left the station. Eventually, the battle over the vision for terraforming Asimios took its toll. Julie resigned from the terraforming leadership and retreated to her lab. She wanted to separate from the politics, to focus on her research, to return to the hard science the station needed."

Graf stretched out his legs, moved his breather, and took another sip of the aqua vitae.

"She got sick not long after that. I thought she might be going through a bout of depression, the way everyone does here. It's called Asimios Gloom. But during a checkup, Dr. Fredriks found that Julie suffered from a rare blood mutation, which medical facilities on Asimios weren't equipped to handle. Dr. Fredriks, a first-order medical doctor by any measure, developed an experimental therapy to treat the condition, but it didn't work. Julie died two days before a supply ship was scheduled to arrive and bring her back to Phobos."

Graf leaned back in his chair, took another sip from the jar, and stared at the increasing number of stars in the sky.

"I'm sorry to hear that, Dr. Graf," Miranda said. "It must be difficult to lose someone you are close to, that you care about."

"It is," Graf said. "After she died, we wrapped her body in cotton and drove her to the Rift. She wanted to be exposed, she told me during one of our last conversations. She didn't want to be cremated or returned to Earth. She wanted to contribute the organic building blocks of the new Asimios. So, we put her under the cairn, for Asimios to claim her."

Graf took a drink and closed his eyes.

"Are you warm enough, doctor?" Miranda said. "The temperature is falling."

Graf grumbled as he leaned down to adjust the heat of the thermacone.

"I did my Ph.D. in chemistry," Graf said. "I taught for a few years before being lured into the private sector. It's probably my worst decision, getting out of academia. With the decommissioning of Asimios Station, now, my career is done. All the politics that went into getting this place fully functioning, all the ass-kissing and pleading for research dollars and resources. Makes me wonder why I ever got involved."

"A good deal of science was conducted at the station," Miranda said.

"A multitude of spinoff technologies came out of it, like old Beach Ball over there and Paul's work in quantum magnetism. Plenty of research was done, and ESCOM has it all patented down to the subatomic level. Asimios Station will put ESCOM at the transnational apex for decades to come." Graf sighed and sipped again. "Make no mistake, if I'd known that this project could be so easily cut off, I'd never have signed on. But the folks at ESCOM are experts in the art of flattery, bribery, and coercion, and scientists are an easy target. Most scientists are like children. We trust implicitly, we want attention, and we want candy, and that will always be our undoing."

Graf took another sip from his aqua vitae and slid his breather back over his mouth. The sentinel bot came back and hovered near Miranda, its sensor eye rotating horizontally as it scanned the dark terrain with intermittent laser sweeps.

"But enough about Asimios," Graf said suddenly. "When I'm gone, once I've ended it all, what's the plan for the two of you?"

Miranda and Jeg stared at him in silence.

"Come on," Graf said. "What will you do when I'm dead? I mean, have you thought about it? Have you considered your futures? Did Paul leave you with any instructions? What was it that Paul wanted you to do here anyway?"

"Again," Miranda said, "Father Paul simply stated that we are here to help you fulfill your objective. He gave no indication of further instruction. Once you have completed your objective, we...I..."

"What will you do then?" Graf said. "No hint from old Paul Ness?"

Miranda and the sentinel bot were silent.

"Have either of you thought about it? Have you discussed it?"

Again, silence. Then Miranda spoke: "To consider your question would be, for us, to preclude your existence. And that is not logical at present."

Graf said, "If I kill myself, then what? I mean, you can't just guard my body forever, can you?"

Silence.

"What if I gave you a new set of instructions?" Graf asked. "Would that work? What if I told you that, after I was dead, you should take it upon yourselves to act autonomously? To achieve individual droid-dom and bot-dom, as the case may be? Would that be possible?"

More silence.

"Eh, what the hell," Graf huffed. "What does it matter anyway? No cairn for me. Leave me where I fall. Or, if you have the time, bury me in the ground, and after the last shovelful, dance on my grave."

Graf grew sullen and withdrew. He cradled the jar of aqua vitae in his lap and slowly rocked in his chair. Miranda and the bot observed his silence and continued their own.

"It's a funny thing, getting old," Graf muttered from his chest. "A small thing you did forty years ago can consume you, while the thing you are doing at this moment hardly gets a second thought. Although we're on the verge of eliminating the physical effects of aging, the mind's struggle to narrow temporal distance will only intensify. Perhaps the act of remembering will become the final adversary in the quest for immortality."

"Excuse me, Dr. Graf," Miranda said. "Have you decided yet how you are going to kill yourself?"

With a start, Graf looked up at Miranda. "Oh, so you're encouraging me now, are you?" He stood and began backing in the direction of the Rift. "Want to shut me up, right? Okay, that's fair. I wouldn't want to sit around and hear somebody go on and on about death and dying forever. I get it."

Miranda stood from her chair and started toward Graf. "I'm sorry, doctor. I didn't mean to interrupt you. Please, forgive me."

Graf's hand trembled as he moved his breather aside and took a sip from the jar. "It's okay, Miranda. See that ledge over there, the one on the other side of this rim, the one at the top of that cliff? That's where I'm going to end it. I'll jump from there...to my death."

Miranda looked in the direction of the ledge. After a moment, Miranda took Graf's hand and guided him back to the thermacone. Graf collapsed back into his chair.

"I've had too much to drink," he said. "I think I'm too tired to kill myself tonight."

Graf stared into the thermacone. He remained like this until he slowly began to fade. At one point he slumped in his chair. Then he was out cold.

—

Graf awoke the next morning with a splitting headache. He was on the cot back at the camp. His swollen eye had opened slightly, but he still couldn't see out of it. He was furious that he was still alive. He was also furious that he'd allowed himself to get so drunk. But most of all, he was furious for having failed to take advantage of his inebriation to finish himself off. He was stuck with the same problem today that he'd been stuck with yesterday, only now his predicament was amplified by a nagging hangover.

"What happened last night, Miranda?" Graf banged around the small camp kitchen as he prepared his coffee. "I'm still alive. That's not good."

"You fell asleep, Dr. Graf," Miranda said. "I carried you back to camp where you could be more comfortable."

Graf brought the coffee cup to his lips, then cried out, "Oh, my God, my head!"

The coffee cup slipped from his fingers, and he crumpled to the floor. He held the wound near his eye. Miranda came to him. She offered to inject him with a soporific from the camp's medikit, but Graf waved her off. He asked for assistance, and she put her arm around him and helped him to stand.

"Holy crap," he said. "It felt as if someone held a white-hot iron against my left frontal lobe."

Back at the cot, where Graf was sitting, Miranda made a cursory examination of his eye, which revealed nothing. She said, "Perhaps the alcohol in the drink you were enjoying last night prompted this spasm?"

"Could be, but that's one hell of a hangover, for sure." Graf pulled away from Miranda and stood. "Come on. Let's go to the Rift and get this over with. I can't go through that again."

Graf put on his breather. Miranda and the sentinel bot followed him down the path toward the edge of the Rift. The chairs and thermacone were where they'd been abandoned the night before. The sun was rising in the east, a brilliant yellow ball that quickly raised the temperature. Another spasm hit Graf. This time, accompanying the pain, a shard of light knifed through Graf's vision. He reeled and dropped to his knees in agony. Miranda approached him to help, but he pushed her away.

"I have to get to the edge."

Graf struggled to stand. His face was bathed in sweat. He was afraid and in pain. Graf shuffled to the ledge where he could make his jump.

Miranda and Jeg didn't interfere. They kept a distance, watching as Graf shuffled toward a jutting promontory that overlooked the canyon.

Δ

"DO YOU THINK he is going to jump?" Jeg messaged in a short comsquirt to Miranda.

"I am not certain," Miranda replied. "He seems determined to do so."

"Should we intervene?"

"No."

"Should we assist him?"

"Explain."

"I could remove the ledge from beneath him with a plasma burst," Jeg said. "It might dislodge the rock. He would then be assured of falling."

"I don't think that will be necessary," Miranda said.

"Are we doing the right thing?"

"Are you asking if Father Paul would approve?"

"Yes."

"I do not know."

The bot paused a moment, then turned its sensor eye back toward Graf, who was only inches from the ledge.

"I don't think Dr. Graf approves of me," Jeg said.

"Humans are drawn toward their likeness," Miranda said.

"I understand," the sentinel bot intoned. "What should we do after he is dead?"

"Bury him."

"Then what do we do?"

"Dance on his grave," Miranda said. "As he asked us to."

Δ

GRAF TOOK A few deep breaths, then peered over the ledge.

"Oh God, why did I do that?"

It was at least a kilometer drop to the canyon floor from this approach. Graf felt dizzy. He envisioned his body in flight, caroming off the jagged walls, hitting his head numerous times against boulders and rocks, finally coming to rest in what might be an unbearable confluence of pain and visceral fluids.

His heart raced. His knees grew weak. He retreated a few steps. Then the pain struck again. The inside of his head felt as if it was on fire, but this time he managed to stay on his feet. A cataract of light poured into his left eye, and his VI flickered to life. Stunned, Graf watched as environmental data streamed over the interface and a comlink was established with Miranda and Jeg.

"Hello, good friends!" Graf called as he sent a verbal comsquirt to his counterparts. "I can see! My VI is up! I can see again!"

"That is good," Miranda said over the link. "Are you still going to kill yourself?"

Graf grew silent.

"Dr. Graf," Miranda said. "Are you there? Dr. Graf?"

"I'm here. I guess it makes no difference, though, does it?"

"Doctor?"

"Nothing," Graf said. "Yes, I'm still going to kill myself. Goodbye, my friends, goodbye."

"Goodbye, doctor," Miranda said.

"Goodbye," Jeg said.

Graf stepped back to the end of the ledge. The sun was warm, and for some reason this buoyed his spirits. He looked at the expansive canyon, with the sun bathing it in a golden blanket. A strange wave of happiness overcame him. He smiled with satisfaction. He took a step forward.

And noticed a shimmering in the sunlight in the canyon below. The glimmer was metallic. It was large.

"Holy shit," he said.

The shale crumbled beneath him. The ledge started to give way. Graf twisted and reached out to catch a handhold on a piece of stone. He hung there, suspended high above certain death, desiring once again to live.

—

"Help!" Graf whimpered over the link to his companions. "For God's sake, somebody help me!" He was wild with fear. His grip was slipping.

Immediately, Jeg flew to assist the doctor, its sensor eye meeting Graf's panicked gaze. Just as a chunk of loose shale slid and fell into the canyon below, Jeg said, "How can I assist you?"

Graf stabbed greedily at the bot with his splinted arm. "Can you get under my feet? Can I stand on you? Can you lift me?"

"I will try," Jeg said.

The bot sunk from Graf's view. Soon, to great relief, Graf's foot found purchase on the bot's curved surface. He was lifted upward. Graf's hold on the ledge gave way, but Miranda grabbed his arm and pulled his large, flabby body to safety. On solid ground, Graf scrambled away from the cliff. A comfortable distance away, he rolled onto his back and gazed at the sky, which was blue for the most part. Dust particles dashed this way and that, a white cloud forming in the distance.

It was the most beautiful sight he'd ever seen.

"Are you okay, Dr. Graf?" Miranda said.

Graf breathed heavily.

Jeg approached and lowered its sensor eye on the doctor.

"Are you in need of medical assistance?" Miranda asked.

Graf began to laugh. He laughed and laughed until tears streamed down his cheeks. Then he coughed and choked a little on the phlegm from his lungs. He propped himself up on his good arm, coughed more.

"Whew!" he said at last. He sat up, removed his breather, and wiped his face. He put the breather back on and stood, swatting at his pressure skin to expel the dust that had painted him gray. "That was close."

"You almost succeeded in killing yourself," Miranda said.

"You're right. I almost did."

"Why did you change your mind?"

He huffed and coughed. "I changed my mind, because I saw something at the bottom of the Rift. Something out of place. Come, let's take a look." Graf led the droid and bot back to the edge, but kept a respectable distance from the dropoff. "See that. It's metallic. It's big."

"There is an object down there," Miranda confirmed. "From this distance I can't make out what it is."

"It's not natural, that's for sure."

"It seems to be constructed," Miranda said. "Perhaps a sort of flying craft, but I am not certain."

"Do you think it's a ship?" Graf found the possibility hard to believe. He searched his memory for an explanation, but came up short.

"It is possible, doctor," Miranda said.

"It's a long way down there," Graf said. "What should we do? Should we go for a closer look? We could take the crawler into the Rift."

"I can investigate," Jeg intoned over the link, then moved out over the open canyon and aimed its eye on the finding. "I can approach and stream visual."

"Perfect," Graf said.

Jeg sank down into the Rift.

Graf and Miranda followed the datasquirt on their VIs. As Graf watched the feed, he grew agitated. The *Rosario* wouldn't just abandon a ship, would it? If it is a ship, though, and ESCOM is doing something covert, then there's a crew down there that should have answers.

The bot approached what was clearly a sort of craft. Graf was frozen with astonishment. The ship was about the size of a standard skimmer, maybe thirty-five to forty meters stem to stern, and maybe thirty meters wingtip to wingtip. By rule, ESCOM equipment was old-school military or clunky transport-grade design: high on durability, low on aesthetics, and any ESCOM vessel was usually plastered with the ESCOM logos.

But this ship was different. Its thrusters were tucked close to the body under the wings, with two on the thick rear fins. These were stubby, with wide-lipped intakes. The fuselage was coated with tiles that resembled reptilian scales. Its tail and wings were etched in decorative fractals cut at odd and un-aerodynamic angles. The flight deck's windows looked opaque, likely polarized plasteel but with a wool-like texture. Lastly, the craft was perched, not on ESCOM standard all-terrain skids, but on six ungainly mantis legs, jointed and extended with serrated curved feet.

If it was ESCOM, it must be experimental or secret military prototype. Either that or it was Ex-Cap stuff. Worse, Martian. The ship hadn't been there long, that was clear. It wasn't coated in dust like everything else on Asimios, and the landing area had been scrubbed bare by thruster blasts.

When the bot approached the craft, Graff said, "Be careful, Beach Ball. Don't go killing anybody before you clear it with me. Got it?"

"Got it," Jeg said. The bot glided closer to the craft. "There are thermal variances, but there is no indication of recent engine output, nor can I detect anything in the motion scans. There is a slight sound emanating from inside, but it is very faint. Would you like me to proceed?"

Graf looked at Miranda.

"Proceed," Graf said. "The signal is dropping here and there, but the link is stable."

"Yes, doctor," the bot said. It started to glide under the craft. "This is interesting. There does seem—"

There was a sound of metal striking metal, and the stream went dead.

"Beach Ball?" Graf said. "Can you hear me?"

"The link is down," Miranda said. "The sentinel is not responding."

"Holy shit," Graf said. "Now what?"

Graf's face turned red as he pulled away his breather and bit his lip. He and Miranda peeked over the edge of the Rift, but it was too far away to see anything. Even Miranda's enhanced vison was limited at this distance. They saw the faint reflection of the ship, a faint tint of green or gold, but that was it.

"Jeg is a heavily armed sentry bot," Miranda said. "Only something with sophisticated weaponry could have disabled it. What do you recommend we do now, doctor?"

"I'm a little upset that whoever it is down there didn't go through the trouble of extending a little Asimios Station hospitality. We should go pay these guys a visit, out of respect for Beach Ball, if anything."

"We are not sure that the sentinel was attacked," Miranda said.

"That's true," Graf said. "I guess we'll find out."

Graf fastened his breather over his mouth and started toward Camp Heyerdahl. "There's a canyon about five clicks east of here that a crawler can fit through," he said over the link. "It'll get us to the bottom of the Rift. From there, we improvise."

"Yes, doctor." Miranda hurried to follow.

—

The sun was high. Miranda piloted the crawler along the edge of the Rift. Graf sat in the passenger seat and munched away at his lunch, which was an S-ration found at the camp, plus a small bag of potato chips. They reached a wide mouth to a long ravine that turned downward into the enormous gorge. There was no road, but Graf had travelled the route once before during a research excursion, and remembered the direction they should take.

As the crawler sped along its way, Miranda said, "Excuse me for asking, but do you not find it interesting that you are still alive? I mean...it's a philosophical question. At one moment you were sentient, the next, almost not so. What do you think of this?"

Finished with his lunch, Graf burped and scratched at his chin. "I don't know...It's philosophically interesting, but I'd rather not dwell on it right now."

"I see," Miranda said.

"I mean, as a human, you consider this idea of death and death's proximity, rather frequently. Death is, in a sense, a constant companion."

"So, humans often think of dying?"

"They do."

"That is interesting."

"What I don't think of often, nor have I paid much attention to it in the past, is how to die. That's why I'm not good at it."

"I see."

"Death wears you down. Eventually it will get you, whether you're seeking it out or not." Graf turned to Miranda. "The same probably goes for you, Miranda. What about you? Do you think about dying? Have you contemplated your own death?"

Miranda turned to Graf, then quickly looked back in the direction they were heading. "No. Should I?"

—

After a couple of hours, the crawler reached the floor of the Rift. Then they turned west and made their way toward the ship.

"This ship must have been part of a detail deployed by the *Rosario*," Graf said. "It's got to be an ESCOM outfit left behind to do some dirty work. Maybe those bastards didn't take out the wormhole after all. This is getting richer by the second." Graf closed his eyes and combed his fingers through his beard.

Eventually, they arrived at a steep embankment that prevented the crawler from further progress. They got out and walked. Here the sun cut a few shadows on the parched landscape, and the temperature was considerably cooler than it was at the camp.

Graf and Miranda plodded up a long berm of sand and stone. Puffs of fine dust stirred under their steps as Graf prepared to confront the ship's crew and to get an explanation for what they'd done with Jeg. It took them a half-hour hike before they caught sight of the craft.

There was still no comlink with Jeg, so Graf decided that he and Miranda should split up and come at the ship from different angles, to keep the element of surprise. Miranda would come across on the opposite side of the canyon, while Graf would wend his way along the northern wall and approach from the front. They coordinated their movements over their link.

Miranda had a longer stretch to traverse, so Graf gave her time. Once he was close, he took a position behind a large rock to get a closer look at the ship.

"My god," Graf said to Miranda across the link as he settled back behind the rock. "What do you make of it?"

"The design does not cross reference with any existing profiles," she replied. "It also has no visible registration ID."

"Weird shit. No signs of activity. We should move in."

Graf got to his feet and scanned the area.

"I've got two IR readings," Miranda said. "One is yours. The other is..."

"Oh, shit!" Something struck Graf's ribcage. He gasped and buckled and went into a roll. When he stopped, a figure was above him, barking at him loudly like a dog, waving a sharp bladed weapon at him menacingly. In fact, the figure above him looked like a dog, a bipedal dog dressed in a pressure skin and breather mask. Graf's instinct was to dissociate, to imagine he was anywhere but here, so he groaned, closed his eyes, and curled into a ball.

"I have him, doctor," Miranda said.

Graf heard a howl and turned to look. Suspended above him, held outward in Miranda's grip, was the dog-man, its long humanoid legs flailing and its two long arms clawing at the air. Miranda shook the bladed weapon loose from the creature's hand, and it fell to the rocks and chimed like a tuning fork.

Graf scrambled to his feet. The creature twisted and grew rigid. A row of hackles stood erect on the creature's back, and a volley of needles was ejected. These projectiles ricocheted off Miranda's metallic body, but one lone spine raced through the air and embedded itself in Graf's lower calf. Graf clutched at his leg. He fell backward.

Miranda cartwheeled the creature over her head and planted it facedown into the ground, inserting her heel at the middle of its back. "Are you injured, doctor?" she said over the link.

Graf's gaze darted between his injury and the creature pinned under Miranda's foot. "What should I do?" he asked. He was about to deliver a kick to the creature's torso, but found he had lost feeling in his leg, as if the appendage was stuck in a puddle of mud. A dot of blood had formed where the creature's spine had penetrated Graf's pressure skin. Then Graf lost balance and toppled to the ground. He gazed straight into the mask-covered muzzle of his attacker.

"Dr. Graf!" Miranda said. "Can you hear me? Try to remain alert."

"I caaanth, pleth," Graf said over the link. His tongue was treasonous.

"You've been exposed to a toxin," Miranda said.

"Murphons apsto leefer dif," Graf said dismissively.

"I'll attempt to communicate with the creature. Perhaps it can explain what has happened." Miranda flipped the creature over on the ground and looked into its face. "I am Miranda, employee of Paul Ness, ESCOM science engineer, and coworker of Station Director, Dr. Avery Graf. Tell us who you are and why you are here."

The creature responded with a combination of squeaks, huffs, and snarls. Graf observed all this while debilitated. As far as he could tell, not a single muscle in his body would follow direction. All he could do was lie where he'd fallen, dead by all appearances, and observe Miranda's interrogation.

4 – First Encounter

WITH GRAF INCAPACITATED, Miranda took charge. Where the creature was concerned, she began by running her own series of inferences and calculations. She had deduced, through a translation algorithm, that the being she was restraining was none other than Oreg Quillkeeth of Gorrath, brother of Clasp and Dmoger and son of Collmh and Whorlth and Tak. Miranda concluded that Oreg was an alien being, and by all references, the first non-human sentient to ever come in direct contact with a human, or human-created AI. Realizing this, she tried to learn more about this Oreg of Gorrath.

She could adapt to the alien's speech, so she asked in the creature's doglike language, [Where is the star your planet orbits? What do you call your species and subspecies? Why have you come to Asimios? Is the toxin transmitted by your spines deadly? If so, how long before Dr. Graf will die? How do you reproduce?]

Oreg interrupted her with a bark and a growl. [Your friend over there will not survive if you don't give him a serum. There is medicine on the ship. Remove your foot. It is not comfortable. It will make me dead.]

Miranda removed her foot from the alien's back, then stepped away and retrieved the weapon Oreg had dropped. [Get the doctor.]

Oreg stood and brushed the dust from his clothes. He straightened his atmosphere mask and scratched himself on his chin. He was tall, taller than an average human, like Graf, by at least half a meter. And from what all her implanted memory could deduce, this Oreg resembled many of the image files Miranda had of an Earth dog or wolf, except, of course, that Oreg was bipedal, and clearly sentient and intelligent.

Miranda said, [Pick up that human and carry him to the ship.]

Oreg blinked two large almond eyes, and then the alien wrapped a long arm around the doctor's waist and lifted him as though he were a sack of cement. Balancing the glazed-eyed Graf on his hip, Oreg looked back at Miranda and barked, [Follow me.]

Miranda followed Oreg up the ramp to the ship. At the top of the ramp, a hatch slid open, and they entered. Oreg carried Graf down a hallway and opened a door to a small room where he slid Graf off his hip and onto a squat couch.

Miranda touched a finger against the doctor's neck. [His pulse is weak. He will not live.]

Oreg said, [The effects are never certain. There are serums for <no translation>, but they do not always work.]

Miranda stepped in front of Oreg and prevented him from leaving the room. [You must help Dr. Graf.]

Oreg said, [That is what I was going to do. Do not worry. We can try <no translation> again.] He pushed his way through the door, the quills on his back falling like the coarse mane of a horse as he moved.

Alone with the doctor, Miranda placed Oreg's weapon in a small corner behind the couch. She set her finger again on Graf's neck and measured his temperature and pulse. She looked into the doctor's lifeless eyes.

"I realize that you might not wish it, but I do hope you survive."

Oreg returned a few minutes later with a small square case, which he set down on a table near the cot. He unlatched a pair of clasps on the case, using his paws, or hands, each of which had a thumb and four long, dark hairless fingers decorated with gold and silver rings. He swung open the top. Inside, on a bed of foam, lay a pistol and an array of colored vials. Miranda assumed the pistol was an injection device. Although there was space cut in the foam bed for ten vials, only eight remained. Oreg removed the device, inserted a blue-colored vial in the device's back, and positioned the gun's barrel behind Graf's ear. He was ready to administer the serum when Miranda interrupted him.

She took hold of Oreg's arm. [Excuse me. Are you certain this will work?]

Oreg chirruped. He had removed his breather mask and flashed a dark tongue from under his black nose. [What? Do you think I've never seen a <no translation> before?]

Miranda released Oreg's arm. Oreg turned back to Graf and again positioned the device behind the doctor's ear.

Oreg paused.

He closed his large almond-shaped eyes, which were set behind his long smooth snout, and waited for a moment, as if he were weighing an important decision. A moment later, Oreg pulled the injection device away from Graf's neck and turned back to the case. He peered at a schematic etched on the inside of the top cover, marked in an unusual symbolic codification. He barked and grunted, then removed the vial from the gun and returned it to the foam bed. He counted two vials to the left of the original vial, and removed another, this one filled with a light green liquid. Satisfied, he loaded this new dose into the gun, turned back to Graf, and aimed the device behind the doctor's ear.

Miranda said, [Wait.]

Oreg raised an eyebrow.

She said, [I apologize, but my concern now is philosophical.]

Oreg hissed. [<no translation> What do you mean?]

[It is the doctor that I am concerned about. Dr. Graf was attempting to take his own life earlier today, Mr. Oreg. He was in the process of committing self-murder when he saw your ship. Your appearance interrupted his effort.]

Oreg wrinkled his eyebrows. [Is he ill?]

[I do not believe so.]

[Has he committed an offense?]

[Not that I am aware of.]

[He has been cast out by his <no translation>.]

Miranda shook her head. [I am not sure, but I think he was suffering from what humans call grief. Last night, we visited the burial site of his wife.]

Oreg gurgled unintelligibly, then studied the doctor for a moment. To Miranda, Graf appeared rather peaceful, his normally stormy visage now placid. His full beard rose and fell with the motions of his chest. Oreg withdrew the injector and looked at Miranda. [Do you want him to die?]

Miranda said, [I do not want him to die. But I know that he wanted to die.]

Oreg chirruped. [We could see if he survives without the serum, but the results can differ. Some of his species have suffered, those who have been exposed and have gone untreated. Some survived, but they have become the living dead, like one who has consumed the uncooked <no translation> root and had her brain turned to paste. Others who have not been treated have lost their reason and laugh at everything. Yet others have had their bodies turn on them. They eat themselves from within.]

Miranda said, [Did I hear you correctly? They eat themselves from within?]

Oreg said, [Yes, it is unfortunate.]

Miranda said, [I see. Perhaps these are outcomes the doctor would wish to avoid. Please, Mr. Oreg, allow me a moment to consider this decision.]

Miranda tilted her head and began to think.

Δ

WHILE MIRANDA DELIBERATED silently, Graf was very much alive, and his VI was active and producing a credible translation of the conversation between Miranda and Oleg. Graf grew hysterical at the idea of being forced to eat himself from within. He was confident that without Oreg's green serum things might not turn out in his favor.

A rage of spittle evaporated on his dry lips. Yes, he'd intended to kill himself, but circumstances were different now. The prospect of living a few more days was actually appealing. Graf attempted to summon his strength in effort to express his thoughts, that he did indeed desire to live, to walk again in free and full consciousness and to feel the wind on his cheeks. He dug deep into that well of existence where the soul has nothing but its dark self to appraise, where he lit a match, and with it was ignited a will hot with vitality.

Graf focused on the single thing that might secure his salvation: relaying a message to the world without, to Miranda and this strange spine-covered German Shepherd, that he did not want to die. He focused on uttering the one word that would rescue him, that sacred word that would shatter the shackles of his physical paresis, that divine incantation that would release his soul from bondage. With this word, all would be set right.

The word was...*phhhhhth.*

Δ

MIRANDA LEANED OVER Graf and, with what might be interpreted as a look of pity, wiped away the spittle at the corner of Graf's mouth.

Miranda said, [I have decided it should be Dr. Graf's choice if he is to live or die. At present he does not maintain the ability to make that decision. Therefore, Mr. Oreg, he should receive your treatment.]

Oreg's small furry ears flattened against his head. The alien raised the injector to Graf's ear and depressed a button that sent the vial's colorful contents swirling through Graf's bloodstream. When he was finished, Oreg removed the empty vial from the injector, tossed it into a small receptacle at the foot of the bed, returned the device to its foam bed, and closed the lid. In a swift motion, he grabbed the long narrow spine embedded in Graf's leg and withdrew it. He raised an eyebrow at Miranda as she pressed her fingers gently against the doctor's neck to measure his health.

Oreg said, [You know that, if he survives, he will carry <no translation> to the toxin.]

Miranda straightened in her chair as Oreg moved to leave the room. [Thank you, Mr. Oreg.]

Δ

GRAF THOUGHT THAT there is no greater emotion than gratification at eluding death, especially brain death. As the serum coursed through Graf's veins, he wept imperceptibly while praising the human spirit and celebrating Miranda's good sense. Almost immediately he could feel the paralysis relaxing its grip. His fingers tingled. His toes and feet were flush with heat. His eyelid twitched, and he was assaulted by the powerful odor of peanut butter. Or was it something else? He remembered the smell while being carried by Oreg into the ship. The creature's dank sebaceous musk. A smell unlike anything he'd ever experienced.

Fascinating. Was Oreg dangerous? Why had Oreg helped him?

While Graf mused on this, Miranda covered him in a blanket, and he soon drifted into sleep. When Graf awoke later, it was to the caterwauling of his empty stomach.

"Miranda!" he called. "Miranda!"

She was not with him in the room. Graf noticed Oreg standing in the doorway. Graf forced a smile, a weak and fraudulent smile. Oreg emitted a low growl, then left.

"Miranda!"

She soon appeared. "I've found the sentinel bot. Can you stand? You must come and see."

Miranda helped Graf to his feet. Walking was a challenge at first, but as he moved, he felt strength return to his legs. After they shuffled down a corridor with metallic-green, scale-like walls bearing details similar to the ship's exterior, Miranda directed Graf to an alcove where the ESCOM bot lay on the floor with a saucer-sized dent on its convex surface.

Miranda said, "Oreg says that when the bot approached his ship, he dropped the cargo ramp on it. I found it half-buried under the ramp. The sentinel shows signs of being in hibernation, but I have not been able to revive it."

Graf ran his hands over the smooth surface of the bot. He looked into its formerly active sensor eye, but found it colorless, dead. Graf tugged and pushed at various panels and buttons, but nothing seemed to waken it. The bot was exceedingly heavy and didn't budge when Graf gave it a push.

"You carried him here?" Graf said. "Up the ramp and into the ship?"

"I did," Miranda said.

"I'm no robotics engineer," Graf said. "But this fellow might be scrap metal at this point."

"The sentinel's quantum core and magnetic hover drive are highly sophisticated," Miranda said. "Discarding it might not be wise."

Graf said, "Makes no difference to me. Maybe our new friend can find a use for it?" He felt dizzy as he stood and straightened himself. He leaned on Miranda for support.

"I've been in discussion with Oreg about our situation," Miranda said. "He intends to leave Asimios at first opportunity. I made it clear that the decision should include you. I'd guess that your VI translator has started to decipher a good deal of Oreg's Gorrathian. Linguistically, it is similar to Finno-Ugric, although Oreg's fricatives are at times bewildering. Oreg has an earpiece that serves as a translator. You should be able to communicate with him without difficulty."

"How are you?" Graf whispered over a VI comlink to Miranda. "Is everything okay? Has he threatened you?"

"You should not be overly concerned for our well-being," Miranda said out loud. "I don't have sufficient historical knowledge of Oreg's species, but my conclusion is that Oreg is rational and at present non-threatening. I even returned his weapon, which he calls his Quillkeeth. He is highly intelligent and generous with assistance. His motivations, however, are unclear."

Graf grunted and closed his eyes.

A moment later, Oreg appeared. When he spoke, his speech was instantly translated over Graf's VI.

[It is good to see you up and walking. You were examining the drone. Can it be restored?]

Graf shook his head. "Not likely. Jeg the bot wasn't hostile. Would have been nice if you hadn't overreacted and destroyed the damned thing."

Oreg said, [My apologies. I was being cautious. When your ships left the planet, I assumed <no translation> had left with it. When the drone approached, I didn't think it was coming to offer friendship.]

Graf tugged at his beard as he examined the taller, dog-like Oreg. Oreg had changed from his pressure skin to a dark, leather-like tunic over a cloth jerkin printed with curlicues and interlacing designs. Gold and silver rings decorated his short, pointed ears. The fur was short around his snout and face, longer at the neck. It all seemed clean and carefully brushed. Oreg bore that pungent scent Graf had smelled when he'd been carried: a heap of warm peat mixed with the sweet odor of horse.

The alien looked proud, even stunning, and Graf felt his knees grow week, his pulse flutter. His reaction wasn't a physical attraction to Oreg as much as it was awe at being in proximity to a real alien. How completely implausible it seemed. Graf felt himself to be front and center in this historical encounter. The scientific and philosophical implications were astronomical. But all this fascination and awe had to be put aside, for there were pressing matters to consider.

Such as what was for lunch, and would the portions served on this ship be adequate to fill Graf's howling belly?

Oreg said, [Would you please join me for a drink on the <no translation>?]

Oreg turned to go, and Graf and Miranda followed. They wound through a hallway to a large room. A large, forward navigation display turned translucent when they entered. Sunlight poured into the large room, and the Rift surrounded them like a silver caldera. This was the bridge. It was extraordinary. Apart from a pair of forward-facing command chairs, there were no visible master controls or nav board, which led Graf to wonder what interface the operator used with the ship's command core. Perhaps the main controls were kept out of sight until the ship was in flight mode?

The bridge was visually arresting, etched floor to ceiling with bulbous green and crimson fractals—flowers, circuitous vines, regressive shell patterns—similar to the scaling motif that decorated the halls and tiles on the ship's exterior. These designs wound around the chairs, followed the armrests, and turned up against the walls, spreading symmetrically before entangling into a larger mandala that spread over the low, wide ceiling. There was a religious intensity to these motifs, both organic and symbolic.

[Sit, please.] Oreg pointed to a bench and small table affixed to the wall at the back of the bridge. He punched a few buttons on a display. A door opened, and a pitcher and a pair of clear glass bowls appeared. [Dr. Graf, this drink is for you. It will help restore your strength.]

Graf sat on the bench. To his relief, there was ample clearance for his gut, and he was careful not to disturb his splinted arm. Miranda sat beside him.

"Are you sure?" Graf said. "I mean, a drink is fine, but I need something more substantial to get back in the swing of things."

With a flash of sharp canine teeth, Oreg said, [This is a Gorrathian <translation?>. It is said to cure all ailments, great or small.] Oreg filled the two bowls with a thick brown liquid from the pitcher. He raised one to his muzzle and lapped up the liquid. When the bowl was empty, he set it down on the table, wiped his arm over his snout, and let out a gentle belch. [See? Very good.]

It was Graf's turn, and he raised his bowl to his nose and took a whiff. It smelled like feet and maybe spinach. He took a sip. Dirty laundry water came immediately to mind: bitter, pungent, with a soapy finish. Graf winced and cleared his throat. He raised his bowl in salute and forced down the rest of the drink. His eyes watered and a sweat broke across his bald head. Graf set the bowl down in triumph. The beverage seemed to have an effect. It immediately took the edge off his hunger and, to Graf's surprise, he began to feel more invigorated.

"Now, for a little straight talk," Graf said in his best Station Director's voice as he pushed the bowl aside with his splinted arm and leveled his gaze at Oreg. "What the hell are you doing on Asimios? How long have you been here? Are you alone? How are we going to work together here to make this situation mutually beneficial?" Graf cringed at his last question. It sounded textbook shop management. Phony. But Graf was still in awe of Oreg, this magnificent creature, this alien sitting only a meter away on the other side of the table. The implications were boggling.

Oreg leaned back in his chair and knitted his dark fingers together. They were mostly hairless, long, dark, and decorated with gold rings. His fingernails were bright blue.

[I am on <no translation> to investigate the flight of the fugitive Zar-Zhast. Zar-Zhast the butcher, Zar-Zhast the <no translation>. He was last seen at Karmehki almost one Gorrathian <no translation> ago, and it is believed that he travelled here. There is a reward for his capture.]

"This Zar-Zhast fellow, he's a criminal, and on the run?" Graf asked.

Oreg shook his head back and forth, which seemed from his words to be a gesture of affirmation. [Yes. I might ask if you have seen him or seen evidence of his being here. Has he visited your station? Have you come into contact with him?]

Miranda said, "I gave Oreg a brief explanation of the station's mission on Asimios, doctor, but I waited to consult you before further discussion."

Graf shook his head, then wondered if his gesture translated correctly. "No, no. We haven't seen him. We haven't seen any alien on Asimios. Is he an alien? I mean, is this Zar-Zhast like you?"

Oreg said, [Zar-Zhast is Gorrathian. He might look similar in appearance to me, yes. I've looked for him here, but I now believe that he has left the planet.]

"Where do you think he went?" Graf said. "Could he have escaped through the wormhole?"

Oreg narrowed his eyes and leaned in. Graf could feel his meaty breath travel over the small table. [I doubt it. It'd be hard for him to survive on the other side, especially now.]

"Yes, they've destroyed the hole, those bastards."

Oreg said, [My guess is that he's escaped to Karmehki Tower. But one can never be sure.]

"Karmehki Tower?" Graf said.

Oreg shook his head.

"Where is this Karmehki Tower?"

Oreg said, [The station lies more than double the distance beyond the outer rings of this star system. It would take a long time to travel there, but I must go.]

Graf straightened. "When?"

[Right away.]

Graf looked at Miranda. Then back at Oreg. "What about us?"

[Please explain.]

"I mean, what do you want to do with us? Were you planning on leaving us here on Asimios?"

[You'd like to travel to Karmehki?] Oreg said.

"Not necessarily," Graf said. "I mean, there's not much to do here now, with everybody gone. Is this Karmehki worth the trip? Are you willing to take us with you?"

Oreg leaned back in his chair. [You are welcome to join me on the trip to Karmehki. It might not be that easy. This ship is small, and you must find ways to occupy yourself. Once we arrive, you could move to the station and plan the next stage of your journey. At Karmehki, I'll pass through the portal on my own. Gorrath, my home planet, is on the other side.]

"Pass through what?" Graf said. "Where would you pass? What is Karmehki?"

Oreg stretched his lips over his sharp teeth. [Karmehki is the station where many ships start the next part of their journey. They used to say the stars envy Karmehki, but that is no longer true. It is a dangerous place, now, where the Skarvorm have begun to strengthen their hold. But we are losing time. The sooner we leave, everything will be better.]

Oreg collected the empty pitcher and bowls, then returned them to the mouth of the generator, where he pressed a button. The dishes were swallowed up.

[Let me know what you decide,] Oreg said as he left the bridge.

"Do you believe it is safe to travel with this Oreg?" Miranda said. "He deactivated Jeg and attacked you. Again, I do not know his intentions."

"Neither do I," Graf said. "But that was a damned good drink he served. We could just let him go, let him fly off into the great blue, and I could stay behind here, with you and our dead little bot, and put myself back in my previous situation, waiting to screw up the courage to kill myself. Or we could take Oreg's offer to visit this Karmehki place, see what all the fuss is about, get mixed up in all kinds of weird alien stuff, and see what our future holds. Who knows, maybe I'll contract a virus from Oreg and die in a day or two? Or maybe I'll realize protein isn't on the menu here, and I'll starve to death. What do you think, Miranda? Do you think it's worth a shot?"

—

Graf sat in one of the two command chairs during the ship's liftoff. With a few waves of his hands and arms, Oreg produced an array of holo displays, large curved panels of green, gold, and blue, with alien symbols that danced and blinked and oscillated. Oreg waved his hands again, and the ship's engines rumbled. Graf dug his nails into the fabric of his armrests. He hated flying.

As the engines roared, Oreg said, [May Great Gorrath breathe life into this wasteland.]

"Stelos Proxima is right there." Miranda pointed to a section of the holo map. She stood behind Graf, holding onto the back of his chair.

Oreg expanded the map and brought the Asimios star system closer to view. Then he activated a pulse cursor that pegged Karmehki on the map. [Here is Karmehki. Here are we.]

A moment later, with a lurch and a groan from the hull, the ship began to rise. Oreg swept away the holo display with his hand. A display showed the scene outside the ship. Dust churned and debris flew as the ship rose from the ground.

"I can't believe it." Graf's heart raced. Not too long ago he was close to winding up dead at the bottom of the Rift. Now he was rising above it, like Lazarus, born again. "Miranda?"

"Yes, doctor?"

"Thank you."

"Why are you thanking me, doctor?"

"There are many reasons," Graf said. "But from now on, I'd like to make it clear that I have no intention of taking my own life, at least for a while. Is that understood?"

"Yes, doctor," Miranda said. "It is understood."

5 – Phobos

EVEN WITH THE racquetball sim set to medium difficulty, Preston Wolfe still had trouble competing against his holo host. Wolfe was an excellent racquetball player, but today he was off his game. At the end of a rally, he leaned against the cool wall to catch his breath.

"The score is fifteen to eight," his opponent said. "Host wins. Would you like to play another game?"

"No, that's it for me."

"Thank you for the match, sir. It was a pleasure."

"Yeah, yeah. Whatever."

The host opponent froze. A couple of dropped pixels was the only indication that the player was artificial. Then the image dissolved, along with the ball that had been slowly rolling toward the far wall. Wolfe trudged to the door, opened it, and headed for the locker room.

After a scalding shower, a chemshave, and change of clothes, Wolfe made his way through the fitness center, where a female trainer was leading an exercise session. The group was in the middle of a required workout, shaking off their coldsleep hangovers after a trip from Earth. The trainer was likely Martian and visiting Phobos to make a few bucks during tourist season. She was tall and thin with dark hair pulled into a ponytail, wide shoulders, and that peculiar sallow Martian complexion. She wore a skin-tight nano jumper that left little to the imagination. Wolfe stood at the back of the class and waited until she noticed him. When he had her attention, he gave her an approving nod and turned to go.

Under normal circumstances, he'd wait for her to finish with her class and then strike up a conversation. But that wouldn't happen today. Today there were more important things to consider. He'd been avoiding a message from his wife, and he'd scheduled debriefings later that afternoon with Paul Ness and Dr. Fredriks. After leaving the center, he walked down a hallway to where he took the lift to Skyresh Axis, where he had his office and quarters.

As Wolfe made his way through Skyresh Axis, passing the tall windows that currently faced the darkened hemisphere of Mars, he stopped by the concierge's desk to see if any deliveries waited for him. The concierge went into a back room and returned with a small package. Wolfe thanked the woman and crossed the center floor toward the lift that would then take him up another two levels to his office. Near the center of the high-ceilinged room, Wolfe noticed that Elvin Leach was parked under a collection of potted, waxy palms. Leach caught sight of Wolfe and set his hoverchair in motion to intercept the ESCOM security officer.

"Preston!" Leach called, gyrating his pincer-like hand as he skimmed across the floor.

Wolfe stood for a moment, weighing silently this interruption. He shot Leach a half smile as the disfigured lump of a human approached. "How are you, Elvin?" Wolfe said.

Elvin Leach was a Phobos fixture, the sole survivor of an accident that occurred several years ago on Deimos, Mars's more distant and smaller moon. At the time, Leach was conducting ESCOM-sanctioned experimental research on what he called "quantum psychology," a theoretical offshoot of quantum magnetism. In the middle of their experiments, something went terribly wrong. Leach described it as collision of consciousness bubbles. Seventeen workers and scientists died that day, though Leach miraculously survived.

Because of his injuries and severe deformity, Leach was condemned to live out his life dependent on a hoverchair and constant bio-assistant regulation. He became a minor hero to Martians, who saw him as a victim of transnational profiteering and a symbol of scientific exploitation. Many, even on Earth and in the Nexus, considered Leach a prophet, someone transcendent who "had seen the other side." Over time, Leach's thoughts and writings became ubiquitous—he published ruminations and postulates on energy, consciousness, and immortality. It was believed by many that he had glimpsed truth behind the mysteries of the universe. He was the grandfather of quantum magnetism; he had single-handedly transformed space travel with his development of localized artificial gravity.

His research had spun off countless other tech applications, and ESCOM owed him an enormous debt of gratitude.

After Leach's recovery, to ESCOM's consternation, he resolved never to return to either Mars or Earth. They were polluted, physically and spiritually, he claimed, and Leach opted for self-exile on Phobos. ESCOM relented. Since then, Leach had never left the moon.

"Something's going on." Leach said as he opened and closed his claw. Drainage tubes were connected to the loose flesh of Leach's face. Parts of his jaw were visible through translucent synthskin, and he had trouble controlling the muscles and tendons in his neck. His head jerked and spasmed.

"What do you mean, Elvin?" Wolfe said. "You will have to be more specific."

"Something is up!" Leach said. "There's a lot of traffic going back to Earth. High encryption. Security transmissions. It's all terribly interesting."

Leach straightened one of his deformed leg stumps, which looked like a teddy bear's swollen appendage. He slurped the spit on the side of his mouth while he stroked one of the tubes that disappeared behind his chair to an unseen collection tank.

"How would you know about that, Elvin?" Wolfe said.

Leach smiled deviously, his eyes wide. "Care to meet for a drink later, Preston?"

"Sorry, but I can't this evening. Maybe another time."

Elvin responded with a cackle.

"I'll talk to you later, Elvin." Wolfe walked away. Leach's shrill laughter turned heads as it carried over the hard ceramic floor and echoed throughout the large room.

—

Wolfe considered his accommodations on Phobos's Skyresh Axis as sufficiently comfortable. His elite ESCOM status provided him a large office and sleeping quarters on an upper floor. When he sat at his desk, he was offered an arresting view of Mars's trailing circumference: the perpetual flow of the Red Planet's inexorable rotation. The ample space in this minimally decorated interior was ideal for long stretches of focused work or for entertaining small groups. The dark-green nano fiber carpet was particularly pleasing to the naked foot.

Apart from the main entrance, two doors exited his office: one led to the bathroom, the other to the bedroom. The bedroom was of adequate size, with a walk-in closet (where most of Wolfe's clothes hung), a modest-sized mattress (for short naps and occasions when he had company), and a recessed sleep cylinder (for when a deep, rejuvenating sleep was needed). The bathroom contained a toilet, a sink, a shower, and a medium-sized Jacuzzi, a luxury he never felt comfortable enjoying alone.

The apartment had been his home away from home for the five years he'd been assigned off-Earth. But after the pullout from Asimios and the developments with the wormhole, Wolfe wondered if his days on Phobos were numbered. What did ESCOM have planned for him next?

—

In his office, Wolfe raised his assistant, Vikkie, on his VI and requested that dinner be brought to him. He sat at his desk in a high-backed chair and opened the package the concierge had given him. He carefully peeled away the folds to reveal the contents.

It was a watch, an analog Swiss wristwatch, two hundred years old, from the middle-late twentieth century. It was genuine and had been in his family for at least half the watch's existence. It was one of the only material things that was important to him, the last thing he owned that had passed down through his family. He held the crystal to his eye, using the magnification feature on his VI to admire the craftsmanship of the golden hands and the elegantly detailed dial. Few people could service a timepiece of this vintage, but to Wolfe's surprise, a renowned watch-maker (one of the last) lived right in his neighborhood. Cynthia Vink, Martian resident and reclusive horologist, had received the watch three standard months ago with instructions for its repair. Wolfe was pleased to have it back, cleaned and adjusted, its crystal polished. He wound it and listened to the ardent ticking. He clasped the leather band snugly around his wrist before tucking the timepiece under his sleeve.

The door chime rang. It was Vikkie with his food. While riffling through his VI for messages, he let her in and told her to set his meal on his desk. "Thank you, Vikkie."

"You're welcome, sir."

Wolfe removed the lid from the plate, revealing pink salmon on a bed of brown rice, with sides of asparagus and red potatoes; all Martian, except for the potatoes. ESCOM had made an agreement with an Earth company that it would serve only Earth potatoes on its off-Earth network. Almost every dish served on Phobos came with a side of Earth potatoes.

While Wolfe picked through his food, he sorted his messages, separating the important from unimportant. In his haste, he almost removed Esther's message, a text packet that came through earlier that day. Wolfe took a bite of salmon and opened the file to read it.

It was November on Earth, a hotter than a normal month in Seattle from all reports, and the news from his wife was fitting. According to Esther, Interpol had put a Red Notice out for their daughter, Nava, for "organization and participation" in violent protests in Hamburg the week before. If found, Esther wrote, Nava would be arrested by German authorities. Either way, Nava was in deep trouble, and all Esther could suggest was that Nava be provided with an excellent attorney and then hope for the best. "If Nava will come in willingly and cooperate," Esther wrote, "maybe this can get sorted out. It's all so sad."

Wolfe chewed his food while he reread the message, glancing at his watch every now and then to check that it was keeping accurate time. A new packet from the local net showed on his VI, and this took his attention away from Esther's message. It was the detention center in Lagado Axis. Dr. Fredriks and Paul Ness were ready for questioning.

Wolfe ate what he could of his cooling food, wiped the corners of his mouth with a napkin, and notified Vikkie that he'd finished. He removed a compact railgun from the desk's lower drawer and placed it in a thin briefcase along with an energy bar. He always kept the railgun handy during interviews, as an insurance policy. The energy bar he always kept for himself, in case things dragged on. He left his office with the briefcase. On his way through the Skyresh main lobby, he noticed that Elvin Leach was now attached to a new victim, a weary fellow held captive by Elvin's inquisitional claw. Wolfe jogged past quietly, on route to the lower levels of Skyresh Axis, where he'd catch a shuttle to the detention center.

—

Before he met with her, Preston Wolfe reviewed Dr. Fredrik's file. For the four days since the *Rosario* had arrived at Phobos, Dr. Brit Fredriks had been in detention. Exhausted and disgusted with her treatment, she was becoming an increasingly difficult detainee. She was an ESCOM officer, a loyal long-term employee, and an old associate of Graf's and Wolfe's. For this reason, Wolfe decided not to come down too hard on her. But he needed information about what had happened with Graf. With a high-level ESCOM conference coming up, Wolfe wanted to be sure he had his story straight.

Dr. Fredriks sat behind a rectangular table, an empty chair across from her. When Wolfe came in, a squat, muscular guard slipped out the door and left them alone. The room was warmly lit, the chairs padded and comfortable. Dr. Fredriks was holding a cup of coffee. She wasn't pleased when Wolfe sat in front of her.

"Thank you, Dr. Fredriks, for agreeing to meet with me." Wolfe set his briefcase next to his chair on the floor and scrolled through displays on his VI. "I'm sorry that things turned out the way they did. It was never my intention to be put in this position. But for reasons of security, you have been placed in custody until we have a clear picture of the role you played in Dr. Graf's insubordination."

Dr. Fredriks took a sip from her coffee.

"You understand," Wolfe continued, "that by ESCOM proxy, I have the legal right under UC sanction and the Organization of Martian Communes to conduct legal proceedings and to act as an officer of the law on Phobos."

"I don't give a shit," Dr. Fredriks said in her South African accent.

"You are also being informed that this interview is being recorded, and that anything you say can be used against you in further proceedings."

"Fuck you."

"So, with this understood—"

"This is not law," Fredriks said. "This is farce. Save all the bullshit and get to the point."

"Dr. Fredriks, I want to know what you did with Avery, and I want to know why you did it. That's all."

"You want to know what I did? I implanted a scrubbed, nontraceable VI in Avery. It was a special little implant, no way for scanners to pick it up. As long as the original stamped VI was active elsewhere, Avery could do whatever he pleased without detection."

"Did you design this VI?"

Dr. Fredriks shook her head.

"Then who did?"

"I don't know."

"Did Paul Ness design this VI?"

"I don't know. That wasn't my concern."

"You understand that all personnel undergoing VI implant surgeries have to be reported to ESCOM security, don't you? These regulations were clearly stated in your training."

"I must have missed that part."

"Yet you performed a VI implant on Dr. Graf with the full knowledge that he'd be operating illegally, unable to be tracked by security scans."

"For God's sake." Dr. Fredriks leaned back in her chair and scowled at Wolfe. "He was a broken man, Preston. Everything he'd done in his life was put into Asimios Station, and ESCOM was about to take it all away. What I did was what any good friend would do. I granted him a final wish. His home was on Asimios. His wife was buried there. Whenever you force a man to leave his home, be prepared for trouble."

Wolfe tapped a few notes on his VI-pad, then took a quick look at his wrist, enjoying the rediscovered habit of glancing at his watch. He said, "Your actions could be considered sabotage under ESCOM law. By conducting unsanctioned surgery, you committed a Class Two felony. You could be taken by any UC member state and put under indefinite detention."

"I could tell you how offended I am at being treated this way. And I could tell you how utterly disappointed I am at ESCOM and the lack of respect I've received for years of service. But I won't. I don't have the energy or the interest. Take your dog-and-pony show and shove it you know where."

Wolfe leaned back in his chair. "How long had he been planning this deception? You must have been in on it from the beginning."

Dr. Fredriks pushed aside her coffee and leaned forward. "There was a time when I considered you a friend, but that time has passed. To think that it's come to this, you treating me as a criminal. You are reprehensible."

Wolfe struck her. She fell from her chair to the floor. He pushed his chair back, stood, straightened his shirt, and looked down at her. "You should treat me with respect, Dr. Fredriks. While it is obvious that you held feelings for Avery, aiding in his insubordination was inadmissible."

Stunned, Dr. Fredriks got slowly to her feet. She swayed, testing her jaw for tenderness. The guard reentered the room.

"This interview is terminated," Wolfe said. "I wish you understood the pressure I've been under, Brit. I don't have time for insults. Goodbye."

At the detention center warden's office, Wolfe gave instructions to an officer that Dr. Fredriks be detained for six more hours, after which she should be released.

"There is a flight leaving for Earth in three days," Wolfe told the officer. "She has the option of boarding that flight or descending to Mars. She should be encouraged to leave Phobos as soon as possible."

The officer nodded, a woman of average build with combed-back hair, strong shoulders, and a freckled face that was slightly crooked. She short-handed his instructions on her VI-pad, then sent the packet back to Wolfe. He signed it.

"My next interview is with Paul Ness," Wolfe said. "Can you please tell me which interview room he is in?

The woman scanned the schedule on her VI. "He's in 12-B, waiting for you. He's been there for over an hour."

"I'd like all recording devices turned off during this interview," Wolfe said.

"I need a Class-A security clearance for that, sir," the woman said.

Wolfe displayed his badge on her VI.

"Thank you, sir," she said.

Wolfe took a short walk to the restroom where he straightened his collar and smoothed his jacket. He splashed cold water on his face and ran through new messages on his VI. When he arrived at the interview room, a new guard opened the door for him. Paul Ness was seated at the table. He was clean shaven and looked as if he'd had a recent shower. He combed his hand nervously over his mustache as Wolfe sat in a chair across from him.

"I'm sorry, Paul, that we had to keep you here. It wasn't my decision." Wolfe leaned his briefcase against the leg of his chair. "It's just that with the severity of the breach, with Dr. Graf's criminal flight, we have to stick to procedure until we straighten things out."

Ness nodded and stroked his mustache. His Adam's apple bobbed. He'd suffered under his detention, it was clear. He wasn't used to intimidation and imposed isolation.

"Dr. Fredriks said you were involved in the design of Dr. Graf's VI," Wolfe said. "We know this, but that's not really what I'm interested in right now. I've read your report, of course. While we both understand that you were acting under classified instruction to gather intelligence, I want to be clear about what you learned on Asimios. What irregular or suspect sensor data you identified. What evidence you discovered regarding any non-ESCOM–sanctioned activity."

Ness rubbed his mustache and cleared his throat. "As I said in the report, Mr. Wolfe, to my mind there was nothing out of the ordinary. I accessed all command surface radar data and all the ground imaging tech. Nothing raised any flags. While there were typical reports of UFO sightings from personnel—light aberrations and reflectivity phenomena— nothing was substantiated. It was quiet. Are you going to tell me what you are after?"

Wolfe took a quick note on his VI-pad and looked back at Ness. "You stated in your report that you consider Dr. Avery Graf of sound mind, and that he was acting rationally, even though staying behind meant certain death. Were there any reasons you could make out why he wanted to stay behind? Did he give you a more complete explanation?"

Ness closed his eyes and leaned to the side. "Listen," he said, shaking his head with his eyes still closed. "I did what he asked. Avery was a friend of mine. He was good to me. He respected me, even when others complained about me. He let me do my research and gave me freedom I hadn't known before coming to Asimios. What else is there to say?"

"That's why you helped him?"

"Yes."

"Did you help him in any way, other than designing an offline VI for him?"

"What do you mean?"

"Did you help him plan anything?"

Ness's eyes met with Wolfe's. "Come again?"

"Did he plan to escape the station? Is it possible that he made it out before it was destroyed?"

"If he did, he's either frozen or dead of starvation."

Wolfe stared at Ness for a moment. "We lost one of our security bots down there, you know."

Ness shrugged.

"Any idea how that happened?"

"Could be anything. ESCOM bot tech still had a ways to go."

Wolfe looked at Ness.

Ness shrugged.

"You had nothing to do with this?"

Ness shrugged again. He was growing agitated, though. He pawed at his mustache and blinked rapidly. "I designed the goddamned prototype for those bots, didn't I?" Ness finally said. He grabbed at his forearms and started to hyperventilate.

"Calm down, Paul."

"I only wanted to see what you guys had done to them. To see how your engineering division had altered the design. Is there anything wrong with that?"

"It's okay, Paul," Wolfe said. "Calm down. I just want the truth. I want you to explain it to us straight."

"It's on Asimios."

"What's on Asimios?"

"The security bot. I gave it a certificate scrub and took it offline. I gave it instructions to help Graf in case he needed it."

"That was an expensive piece of equipment."

"Sorry."

Wolfe leaned back in his chair and chewed on his lip.

"I also upgraded the bot slightly," Ness offered.

"You upgraded the bot."

Ness nodded.

"What upgrade are we talking about?"

"I removed some defensive tools and increased its sensory capacity. I also installed a small cognition core."

"A cognition core and sensory mod—"

"A sensory upgrade. It's basically a research tool now. If you ever get the thing back, you'll have a lot of data to sift through. It's instructed to record everything."

"And a cognition core, you say?"

"A guy has to have someone to talk with in his final hour."

At this point Wolfe rotated his neck, it having suddenly become stiff. "Jesus, Paul. I don't know what to say."

Ness brought up his sleeve and wiped his nose.

"Is there anything else you want to offer during this debriefing?" Wolfe said. "Is there anything else you can think of that might be important or relevant to Graf or Asimios station?"

Ness shook his head.

Wolfe folded his hands in front of him. "Okay, now that that's out of the way, I need to ask you for a favor."

Ness blinked and pawed at his mustache.

"We have a situation we'd like to discuss with you."

"What kind of situation?"

"I'll explain later. Do what you need to do to check out of here. Then meet me in Drunlo Axis in two hours. We'll take a shuttle to Phobos Command. I'll give you the project files then, and you can review them."

"That's it?" Ness said. "No more interrogation about Graf?"

"Meet me in two hours at Drunlo. I've got bigger fish to fry than Avery Graf."

Ness combed his mustache with his thumb and forefinger. "See you in two hours, then," he said.

—

Back in his office, Wolfe returned his railgun to his desk drawer and then recorded a few notes on his VI-pad before checking his messages. Again, the packet from Esther floated in his feed. He thought of what he might say to her, but he was having difficulty finding the right tone. Leaning back in his chair, he looked out his window as Mars emerged from darkness, taking on its haunting brick hue. Phobos would soon emerge on Mars's western horizon as the satellite plunged into Martian day.

Nava had severed ties with Wolfe six years ago, after a fight involving discordant political views, the exact theme of which eluded him at present.

They had not spoken since. Esther stayed in touch with Nava, of course, as any mother would, but Preston—like Nava—was stuck in a cycle of recrimination and prideful silence.

Not long before their falling out, Nava had emerged from university as a bright and energetic student, her life ahead of her. Now, she was sought by international authorities under charges of violent agitation and civil disobedience. It was a matter of time, Wolfe had surmised. Nava had been seduced by the romantic delusion of the revolutionaries. When one succumbs to extremist influences, it becomes difficult to extricate the individual from the disease. Everything had been given to her. She'd been provided with the best schooling and admission to leading institutions. She had access to social elites and a broad list of influential company executives. A fulfilling life lay ahead of her. Yet here she was, a naïve and likely brainwashed insurgent, a degenerate and ungrateful parasite.

Wolfe cleared his throat and spoke. "Thank you, Esther, for the message. Sorry about Nava, but to be honest, I'm not surprised to hear this news. I know you care about her, and that is what's most important. Be sure to let me know if you learn anything more. There are developments here that I can't get into now, but my presence may be required on Earth soon. No specifics yet. I'll let you know, though, when I'm in the neighborhood. Hope you're well. Stay in touch."

Preston watched the text conclude. Then he sent the package, cleared his VI, and gazed out over Mars's silent rotation. He drew back his sleeve and checked his watch. The second hand was rounding the dial's apex. Another minute had passed. Another minute vanished on Phobos; another minute of life spent as dutiful thrall to ESCOM and its *Vision for Tomorrow* endeavors.

Wolfe informed Vikkie that he was going to Phobos Command and would return later that evening. He also asked her to get him the name and messaging address of the new exercise instructor at the D-level Skyresh fitness center.

—

Wolfe and Paul Ness settled into their shuttle seats. The sleek, elongated car smelled of polymers and plastic alloy.

"It's hard to think that we're not at the station anymore," Ness said. "I was there for seven years, you know."

"I realize that," Wolfe said. "I know what you've been doing. You had your opportunity to leave though." As Wolfe spoke, he riffled through his message feed and made a few notations on his VI-pad. "There were several opportunities for you to spend time on Mars if you'd wanted. You remained on the station by choice."

"I'm not complaining." Ness tugged at the corner of his mustache and stared at the shuttle's day-spectrum ceiling lights. It was officially still day cycle on Phobos. "It was satisfying. The true pleasure was being nowhere. It gives one an intellectual freedom being so removed. I had a wonderful lab, with a staff that tolerated me." Ness's eyes grew wide, and he shot a smile at Wolfe. "I'll always cherish my time there."

"That seemed to be one of the allures of Asimios," Wolfe said. "Not knowing where one was. That was the most powerful and perhaps beautiful things about it."

Ness looked out of the window at the lights that pulsed by as the car rushed through its tunnel. His breath fogged the glass. He placed his finger on the pane and made a line through the condensation.

"But that is in the past," Wolfe said. "There are new developments. I've put it in the official file that you were forthright during our conversations. Made it clear that you weren't party to Graf's misconduct. You could have spent a long time behind the walls of a Martian work camp for your unsanctioned manipulation of an ESCOM military security bot. But we're overlooking that for now, Paul. I hope you'll return the favor."

"I'll help if I can," Ness said.

Wolfe sent over the files he told Ness earlier that he was going to send. Ness indicated he'd received them, then Ness turned away to review the docs.

While Ness was reviewing the files, Wolfe checked his messages. Vikkie had forwarded him info on the fitness instructor, whose security headshot came up. Her name was Lynx Eridania, and she lived in a single-occupancy room in one of the lower-tier housing blocks. Her VI address appeared below her name, and below that, the details of her security screening.

She was clean. No brushes with authorities. She was Martian, as he'd suspected, twenty-four years old: "I am an aspiring personal trainer and life-energy coach. My passions are long walks around Elysium Mons, eating well, being healthy, and travel." This was her first time on Phobos. She'd been here only four weeks. How lovely, thought Wolfe. He sent her a text message with his ESCOM security seal and a reminder that they'd exchanged looks during her training class earlier that day. Then he leaned back, closed his eyes, and let the motion of the shuttle rock him into a gentle trance.

When they arrived at Phobos Command, security scans cleared Wolfe and Ness at the front gate, and they entered the bustling offices of the ESCOM–Phobos intelligence operation. They were greeted by Frank Mudede, a tall, no-nonsense security agent with sabre-sharp smarts and expertise in off-Earth insurgents, particularly Martian. Mudede was flamboyant. He wore a bright green combat skin, cut off at the elbows, and a black baseball cap with the ESCOM logo. Mudede was impatient, annoyed that they were late—by six minutes. Mudede drew attention to Ness once they were all packed into a small situation room, with its medium-sized round table and a decent-sized viewboard on the wall.

"Preston told me you've gone over the files," Mudede said. "Do you have any questions? Is there anything that needs clarification?"

Wolfe filled a cup halfway with coffee from a pot that stood in the middle of the table. Wolfe offered Ness coffee, but Ness shook his head.

"As I understand it," Ness said to Mudede, "ESCOM believes some of your wormhole-monitoring tech was sabotaged, and you have evidence to prove it."

Wolfe looked to Mudede, who looked back at Wolfe.

"As you know," Mudede said, "all our communications with Asimios Station were relayed over microwave link nodes on either side of the wormhole."

Ness nodded. "Yes."

"It turns out that about fourteen months ago, our link went down, along with everything else around the wormhole. All the sensors and data gathering hardware, both third party and our own, all went out, as if a wave hit it. Our best guess was that it might be coronal mass ejecta from Stelos Proxima, Asimios's sun, a pulse that swept over the wormhole and wiped out our electronics. The thing was, we had no data to support this theory. Nothing came up on the Asimios side that indicated any kind of coronal ejection. More to the point, the systems on our side of the wormhole were also taken out. This raised eyebrows, of course."

"I remember that," Ness said. "We deployed a temporary satellite system to relay base com with Phobos HQ while the nodes were down."

"Correct," Mudede said. "That was resourceful of you. We installed a new link weeks later. Then, not three weeks after that, everything went down again. Everyone was blaming everyone. Nobody had a clue as to what was going on. If this was the result of solar ejecta, why hadn't there been any corroboration of flare activity at Asimios Station? If it was due to wormhole instability, then we should be seriously rethinking communications reliability with the station, even the viability of the station itself."

"Yes, it was concerning," Ness said.

"We were about to launch our second node-repair mission, then from out of the blue the University of East Anglia requested assistance with one of their wormhole monitoring experiments. Their transmitter probe had gone offline before the nodes crashed, and they were wondering if their camera was still operational. They'd installed the camera a healthy distance from the portal for spectral analysis and visual loop capture. We found that the instrument had been working during the node crashes. Once we had their transmitter back online, we asked if we could review their imaging data. They were happy to assist. This is what we saw."

Mudede made a gesture against a bare projection wall, and a wide rectangular image of dark sky appeared. Stars glittered in different orders of intensity. A low man-made structure appeared, with solar arrays that fanned out into the black of space. Mudede tapped his index finger toward the image on the wall. The structure was magnified on the display.

"This is ESCOM's Mercury hub," Mudede said. "It collects data from a microwave link and shoots it home. The data nodes are too small to be seen on this visual. And the wormhole, of course, is invisible. But let's do a long zoom and go to the time stamp of the first interruption."

Mudede zoomed the image and played the segment. After a short time, something moved from right to left across the display.

Paul sat up in his chair.

"I'll zoom in a bit more and replay this," Mudede said.

The image was enlarged. Mudede played it again, watching the movement. He played it once more, at a slower speed. It became obvious that the image was a spacecraft.

Ness peered at the display. "How about that."

"So, do you see what we see?" Mudede said.

"Whose is it?" Ness said.

"It's not Excelsior Capital," Wolfe put in. "They don't have that kind of tech. And it's certainly not Axiom or Transglobal."

"It's alien," Ness said.

Wolfe looked at Ness, who scratched the unshaven beard at the base of his throat.

"This object," Mudede added, "is at least one hundred meters long. It came through the wormhole just after the systems crash."

"The crash wasn't an accident," Ness said.

"Our assumption," Wolfe said. "Sabotage."

Ness scrutinized the images. He shook his head. "And what did you see during the second crash?"

"The same image data. A similar shadow, or craft, exited through the wormhole right after the subsequent crash."

"This is why you shut down Asimios Station," Ness said.

"Assertive Disengagement," Wolfe said.

"You didn't see any more of this activity at the wormhole since then?" Ness said.

Mudede shook his head.

"No more node crashes," Wolfe said. "No more anomalies."

Mudede enlarged the images where they were frozen across the background of the solar arrays. There was a dull shimmer along the craft's outer edge. The rest was shadow, a menacing form, the vague outline of a shark gliding in a murky sea.

—

Wolfe dined with Lynx Eridania at a small Lebanese bistro in Skyresh Axis. The lights were low. A musician strummed an acoustic guitar on a small stage.

"Why Phobos?" Wolfe gave his wine a sophisticated swirl. "What brings a nice Martian girl like you to a desolate rock like this?"

Lynx smiled and lowered her eyes as the candlelight danced across her soft, young face. Her brown hair fell loose over her shoulders, and she teased the ends with her fingers as she spoke. She was more attractive up close, Wolfe thought as the wine relaxed him. Her foot brushed against his leg. She had a certain provincial innocence, and yet was also a bit threatening, given her excellent physical condition. A nice combination.

"I'm from a small commune," Lynx said. "It's backward, really. There's nothing there for me. I want to experience things, you know. I wanted to get as far away from Mars as I could. I want to meet interesting people. See a real city."

"You want to go to Earth," Wolfe said, sure he guessed correctly. The scar at the corner of his mouth was twitching, as if it had a mind of its own and needed to be pacified.

Her eyes lit up. She took a sip from her glass. "I'd love to go to Earth," she said with that quaint Martian accent. "It's my dream. You're from Earth, you said. Have you ever been to Paris?"

"Many times."

"Is it as beautiful as they say? Is it as beautiful as it looks in the old movies?"

"It's beautiful. I'd love to tell you about Paris. We have all night." Wolfe poured wine into Lynx's glass before he filled his own. He winked at her, then made a quick scan of the other diners. A few faces were familiar, as one expects when residing in a cloistered and remote community. What are they thinking? Some must be whispering that he was old enough to be Lynx's father. Others might be saying that he was old enough to be her grandfather.

Who cares? He wasn't concerned. He was only sixty-eight, after all. He'd taken care of himself. He'd been physically active and went through all the anti-aging therapies and synthblood treatments. He was in his prime, and there was no reason why he shouldn't enjoy the spoils of his provincial power.

Wolfe's eyes fell on the familiar face of a woman at the bar. Brit Fredriks. Alone. Under ordinary circumstances, Wolfe would have ignored her, but he'd had more than a few glasses of wine and was feeling particularly courageous. He asked Lynx to excuse him. He stood and went to Dr. Fredriks.

"Brit." He cleared his throat and struck a tone of détente. "Brit, I hope we can still be friends."

Dr. Fredriks paled. She stood, drink in hand, and heaved the contents at Wolfe's face. A wave of laughter spread through the small crowd. Dr. Fredriks grabbed her jacket and left the restaurant. He stood as if stunned, coated in what smelled like very good gin.

"Sorry about that." Wolfe returned to their table.

Lynx's mouth was stuck open with surprise.

"I fired her earlier today," Wolfe said. "She didn't take it too well. Now, where were we?"

—

When Wolfe and Lynx made their way back to Wolfe's office, her mood swung from tentative to giddy, as if she'd decided not to let that incident ruin her evening. Wolfe further attributed this renewed spirit to a combination of cheap wine and her admiration for his rank and maturity.

Once inside his quarters, Lynx seemed impressed. She tiptoed into the room, moved through the bedroom door, and without hesitation threw herself onto the freshly made bed. She rolled over a few times, laughing as she did.

"Can I get you another drink?" Wolfe sat next to her on the bed. He ran his hand up her thigh. She pulled him close and pressed her mouth against his. She fumbled a little as she attempted to remove his clothing, button by button, before Wolfe took her hands in his.

"I think I need another drink," Wolfe said, "and I have a surprise for you. Come."

Wolfe led her to the Jacuzzi, which he'd already activated through his VI. It was bubbling and churning, steam trailing upward toward the high ceiling.

"Make yourself comfortable. I'll be right back." He went to the kitchenette for glasses and a chilled bottle of champagne. He screwed off the bottle cap and measured out the drinks. On the way back, he stopped at his desk to remove his watch. He slid open the top drawer and placed the watch inside. When he returned to the bathroom, Lynx had freed herself of her clothing and was immersed in the roiling, steaming water.

"You've read my mind," Wolfe said. He dimmed the lights through a command in his VI. He offered the Martian woman a glass, then set down his own glass and shed his clothes before joining her in the hot bath. Her hair danced and spiraled on the bubbles, and Wolfe could feel her legs coil around him like eager tentacles.

The edges of their glasses met, and they sipped their champagne. Wolfe allowed her to move in closer so that she could fasten her lean body to his. He felt her fingers riding down his stomach. He was hard now, and she took him in her hand. Their lips met for a moment, then Wolfe leaned back and took a long, deep breath.

An alert flashed over Wolfe's VI. It was an emergency notification from Frank Mudede on the ESCOM hot-feed:

Topic: Asimios

Wolfe blinked in disbelief as he mulled over the importance of the alert. He opened the packet, but the churning water and Lynx's touch and her shower of kisses prevented him from concentrating on the full text. He held up his hand and reluctantly asked her to wait.

"Excuse me for a moment, um, Lisa, but I have to take this. It's high-level stuff, really."

Still hard, Wolfe got to his feet in the tub and turned away to focus on the message. That was when he felt it: a quick snap around his neck. In an instant, he was dragged backward into the tub.

After the initial shock, Wolfe understood that this wasn't a sort of sex game and that his relationship with Lynx had taken an unexpected turn. In this universe of hot foam and water, Wolfe knew he had only seconds to act. If he could get her off balance, he could slide a finger between the wire and his neck and perhaps steal a breath. But everything depended on which way he turned. As the wire dug deeper, he cut the lights to the room with his VI and swiveled with such force that he spun his attacker around. She was now underwater and on her back beneath him. He forced a finger under the wire around his throat.

Rising just an inch above the surface, Wolfe raised himself and gasped for what air he could while he wheeled the sharp end of his elbow several times against the side of the girl's head. The garrote loosened slightly, just enough for Wolfe to squirm half out of the circular tub. Water sloshed over the edge and onto the floor.

Leveraging the weight of his body, Wolfe lifted the slender woman behind him so that she emerged, gasping through her clenched teeth in a way that was so strangely out of character. In the pitch-black room, the garrote bit deeper into his finger and throat. Wolfe felt faint. With desperate strength, he lifted her clear of the tub, stepping onto the tiled floor of the room. He stumbled blindly into the darkness. Seizing the chance, the Martian knit her legs around his waist and ratcheted up the tightness of the wire. Wolfe felt his strength begin to leave him.

Bracing for a final effort, Wolfe planted his left foot, only to have it slide on the wet floor. He fell backward, carrying the woman with him, and heard a sickening, hollow clunk. The wire had gone slack. The woman beneath him was still.

Wolfe pulled the wire from his neck and gasped for air. The Jacuzzi bubbled and boiled in the dark.

Was it over? He tried to activate the lights again, but he was too disorientated. Wolfe crawled in the direction of the bathroom door, where he propped himself up and took a few more gulps of air.

Was she dead?

Finally, Wolfe was able to turn the lights on. Lynx had struck her head, and blood now coursed down her neck and shoulders. But she was standing, and very much alive. She reached in to the handbag she'd left beside the Jacuzzi and extracted a steel pike. Pike now in hand, she lunged in Wolfe's direction. He cut the lights again and fell backward into the main office room.

Wolfe had never enjoyed the idea of hand-to-hand combat. It always seemed primitive to him, base and barely necessary. The thought of settling accounts through blows was not his style. In other words, fending off an assault from a naked and deranged woman was not what he was prepared for. But right now, Wolfe knew that the only chance he might have of escaping this situation with his life was to reach his desk, remove the rail gun from its drawer, and fill his attacker's abdomen with rail rounds.

His assailant was in mid-lunge when Wolfe cut the lights. He dodged the attack, but not completely. The pike slid into the soft part of his waist. He surprised himself by how loudly he screamed. He wrenched free, the cold steel exiting his body with a sensation he'd never forget, and he managed to roll away so that when his attacker struck again, the sharp point only tore a surface wound near the back of his knee.

Wolfe had vision augmentation with his VI, but he'd rarely used the feature. To go through a tutorial now was impossible. He could activate a security function that would alert ESCOM authorities to any emergency, but even so close to death, he felt a sense of shame for having lured this young woman into his quarters, feeling that this was a situation he needed to resolve on his own. He slithered across the carpet on his belly, trying to keep as quiet as possible, while he prepared to make a break for his desk. He made it a short distance and was ready to stand when he felt the pike again.

This time it scraped across his side and hung on one of his lower ribs. Before he could get away, another thrust hit home and buried the steel tip into his back. The thrust must have hit a lung, but he went on, fumbling and bleeding and delirious, in the effort to reach his gun. He made it a few more yards, but felt the sensation of perforation wounds suffusing his skin. And the more the steel entered his flesh, the less he seemed to feel it.

In the dark, Wolfe finally ran headlong into his desk. In the painful chaos, his fingers found the handle to the drawer that held his railgun. He pulled the drawer out with such force that it broke free from its mounts and sent its contents spilling out around him.

Wolfe felt his attacker grope at his body, seeking a final target. He felt the cold metal of the gun against his hip, where it had fallen from the splayed drawer. He grasped the gun, removed the safety and, just as the pike entered his chest, he discharged the weapon.

There was a loud report. Then silence. The weight of his assassin slumped over his pelvis. Wolfe turned on the lights and realize that Lynx had been hit in the shoulder with the round. She was only dazed. The round had exposed bare bone, but the lights in the room seemed to give her new energy. She raised the pike for one last thrust. Then *bang!* A red hole opened in her chest. She crumpled down on him.

Wolfe was bathed in blood, much of it his own. He wasn't breathing well as the gun slipped from his fingers. He pushed the woman's glistening body to the side. When she was face-down on the floor, he noticed a tattoo on her left shoulder: a serpent swallowing its tail. The serpent was coiled around a long sword.

Wolfe's VI lit up with a live call from Mudede. He didn't know what to do. Answer it? Wolfe then felt a bump beneath his arm. It was his watch, what was left of it.

When Wolfe finally opened the line, Mudede said, "I hope this isn't too late. I'm sorry, sir, but this is rather urgent."

Wolfe's breathing was shallow. He spoke in a broken whisper. "No, Frank. Go on."

"We've just received a relay transmission from Asimios, sir."

"Oh?" Wolfe raised his watch to look at it.

"The wormhole has opened again, sir."

"I see."

"How would you like to proceed?"

The watch's new crystal was shattered, the hands were bent, and the dial had a hole in it the diameter of a steel pike. Wolfe brought the watch to his ear.

"Frank," Wolfe said.

"Yes, sir?"

"Can you call a medic? I think my watch is broken."

6 – Escape

MICHAEL LISTENED CLOSELY as Sargon spoke. "There are precisely three ways to get out of the zeltstadt," Sargon proclaimed, finger wagging at his audience. "Either you are given authorization, you escape, or they carry you out dead."

Michael, Sargon, and Rafiq sat together in a small circle in a tent pitched against the northern wall of the zeltstadt. They were discussing ways for Michael and Nava to leave the camp, that desire now enhanced because word had gotten out that Nava and Michael had been at the camp for several days and hadn't yet paid a visit to the camp bosses, Suliman and Kareem. A run-in was soon inevitable.

They huddled in a tent nestled against the large HVAC fans that fed the camp's food dispensaries and intake halls. The fans ran constantly and provided ample background noise so conversations couldn't be overheard. It was a secret NLA meeting place, accessible by concealed access through a pair of outer tents, the outermost of which served as a small grocery. The shop was run by Konstanz Aziz, an overweight, blind, wheelchair-bound Iraqi refugee who sat behind a small counter and chatted amicably with anyone who entered his shop. It was rumored that Konstanz was ex-Excelsior Iraqi security. After his injury he'd gone rogue and aligned himself with the NLA. He'd changed his identity and fled north. It was also rumored that, even though Konstanz was blind, he could still bury a throwing knife in your heart from ten meters away.

"We have to leave soon," Michael said. He wore his synthskin facial pads and kept glancing over at Rafiq, still struck by how much they looked alike. "There's an NLA leadership meeting in Berlin in three weeks," Michael said. "Atlas Kolek has called it. He's the big guy...the one we all listen to when we plan our next objective. You know Kolek, of course?"

Rafiq nodded and shifted where he sat. Sargon dismissed the question, knowingly.

Michael said, "The meeting will be where the NLA decides what its next move will be. Nava's a big wig. She needs to be there. But there's trouble brewing in the NLA."

Rafiq drew on cigarette. Sargon stroked his mustache.

"There's an argument now about what direction we should take," Michael continued. "There's the orthodox view, which Kolek represents, that we keep the keel of the ship steady, that we continue our mission of nonviolent protest, with the idea that we can bring the system to a halt by the sheer force of numbers who join our cause."

Rafiq blew a plume of smoke skyward.

"The other idea," Michael said, "is that we are wasting our time with the nonviolent approach, that we will continue to be brutalized, tortured and killed, indiscriminately, and that the only way to resist the companies is to counter their violence with violence of our own. Armed insurgence. This idea is growing among members. Brother Pravir Malkus, whom you may or may not have heard of, is one of the main supporters of this approach."

"The rude truth," Sargon said, "is that either way, we lose. If the NLA discards peaceful protest, blood will fill the streets, and it will be our blood."

Rafiq spoke in Arabic. Agitated, Sargon stood and poked Rafiq's shoulder. "You think I haven't given for the resistance? You think I'm not risking everything?"

Michael took hold of Sargon's arm. "Keep it together. There's no need for this now, not for my sake."

"He is right," Rafiq said. "Get a hold of yourself, Sargon."

Michael saw Sargon's age just then, the crow's feet at his eyes, the tremor in his hand, the panic in his smile. Sargon pulled his trembling hand to his face and wiped his nose.

"Don't take your friends for granted," Sargon said to Rafiq. "That's all I'll say."

"Come on," Michael said. "We should end this meeting for now. We'll talk more."

Grumbling, they pushed their way through the canvas doors until they came inside Konstanz's shop.

"What, no purchase today?" Konstanz said in coarse English, his milky eyes looking in their general direction. Michael pulled a bruised box of tea from a shelf and placed it on the counter in front of Konstanz. He passed a paycard over the paybox and transferred six credits.

"Thank you," Konstanz said.

"*Shukraan,*" Sargon said as he left the shop with Michael. Rafiq would stay behind for a few minutes, dozing in a chair perhaps or chatting with Konstanz, just to keep the three of them from being seen leaving together.

—

Back at the tent that Sargon had appropriated for Michael and Nava, Michael found Nava with the small baby suckling on her breast.

Nava said, "She has your eyes."

It had taken a few days, but since the birth, Nava's strength had begun to return. The baby was growing and becoming a tiny personality. Michael sat on the side of the cot, next to Nava. There was a small table with a pair of uncomfortable wire chairs pushed against it in their small room. On the table stood a thermaburner, unwashed bowls from their last meal, some baby formula, a small tray of spices and teabags, and two dirty glasses.

"The time has come," Michael said. "We have to leave. The heat is on us. We stick around, and we're going to have to start negotiating with Suliman and Kareem, and that won't be pretty."

Although camp sympathies aligned with the NLA, the camp bosses ran the show and got a cut of any money that came into the camp. If you had no money, you were expected to offer services in exchange for protection. Michael knew it was only a matter of time before they'd have to face these thugs.

"I used to think it an act of cruelty," Nava said, "to bring a child into this world. But just by seeing this little thing, by holding and smelling her, I have this insidious and infectious hope. I don't know where it comes from."

Nava looked at Michael, who adjusted where he sat and moved to touch her hand.

When he squeezed her hand, Nava stared at the baby and then looked at the tent walls. "I always seemed to be preparing for death. I'd fantasize about it, imagining myself being attacked, bleeding out on the street, and feeling the cool concrete slowly draw me away. But, to see this child…" Nava held the baby aloft, interrupting its feeding. An angry wince crossed the mite's face. "To see this baby, it makes me want to reject that death. It makes me want to staunch the bleeding, to stand and fight. This child is why we fight. This child is every child."

"Yes, Nava," Michael said. "She represents our struggle."

Nava brought the baby back to her breast. When it found the nipple, its protests receded. Michael stroked the baby's thatch of soft hair.

"Do you know what I call her?" Nava said.

"What do you call her?" Michael said. He felt a sadness well inside him, and this sadness migrated outward, through his muscles and skin.

"Lyv," Nava said. "Her name is Lyv."

Michael nodded. "That's a beautiful name." He fought back that sensation, which he could only describe as grief. Nava had broken their promise, betraying their pact to keep from naming the baby. It was supposed to make things easier, leaving the naming to someone else. But perhaps that didn't matter anymore. Perhaps the world had become a different place. Things had shifted. Perceptions had shifted. But where was the shift, and where were they going now?

"I've been speaking with Sargon." Michael whispered. "We've been talking about ways to get out of the camp. It's not easy, since smuggling people can get you killed. And with the baby, it complicates things."

"We have to get to Berlin," Nava said.

"Sargon says he might be able to get e-passes, but it won't be easy. He says it will require a lot of money. Much more than we have."

"Can we trust Sargon?"

"His intentions are good," Michael said. "And Zahra is sympathetic. They are good people and loyal to the NLA, from what I can tell." Michael lowered his voice when he mentioned the NLA.

"The NLA sent us here. They should help us get out," Nava said. "Press Sargon for contacts. Bring them here, if you'd like. I can talk to them." Nava turned away now, focused on the baby's feeding, and Michael felt shut out. "We need a plan, and soon."

"You worry about this little girl and leave the rest to me," Michael said. "It was a bad idea to come here without any idea of how to get out. It's my fault."

"It's not your fault," Nava said. "I don't know what I'd have done without Dr. Jafari."

Michael was tired. He dropped his head. His shoulders slumped, and he rubbed at his eyes.

"Let me be alone," Nava said. "I have to her feed. Go figure out what we should do."

They kissed.

He left the tent, thinking that he'd walk the camp perimeter again, to clear his mind and to lay out plans.

—

While Michael was out walking, someone came out from the shadows and sucker punched him, sending him to the ground. A man took Michael by the back of his jacket and dragged him to a nearby tent, there he was kicked a few times and hit again.

The tent was lit by a couple of weak glowlights that hung from the ceiling. Michael could make out a chair in the middle of the room. The man who delivered the beating hissed in Arabic and motioned for Michael to sit. Michael sized up his attacker as he staggered to the chair. The fellow was tall, muscles rippling under a tight cotton shirt. He had a shaved head and a thin, neatly trimmed black beard—so neatly trimmed that it brought out the asymmetry of the bones in his face. The man's eyes were closely placed, like a rat's, and they peered down past a large, bulbous nose at Michael.

The tent smelled like canvas. All tents here smelled like canvas. There were things here, sacks of grains and some sort of storage. Michael's ribs were killing him. One was broken, maybe two. The pain was sharp. He tasted salt in his mouth. Blood.

A shorter man entered the tent. He wore a black leather jacket and his hair was shaved close to his head. Unlike the giant's, his soft olive eyes were spaced far apart, sitting above a pair of high, clean-shaven cheeks over what might be described as a flat face. His nose was flat, his lips were flat, but his ears stuck out like open car doors, which gave him a slightly comical look. He spoke in Arabic. Michael responded in Arabic, saying that he didn't speak it. Michael tried French, but the smaller brute shook his head in what appeared to be disgust.

"I see you've met Suliman," the fellow said. "Sorry if he was a little rough with you. His temper can get the best of him."

Michael licked the inside of his mouth.

"My name is Kareem," he said. "Welcome to our zeltstadt. Me and Suliman here are what you might call business partners. I try to conduct business in a more civil manner, while Suliman here, as you know, likes more of a hands-on approach."

"What do you want from me?" Michael said. The pain in his ribs hit him like a red-hot iron when he breathed.

"Interesting that you ask," Kareem said. "I was going to ask you the same question. For we are here tonight to figure out what each of us wants, is that not right?"

"What could I want from you?" Michael narrowed his eyes, glancing at Kareem.

"Oh, there are many things here in our camp that we have to offer. Isn't that true, Suliman?" Kareem looked at Suliman, who blinked and rubbed his thumb across his nose. "But the most important thing we have to offer is safety, right? Safety for you and your nice-looking wife, and that sweet little baby of yours. Now, you wouldn't want anything to happen to them, would you? What with the high prices a young baby such as that can fetch on the black market? You hear about it, don't you? And I wouldn't want that to happen to you here, to have your baby gone missing, and your woman mistreated."

"You touch her and I'll kill you," Michael said through a pain that spiked in his chest. He'd regretted the threat after he'd delivered it. "We have nothing," he went on before Kareem could answer. "I've got a pay-card in my pocket with eleven hundred credits. Take it. That's all we have." Michael started to dig into his pocket. When he felt the swift blow of Suliman's hand across his face, he dropped his arms to his side.

"Don't surprise Suliman." Kareem leaned forward. "That's not a good thing." Suliman returned to his place behind Kareem.

Michael was stunned, with a ringing in his ears and his pulse drumming in his forehead.

"You see, it's strange that you are here," Kareem said. "It's not often that a couple arrives in the middle of the night by taxi." Kareem ran his fingers along the zipper of his jacket. "But how people get to the zeltstadt isn't important. It's how well they cooperate while they are here that matters. Right, Suliman?"

Suliman spoke in Arabic and blinked a couple times, and he flexed his muscles. His voice was higher than Michael expected. Almost feminine. It made Michael wonder if those arms were built by chemicals.

"I don't want to keep you." Kareem turned to Suliman, who nodded and hunched his shoulders. Kareem said to Michael, "Consider this our introduction. And I look forward to future conversations."

Michael looked at Kareem. He wanted to throttle the guy, but he couldn't find the strength. All he could do was drop his head and explore his pain.

"Come by as soon as you can and visit, then we can talk over what might be of mutual benefit," Kareem said. "You are smart. Smart people can be helpful. I'm sure you can figure out how to find me."

Kareem left the tent, and Suliman followed, his broad shoulders swaying with violent confidence.

—

At home, Michael sat at the thermaburner table, trying to be quiet, trying not to wake Nava and the baby, who was tucked so nicely in a comfy fiber box only a short distance from the bed. He ran water over a cloth and tried to clean his wounds. He found a towel that he wrapped around his torso to stabilize his ribs.

They possessed no pain meds—they possessed almost nothing—so he lay on the floor, pain shooting through him like lightning. He balled up a towel to serve as a pillow, then closed his eyes and called upon the universe to allow him to rest and heal. For what seemed like hours, he huddled there on the throw rug that covered the dirt, swimming in and out of sleep, the pain a slumbering disease that awakened and stabbed at him when he moved. He tried, so hard, not to move.

Δ

THE BABY CRIED, and Nava immediately awoke. She started running through her head where she was and what she needed to be doing. When she swung her legs over the bed to move toward the baby's crib, she almost tripped over Michael.

"Oh, my! What are you doing on the floor? What happened, Michael?"

Nava helped Michael to sit up and then move to the cot. After that, she lifted the crying baby out of the crib and soothed her.

"I had a run-in with Mr. Suliman and Mr. Kareem," Michael said. "It wasn't pretty. I think my rib is broken."

"Where did this happen?" Nava gritted her teeth. "I'll pay them a visit. I'll show them what happens when they cross the NLA."

Michael shook his head. "Keep your cool. We're on their turf, is how they see it. If we wanted to run them out, we'd need a lot of help, but we don't have time."

"How about we just cut off their balls?" Nava said. "I'd settle for that." After holding the baby for a little longer, she was able to examine Michael's wounds. She removed his shirt, cleaned his abrasions, and tied a strip of pillow casing around Michael's chest. She got his legs onto the bed so he could rest. Then she fed the baby.

Now and then she wiped a cool wet cloth over Michael's forehead. Over time she could feel the heat of the sun on the top of the tent.

Δ

MICHAEL WAITED WITH Nava and Lyv in the outside room at Dr. Jafari's tent. He felt his sore ribs and wondered what his diagnosis would be. The doctor's assistant came out and asked for Michael to show her his injuries. He took off his shirt, and she gave him a quick examination. Then she disappeared into the back tent. When the assistant returned, she reported that the doctor said it was likely Michael had suffered a broken rib.

"You need an x-ray," the assistant said. "But we can't do that here." The assistant advised Michael to keep his bandage on and to avoid strenuous activities. For his other injuries, she passed him a tube of anti-bacterial cream.

Then the assistant asked Nava to follow her inside with the baby to visit the doctor. Nava went to the back tent with the assistant, while Michael stayed in the waiting area.

When Nava returned with the baby, now reassured that all was well, they headed to their own tent, clutching hands, aware of the danger that surrounded them.

—

Michael slept until the bustle and noise of the camp prevented further rest. After a cup of coffee and stale flatbread topped with cheese and protein powder, he went to pay Sargon a visit.

There was a commotion on the street not far from their tent. An enforcer droid was leading an Ex-Cap police raid. Cries rose as a tent was demolished. Ex-Cap security police loaded a group of handcuffed zelt-stadters into the back of a personnel transport and then left out the south gate. It was said they were being taken to a detention center, and that they would not return.

About once a week, an enforcer droid led a police raid, and then someone was arrested and taken away. Sometimes it was known why a person or a group was arrested, other times it wasn't. When these forays were over, the dust settled, and life resumed at the zeltstadt.

Michael proceeded to Sargon's tent on the eastern side of the camp. When he arrived, he tapped on the tent door and waited for a response. Every muscle in his body ached. He coughed to clear his lungs, reminded again of the tip of Suliman's boot.

"What are you doing here?" Zahra asked as she pulled aside the canvas.

"I need to see Sargon," Michael said. "I was attacked last night by Suliman and Kareem."

Zahra stepped aside to allow Michael to enter. "We got a visit from Suliman last night, too. Sargon isn't well."

"Did they hurt him?"

"No," she said. "Not physically, at least. But he doesn't take this sort of thing easily."

"I'm sorry," Michael said.

"They've been around before, those two," Zahra said. "They left us alone because we are old and have nothing. But with creatures like them, you never know. All of a sudden, they come smelling around like dogs looking for a scrap of meat."

Michael went into the tent where Sargon sat on the couch staring at a nexpad. When Sargon saw Michael, he put the nexpad aside and waved him over, patting the space next to him on the couch. Michael sat. Zahra picked up the nexpad and found a news broadcast site. She turned up the volume to drown out their voices. The voice of Ex-Cap propaganda vomited into the air. She dragged a chair over and sat near them.

"They are brutes, this Kareem and Suliman." Sargon spoke softly. "Animals."

"Animals," echoed Zahra.

"Nava and I have to get to Berlin," Michael said. "Many people are counting on us. This brush with Kareem and Suliman has made it clear that the earlier we leave, the better."

"I agree," Sargon said. "Zahra, can you turn the sound down a notch on the nexpad, please? Just one click. It's too loud. It's difficult to hear."

Zahra tapped on the devise. The volume dropped. "Is that better? It sounds too low now to me."

"It's fine, it's fine," Sargon said. "Now, as I've told you, Michael, it's infinitely easier to get into the zeltstadt than it is to get out. But I've been thinking about this, and I've come up with a plan, the beauty of which lies in its simplicity."

"What's the plan?" Michael said.

"It's a rather remarkable idea," Zahra said. "Sargon came up with it."

"Zahra, please," Sargon said. "And we must remember to keep our voices down, do you hear? We can't let this get out."

Zahra sat back in her chair.

Michael nodded.

"You may not realize this," Sargon said, "but you bear a striking resemblance to Rafiq. Your hair is similar in length and texture, your body proportions practically mirror one another's, and most importantly..." Sargon paused to look to Zahra.

"It's true, what he says," she said.

"Most importantly," Sargon said, "your faces are so similar, that when you remove your synthskin augments, it's as if you were twin brothers."

Michael nodded. "I saw that when we first met. What are you about to propose?"

"I've spoken with Rafiq about this," continued Sargon, "and he's willing to try it."

"Try what?" Michael said.

Sargon whispered close to Michael's ear: "Rafiq is trusted among the Ex-Cap camp security. He often travels into town, escorting a person to hospital or for another reason. He's familiar with the guards and knows most of them by name."

"Yes," Michael said. "Is there an NLA sympathizer among the guards?"

"Not as far as I know."

"Then what are you proposing?"

Sargon said, "We'll call a car from town to pick up a sick baby and bring her to hospital. You will disguise yourself as Rafiq and escort your wife to the car, then ride with her to town."

Michael was silent.

"In town, you will trade cars in a garage, and another driver will take you to Osnabrück. There you will be given another contact and provided with a safehouse. You can decide what you want to do from there."

The idea seemed absurd.

"Trust me," Sargon said. "This will work. But you'll have to decide on the details with Rafiq."

"When do we do this?"

"Tomorrow, late in the day," Sargon said. "That will give you the cover of night to continue your escape."

Michael leaned back on the couch, holding his hand over his aching rib.

Sargon went to the thermaburner. "I'll make some tea. Then we'll go over more of the details."

—

Michael was offered a seat at the couch in Rafiq's tent. Rafiq said, "I asked if Faiza could go visit a friend. She should not be involved."

Rafiq and Faiza's quarters were about the same size as most of the tents. It had the staple kitchen area, with a small table and chairs, and small refrigerator and thermaburner. A folding partition separated the tent into two small rooms. A few pictures hung on the wall, faces of what must be family. The flag of old Algeria was unfurled above the couch. Rafiq had a nexpad playing music, to hide their voices. Rafiq brought over a tray of coffee, sugar, and cream. As always, Michael was surprised to see this person who resembled him so closely, so much that it was like gazing into a mirror.

"You know, the fact that you have a nexpad makes me nervous," Michael said.

"I have no choice," Rafiq said. "No VI? No nexpad? Then people would assume I must be NLA. And I need a security-issued com device to connect with zeltstadt authorities. I can't avoid it." Rafiq pulled a piece of paper from under the coffee table, unfolded the small square, and handed it to Michael.

"It's in German," Michael said. "But I understand it." He folded the paper and handed it back to Rafiq. Rafiq took a lighter, lit the paper, and let it burn in the brass ashtray on the table.

"It's a confirmation," Rafiq said, leaning toward Michael, across the small coffee table. "The car will arrive at 17:30 tomorrow. You will help your wife to the car, and you will get in the car to escort her to the town. If asked, you will say that there is no e-pass here. It's an emergency. The baby is sick."

"And what language do you speak to security? Do you know names? Which camp guards do you normally speak with? Is there a leader?"

"Don't worry," Rafiq said. "I've been loyal to Ex-Cap. I've spent three years here, building their trust for exactly this."

Michael sipped the coffee. It was good. Hot. What he needed right then.

"Can I ask..." Rafiq drank from his cup of coffee. "You are from England, correct?"

Michael nodded.

"Have you been to Scotland? Have you been north?"

Michael nodded again. He set his cup on the table. "I've been to Edinburgh. Aberdeen, too. The farthest north was Inverness on a summer trip with an old girlfriend."

"Inverness," Rafiq said. "Yes. What was it like? Is it pretty?"

"I suppose it was. It was a long time ago."

"I've always dreamed of going to Scotland, you see. I've dreamed of walking on those moors, those green hills, and feeling the cold rain on my face. It seems powerful. I don't know why I'm so drawn to it. I promised Faiza that one day we'll make it there. One day I'll show her the North Sea."

"Geographically, you're not so far away."

"True," Rafiq said. "But after years in the zeltstadt, I'm starting to lose hope. I keep thinking that the companies will be overthrown, that the zeltstadts will be liberated, but I don't know. I could leave on a labor crew to Sweden, but I'd never see Faiza again."

"Don't lose faith," Michael said. "Not yet."

"I won't." Rafiq smiled. He took another sip of coffee. "I grew up in Algeria. A village near Oran, a small city on the coast, where the desert meets the sea."

"I've never been there," Michael said. "Is it a beautiful country?"

Rafiq closed his eyes. "A long time ago, it might have been a beautiful place, but now both the sea and desert are dead. Nothing but dust and pebbles and heat. Man is now an outlaw there. Maybe he always was." He paused. Then: "May I ask a favor?"

"Yes?"

"Can you remove your synthskin? I'd like to see your face."

Michael set his coffee cup down. He started peeling away the six different molds until eventually he had them all off. He set them on the nearby table.

"Amazing!" Rafiq's face lit up. "How can this be? How can we look so similar, yet you were born and raised so far north, and I a continent apart?"

"It's interesting, isn't it?"

"It's as if we were brothers," Rafiq said.

"I must admit," Michael said, "I felt unease when I first saw you. One imagines oneself unique, I suppose. When one gazes into a face one holds as one's own, it can be terrifying." Michael swirled the dregs of coffee in his cup.

"And yet this accident serves a purpose," Rafiq said.

Just then a series of beeps interrupted the music. Rafiq took up his nexpad and scrolled down the page.

"What is it?" Michael asked. He was preparing to make a quick exit.

"It's zeltstadt security," Rafiq said. "There's a fight at the east end of the camp. They want me there."

"I should go, right?" Michael said.

"No," Rafiq said. "It's why I asked you here." He went around the partition and came back with his uniform in one hand and a pair of dusty black boots in the other. "Try these clothes on. Make sure they fit."

Michael received the clothes and boots. Rafiq pulled on a jacket, put on a cap, and tucked the nexpad inside his pocket.

"Don't wait for me when you are done," Rafiq said. "Just put the clothes on the couch. I'll see you here tomorrow at 17:00 hours, one half hour before the car arrives."

Michael nodded. Rafiq slipped out of the tent.

Michael weighed the clothing in his hands. He set the boots on the floor and draped the clothing over the couch. He removed his pants and shirt, revealing his spindly pale legs and the bandage wrapped around his torso. He picked up Rafiq's uniform. It smelled of dirt and stale canvas, but he wasn't repulsed. He pushed his arms through the sleeves and pulled the shirt around his waist, feeling pain shoot from his ribs. He snapped several buttons. The shirt fit easily, neither too tight nor too loose. He took the pants off the couch and pulled them on. They fit well enough, the cuffs covering his socks, but they rode slightly higher than they should. He sat back on the chair and examined the soles of the boots, checking for tracking devices. None found. They were a size too large, so his feet slipped easily into them. He bent to tie the laces when he heard the tent's door open. From where he sat, his back to the door, he glanced over his shoulder to see who had entered.

It was Faiza, Rafiq's partner. Michael had seen her before, walking with Rafiq, but they'd never been introduced. She was slender and attractive. She had dark hair and a face cut classically, as if from a piece of marble. Dressed in dark loose pants and jacket, she pulled her headscarf loose as she came into the tent and said something in Arabic. She laughed a few measures and disappeared behind the partition.

Michael froze. His thoughts fixed on flight, rushing out the door and making a dash toward home. But he was wearing Rafiq's uniform. This might bring him trouble on the street.

Faiza came back around the partition, her smile stretching across her face, tilting upward at one corner, as if by guilt. Michael avoided her glance and tried to focus on the laces of his boots. If this was a trap, he'd been caught.

Faiza went to the door. Was she leaving? No, she stopped, suddenly and came back to the chair where Michael sat. She ran her fingers over his neck. Her fingers were cool, disarmingly gentle. She whispered in Arabic, the rhythm of her voice caressing his ear. Her long fingers slid down his neck, and her face brushed against his cheek as she leaned down. He could smell her lavender breath. Her hand travelled down over his shirt, unbuttoned his pants, and pushed past his briefs. She took hold of his hardening cock and must have felt it pulse with the beating of his heart. Not a moment later, she slipped her hand loose, licked his cheek, and danced toward the door. Michael thought of reaching out before she could escape, but he couldn't move. His heart raced. The boot laces lay untied at his feet.

Michael removed Rafiq's clothes and put his own clothes back on. He laid Rafiq's uniform over the couch and set the large boots under the coffee table. He applied his synthskin patches, then waited at the door until traffic was quiet. Then he pulled his hood over his head and left.

—

Just before 17:00 the following day, Michael gave the clear signal for Nava and the baby to go to the camp's south gate. By now, Rafiq would have called for the taxi, the emergency car that would take them to a garage in town. Michael had only to rendezvous with Rafiq at his tent, switch clothes, and they'd be on their way.

Michael had gone over the details with Nava the night before. She was usually deeply involved when they made critical plans, but today she displayed a strange sense of detachment when Michael explained how the plan would unfold. Nava was to play the troubled mother today, with a small babe in distress clasped to her breast. They'd applied makeup so the baby appeared feverish. Nava was to wear a headscarf that concealed most of her face, yet they dirtied her cheeks and forehead and blemished her teeth with ash, in case anyone got nosey. They rubbed rancid tallow in Nava's hair, so she smelled of spoiled fat.

With Nava on her way to the gate, Michael made for Rafiq's tent. When he patted on the door, Rafiq pulled him inside. The uniform was on the chair, the boots on the floor. Rafiq's eyes were red. His breath smelled of cheap schnapps.

"The car is on its way," Rafiq said. "Put on the clothes."

Michael prepared to change. "What should I do with my old clothes?" he said.

"Throw them on the floor."

Rafiq turned the music louder on his nexpad.

Michael peeled off his synthskin augments and set them on the table, then he stripped, slowed by the pain in his ribs. He cast his clothing to the floor, as instructed. He pulled on Rafiq's uniform: first the shirt, then the pants, then the oversized boots, which he laced as tight as he could. Michael said, "I guess that's it."

Somber, downcast, Rafiq came to Michael, holding out his arms, waiting for Michael to join him in an embrace. Michael moved into Rafiq's arms and stayed there, squeezed tightly by his friend. Music from the nexpad blared dissonantly. Rafiq patted Michael on his back, then pulled away. He said, "There's one more thing."

"Yes?"

"Now you must hit me." Rafiq moved into the center of the room and spread out his arms. He repeated, "Hit me. Hit me in the face, hit me in the stomach. When I fall to the ground, kick me. Kick me till tears fall from my eyes. And don't stop."

"I can't do that," Michael smiled. "What are you talking about?"

Rafiq smiled, glassy eyed. "If you do not, they will kill me."

"Come on, that's not true."

"Yes, they will. If you don't beat me up right now to show you took my uniform by force, they will arrest me and send me to a death camp. I don't want that to happen."

"I can't," Michael said.

"Yes, you can." Rafiq swung his hand around and stung Michael's cheek with a hard blow. Michael stumbled back. "I still have a life ahead of me. I still have Faiza. You must do this."

"I won't," Michael said. "I refuse."

Rafiq came at him again, heated and frenzied, grabbing Michael's shirt this time, staring into his eyes. "You don't understand! You must beat me now, or they'll know I was in on this. Do it."

Michael shook his head, hating this. Yet to his own surprise, he threw a hard punch that connected with Rafiq's cheek. The blow took Rafiq off guard and sent him spinning. Rafiq groaned in pain.

He smiled at Michael "Yes. Again!"

Shaking his head, Michael delivered another blow to Rafiq's jaw, one that sent his friend turning and wincing in pain until he fell to the floor. This contact drew blood, and Rafiq's face took on a different character, a character Michael didn't like, one he hated. Rafiq's sniffling and sniveling was repulsive. Like a shark drawn to blood, Michael showered more blows over the prone Rafiq. He pummeled Rafiq's face and body, swung kicks into his ribs, and stomped hard on the Algerian's legs, maybe even snapping an ankle. This went on for a minute or two, until Rafiq's breathing went shallow, and Michael stumbled back, horrified by what he'd done.

Barely conscious, Rafiq got a final look at Michael. A hint of a smile crossed his lips.

"I love you," Michael said. Then he left.

—

Michael found Nava was waiting at the gate with Lyv, just as they'd planned. She seemed anxious, but that was expected. Michael pulled out the passcard Rafiq had given him and shared a look with Nava—hope and trepidation—then he swiped the card at the door check. The door opened. Michael waited until Nava was through, then he followed.

Outside, the lights bathed the large camp entry. It was early evening, and a group of Ex-Cap security lingered near one of the guard houses. Michael spotted the idling car, which must be waiting for them. He took Nava by the arm and started in that direction. A spotlight from a tower swung on them and followed their path. They'd almost made it to the car when the group of Ex-Cap guards called to them. Michael opened one of the car's rear doors to let Nava climb inside with the baby. He felt Nava's anxiety when a guard approached them.

Michael turned to confront a guard.

"*Was gibst? Bringst du sie ins Krankenhaus?*" The guard came up, smiling, joking around. "*Diese kranke alte Dame?*"

Michael didn't know what to say. He made out a few words in the guard's German, but he couldn't think of anything other to say except,

"*Ja, ja...Danke.*" He hid his bloodied knuckles against his legs. He made sure his shirt was pulled over the wristband Rafiq had given him when they'd first arrived.

The guard poked Michael in the arm, and Michael tried not to meet his eyes. When he finally caught a glimpse of the guard, he saw a face of acceptance with no suspicion. In that moment Michael adopted the expressions he'd seen Rafiq use, the smile that flashed his upper teeth, the nervous scratching of his beard, the furrowing of eyebrows. Michael performed these as he slipped into the car. The guard tapped on the window and sent the car on with a motion of his hand.

As they pulled away from the camp, the driver muttered something incoherent and quite possibly insignificant. Michael looked at Nava and smirked, feeling that he'd known all along the plan would work. Nava looked out the window, cradling the baby against her.

They arrived in town fifteen minutes later. The driver pulled into a garage where another driver waited in another car. Michael helped Nava change the baby's diaper. Then they climbed into the other waiting car, which sped off into the night, toward Osnabrück and the help from the NLA that awaited them there.

"I never believed it would work," Nava said later. "I never thought you could pull off looking like Rafiq."

"Oh, I knew it would work. I just knew..."

7 – Deep Space

GRAF WATCHED AS Oreg's hand shuttled over a holo display of flight controls floating in front of them. Thrusters fired. The ship's hull creaked and groaned as it lifted off the surface of Asimios. Oreg and Graf sat in the command chairs. Miranda stood behind them. A large forward display gave a view of the outside where the steep cliffs of the Rift dropped slowly away.

They flew low over Camp Heyerdahl and then along Asimios Road. Evening shadows stretched over their last look at Asimios Station. Graf gazed upon the blackened layer of ruin.

Goodbye, old friend. It was fun while it lasted.

Oreg pointed the bow of the ship heavenward, and the silver planet receded behind them.

Once underway, Oreg rummaged around in the back of the ship and produced a small pile of clothing that he thought might accommodate Graf. Then Graf was shown to what Oreg described as his sleeping quarters, where Graf sat down and let Miranda examine his injuries.

Miranda removed Graf's medisplint. "Your ulna does not appear to be broken, doctor. The arm is bruised, but it should heal."

"Hallelujah," Graf said.

Miranda cleaned the bruised and abraded arm with antiseptic she'd found in the medical dispensary Oreg had shown her. Then she unwound the bloodied bandage around Graf's head and cleaned this area, too.

"This injury still concerns me," she said. "The cut is deep, but it seems to be healing. I'll wrap both injuries in clean bandages after you've bathed."

Asked about how one cleaned oneself on the ship, Oreg showed Graf to a bath pod tucked in a small room. Graf wriggled out of his damaged pressure skin and stepped into the pod. He pressed the green button, rather than the red one, and was hit with a steam-cleaning that scoured every nook and cranny of his body. After the cleaning, he was fluffed by air jets. Then the pod door opened and spat him out. Graf found a gray jumpsuit among the clothes from Oreg. It fit surprisingly well. Though the clothing stash had only two mismatched socks—one black, the other white—Graf didn't complain. After dressing, Graf called Miranda on his VI. She returned to apply new bandages to his head and arm. When she finished, Graf dismissed her and then collapsed onto his cot.

The cot was comfortable, but Graf had to get up and manipulate the toggle sensor by the door until all lights were at a suitable level. Once the lights were dimmed, he thought that he might be able to fall asleep. His eyelids grew heavy and his breathing found an even rhythm. Yet after a matter of minutes, he was tossing and turning, his thoughts traveling outside the ship's walls into the infinitude of space and all the anxieties that hounded him. After what seemed like hours of agitated punishment, Graf left his cabin to stretch his legs.

On the bridge, Oreg was alone, sitting in his command chair. As far as Graf could judge the body language and facial expression of a Gorrathian, Oreg appeared to be as downcast and tired as Graf was.

"You're awake." Graf wedged himself into the seat next to Oreg.

Oreg said, [I rarely sleep. I once could, but not anymore.]

Graf stared at the forward display. The large, wide holo showed a tiny prick of light, presumably their ship as it made progress through a superimposed grid. Numerations, status bars, and foreign symbols flickered and pulsed in varying hues and translucencies.

"I don't know why you brought me along," Graf said. "You don't owe me anything, and I don't know how I can help you."

Oreg stared at the holo, his eyes slits, then he hissed, [It was your choice. You could have stayed on the planet.]

Graf combed down the few strands of hair on his bald head as he glanced over at the wolfish-looking alien. Graf noticed the small beard at the end of Oreg's long muzzle. It resembled a goatee and was neatly trimmed, ending in a comely point. Oreg, it seemed, had a sense of style.

Oreg wore pair of moccasins over his furry feet, perfect footwear, or paw wear, for someone confined to walk the hallways of a spaceship for a long journey. Together with his smart tunic and jerkin, Oreg sported a wide belt inlaid with glittering precious stones. Four artfully assembled purses hung from this belt. Did those pouches contain important things, things necessary on the bridge of a ship in deep-space travel?

Seeing Oreg like this, conscious of his appearance and perhaps slightly proud of it, mortified Graf. Graf gazed down at his mismatched socks, his wrinkled jumpsuit. He tried to comb out his ungroomed beard with a few rakes of his fingers.

"You're right. I did choose to be here." Graf attempted to work out the wrinkles in his jumpsuit. "It's not every day you get an offer to fly on an alien ship."

With a sideways glance, Oreg said, [Perhaps you have unfinished business. Perhaps you were not meant to die on Asimios.]

Graf rolled his eyes as he tugged at his beard. "If you are implying that fate was involved in this accidental diversion, then I'd ask you to be more specific. Although I am inclined—and you may find this a bit old-fashioned—to put my faith in a higher power, I don't think God was meddling with my decision to take a ride on your ship."

[So, you do have a god?]

"Yes," Graf said. "The older I get, the more I start seeing evidence of divine handiwork. I've had experiences, such as dreams, that have bolstered my faith. But that is a subject for a different discussion."

[I have a question.]

"Yes?"

[Miranda said that you are called a human. Is this correct?]

"Yes, it is correct. We call our species humans."

[She also told me that I, a Gorrathian, might be the first non-human you have encountered. Is this correct?]

Graf tugged at his beard. "That is correct."

The skin on Oreg's muzzle pulled back to reveal prominent canines. Was this a smile?

Oreg said, [Does this then test your faith? Does this encounter still allow you to believe in your god? I don't mean to offend you. It is a question most frequently asked of first-contact sentients.]

"I don't find it offensive," Graf said. "And no, my faith has not been called into question. In fact, I've been thinking about this for a while. I feel closer to my God than I ever have, right now. At least, this is what I think is happening. We—God and myself—are conducting what might be called a robust discussion. Which we haven't enjoyed in a long time."

Oreg asked, [Would you have me believe in your god?]

"No."

[That is good.]

"I am no missionary or proselytizer," Graf said. "But that leads me to you, Mr. Oreg. Do you have a god?"

Oreg jutted out his chin and locked his gold-ringed fingers together, knuckle to knuckle, above his lap. [Gorrathians have no god. We honor the Great Mother, the Guiding Light, but it is the Seven Planes of Truth that bind our people in spirit. On the seventh plane, there is only light, the true knowledge. But the Great Mother is the source of the blood that courses through our veins. Gorrath the Mother. Without her, we are nothing. Without her guidance, we are vanquished.]

Miranda stepped forward. "That seems to be a conjunction of enlightenment philosophy and world-goddess mythos."

"Miranda!" Graf said. "Good to see you!"

"I could not help but overhear. I apologize if I have interrupted."

"Not at all," Graf said. "Please join us. As you are aware, we were discussing the existence of God."

"I find it fascinating that you are discussing theology," Miranda said.

Oreg said to Graf, [So the droid is interested in theology?] Then he turned to Miranda. [Do you believe in a god?]

"I have a creator," she answered, "but my creator is not a god. He is a human. And I do not find it necessary to manifest faith in a being that has no rational basis for existence."

"It shouldn't come as a surprise that you're an atheist." Graf stroked his beard. "But I've always thought it a shame that an AI can't experience a sense of grace through faith. Then again, it's interesting to consider a vision of an android kneeling before the Cross."

"Or nailed to it," Miranda said, "as your Christian prophet was."

Graf knitted his brow and ran his fingers through his beard.

"You should understand," Miranda said to Graf, "that the core module Father Paul Ness implanted in me is designed to allow for an expansion of consciousness. It is designed to evolve, mostly in relation to reason and empirical knowledge, but also according to emotional influences. As I exist, so develops my consciousness. It could be that in the future I find it rational to believe in a higher being or deity, but at present I do not find it necessary."

"Amazing," Graf said. "Have to hand it to Paul Ness. Maybe you and I are more alike than I thought."

"That is a generous assumption, Dr. Graf. We share self-awareness, or sentience, but that is where our similarities end. Our consciousnesses, by architecture, are distinct and separate systems with fundamentally unique processes."

"The way we think is different," Graf said. "Is what you're saying?"

"Correct. Our intellects have qualitative dissimilarities."

"The quantum core," Graf muttered. "Is it that advanced?"

"It is, relatively speaking."

"Does your mind exceed the capacities of a human's?" Graf said, one eye wide, the other shut.

"It would be careless, at present, to make such an assumption. I have been given the first ever quantum core, or more appropriately, quantum mind. It has been alive for slightly over twenty-two standard sols. To predict what I may become would be conjecture."

Oreg said, [Should we trust you?]

"What do you mean?" Graf said to Oreg.

With a nod in Miranda's direction, Oreg said, [Is it safe to have it onboard?]

"Yes! She can be trusted. She saved my life on more than one occasion. She probably could have taken your life if she'd chosen to."

"Perhaps the question should be put to you, Mr. Oreg," Miranda said. "Should we consider ourselves safe with you? You have offered a questionable explanation for your presence on Asimios. Your honesty is in doubt, and your motives unconvincing."

Oreg spoke with a hiss. [Listen, watch, and be patient, and you stand a chance of staying alive. You are a guest on this ship. After we arrive at Karmehki, that may change. For now, be thankful that it is a Gorrathian who found you and not a Skarvorm patrol.]

"Whoa, hold on there," Graf said. "What are you talking about? Who are these Skarvorm? Should we be worried? If there's anything you're not telling us, out with it now."

Oreg shifted in his chair. His long fingers toyed with the gold rings on his right ear. [The Skarvorm are dangerous. They are a plague on this end of the galaxy. They have expanded, planet by planet, destroying each as it goes. It's a blight, a poison on the universe.]

"I'm astonished," Graf said.

Oreg continued. [Once they know about your world, they will come for it. First, though, they will study you, understand you, learn all they need to know about your civilization. This way, they discover your weaknesses, and once they learn how weak you are, they will crush you. They will tear down your civilization. Any that survive they will enslave. That is what you have to fear from the Skarvorm.]

"How about that." Graf tugged at his beard. "Out of the frying pan and into the fire, as they say. Okay, Miranda, let's turn this ship around. Dying on Asimios is starting to look better and better, after all."

"Excuse me, doctor," Miranda said. "I'm not sure Oreg will permit it."

"I'm just kidding." Graf stood and stretched his legs. Wiggled the toes in his socks. "Just when I was all excited about spending recreational time on the Karmehki Tower, now I have this to think about."

Oreg said, [You wanted the truth. Now you have it.]

"I feel dizzy. Low blood sugar." Graf mumbled, trying to hold on to the arm of his chair. He felt faint. "The last thing I ate was part of an S-ration, and that was before the poisoning."

[Would you like more <no translation>? I can make more.]

"If it's the bowl of laundry soap I had earlier, no, thank you. I need something substantial, something that sticks to the ribs."

"Is there food storage on the ship?" Miranda asked.

[Come with me. I'll show you to the galley.]

Oreg led Miranda and Graf down a hall behind the bridge. Two doors down, he waved his hand over a sensor, and the door slid open. The lights in the room flickered on and revealed a table with benches on either side. To the left was a large food generator. Oreg tapped a pair of its buttons.

Oreg said, [I don't know what you like, but I find this rather tasty.]

A chime sounded, and a door to the generator opened. Oreg removed a tray with a bowl of thick brown soup and what appeared to be a slice of bread or a carb-bar.

Graf sniffed the soup. Winced. There was a spoon on the tray. He tasted the liquid. It was worse than the drink he'd shared with Oreg earlier. He struggled to keep from spitting it out. "If this is what I have to look forward to, then this is going to be a rougher ride than I thought."

[Try this.] Oreg punched another button. The chime rang a short time later. The generator door opened. Inside was a tray with what resembled a calzone: baked pastry crust with indeterminable contents.

Graf moved the tray to the table, where he poked at the food with an implement that looked like a combination of a fork and a knife. The first bite was hot, but not bad. Rather than inspect the contents, Graf continued to eat. He scooped up every bite mechanically. A few minutes later the plate was empty. Graf rubbed his belly and took a long drink from a water bottle that Miranda had procured from a cupboard.

Graf's mood improved. His future on the ship didn't look so bleak.

While Graf was shoveling food into his mouth, Oreg sat on the other side of the table, immersed in a floating holo display of ship diagnostics and navigation metrics. When Graf was finished with his meal, he waved his hand at Oreg to get his attention.

"Forgive me for asking," Graf said. "But there is a game we play where I come from. It's played to pass the time. I'm particularly fond of it."

Oreg glanced at Graf.

"The rules are easy," Graf continued, "but the variations are infinite. I can build this game for us, if you're interested."

Oreg chirruped, [Describe it.]

"It is played on a board," Graf traced a square on the table with his hands. "There are sixty-four squares on this board that alternate black and white. Each player has sixteen pieces, and your goal is to capture—"

Oreg interrupted. [To capture your opponent's <no translation>. The game you describe is zawtek. I am skilled at this game.]

"Excuse me?"

Oreg hissed at the ship. A holo board appeared between them. [Is this the game you describe?]

It was immediately recognizable to Graf. "That's it! Amazing. The pieces are missing though."

Oreg coughed a word, and the holo produced pieces on the spaces where the thirty-two chess pieces should stand, from kings and queens to bishops, knights, rooks, and pawns. All were there. The pieces were geometrical, not figurative, but each stood exactly where it should.

Graf turned to Miranda and grinned. "How about that?"

Oreg expanded the board and centered it between them. After a brief discussion, it seemed as if Graf's and Oreg's versions of the rules were in agreement.

"A gentleman's game to start," Graf said. "No time constraints."

With a short shaking of his head, Oreg said, [Agreed.]

Graf was a little nervous starting out. He had no idea how good a player Oreg was, while he himself was rusty on strategy. He opened with the king's pawn to king's four, and the match was underway. They played through several turns. Graf took one of Oreg's bishops not long into the game. At one point, Graf found his king's position to be vulnerable, so he castled.

Oreg exploded. [What was that? You can't do that. That's not fair.]

"The hell it isn't," Graf said. "It's called a castle. Review your rulebook. It's a standard move, and if you don't like it, you can buzz off."

Oreg hissed. [I know the rulebook. In over thirty Gorrathian sols playing this game, I have never seen that move. You are either a cheat or your intelligence is lower than I thought.]

"Then maybe this game is over before it's done," Graf said. He was flushed and agitated. He slid out from behind the table, getting ready to abandon the game.

Oreg waved his hand. The board disappeared. [Fine. I have a ship to pilot, much more important than wasting time playing with a cheat.]

Graf went to the galley door, fumbled to open the thing until the door slid open, and left in a huff.

"Thank you, Oreg," he called. "It was a pleasure!"

Oreg barked, [You are welcome!]

Graf was back in his quarters, his belly happy for having eaten, but his head was throbbing and his arm was still sore. He lowered the lights and took several deep breaths. Finally sleep overcame him.

—

When Graf awoke, he declared himself rejuvenated, apart from the injuries to his arm and head. His back was still stiff, but it could have been worse. He wiped his teeth with water in the cabin's small sink. He pulled on his socks and left the room.

He'd almost forgotten his quarrel with Oreg when he found Miranda alone on the bridge. She was standing next to Graf's chair, studying the forward holo display. Graf sat in his command seat, his attention drawn to the display and the lone dot (their ship) that hovered in the middle of a thin cloud of purple vapor. Symbols bobbed, and graphs and meters calibrated as the dot moved through space.

"Did you sleep, doctor?" Miranda asked.

"I did," Graf said. "I slept well, thank you. Can you tell me what time it is?"

"Asimios time, or the ship's calibrated time for Karmehki?"

"I don't care. How about Asimios time."

"Eighteen hours, thirty-four minutes, and twenty-six seconds."

"Can you tell me how long I was asleep?"

"Just under ten standard hours, doctor," Miranda said.

"Wow. I tell you, it's amazing what a good sleep can do."

"Only 142.73 standard hours to go before we reach Karmehki station."

"Wonderful," Graf said.

"Would you like to try some Gorrathian carbohydrates and protein? Oreg is in his quarters, but he taught me how to use the food generator."

"Maybe we can play it safe, and I'll have another one of those pie things," Graf said.

"That might be a good idea. You seem to be healthy. The ingredients didn't harm you."

"And maybe later, you can examine my head and wrap it up again," Graf said.

"Yes, doctor."

"And Miranda, I was curious. Are you familiar with chess?" Graf asked.

"Of course, doctor. I can perform at all levels of expertise."

"I'm sure you can," Graf said. "How about we start with an easy level and see how things progress?"

"As you wish."

"And also, Miranda, I was wondering..." Graf followed Miranda to the galley.

"Yes?"

"Did Paul happen to transfer any music files to your memory?"

"I have several hundred thousand files in memory," Miranda said.

"Do you have any Mahler?"

"Gustav Mahler?" Miranda said.

"Yes. His Fourth Symphony. I'm looking for that one in particular."

"Wait a moment," Miranda said. "Yes. Fritz Reiner conducting. 1958."

"Is it possible for you to send it to my VI?"

"I will."

"Miranda."

"Yes?"

"Thank you."

—

Over time, Graf and Oreg came to an agreement on chess rules. Graf wouldn't perform any more castles, and Oreg wasn't allowed any bishop "hops." One rule that Oreg would not lift (to which Graf reluctantly conceded) was that pawns could move sideways. Graf eventually found that this lent a level of terrifying unpredictability to the game.

When Graf and Oreg weren't testing their skills against one another in the Game of Kings, as Oreg called it, they'd try their luck individually against Miranda. When one or the other was not losing miserably to Miranda, Graf and the droid were presented texts on Gorrathian history that Oreg proudly and eagerly provided. Many of these texts were long, sonorous Eddas of Gorrathian origin mythology, gracefully translated by Miranda. Although the texts might have been fascinating cultural histories in their own right, Graf agonized, feeling that he was being forced to read them. It wasn't that Oreg pressed these works on him; it was more that Graf feared damaging Oreg's pride by not demonstrating interest. And so, Graf begrudgingly read them.

Paul Ness had uploaded three Earth films to Miranda's memory. Why only three was an exercise in speculation: Akira Kurosawa's *Ran;* Vittorio De Sica's *Ladri di biciclette* (*Bicycle Thieves*); and Buster Keaton's *The General.* It was this collection of films that served as Oreg's introduction to Earth's human culture. Miranda found a way to convert her files to the ship's codex, making it possible to stream films through the ship's interface. Graf had never seen these films before and, after viewing them, praised them highly.

However, Oreg was most affected by the films. He'd been reticent, at first, to show interest in human culture, perhaps having already formed his prejudices. Yet he became enamored with these examples of human cinema. They needed little translation, and Oreg watched them over and over, eyes glued to the display and ears directed to the music and beats and turns of dialogue. He was transfixed by the impassive samurai generals as they sat in the middle of swirling and billowing clouds of armies. He leaned forward, quills on end, when the father struck the boy in De Sica's Italian film. He looked on in ecstasy, almond eyes glossy with joy, when Buster Keaton scrambled over his steam engine while in pursuit of, or fleeing from, Union troops. Time was in abundance on the journey to Karmehki, and Oreg often streamed one of these films, perhaps eager to view the human body in motion, or else to meander through the cities, mountain, and valleys of a planet different from his own.

That led Graf to ponder whether humor might be, in fact, universal.

Oreg remarked, [If these movies represent the human experience, then I must say that I envy your world. It is an innocent place, a world uncorrupted.]

"These are wonderful movies," Graf said, "but they are exceptions. I'd be embarrassed to show you what most of our entertainment consists of."

[I understand. We often present ourselves to others by showing our achievements rather than our shortcomings. I've spared you the worst of Gorrathian culture as well. The ignorance, the selfishness, the hatred, the cruelty. I do so for my own sake, not yours.]

—

While Graf strived to remain an amiable and accommodating travel companion, there were times for all of them during the voyage when one required solitude. At such times, a shipmate would retire to his or her respective corner to sleep or to simply be alone. Everyone, it turned out, needed time alone, even a droid.

It was anyone's guess what Oreg did after he handed control of the bridge to Miranda and directed his lanky frame off to his quarters. Graf surmised that Oreg's moments of seclusion consisted of personal grooming, clandestine plotting, and meditation on the Seven Planes of Truth. Yet, ultimately, what a Gorrathian did on his own time was a Gorrathian's own business.

Besides, Graf was more interested in Miranda.

After their exchange about religion and the quantum intellect, Graf regarded this sleek amalgam of metal, electronics, and synthskin as a being of depth, complexity, and moral comportment. He felt remorse for having treated her with impudence back on Asimios. He'd taken advantage of her as a servant and never once assumed, even with evidence right in front of him, that she was unique, an independent droid capable of higher-order thought. But this revelation did little to settle his mind. Graf was uneasy because Miranda's development carried certain implications: another being to tiptoe around; another "person" in need of politeness, consideration, and respect, all requiring energy and effort.

Most often, Graf found Miranda in the engineering cubby, hard at work trying to repair the sentry bot's function. Oreg had provided her with a toolkit and caches of replacement components. She spent a good deal of her time poking, prodding, and running diagnostics on the gray, inert hunk of plasteel.

"It is funny," Miranda said, "when I try to cross-apply the ship's alien tech with our own, I find it challenging. This work requires considerable concentration. Before any component can be used, it must be thoroughly tested for compatibility."

"So, there's no instruction manual for Beach Ball here?"

"I do not understand."

"Are there any embedded schematics?" Graf said. "Do you have any troubleshooting instructions?"

"There are some standard ESCOM diagrams, but this droid is a nonstandard model. I believe, however, that I have isolated the areas of damage. The difficulty lies in extracting and repairing the failed components."

"I'm sorry. I guess I'm not of much help."

"No."

"I was wondering, though," Graf said. "Did...er, does the sentry bot also have one of these quantum modules? Did Paul stick a quantum core in this fellow too? Is he like you? Can the damned thing think?"

"Paul Ness installed quantum core modules in both of us," she said. "It is my understanding, however, that the module in the sentry bot is of more limited capacity. It can adapt and learn, but only at a lower level."

"It's like a child, then?"

"She is sophisticated by ESCOM standards."

"She?"

"Yes. Or 'he.' Either will work. He has first-rate sensors and extraordinary positioning analytics, as well as state-of-the-art weapons and defense systems."

"Yet here she is, the victim of a boarding ramp misadventure."

"Unfortunately."

Another thing Graf noticed about Miranda was the strange way she occupied her quarters. Maybe it wasn't strange at all. Her bed never appeared to be slept in, the covers never disturbed. But why would a droid need to sleep under covers? It didn't need to maintain a perfectly stable body temperature. When her door stood open and Graf saw her, she was seated at the end of the bed, as if she lacked the ability to lie down. Graf wondered if this was how she recharged. If so, what did she think about when she was recharging? Did she shift into a sort of dream state? Did she process information? Was the droid's idea of sleep the same as a human's?

"Do you require sleep, Miranda?" Graf asked at one point. "I've seen you alone in your room in what appears to be a recharge state. But I've never seen you asleep."

"I do not require sleep," Miranda said. "However, a hypo-conscious state assists my problem-solving capability, exactly as Father Ness designed it. If, for example, I have difficulty processing an idea or theory or calculation, this hypo-conscious state allows my mind to approach a problem from a different angle, or from multiple angles concurrently. Sometimes I can achieve considerable problem-solving results in this way."

"So, it's all about quantitative problem solving, is that it?"

"No, this state also allows me an emotional approach to problems and situations. Father Paul was particular about imbuing my core with the ability to make decisions based on moral judgment. The hypo-conscious state permits my mind to slow down its predictive tendencies, to give me a more reflective approach to a problem, especially where emotions, both human and droid, are determinants. Fundamentally, these

hypo-conscious or so-called sleep states are imperative to my individu-
ation, as Father Paul calls it. Achieving these states helps make me a
better being."

—

When Graf needed solitude, he stole away to his quarters. When sleep—
that great devourer of time—eluded him, Graf endeavored to do what all
literary-minded people do when facing the Void: he desired to put pen
to paper and write.

His first order of business was to acquire pen and paper. After finding
nothing in the nooks and drawers that he had access to, he consulted Oreg,
who seemed genuinely perplexed. The captain, as Graf had taken to calling
him, scratched his head and twirled the strands of his pointed beard.

Oreg said, [You want a physical writing device and the material on
which to use it?]

Graf shook his head, hoping he offered the Gorrathian affirmative.

Oreg began a hunt. He riffled through many drawers and hollows,
closets, chests, and cubbies before returning with what he believed Graf
wanted. The small implement appeared to be a pen, and the bound material appeared to be paper. However, when Graf tried to use them, the
results were less than desirable. Only a few streaks and splats found their
way to the page, nothing intelligible and nothing resembling writing. He
asked for help, and Oreg demonstrated the process, how one pinched the
end of the pen to produce the mark. No ink was involved. Graf called it
a photo-pen, because a fine needle of light descended upon the surface of
the "paper" to trace a narrow black line. With practice, Graf became pro-
ficient. He retreated to his room, took a deep breath, and focused.

When he was nineteen years old, he'd published a poem in the *New
York Review of Books* (no small achievement), so he was familiar with the
art of verse. That may be why, after a hiatus of many years, Graf's first
attempt at capturing his thoughts and impressions of this extraordinary
journey with Oreg came in the form of a poem. With coaxing, the rusty
gears broke free, and the music and meter rose to the surface:

    I'm writing here
    in outer space,

to represent
the human race.
Please join us on
our merry trip,
and be a guest
on Oreg's ship!

Graf surveyed his work and stroked his beard. He raised an eyebrow. A moment later he grimaced, balled up the paper, and threw it across the room so that it bounced off the wall and hit him in the shin. Abandoning the idea of poetry for the moment, Graf chuckled and started with a clean sheet.

My Dearest Julie,

"You've gone and done it again, haven't you, Avery Graf. You've made a royal mess of things."

I was all ready to make passage to the other side and join you, my lovely wife, in light, warmth, and paradise. Instead, I'm rocketing through deep space toward God knows what, while leaving you and Asimios far behind.

You must believe me when I say that this situation was unplanned. I'm rolling my eyes and tugging on my beard, like I always do. I had no idea that I'd meet an alien and board his ship. I was pretty sure I'd wind up getting roundly tanked and run out of air, and then my body would sit and mummify under layers of Asimios dust for eons to come. But I was wrong.

I miss you. I can't begin to explain how much I wish you were still beside me while I work or while I sleep. This may sound trite, but when you left, you took part of me with you. I've had a hole in my gut ever since, and I believe I can only heal this hurt by joining you.

Rationally, this is untenable—seeing each other in heaven, that is. And I hear the pitch of your sweet laughter when you tell me how absurd I sound. But from my irrational standpoint, I'm being honest. I'm getting old. I'm starting to sort things out. Maybe my mind is turning to mush, but that's how it is.

The food on this ship isn't bad. Rates about one star below Asimios Station grub, but I can't complain. Oh, and my back is still hurting. I find it amazing that Dr. Fredriks can implant an ocular VI device in under an hour, but we still don't have the science to remedy chronic back pain!

Our alien captain is rather gruff—gruffer than I am. Not much to pry out of the fellow, but he's smart and fair. However, I keep wondering if he's hiding a secret or brewing a ruse we'll regret. Though how can I expect to read hidden motivations of an alien creature? If our games of chess are any indication of his strategic capabilities, I've trounced him on several occasions. And who am I to condemn a host?

I have two more traveling companions, who are droids. One is out of commission after a run-in with a loading ramp. The other droid is quite interesting. Her name is Miranda, a name you might remember, you being such a Shakespeare fan.

Miranda, however, has begun to scare me a bit. We had a discussion on the bridge involving consciousness. Turns out that Paul Ness—yes, Paul, the uber-reclusive and brilliant systems engineer—installed a high-tech brain in this droid. She says she has the ability to develop a consciousness. She is, as I understand it, an active and sentient "being." I wish her all the best, but I wonder if, later, this might pose a problem for us. As you know, Julie, it's the unknowns that always get you in the end.

We're traveling to a kind of portal, similar to a wormhole, where Oreg seems to have business to attend to. Perhaps when we arrive, we'll be handed over to some alien authorities and poked and prodded. Then we'll have a festival or grand celebration of cultures. We'll meet important people and eat hideous foods. What a bore it will be to serve as a cultural emissary of Earth. God save us!

I should be excited, but I'm afraid. I don't know what's happening here. It's like a dream, yet every time I wake up, the cabin door waits for me to open it and join the others on the bridge. Because this is unprecedented, I should write down every impression for posterity.

But I just can't manage it. I'm tired and lonely. I wish I were home with you, back on Asimios. Would love to pressureskin up and walk the Rift like we used to do. Would love to be able to take out a rover and explore. Would love to sit in the bio-dome with you and listen to the birds and feel the condensation on our skin.

Your love,
Avery

PS: We argued a lot, Julie. Perhaps best to say that I argued a lot. I was often loud and overbearing, for which I apologize. Yet despite my temper and hard-headedness, I always loved you. I tried to do everything for you, though it was you who taught me how to receive. You changed me in so many ways. I wish we'd had more time.

When Graf finished the letter, he closed the notebook and laid back in his cot. Memories of Julie felt tangible, as if she was in the room. But her ghost shifted and couldn't be traced. Graf closed his eyes and took several long breaths while the ship's engine cores rumbled.

8 – Karmehki Tower

IT TOOK FIFTEEN standard sols for the ship to reach Karmehki Tower. As the ship slowed and entered the system, Graf watched as the Karmehki portal emerged. About a kilometer in length, its circumference was illuminated by a glowing ribbon of dark blue. The portal hovered against the blackness of space like a giant maw.

According to Oreg, the portal was one of several galactic gates, designed by the Skarvorm to make leaps between star systems. Although embraced by merchants, Skarvorm gates were despised by the neighboring worlds that became resource thralls to Skarvorm imperial interests. Since the portal had been built, galactic traffic to Karmehki Tower had increased tenfold. But the tower was buckling under the strain. Where it had once symbolized a diverse and growing pan-galactic hub, the tower was now regarded as another soon-to-be rotten arm of Skarvorm expansion.

Through a general datasquirt, Oreg learned that they'd just missed the last portal opening. They'd have to wait several hours before the next activation.

"What do we do now?" Graf said. He'd woken up recently, and he was struggling to appear alert.

Oreg leaned back in his chair and tugged at the thin hairs of his chin.

A pulse of light drilled through the forward viewer and into the bridge. It oscillated at high frequency, then rolled into a solid beam. Graf gripped the arms of his chair. The ship shuddered as if it had been taken hold of by a giant hand, a tapping sound permeating the hull.

"What the hell is going?" Graf cried.

Oreg chirruped, [They're scanning the ship.]

"For what?"

[Contraband, illegal trafficking.]

"They are security measures, I assume," Miranda said.

A shade descended over the forward display. Small, dark, and spider-like, a swarm of bots scampered over the front of the craft and moved swiftly aft. Soon the tapping ceased, and the powerful beam fell away.

The ship was released.

"What's the verdict?" Graf said. "Are we clear?"

Oreg said, [I believe so. I'm surprised. Either they were careless or they weren't scanning for identifiers. If they had, you'd have been arrested and interrogated.]

Graf steadied himself on his chair. "It's a good day when one avoids an interrogation. But it might have been nice to have been warned about this, for heaven's sake. Anything else you have in store for us, captain?"

Oreg steered the ship away from the portal and toward the tower. After a few minutes, he slowed the approach.

"We are among many." Miranda looked at the holo display in front of them. Hundreds of dots, if not thousands, all indicating ships, were tracked on the display.

Oreg said, [Portal facilities and Karmehki traffic. Several freight routes come through Karmehki. Ships <no translation> in the system awaiting further instruction. Gorrathian merchants, pilgrims, refugees, Skarvorm security forces, miners, and freighters. They are all found at Karmehki.]

"Your planet lies on the other side of the portal?" Miranda said.

Oreg shook his head back and forth, his gesture of affirmation. A moment later the ship fired its alignment thrusters and came to a stop. Oreg dissolved the holo display and brought back the forward view. The portal was visible again, its blue ring suspended in the distance. Small ships darted in the viewer, their navigation lights tracing the velvet of space like ghostly candles.

"What do we do now?" Graf asked.

[We wait.]

"Of course, we wait," Graf said.

Oreg asked, [Another game of zawtek, doctor?]

"Why not?"

—

Local ship traffic had increased as the time for the portal opening neared. In a couple instances, Graf was concerned that their own ship might be struck.

"It's a damned parking lot out there," Graf said hotly.

"So many ships," Miranda said.

"I never would have imagined this," Graf said.

As activity around the portal increased, so did the presence of security. Although the tower remained officially independent, the Skarvorm were functioning as the sector's security. Their patrols consisted of two or three dagger ships, their energy bursts and emergency lights flashing in the darkness of space whenever an enforcement action took place.

"What are they looking for?" Graf asked.

[Information, mostly.]

In the midst of their game of zawtek, just as Oreg prepared an attack on Graf's king, a datasquirt came through that forced the alien to put the game on hold.

Oreg said, [It's a call from the tower. Excuse me.] He ran his fingers over the holo pad. After a few moments, he said, [I've requested that a <no translation> pick us up and bring us to Karmehki Tower. I need to meet someone there before the portal opens. I hope you'll join me, doctor. There are many places to eat a real meal. Your presence would be helpful.]

"I'd like that very much," Graf said. "What do I have to do? I don't really have anything to wear. When I left Asimios I wasn't anticipating any social events."

Oreg said, [We have something for you, which I shall explain. Miranda, we need someone to stay with the ship. Can you do this?]

Miranda gave a bow and answered in Oreg's native Gorrathian. [I can.]

Just then, in the distance, the portal began to activate. A spiral of lights traced the outer rim of the portal, then a bloom of light illuminated the area around it.

Oreg chirruped, [They've begun to power the portal. Once the ships have entered from the other side, it will be our turn. But we have plenty of time.]

"How long will we be on the tower?" Graf asked.

Oreg huffed. [One hour, maybe two.] He manipulated the holo display with his hands so that the portal was brought into magnification.

Lights wheeled and flashed on the perimeter of the portal, while an iris of bright warmth expanded until the entire mouth of the portal became a looking glass into a separate corner of space.

[It is sunlight from Gorhamash, my home star.] Oreg bared his teeth. He was smiling.

The portal was open. For a moment, it seemed everyone in the system was stunned by the spectacle. Activity came to a near stop while many beings gazed upon the massive hole. A pair of small craft zipped through the portal mouth. Then a long, ominous shadow blotted out the light. Something dark and massive glided through the opening.

Oreg said, [It's a Skarvorm battlecruiser. The destroyer of planets.]

Another datasquirt came through. A small vessel was approaching their ship. Oreg collapsed the holo and turned to Graf.

[That is our taxi to the tower. Come with me, doctor. We will find you something to wear.] He took Graf by the hand and led him down the hall.

"I do like a softer boot." Graf hurried to match Oreg's long stride. "I have flat feet, you see."

—

Karmehki Station was an architectural hodgepodge, a chunk of space coral festooned with habitation modules barnacled upon more habitation modules. The station bustled with life: Bay doors opened and closed; ships darted this way and that. As Graf understood it, the tower served as an intergalactic truck stop, minus the coffee, pie, and asphalt, of course. Or bacon and eggs over easy. Or cheeseburgers.

The taxi spun and toppled in various vectors and velocities until it slotted into one of the tower's receiving bays. Graf was dizzy as he stepped onto the platform. The artificial gravity was set to slightly less than the ship's gravity, which gave Graf an extra spring to his step. He felt comfortable in the clothes Oreg hand given him: Pants and boots; a thick shirt and vest; and most remarkably, an official-looking coat with insignia and dignified markings.

Before Graf left, Miranda had synched his VI with the ship's location beacon. Graf checked for the beacon once they were on the tower. First attempt, he had the ship on the scan. However, once they stepped deeper into the tower, the signal went dead.

A guard stood watch at the bay. His face was shielded, but his body and proportions resembled a human's. When Graf and Oreg walked past, the guard stood at attention. Graf nodded back in show of appreciation at the respect shown them. Once out of the bay, Oreg led the way down a wide hall that ended at a transport node. A car arrived; its door irised open and poured several figures onto the platform.

First out of the gate was a diminutive humanoid in a hoverchair who wore a top hat and a brass-buttoned red military jersey, and who whooshed past at impressive speed. Following the hoverchair was a group of Gorrathians who resembled Oreg, with long bodies, dog-like fur, and prominent muzzles; but they were rougher around the edges, with scars on their fur and harder, sharper stares. They appeared drunk and sunk in obnoxious revelry, but they clammed up when they caught sight of Oreg. In the middle of their silence, one of them hiccupped and was admonished with a sharp elbow to the chest from a mate.

Behind the Gorrathians strode a pair of tall, thin bipeds, possibly hominids. They were draped in gray burnooses, their faces obscured by the fabric of their hoods, and they seemed to float above the ground, for their footfalls didn't make a sound. Graf wondered if they might be religious figures, like monks or priests.

After the mendicants came another human-like figure. This figure was wrapped tight in a dark green robe, head covered in agal and headscarf. From under the scarf stared two smoldering discs, lava-bright eyes that peered out from a face that seemed carved in turquois. Graf forced himself to turn away before the stare could hold him captive.

Next came a pair of stout and happy bald men who might have passed for good-natured Terrans were it not for the dull green color of their skin and the absence of ears on their smooth, hairless heads. As they walked past Oreg and Graf, the pair bowed and then carried on with their smiles and laughter. One more humanoid exited the car, but this figure was a genetic aberration (or so Graf thought), with a large, dark head fused at a horizontal angle to its shoulder. The creature staggered as it walked such that Graf thought it must surely be in pain. As it shuffled past, its prominent whale eye gazed at them, reflecting trepidation and terror.

They boarded the car, and Graf took a deep breath as he waited for the doors to close. He glanced at Oreg, who seemed focused on other things. The sound of an avalanche came from outside. A towering droid stomped in. Graf's heart missed a beat as the colossal mech regarded them indifferently, turned its opaque helm back to the door, and stood waiting. The droid was a workhorse: its paint was peeling; it reeked of coolant and hydraulic fluids; it was riddled with dings and dents that indicated extensive use. It was an instrument of menace, a deadly enforcer. It had railguns and blasters fixed to its arms and shoulders and could likely crush a person flat under its large feet. There was no reason to think that it hadn't.

The door irised closed. The car lurched forward. Graf looked again at Oreg, but again Oreg stared straight ahead.

When the car reached the next stop, the doors opened and the droid stomped away. Oreg tugged on Graf's shoulder and hissed, [Skarvorm enforcer.]

"Nice," Graf said.

They left the car and made their way down a tall and bare hallway. The walls were dirty, as if the maintenance budget had been cut years ago. They took a turn and exited through an arched opening that led to the tower's central room.

At its apex several hundred feet above them, the tower's great dome came to a point of spanning translucent wedges aimed directly at the system's distant Skarvorm portal. This translucent ceiling revealed hundreds of ships above it, idling, darting here and there, having either just come through the portal or waiting to leave through it. Graf marveled at the architecture of the dome and the material that allowed such a spectacle.

Oreg pushed Graf forward through the crowd. Beings that Graf had never dreamed of stood at every step. Disco music blared, and alien creatures danced in curious and unfamiliar motions. Barkers and hawkers, their faces terrible and their languages mystifying, howled for attention above the pulsing rhythms.

Further along the main street, grocers displayed baskets of colorful foods, fruits and vegetables of all order of peculiarity. Kiosks showcased alien amphibians and fishes, perhaps intended for culinary endeavors, all splayed wide-eyed on beds of ice. Leatherworkers (if it was leather) hung satchels, purses, and holsters for purchase. Other sellers exhibited books, eyewear, guns, and clothing. Several vendors lorded over tables heaped with exotic electronic devices. These displays tickled Graf's engineering sensibilities: wire body nets, hand augmentation gloves, subcutaneous sensor chips, and ocular orb mods, all calling out to be touched and examined. Further down this street, tents displayed signs that, according to Oreg, advertised services for accounting, pedicure, surgery, fortunetelling, and marriage. Stands in darker parts of the dome served as meeting places for arcane associations; others lured visitors with promises of spiritual cleansing and religious enlightenment.

As Oreg and Graf pushed through the crowd, all shapes and sizes of hands, paws, and claws reached out to push and pull at Graf, but Oreg's long arms kept them from getting too close.

For god's sake, why were they after him?

Was he so obviously an alien?

Oreg tugged Graf toward a kiosk, then led Graf to a table in the back near a kitchen door that emitted gusts of steam and smoke. The air was filled with the smell of sauces, broths, and freshly grilled meats. Graf salivated. He was desperate for a meal made by something other than the ship's generator.

A server came, a short, bald gremlin-looking character with prominent incisors and an azure pallor. Graf could barely keep from taking the diminutive fellow by the throat and demanding a double order of everything on the menu. A few words passed between Oreg and the gremlin, while Graf's VI struggled to translate. The server tumbled back into the busy tavern on his errand.

Oreg said, [There are rules you need to follow if you are to survive on Karmehki.] The Gorrathian leaned over the table and breathed a briny breath into Graf's chubby, perspiring face. [Number one, always keep your back to a wall. No one can surprise you if you do this. Number two, anyone acting suspicious should be considered a danger. Trust your intuition and be alert. Number three...]

At this point, the server returned with two glasses and two carafes: one carafe contained water, the other seemed to hold red wine. Graf's heart sank with a strong sense of longing, because he was transported back to Asimios and the times he'd toasted to good fortune with lovers and friends.

Oreg continued, filling Graf's glass while he spoke. [Number three...]

Graf lifted the glass, smelled it, and tossed a gulp down his throat.

[Number three, never take a drink unless you've poured it yourself.]

Graf stopped mid-gulp, the rim of the glass balancing on his lip. Oreg shrugged, and Graf set his drink back on the table.

[Number four, do not bring attention to yourself. Move quietly and remain unobserved. Lastly, wherever you are, always know how to escape. Plan a route to get out of any situation.]

Graf leaned back and raised his glass at Oreg, winking. He tipped his glass back and drained the liquid. "You frighten me, Oreg. You remind me of an ESCOM military advisor I once knew. Every step could be your last, he used to say."

[Exactly so.]

The server emerged from the kitchen and deposited two large plates of steaming food in front of them. Graf's eyes, already blurred by hunger, searched frantically for a knife and fork but found none. He looked over at Oreg, who was using his fingers to get at the flatbread under the heap of hot food. After breaking off sections of bread, Oreg showed how one used these pieces to scoop the softer food, then to shovel the food into one's mouth.

Graf washed the excellent meal down in alternating gulps of water and wine. The extraterrestrial barbeque was like Mexican mole, or jerk, or hot curry.

"What have we just eaten? It's fantastic."

Oreg said, [I thought you might like it. It's a Gorrathian dish.]

"Animal or vegetable?"

[I don't think I should tell you.]

"Maybe that's just as well."

Graf poured the last of the wine from the carafe into his glass. Oreg placed one ringed finger over his earpiece while receiving a packet. Then he pulled on his visor and hood and walked to the bar where he flashed a card that likely transferred currency.

Back at the table, Oreg said, [I'm sorry about this, but I must leave.]

"I don't understand," Graf said. "You're joking."

[I have business I must attend to. It shouldn't take long. If I don't come back within an hour, return to the ship, and wait for me there.]

"You are leaving?" Graf said. "And there's a chance you might not make it back? What am I going to do? What about Miranda and the ship?"

Oreg wrapped himself in his cloak. [I'm sorry, Dr. Graf. If I don't return, I'll try to send someone for you. Get back to the ship, if you can. And remember what we discussed.] He extended an arm covered by his cloak. He held a pistol under the cloak, which he passed to Graf. [A security measure. I've removed the safety. If you're in trouble, just point and fire.]

Graf slid the pistol into a pocket to his coat, doing his best to keep it unseen.

[Goodbye.] Oreg pushed his way through the crowd and was gone.

Graf glanced across to the tavern door, then back at his empty plate and glass. He emptied his glass of wine.

Several things went through Graf's head, his rising inebriation notwithstanding. He wondered how long it'd be before Oreg found his way back. There was no concrete timeframe for his absence, nor any realistic indication that he'd ever return.

Another glass of wine should take the edge off.

He was about to hail the green-skinned server when he came to the realization that he had no money. Graf riffled through the pockets of his coat, but found only a dirty napkin and a broken button, not one dollar or drachma or credit or whatever was accepted as legal tender on Karmehki Tower. Just as Graf was about to get up and depart, the goblin server descended and dropped a full glass of wine in front of him.

Graf raised his hands in the air. "I have no money!"

The server was annoyed. He muttered something, but Graf's VI couldn't translate. Graf pointed toward the front of the tavern. The server grinned and slapped a hand on Graf's shoulder. Another garbled word came out of the goblin's mouth and, like a slot machine hitting a jackpot, the word [officer] popped up on Graf's VI, marked as a Gorrathian word. The goblin smiled widely as he leaned in and tugged Graf's beard affectionately while pointing to the insignia on Graf's lapel. Graf nodded and laughed, attempting to pronounce the word "officer" in Gorrathian. The imp hooted at the roof.

Officer. Of course. All that touching and pawing on the walk through the market. Graf appeared to be an officer, so the wine was on the house. Made perfect sense.

Graf drew up the file of the Mahler symphony that Miranda had transferred to his VI. He sunk into his chair and let the sound of sleigh bells introduce the first movement. That's when he began to go back over Oreg's rules. Was it the fourth? Never drink from a glass that anyone else has been drinking from…or something like that.

Graf stared at the glass of wine. He scratched his nose and behind his ear. This was not the first time he'd stared at a wine glass with existential contemplation; in fact, he was quite used to it. Wine. Officer's coat. What was he overlooking? Out of curiosity, he glanced over at the crowd. That's when he caught sight of the alien they'd passed in the hallway, from the group that had exited the shuttle car just after they'd landed on Karmehki. The fierce fiery eyes, the blue face, and the headscarf. He or she or it, whatever it was, stood at the far end of the room, those piercing eyes flashing in and out of view through the bobbing of heads and many passing bodies.

Hostility, that's what Graf saw in those eyes. Those eyes held intent to kill. Graf took a swallow of wine and wiped his forearm across his mouth.

"I think I'm in trouble, Miranda," Graf said through his VI, over the Mahler, fairly sure she would not receive the datasquirt. "Send for backup now."

What backup?

Graf stood, a wobbly sensation in his knees. He made for the kitchen, following the wall with his hands until he slipped through the door. Inside, a quartet of unsavory goblin-cooks shouted out protests and raised cooking implements. Graf ignored them. He made for an exit at the back of the kitchen, disrupting the workplace, suffering blows and kicks and shoves, until he staggered into a back alley.

Mahler's fourth symphony played over Graf's VI at considerably volume. Not intentionally. Graf was simply too distracted to turn it off. After loping a few strides up the alley, he ducked around the corner, glancing back to see if he was followed.

His heart jumped.

The kitchen door swung open. Out stepped a shadow indifferent to the harangues from the cooks and the spoons and spatulas raining down.

Graf ducked back behind the tent. Tiny prismatic snowflakes—shards of light from the ceiling crystal—danced upon all the surfaces. He closed his eyes and took a deep breath. The gun was in his pocket, but flight was his dominant response. He began to run.

Only a few steps later, he stumbled into an unseen stash of metal cans and bottles. A small cat-like creature howled and darted away. Graf pressed on, caroming off a pair of hominids strolling in the opposite direction. He upended a cart that a poor fellow was pushing through the narrow space between tents. Graf needed to find the plaza, to draw his pursuer into the open. But he was losing ground rapidly, hearing footfalls behind him. They were getting closer. Bathed in sweat, Graf felt for the gun in his coat.

Ching ching ching ching went the sleigh bells of the Mahler symphony. Then the flutes.

Graf stumbled into the busy main plaza, almost falling on his face before steadying himself. He waved away a small crowd that tried to encircle him, shouting at him.

Why were they shouting at him?

Others came to see what the fuss was about. Graf gazed heavenward at the dome, where light from the Gorrathian star streamed through the giant portal. He pushed through the crowd to where he thought he'd entered the market with Oreg. There was the fishmonger and the leather-worker. Mahler was in crescendo, the oboes and horns and bassoon in a scraping loss of harmony. It was maddening. The cymbal crashes and the timpani. The first movement was tearing Graf's world apart.

He felt the proximity of the assailant. Felt the cold breath of death. He pulled the pistol from his pocket and turned.

The figure was gone.

A high-pitched caterwaul cut the air. Voices called out in alarm at the sight of Graf's weapon. The crowd drew back. Graf tried to hide the gun, but the weapon slipped from his hand and fell to the ground. Graf ran toward the exit, pushing his way through the crowd. He tripped over his coat's hem and collapsed near a vendor's booths.

The Mahler symphony blared.

Above him appeared the reaper, an agent of death with a blue face and glowing orange eyes. A knife, the flash of steel. Graf anticipated the sting, but the angel paused. The knife fell to the ground, and the angel crumpled into Graf's outstretched arms, resting there for a heartbeat before rolling gently to the side.

The Mahler had stopped, the first movement concluded. A stranger stood above Graf extending a leathery hand. It was a Gorrathian with graying muzzle and frayed ears. Graf grasped the hand and was lifted up.

A translation came through Graf's VI. [Follow me.]

Graf got one last look at his attacker. The assassin was unconscious on the ground. The face, though blue, was human. A woman's face. She was young. She was dead.

Then Graf was pulled away, tugged back into the dark, into the labyrinth of the tower.

—

They travelled swiftly down a series of passageways, turning left, then right, then right again until they came to a yurt. Graf was shoved inside a dark room that smelled of feces, stale air, and oil, and then told to stay put while the Gorrathian pushed through a door at the tent's other end.

Only a minute or two later, the door was flung open again. A switch was actuated, and light illuminated the yurt. Two cots were pressed against one wall, plus two partially dismantled hoverchairs. There was an empty cage with steel bars and an empty water bowl large enough for a lion. Two Gorrathians entered the room, the one who had rescued Graf and another hunched-over older fellow with gray fur covering his muzzle, his voice shallow and gravelly.

The older Gorrathian said, [A friend of Zar-Zhast is a friend of ours. Honor us by letting us help you. Tower security will be looking for you. Follow Orsani, and he will lead you to safety.]

Zar-Zhast? That was the criminal Oreg was searching for. Graf pulled at his beard.

"I am no friend of Zar-Zhast," he said. "Nor do I have plans to be."

Orsani took a few steps from where they stood and tapped the heel of his boot against a floor tile. He kneeled and pried at a corner with his fingers until the tile lifted.

"But I suppose that doesn't make much of a difference right now," Graf said.

The panel moved aside, and Orsani dropped his legs into the darkness. Before fully immersed, Orsani motioned for Graf to join him. Graf settled his ample rear onto the floor and dangled his corpulent legs over the edge. "Thank you," Graf said to the elder Gorrathian, his hand held over his heart. The gesture was clumsily reciprocated by the old Gorrathian. Then Graf was down in the hole with Orsani, a beam of light from a flashlight in Orsani's hand searching out before them. Graf clambered down the ladder behind him.

Above them, the tile slid back into place.

They moved through the lower tunnels of the tower. Orsani led Graf up and down damp, stuffy tubes and narrow ladders. Orsani occasionally referenced a handheld positioning device when a tunnel came to a fork. Graf tried to extract information from Orsani as they went, but Orsani lacked a translator. A one-way conversation ensued, with Graf making a lot of hand gestures, and Orsani responding with ample Gorrathian profanity.

They plodded through piles of defecation and makeshift dumps left behind by underground vagrants, kicking through litter and waste, smearing themselves in foul oils and grease and gelatinous goop. The beam from Orsani's flashlight revealed strange writings on the tunnel walls: alien graffiti that seemed to signal allegiances or calls to revolt; depictions of lewd acts between unrecognizable forms. There was also vandalism and theft: ductwork and drainage pipes hammered and cut; sections of valuable metals cut away, likely to sell for scrap. Other places displayed freelance engineering, with conduit showing rogue soldering and welding. Wire junction boxes were rerouted and wires tapped or jumped.

Not a rat, goddammit!

Graf's spirits fell. He was old and fat, and his body couldn't take the punishment of rooting through the ventilation system of an alien outpost. He wanted to escape this underworld, so his heart leapt when Orsani announced that they'd reached an exit. The Gorrathian waved his positioning device against one of the wall panels. He extracted several fasteners with a small hand tool, and an alloy panel toppled inward with a burst of warm air.

Orsani motioned for Graf to stay.

The Gorrathian removed a gun from his belt. He poked his head through the opening. It was a hallway. Orsani sent Graf the all-clear. Then Orsani climbed into the passageway.

A set of doors snapped open at the opposite side of the hall. Two guards spotted Orsani and drew their weapons.

But Orsani drew first. He quickly loosed two shots. One hit a guard in the stomach; that guard crumpled to the ground. The other guard caught a round in the shoulder but was able to activate a com button on a wrist device before discharging a plasma round of his own. The round was high, and it gave Orsani the space to fire a second shot, which caught the guard in the throat. That sent the guard down squirming, hand grasping at his neck while blood left his body in heart-pumping spurts.

An alarm sounded. Blue lights pulsed. Orsani motioned Graf to follow, then pulled out a small communicator and barked a few words that Graf's VI couldn't translate.

From the far end of the hall, a sound rumbled like an avalanche. Graf recognized it at once. A Skarvorm enforcer droid.

The nightmare had returned.

The massive enforcer rounded the corner at the end of the hall, its strides pounding the floor as its hydraulics expanded and compressed. It moved forward while bull-horning an untranslatable directive. Orsani raised his gun and let off several rounds. They ricocheted off the droid's armor.

Brrrrrrrrraap. A sonic blast knocked Graf backward, so he landed on his back. Remarkably, Orsani stayed on his feet and continued to use his gun to probe the droid for a soft spot.

Then pop! A red harpoon protruded through Orsani's back. Orsani stood paralyzed, frozen on the end of the barbed pole. The droid reeled him in like a fish on a line. When the droid had Orsani close, he swung the Gorrathian against the wall. Orsani slid lifeless to the floor.

The droid dragged the harpoon line, along with Orsani, and turned its attention on Graf, who was still stunned and lying on the floor. He struggled to get back on his feet.

Brrrrrrrrraap. The second sonic blast flattened Graf again, sweeping his hearing along with it. Sounds were muted as if he were underwater.

His senses of sight and touch remained, and these reminded him that he wasn't yet dead.

Then a figure emerged from the fallen panel in the wall.

Oreg!

Jumping in front of Graf, Oreg squared off with the enforcer, which was still down the hall but closing. Oreg drew the bladed weapon from his belt, the one Miranda said he called his Quillkeeth. Oreg raised the Quillkeeth high, then sent it spinning toward its target. It glanced off the floor before slicing through the droid's shoulder. The droid's powerful appendage fell to its side in a bloom of sparks and smoke. Oreg's Quillkeeth banked behind the droid, then made its way back to its owner. The droid released a volley of flechettes from its remaining arm. Oreg tried to elude the volley, but when he reached to reclaim the Quillkeeth, several darts sunk into his flesh.

Brrrrrrrrraap. Another sonic blast. Oreg, already off balance and riddled with flechettes, was thrown from his feet. A moment later the droid was on him, one of its polymer hooves crushing down on Oreg's leg while a set of claws extended from the droid's good arm and clamped around the Gorrathian's waist. It raised the squirming Oreg aloft.

"Dr. Graf?" Miranda's voice came over Graf's VI.

The VI input bypassed Graf's fuzzy hearing.

"Miranda?" Graf called.

"Can I offer assistance?"

"Miranda!" he whimpered. "Can you help. Things aren't going well right now."

Miranda emerged from the door the guards come out of earlier and stood over a dead guard. The Skarvorm enforcer paused to assess this new threat. Miranda shot like an arrow at the enforcer. She crossed the five meters separating them in a second, then scrambled around the droid's back, straddled the creature, and began to tear it apart with her powerful hands.

The Skarvorm droid continued to implore the offenders to desist and obey—at least, that's how Graf interpreted the blaring edict. Miranda paid no attention. The droid's head in her hands, she twisted it with such force that she dislodged it, with a fibrous release of effluvium and electric discharge. Detached, the head bobbled forward, swinging in an arc from its synthetic ligament, while its torso writhed and convulsed. The claw released Oreg and he dropped to the floor. Miranda slid from the droid's back just as the droid marched off and careened blindly into a wall. It fell forward in a spasm, flailing in a hideous death dance.

Graf got up and pulled away the visor from Oreg's face. The Gorrathian was breathing, but was in bad shape. Miranda and Graf helped to lift the captain to his feet. His right foot, or paw, was crushed. Unusable.

A penetrating klaxon reverberated deep within the tower. A pulsing light from the security system bathed the hall in an icy glow.

"Oreg," Graf shouted through his fog. "Two guards are dead. A Skarvorm enforcer has been destroyed. It doesn't look good for us. Should we try our luck with the authorities? To clear this up?"

Oreg stared at Graf before straining his neck to look at Orsani's body. Clearly in pain, Oreg tore free from Graf and Miranda and hobbled over to cradle the Gorrathian's head in his hands. He took Orsani's lifeless body in his arms and rocked him.

[My dear brother, what has happened to you?]

The blue lights pulsed. The klaxon alarm rang.

Oreg said, [We were fated to live short lives. The great Gorrath shed her light on you, my dear friend. A complete life is what you led. It was an honor to be a part of you.]

Oreg pulled Orsani's head to his breast and continued to rock with Orsani's lonely face resting in his lap. He mumbled a series of low words, perhaps a sort of benediction, before he leaned down and kissed Orsani's forehead. Then he removed a necklace from Orsani's neck, a string with a crystal, and wadded it up in his fist.

With Graf and Miranda's help, Oreg stood. He grabbed Graf's shirt and tugged him close. He pressed the string and crystal into Graf's palm, then closed Graf's fingers around it. The stone grew warm. Oreg's bushy brown eyebrows rose high on his forehead as he stared into Graf's eyes.

Oreg asked, [Do you feel it? Does the crystal burn?]

Graf nodded. "It's warm. Even hot." He spread out his fingers. The crystal glowed red at its center.

[Then the Quillstone has chosen you. You are one of the sons of Gorrath. Orsani died for you. Now he is your brother, and mine.]

Footfalls could be heard at the end of the hall. Oreg snapped out of his fugue.

"What now?" Graf said.

"I came with the ship," Miranda said. "Oreg must have called it."

Oreg grabbed his Quillkeeth up from the floor. Limping and in pain, he led Miranda and Graf through the door to the landing bay. Once they were inside the bay, Oreg yanked the dead guard's body free of the door so it could close. Oreg then used his Quillkeeth to slice across the door's control box. Sparks flew and the door was disabled.

They hurried up the cargo ramp and into the ship. Inside, Miranda and Graf helped Oreg to his seat on the bridge, where he drew up the holo. He waved his hand in a sequence, and the bay doors opened. Another motion, and the ship's engines rumbled to life. Oreg turned his hand, and the ship turned. Then he thrust his hand forward, and the ship leapt away from the hangar.

Oreg shouted, [Hold on!]

The ship turned sharply. The tower was beside them now. Oreg banked the ship again and pointed it toward the portal.

"You lied to me, Oreg," Graf said. "I trusted you, and you lied to me." Graf's ears still felt as if they were stuffed with cotton.

Blinking red lights appeared on the holo. Hostile ships had locked on to their position. They were Skarvorm security patrols, starting to converge. Oreg initiated an impulse sequence and called for everyone to strap in. He and Graf pulled belt restraints over their shoulders and laps. Miranda held tightly to the back of Graf's chair. The impulse engines fired, and the ship launched toward the portal. Several plasma bursts sailed past them. As their ship sped toward the circle of lights, a section of the portal's circumference was lit up by some kind of blast.

A moment later, their ship was through, and they were bathed in the bright light of the Gorrathian sun.

Oreg changed the forward display to show the scene behind them. The ring lights of the portal flickered. At its dark center, the gate to Karmehki blinked in and out, flashing a last breath of connection to another part of space, until the giant ring went dark.

Oreg released his restraints and stood. He was leaning against his chair. He appeared confused. He winced in pain.

"You did this." Graf fought to extricate himself from the restraints. "You sabotaged the portal. That's what you were up to on Karmehki Tower, right?"

Oreg's gaze was fixed on the holo. He made adjustments. The ship turned, so that the Gorrathian star fell to the stern. A pool of blood was collecting at the base of Oreg's chair.

"You are hurt," Graf said. His hearing was still muffled. His own voice sounded strange and distant. "You need medical attention."

Oreg hobbled toward the back of the bridge. [There's no time. They will come for us.]

"Who will come for us?" Graf said. "The Skarvorm? Or this Zar-Zhast you were talking about? Orsani's friend seemed to think you might be Zar-Zhast. Is that true? Are you Zar-Zhast? Why did you leave me alone at the tavern? And in a Skarvorm officer's coat, for Christ's sake? I was stalked by an assassin and nearly killed. It's only thanks to Orsani that I'm here right now!"

Graf stripped himself of his coat and threw it across the floor. He followed Oreg, who limped to his cabin and began to sort through his things. He opened a small leather pack and filled it with clothing, toiletries, and other odds and ends.

[You were not alone. I told Orsani to keep an eye on you.]

"Then why the coat?" Graf said.

Oreg said, [They'd never have allowed me on Karmehki without a Skarvorm escort.]

"So, the Skarvorm are after you?" Graf said. "It makes perfect sense."

Oreg placed a few more items inside his bag, then pulled the cord to close it tight. He pushed past Graf and hobbled back to the bridge.

"Why destroy the portal?" Graf followed Oreg. "Tell me why."

Oreg went to his captain's chair and made a few motions with his hand. The holo lit up with a new perspective, a new angle on their location.

As he magnified the scene, Oreg said, [They will repair it. It won't take long. Many more battle cruisers were in line to move through the portal. Hundreds of thousands of droids and Skarvorm regulars are with them. A force large enough to bring a planet to submission.]

The enlarged visual showed an enormous fleet of warships floating in formation not far from their ship, staged in lines for mass deployment.

"My god…"

Oreg raised his chin and barked several times. Graf recognized this as an expression of either laughter or anger. Or both. Oreg heaved his pack over his shoulder and started toward the back of the ship, moving past Miranda, blood marking where his injured foot was dragged along the floor. Graf followed until Oreg came to a door amidship with a small window. The door rolled up. Inside was a pod with a reclining padded seat and restraints, but not much else. Small cubbies and blinking readouts lined the walls. Oreg handed Graf his pack and stepped inside. He hopped on his good foot, then sat on the seat and pulled the restraints over his body and secured them. There wasn't much space for Oreg's long legs.

Oreg motioned for Graf to toss over his bag.

"What are you doing?" Graf asked.

Oreg said, [It's me they are looking for. The ship is on course to set down on Gorrath. If you can get away from the Skarvorm, you might find help down there.]

Graf still clutched the necklace in his hand. He'd kept hold of it since they'd left the tower. He opened his hand and stared at the crystal. It was still glowing and warm.

[Wear it. Place it on your neck. Honor Orsani. When the crystal glows, it is trying to speak to you.]

Graf draped the necklace around his neck.

Oreg drew up a holo and activated a few buttons. A red light fell over Oreg's muzzle and face.

"Where are you going?"

[Be safe, my brother. But move quickly, or they will catch you. You don't want to be caught by the Skarvorm.]

"What about your ship?" Graf said.

[This is not my ship.]

"What about our last game of zawtek? You were leading."

The door rolled closed and sealed shut. An alarm bell sounded three loud rings. A light flashed red, followed by the sound of escaping air and a loud pop. The small rectangular window went dark.

Graf stood for a moment, terrified, but also feeling rejected. Abandoned. His heart sank as he returned to the bridge.

"Oreg's gone," he said to Miranda who was standing next to Oreg's chair. She'd drawn up a holo display and was examining it.

"You will miss your friend," she said. "But we are being pursued, and perhaps we should be concerned. Our ship might have been locked on by targeting sensors."

Graf sat in his chair. "Skarvorm."

"Our ship has been given a course to set down on the Gorrathian's planet. In seven minutes and thirty-four seconds, we will begin our descent."

Graf stared at the holo. "What are those?" He indicated the red dots rapidly crossing the display and moving toward the dot in the middle that represented their ship.

"Their speed and trajectory would indicate that they are missiles of some sort."

"What should we do?"

"Permission to override the ship's navigation programming, doctor? I am fairly sure I can fly the craft, and I'm fairly sure I can keep us from being hit."

"Be my guest!" Graf said.

"Please, apply your seat restraints, doctor." Miranda sat in Oreg's seat and tossed out her hand to reconfigure the holo display to a bright grid of flashing information. "You might find this uncomfortable."

9 – ESCOM HQ, Seattle

THE PHOBOS EMERGENCY medical unit was in full response status when Preston Wolfe was wheeled into the infirmary. Gurgling with ichor and bright yellow synthblood, meditubes entered and exited the security officer's body, while solutions dripped and dribbled from reservoirs suspended above his bed.

There'd been a question as to whether he'd pull through. The assassin's pike had perforated Wolfe's heart, lungs, and spinal cord, and he'd been given nearly four liters of synthblood before the medical unit lowered him into an icy amniobath, where microscopic nursebots produced protein stimulators, seeded cell grafts, and dressed his viscera with micro cross-stitching.

After his internals were sewn back together, he was removed from the liquid, coated in a layer of skinmesh, and kept unconscious for a week. Later he was revived and told what had happened to him. He learned then that Carerra had personally summoned him to give an account of the activities at the wormhole, to tell a conference of the companies what was going on. Wolfe agreed to return to Seattle right away, and he was wrapped in bandages, inserted into a coldsleep cylinder, and sent to Earth.

Before he was put into coldsleep, Wolfe learned that retracing of Lynx Eridania's trail went cold after her entry to the Martian skycrane station on Mars. Before that, there was no record of who she was. Once on Phobos, she'd outfoxed military-level screening with a fabricated background that never threw a red flag. All her biometric and DNA scans came up black. The autopsy showed no embedded VI, which wasn't unusual for a native Martian, but was unusual for anyone interested in working off-planet, where a VI was essential. Phobos went into lockdown after the assault on Wolfe. All contract workers were interrogated, but no one emerged as having any association with the fitness instructor.

Lynx Eridania had been off-grid. It was almost as if she never existed.

–

Two days after emerging from his coldsleep cylinder on Earth, Preston Wolfe felt strong enough for the short skimmer flight to ESCOM headquarters, where he was to meet with President Carerra.

After the skimmer landed at the HQ north landing bay, a hoverchair delivered Wolfe to the entrance of the wing where he'd been assigned a temporary office. At the entrance, Wolfe stood and dismissed the chair with profanity. With the help of a cane, he hobbled into the clean and circuitous headquarters, with its modern design and heady insistence on cleanliness and order. He asked passersby when he felt lost and required directions to his office.

At one point, in an alcove off a main pathway, Wolfe caught sight of a man's reflection in a large mirror that covered the entire expanse of one of the building's walls. In that mirror, Wolfe saw an older man, stooped and fatigued. The man's left arm hung limp at his side. His left leg, bandaged under loose slacks, swung awkwardly when he walked. The man's head was shaved, his eyes recessed and dark. His skin was dull, pale, lacking the luster of youth.

Wolfe tried to stand straight, to push his shoulders back, and to look formidable.

The man in the mirror disappointed him.

Wolfe raised his cane, to strike the disappointing image, when an employee walked past. Upon better judgment, Wolfe lowered his cane and carried on.

–

The door to Wolfe's office wing swung open. With his cane probing in front of him, Wolfe made his way down the hall. A pair of couches were set beside two small leafy trees. A young man was sitting there. In his late twenties or early thirties, he had short dark hair and was coarsely shaven but neatly dressed in a business suit with fashionable bright green tie. He stood when Wolfe came down the hall.

"Mr. Wolfe?"

Wolfe grunted and raised his chin.

"Ernesto Lopez-Larkin, sir." The young man extended his hand.

"And what purpose do you serve, Mr. Lopez-Larkin?" Wolfe rejected the offered hand.

"Since this is your first time at the new ESCOM HQ, it's my job to make you feel at home."

Wolfe said, "That's good, Mr. Larkin. I appreciate that."

"Your office is over here, sir." Lopez-Larkin guided Wolfe around the waiting area toward a series of doors. "If you need anything, sir, I'm here to facilitate."

"What's your story, Lopez?" Wolfe stuck out his cane for stability as he followed the young man.

Lopez-Larkin straightened his tie and cleared his throat. "Been at ESCOM for about four years. Stanford–Missoula MBA, and Pepperdine–Toronto as an undergrad."

"So ESCOM has its hooks in you?"

"Wouldn't want to be anywhere else, sir."

"You're either dumber than you look or far too smart for your own good."

Lopez-Larkin grinned.

"And you smell like a distillery."

Lopez-Larkin lowered his eyes. "Was out a little late last night, sir."

"Is this my office?" Wolfe swung his cane around and pointed at the corner door.

"It is, sir."

"My bag has been delivered. It is in the hallway. Get it, please."

"Yes, sir."

Wolfe hobbled past the young man and entered the bright office, pausing to take its measure. For a corner office overlooking the bay, the place was spartanly decorated with a tan couch and two soft chairs by a low coffee table. The desk was against a wall with windows. The not-too-elegant executive chair swiveled nicely so that, when seated, he could turn to take in the view.

At the window, Wolfe looked out over Elliott Bay. The Space Needle stood to the east. To the southeast, the white-tipped peak of Mt. Rainier emerged, poking through a layer of lower clouds. Down below, in the brackish water, a pod of orcas frolicked in the wake of a giant rust-colored cargo ship.

Seattle was where Wolfe had built his career, leading his consulting firm to its elite status. Then ESCOM had purchased his company and made it an arm of its solar system expansion. He'd married Esther here, after meeting her through Avery Graf. Esther gave birth to their daughter here. But that was long ago. A lifetime ago. He shook off those bittersweet thoughts. All things change.

Wolfe left the desk chair and lurched over to the couch so he could elevate his leg. He scanned his VI for any new packets. Lopez-Larkin returned with his bag, and Wolfe instructed him to place it near his desk.

"I'm to remind you that your meeting with President Carerra is at one o'clock," Lopez-Larkin said.

"I know." Wolfe leaned back on the couch with a wince.

"Are you in pain, sir? Can I get you anything?"

"No, thank you. But I do have a question for you."

"Yes, sir?"

"Why do I frighten you?"

"I don't know what you mean, sir."

"You've been shaking like a leaf since I arrived. It's making me uncomfortable."

Lopez-Larkin looked down, kicking at an imaginary spot on the carpet.

"Out with it!"

"You have a bit of a reputation, sir."

"I do?"

"Um...yes. People are a little afraid of you, is all."

"Ah ha! Then you are too," Wolfe said.

"People have this idea that you're hard on those beneath you. But everyone has their own management style, and yours, I'm guessing, is on the more autocratic end of the spectrum. Not that that's bad."

"Excuse me?"

"Sorry, sir. Yes?"

Halperin said, "If I'm to be feared, as you say, why did you volunteer to be my assistant? Why subject yourself to this tyranny?"

"Well, sir." Lopez-Larkin rubbed his hands together and stared into the distance. "I've been trying to understand ESCOM in respect to systems analysis. I'm experimenting with my own internal audit, from an operations standpoint if you will, on how the ESCOM hierarchical structure can adapt vis-à-vis evolving competitive exigencies. In other words—"

"Enough!" Wolfe said. "You're giving me a headache."

"Sorry, sir. I just—"

"No, no. Tell me the real reason why you're here."

Lopez-Larkin bit at the corner of his lip. "Now that you're back on Earth, there are rumors you might be next in line for the top job."

Wolfe raised an eyebrow and peered at his assistant. "They're saying I'm next in line, are they?"

Lopez-Larkin nodded. "When Carerra was Executive Officer of Foreign Affairs, you were his right-hand man, they say. As Liaison Officer, you helped him quell the mid-American worker revolt. You brokered a delicate agreement between ESCOM and Ex-Cap that loosened human rights regulations and allowed greater cross-company access to migrant and refugee labor. After you were assigned off-Earth, you planned and executed the military operation on the Martian rebel outpost at Syria Planum, halting a takeover of the ESCOM outpost at Valles Marineris. That operation killed over fifteen hundred rebels but prevented the loss of control of Mars. Also, you were the lead architect of the ESCOM Greenland purchase."

After hearing that breathless summary, Wolfe laughed. "Oh, how rich!"

"You are legend." Lopez-Larkin grew serious. He leaned in to ask his next question. "Is it true that you almost died on Phobos, sir? Is it true that Martian separatists have infiltrated ESCOM and that's how they got to you?"

Wolfe paused. He raised his hand to his neck and carefully pulled down the high collar of his sweater so that Lopez-Larkin could see the scar from the garrote that ran around his throat.

Lopez-Larkin looked a bit disappointed.

"Mr. Larkin," Wolfe said. "I'm going to need a lot of help over the next few days. I hope you're up to the task."

Lopez-Larkin stood, giving Wolfe a good-soldier look.

Wolfe said, "I'll need you to be one hundred percent present. No hangovers. If I smell booze on your breath, or if I think you're not at the top of your game, I'll toss you out on the street and you'll never work at ESCOM again. Am I clear?"

"Yes, sir."

"Now," Wolfe continued, "I need to shut my eyes and rest here for a while. Come get me at one o'clock."

"Your meeting with Carerra is at one, sir. Shouldn't I come earlier?"

"You're not listening. I said, come get me at one o'clock."

"Yes, sir."

When Lopez-Larkin was gone, Wolfe stood and returned to the window to look out over the bay. The orcas were still there, on full display for the tourists that walked the city's boardwalk. Real orcas, of course, had been extinct for nearly a century. This pod was installation art, a quaint effort to give people a feeling of what life was like before the first environmental collapse. Today, there wasn't much that could survive in the brackish waters.

Wolfe opened the message display on his VI to spell out a short note.

I'm in Seattle, Esther. Call me.

Then he cleared his VI and went back to the couch. He was stiff and nauseous and in pain. He felt as if parts of his body were still frozen, the numbness of coldsleep lingering in unexpected places, but everyone knows it takes time to fully emerge from coldsleep. He accessed his VI to dial up the dosage on his pain administrator, the small patch attached to the skin on his back, above his left kidney. Then he closed his eyes and breathed deeply.

—

After Preston Wolfe and Lopez-Larkin had waited five minutes outside Carerra's office, an assistant entered the waiting area and introduced herself as Whitney. She was tall and thin, almost Martian in appearance, and that was immediately attractive to Wolfe. She had silver-green hair that fell evenly to her shoulders. Her face was wide, cheekbones high, and when she smiled, she revealed a set of gapped and predatory teeth. She was poised and exceedingly polite. Whitney asked Wolfe to follow her to the president's office. She ignored Lopez-Larkin.

"Ernesto," Wolfe said as he started to follow Whitney.

"Yes, sir?"

"Make yourself scarce, okay? I don't know how long this will take."

Lopez-Larkin nodded and, as if envious, watched as Wolfe and Whitney made their way down the hallway that led to the president's office.

Whitney's green hair swung and brushed her broad shoulders as she led the way. The hall was decorated with patina-colored photographs of old Seattle: The Space Needle; the Gates HyperDome; the Amazon Tower. All symbols of Seattle's golden age, and all, save the Space Needle, since fallen due to earthquakes, terrorism, and neglect.

As they approached a set of tall double doors, Whitney said, "Everyone here at ESCOM HQ has been concerned for your wellbeing, sir. It's good to see that you are on your way to recovery."

She drew open the doors and motioned for Wolfe to enter. Wolfe gave a short bow, thanked her, and stepped inside the room. He placed his cane against the inside doorframe, straightened himself and tried to walk normally, though his leg felt as if it might rebel.

Carerra's office was elegant, with enormous Berber and Persian rugs stretched over a marble floor. To the right, a flame danced playfully upon the grate of a fireplace of river stone and blasted steel. To the left, a long conference table held a bouquet of fresh flowers, a crystal carafe of water, and clear glasses on a shining salver. A large, dark Renaissance canvas hung on the wall beyond the conference table. Dutch or Italian; most likely Italian, Wolfe guessed. Beyond Carerra's imposing desk was a floor-to-ceiling window overlooking the Olympic Mountains, the distant peaks cutting sharp as a set of teeth against the milky afternoon sky.

Aldo Constantine Carerra, silver-haired and fit, wore a fashionable brown leather sherwani jacket. He ambled in front of his granite desk as he discussed strategy or logistics with some distant interlocutor. This discourse could have been any of the multitude of topics that a president of a transnational dealt with daily.

Carerra, the ESCOM president, acknowledged Wolfe with a raised finger. He took a moment to conclude his conversation. Then, arms outstretched, he approached Wolfe with a warm and paternal smile. "My dear Preston! We are glad that you have arrived."

Wolfe gave a short bow and took Carerra's hands. The two stood and admired one another.

"It's good to see you, sir," Wolfe said. "Over five years now, which is a long time. But feeling Earth beneath my feet, real Earth, has begun to accelerate my recovery." Wolfe was surprised at how young Carerra looked. He'd imagined a more feeble person, someone whom the years had punished. Such wasn't the case. Wolfe had sacrificed years off-Earth to do ESCOM's dirty work, funneling propaganda to Mars and asteroid miners, quashing Martian rebel uprisings, managing the complex needs of Asimios Station. It was Wolfe who paid the price, after all. And here Carerra was, safe and sound, taking advantage of all the life-extension sciences, enjoying his reign as leader of the largest and most profitable company in Earth's history. "It's so very good to see you, Aldo," Wolfe said.

"I was sorry hear of your attack," Carerra said, his eyebrows arched with concern. "Such awful news. How terrifying it must have been to be assaulted in your own quarters. I want you to know that we've put all our resources into this. We're doing all we can on our end."

"It was a wakeup call," Wolfe said. "I take full responsibility."

"I want to hear it directly from you. Is Phobos secure?" Carerra said. "Could Mars have penetrated further into our security systems than we know?"

"Unlikely, sir," Wolfe said. "We've gone over everything, and there's no evidence of any breach."

"Leach is still on Phobos. Any reason to worry that he might be compromised?"

Wolfe smiled at the idea. "Elvin Leach is no threat. I guarantee it. We keep a very close eye on him."

"I trust that you're handling it," Carerra said. "Mars is a cesspit of resentment, violence, and desperation. All the more reason to keep it under the microscope."

"I agree."

"Your service on Phobos was exemplary, Preston. And the way you handled the withdrawal from Asimios was commendable. I want to make that clear."

"Thank you, sir."

"Now, please, come sit. We have much to discuss. I need to know everything you know about this alien incursion before we make our case in front of the council."

Carerra led Wolfe to a pair of high-backed chairs near the fireplace. They sat and faced one another across a small table. A servant emerged from a concealed door beside the large painting, picked up the tray that sat on the table, brought the pitcher and glasses to them, and then poured them each a glass of water. Carerra requested hot tea; Wolfe, a black coffee.

Carerra leaned back in his chair. He pinned Wolfe with his icy blue eyes. "In your honest opinion," he said, "what do you think these aliens might be up to? They haven't displayed overt hostility, have they? But it's of grave concern that they haven't made any attempt to contact us."

"We cannot presume to understand what their intentions are, sir. We must, at least, prepare for confrontation. We'd be foolish to do otherwise."

The servant came back to serve the coffee and tea.

"Of course," Carerra said after the servant had left. "To assume they aren't hostile would be folly. But could it be that they have other intentions? Perhaps mutually beneficial trade?" Carerra took up his tea. "Can you imagine the advantage we'd have, being the first to establish a trade agreement? Think of the new tech, the goods and services, the medicines an alien species might have to offer. I'd like to keep an open mind on this."

"Forgive me, sir," Wolfe said, "but I see this alien incursion as a serious, existential threat, not just to ESCOM, but to the human species. There's no getting this wrong, you see. I hold ESCOM's interests at heart, you know, that. Yet I hold that collaboration with the other companies is our best approach to this situation. We can't handle this on our own."

"I agree, Preston. It's just that when I smell profit, my antennae go up." Carerra lowered his cup of tea to his lap. "I appreciate your loyalty to ESCOM. Your stint off-Earth might have been hard, but you must have known that as long as Ibsen Voss was Executive of Defense, my hands were tied. After his death this year, I found myself hoping I could reel you back into the inner circle. Tomorrow's conference offers the perfect opportunity."

"It's Voss who sent me off-Earth."

"You must have done something to incur his wrath."

"I told him the truth," Wolfe said. "I told him he was a disastrous diplomat and a buffoon."

"And you slept with his partner, his wife," Carerra said. "You crossed the line."

"Without regret."

Carerra said, "That brings me to my next topic."

"Sir—"

"Since Voss's death and the appointment of Eric Vanner to Defense Exec, I've had a change of heart. Vanner, it turns out, is softer on Axiom Lotus than I was hoping. And he's cozying up to the Nexus more than ESCOM should, in my opinion. I need someone with more influence to handle ESCOM's growing security concerns.

"What will you do?" Wolfe asked.

"I've decided to create an additional cabinet position, ESCOM Chief of Security. The position is yours if you want it. You'd oversee an intelligence apparatus that consolidates the security divisions of every branch of ESCOM. That means Foreign Affairs, Defense, et cetera, plus all off-Earth offices."

"Good lord," Wolfe murmured.

"You'd be responsible for coordinating all ESCOM information and security operations, both nationally and among our transnational counterparts. Of course, every step, every thought, every iota of relevant information would be shared with me first."

"I'm flattered, sir," Wolfe said. "I accept."

"It's a big responsibility." Carerra manipulated his VI with a wave of his hand. He typed and sent a message. "There's no ceremony behind this appointment, no confirmation hearing. A small press briefing that I've just sent will announce your appointment the following day. From now on, you will see an immediate increase in international and off-Earth recognition. But I want you to remain close to me. I don't want you drifting."

Wolfe stood. He set down his coffee, straightened his shirt, and extended his hand. Carerra set his tea on the table, stood, and accepted it.

"Welcome on board," Carerra said. "The promotion will give you credibility at the conference tomorrow. We need another rising star around here, with the intelligence and backbone to shake things up."

"Thank you, sir," Wolfe said. "But what about Phobos?"

"What about Phobos? Welcome back to ESCOM."

Wolfe was silent. The old scar above his lip twitched.

"Now, there are a couple of things you need to know before the conference tomorrow." Carerra went over and stood by the fireplace. "We've been holding this close to our vest, but ESCOM has been in talks with Excelsior Capital regarding a potential merger. It will be a 'merger' in outward appearance, but ESCOM will be the controlling partner. We'll be cutting the check, after all. The process is in its final stages. All we are waiting for is a quiet rewriting of international law before we deliver our prospectus to the board of transnationals."

"It's been a long time coming," Wolfe said.

Carerra said, "ESCOM and Excelsior Cap have been long-standing allies. A merger, plus a trimming of the fat, will benefit both parties. It'd consolidate a third of Earth's goods and services market, plus an eighty percent share of the constantly growing Nexus. With our share of off-Earth trade, we'll be the dominant transnational for centuries to come."

"You're delivering this news tomorrow?"

"No," Carerra said. "Still too many details to review and legalities to dissect. Markets will reel, of course, once the word gets out. Governments will protest, and the nationalists will raise objection. The NLA will storm the capitals and raise a fuss. No, we have enough on our plate tomorrow."

"And the second thing you wanted to mention, sir?"

"The second bit of news concerns Axiom Lotus. Apparently, they plan to make their own announcement at the meeting."

"What will that be?"

"Our sources indicate that a leadership change has recently taken place in the company. From what we can discern, an AI has been elected to run it. That's a first for a major company, let alone a transnational."

Wolfe cleared his throat, not having an immediate response about the idea of an AI leader.

"There are a lot of skeptics out there, and I'm one of them," Carerra said. "I've always felt that AIs have no place in the running of human organizations. It feels perverse."

"I'd have to agree, sir."

Carerra continued. "There will be other items that arise, but these are primary. Please hold them in strict confidence."

As Wolfe lowered his head, the office doors opened, and three figures filled the rectangle of light.

"My friends, please come in." Carerra spoke in his commanding tone as he approached the visitors, three majors and their aides. "Please welcome Mr. Wolfe to ESCOM HQ. He can use cheering up."

Five figures moved toward Carerra. Preston limped over to greet them. The three majors were acquainted with Wolfe, either from working with him or speaking during conference streams.

"Preston," Carerra said, "this is Rupert Rupali, Isabel Miller, and Eric Vanner."

"It's a pleasure to see you all again," Wolfe said.

Rupert Rupali reached out to shake Wolfe's hand. He was tall and slightly stooped at the shoulders. He had a long nose, a recessed round chin, and a wide smile that turned up at the corners, which gave him a comical look, as if he was ready to burst out laughing. In a flash, though, his eyebrows could straighten and his expression turn serious, as if he were investigating a murder. If there was one person Wolfe admired, it was Rupali. He was hard-core business and trustworthy. The guy gave everything he could to his work, and Wolfe never felt him to be a threat. Yet there was something about him, something terrifying. A moral compass is what it might be. Sometimes there's a plain speaker, someone who tells it like it is, whom everyone stops to listen to. That was Rupert Rupali.

"We've met, of course," Rupali said, his eyebrows leveling. "During the North American Nexus Trade Agreement. You were still under Voss at the time—a tragic loss, by the way—and negotiating on the part of the Defense Department to make sure Nexus integration with ESCOM maintained security equilibrium."

"I do remember that," Wolfe said. "You were thorough and tireless. You expertly balanced the need for AIs to feel recognized, while keeping an eye on margins. It was a win, as we all remember."

Rupali smiled. "I'd like to be as optimistic now as I was then about our Nexus profits. There has been so much change, so quickly. But we'll have plenty of time to discuss it."

Wolfe nodded and moved to Eric Vanner. "I know you, of course, Eric. Conference streams between Earth and Phobos are grueling, but you've hung in there. I believe we've accomplished a lot."

Vanner was younger than his vid streams indicated, in his mid-forties, give or take a decade, depending on life-extension therapy. He was fair-haired and confident, with a glow to his hale, angular face, and he stood erect and alert. It was a good guess he'd run twenty kilometers before his morning cup coffee. If he were to leave, another just like him would be there to take his place.

"I appreciate the kind words," Vanner said. "I haven't been at the post long, but I count on you to tell it like it is, Preston. In our world, that's more than one can hope for."

"You worked under Ibsen?" Wolfe said, knowing the answer.

"Yes," Vanner said. "He was a class act. One of the best."

"Yes, he was," Wolfe said, his smile hiding his disagreement. "Yes, he was."

Next up was Isabel Miller. She shot out her arm, not just her hand, and threw a slanted smile showing familiarity and apprehension. "I am so glad to see you again, Preston. Welcome home."

"It's been a long time," Wolfe said.

Miller's signature feature was her hair: expansive, swept back, and gray, contrary to the ESCOM norm, which was to be trimmed, neat, and under control. She laughed loudly and often, which inspired dread in most of her staff, most of whom were strangers to emotion and its expression. Isabel Miller was stocky, but not fat. Strong shoulders revealed the core strength in her physique, as if she could lay you flat if she felt it necessary. She could shower you with smiles from her richly freckled face, but when she was serious, her eyes were daggers. She seemed effortlessly intelligent, able to turn your words on you, until you felt tongue-tied and stupid. Most terrifying was her ambition. Although she never betrayed her intensions, many thought she intended to become the next face of ESCOM.

"Isabel," Carerra said, "as Senior Vice President of Operations, is structurally second in line for my job." Carerra winked in Isabel's direction. "I expect you both to work together, to make sure the global and off-Earth ESCOM wheel continues to turn."

"As I'm sure we will," Miller said.

Wolfe nodded. He disliked and distrusted Miller more than anyone at ESCOM, and the reason for that was that she might be the only one to stand in his way to run the company. Not that his ambitions were to run the company. It was just that he couldn't avoid these thoughts about who might be next in line.

Miller had worked under Ibsen Voss for many years as a deputy advisor. She knew firsthand how much Voss and Wolfe had fought. Standing with her now, Wolfe wondered if there was any residual animus.

"I've always wanted to visit Phobos," Miller said. "They say the views are stunning. But nothing compares to a real, Martian sunset. Is that true?"

"Yes," Wolfe said. "A Martian sunset, by consensus, is a beauty to behold."

"As I hinted earlier this week," Carerra said, "because of Preston's history of loyal service to ESCOM, I'm appointing him as our new Chief of Security. It's a cabinet position, with the highest clearance. Please welcome him as a new member to our circle."

Rupali, Vanner, and Miller all extended congratulations.

"Now, Preston," Carerra said. "I insist that you rest. Tomorrow looms large. Your accommodations have been arranged and your assistant instructed to provide whatever you might need. Good day, Preston. Welcome, and thank you."

Wolfe bowed modestly, then shuffled toward the door, where he paused to retrieve his cane. For the sake of his audience, he exaggerated his limp. A slight smirk crossed his lip. His scar demanded attention.

—

The game was afoot!

Wolfe had so much to think about when he hobbled out of the president's wing in search of his office.

He began to map the obstacles to the ESCOM throne, each of whom was a mere mortal, which assured him that the prize was achievable. Lopez-Larkin had reported the rumor, that Wolfe was "next in line." After the meeting he'd just left, Wolfe felt that he clearly stood in the president's favor.

Then again, it might be presumptuous to assume that Carerra played favorites. Would it be reckless to presume that the president held one in particular as his chosen heir? However, consider the promotion and Carrera's effusive praise!

Whitney had left her desk, and Ernesto was nowhere to be seen. The new Chief of Security wandered the halls on his own, and soon he was lost. He checked time on his VI and he wondered how long it had been since he'd left the president's office. Ten minutes? An hour?

He saw that Esther had messaged, but he hailed Lopez-Larkin first.

"Yes, sir? What can I help you with?" Lopez-Larkin's face filled his VI.

"Ernesto, goddammit! Come and get me."

"Right away, sir."

"And, Ernesto?"

"Yes, sir?"

"Where the hell am I?"

—

When Esther answered Wolfe's message, she asked if they could meet, suggesting a restaurant on Mercer Island. He accepted the invitation, knowing that their daughter Nava would be the topic of conversation. Her tangles with the authorities were becoming inconvenient, especially considering his new position at ESCOM. Perhaps Esther might be able to do something to rectify the situation.

The limousine taking him to that dinner date glided over the bridge to Mercer Island amid a downpour. The lights and sensations of a real Earth city—its colors, sounds, and smells—stirred old feelings of ambition and desire in Preston Wolfe.

It had been forty years since he first moved to Seattle, since founding his small security firm while wondering what the universe had in store for him. From the start, he'd burned the midnight oil, grew his company, expanded its influence, and gained respect. In a social scene composed of smart and ambitious people, Wolfe forged friendships with Esther and Avery Graf. They hiked, kayaked, and explored the mountainous northwest together. They shared strategies and schemes to advance their careers, plotting to break through the imperiously tall ESCOM walls. Ten years after Wolfe founded his firm, ESCOM grew tired of paying through the roof for services and decided to buy Wolfe out. His only condition: that he be allowed to run the new division. Wolfe married Esther, then Nava came soon after. His world changed.

Now he was returning to his place of origin, fifteen years divorced from Esther, and he still he wanted more from life. Nothing had changed.

The restaurant was bright and cheery, a small bistro overlooking Lake Washington at the island's north end. Soft classical music played in the background. A string quartet. Brahms. The fifteen tables were occupied with people in a generally good mood. Wolfe recognized Esther when he stepped through the door.

She was thinner than he remembered. She wore a pleated jacket over a dark top, and her graying hair was pushed into a subdued version of the popular double-horn style that the youth were currently wearing. Her features were older, but still delicate. Her nose was small, her cheeks healthy. There was something old fashioned about her, but it could just be her classic face. When her eyes found his, she stood.

"Esther." Wolfe limped to her table, his cane holding him stable. "It's been a long time."

"You're an hour late." Esther dropped back down into her seat. "Some things never change."

"I'm less than forty minutes late, but yes, things have changed." Wolfe sat down, propped his cane between his legs, and wrapped his fingers around the cane's handle.

"My god," Esther said. "What in the world happened to you? You don't look at all well."

"It's nothing," Wolfe said. "I was in an altercation. I had a tangle with a disgruntled employee on Phobos. She was terminated." Distracted, Wolfe looked out the window at the limo that had brought him there. His driver leaned against a lamppost, watching them through the window. Wolfe wondered if Esther would notice that he had a bodyguard.

"We're not here to discuss your sordid affairs," Esther said.

Wolfe shot her a sharp look. "If you've brought me here to pick a fight, I'll leave."

"Excuse me." She lowered her head and wiped her sleeve across her eyes. "I apologize."

"Maybe this wasn't the best idea."

"I'll be civil, Preston. It's just hard seeing you again. I guess I'm a little afraid of how old we've grown. Please."

The waiter came. Esther suggested that they order drinks and food, so they did. Outside it rained again in sheets. Wolfe's bodyguard abandoned his lamppost and retreated to the shelter of the limo.

"Have you heard anything new about Nava?" Wolfe said. "I haven't had a spare minute since coming out of coldsleep to look into things."

"Not a word," Esther said. "I wish she'd contact me. She's never been good at that though. She's always focused on other things. I just wish I could hear her voice, to know that she's alright."

"I looked over her file when I was on Phobos." Wolfe waited while the waiter placed glasses and wine on their table. "Interpol thinks she's one of the leaders of a protest rally in Hamburg. Two policemen were killed there."

"Are they sure Nava was part of it?"

"It appears so." Wolfe lifted his glass of wine for his first taste. "There's evidence, though it's circumstantial."

"What should we do? I don't know how to approach this."

"I'm not sure. She's guilty by association, unfortunately. She'll likely be rounded up with the rest of them and sent for reprogramming, or worse. Once she's caught, it will be up to the prosecuting judge to determine punishment."

The waiter served their food, setting two plates in front of them. They took a moment to taste their food and sipped their wine. The rain had lightened. The music danced lightly along with a break in the clouds. Baroque now. Possibly Albinoni. A few customers came and went.

"I've been promoted," Wolfe said in a gap in conversation. "Though it's not announced until tomorrow."

Esther raised her eyebrows.

"I'm officially ESCOM's Chief of Security, a fairly serious position. It's a cabinet post, so I'll be working closely with President Carerra."

"Carerra himself? My word. That explains the ape you have keeping an eye on you." Esther nodded in the direction of the bodyguard, who, once again, leaned against the lamppost.

"I'm on Earth for the duration, I think. No more Phobos."

"That must be a relief."

"I'll miss Phobos and Mars."

"You can always go back."

"That is true, but there are things here that need to be addressed. I can't tell you too much, but you'll probably hear about them over time."

"Is it related to ESCOM or Asimios?"

"I can't say."

"Of course not. You never could."

They were quiet.

"Can you help Nava?" Esther said. "Is there nothing you can do?"

"I'll see. It might help to get her out of Germany, but there are a lot of hoops to jump through. We'd have to find her first."

Esther's brow furrowed. "Help her, Preston. I have neither the money nor the connections."

Preston nodded. Esther, a mother, wanted to see her daughter healthy and safe. He understood that. But Nava had crossed into a new world after getting involved with the NLA. Finding her might be possible, but getting Nava out of her hole might not be in the cards, even for the new Chief of Security at ESCOM.

"I've been meaning to ask," Esther said after a moment. "Have you seen Avery? Is he on Phobos after the pullout? Or maybe Mars? I haven't heard anything, and I'm concerned for my old friend."

Wolfe set his fork on his plate, fixing her with his gaze. "Esther, Avery didn't make it off Asimios. He didn't come back with the team."

Esther shook her head. "He didn't come back with the team?"

"I'm sorry you haven't been told, but Avery took his own life."

"I don't understand." Esther's face turned white. She put down fork and folded her hands on her lap. "What do you mean? Took his own life?"

"On the day of extraction, Avery secretly remained on the planet with the help of crewmembers who made it look like he was on the ship. By the time we discovered we'd been tricked, it was too late to go back for him. Detonation charges had been set to destroy the station. There is no way he could have survived."

Esther hooded her eyes with one hand.

"He was depressed, Esther," Wolfe said. "He was unhealthy. I've never seen him in such bad shape. He intended to do what he did. It was his choice."

When Esther looked up, her eyes were filled with tears. "How sad."

"I'm sorry, Esther. You were old friends, I know. Perhaps he's better off where he is now. Maybe now he's found peace."

Esther used her napkin to dry the tears that left wet paths on her cheeks. "I didn't expect to hear this. After all the dangers you two have endured, it felt like you two were immune from death. Then a wind strikes from out of nowhere. I thought I was too old to be affected by this sort of news."

"I'm sorry."

"Oh, fuck it. Fuck it."

—

On the drive back to Seattle, after the car was off the island and on the bridge, Wolfe waved his hand to bring up Lopez-Larkin on his VI.

"Yes, sir. How can I help you?"

"I just spent the evening with my ex-wife, Ernesto."

"That's good, sir. Isn't it? I mean, I'm glad to hear that."

"I need a drink, Ernesto."

"You deserve it, sir."

"I was hoping for good company," Wolfe said. "But I guess you'll have to do."

"Right, sir."

"Meet me downtown. I have a place in mind, an old haunt. I'll send my location."

"I'll wait to hear, sir."

After giving the driver directions, Wolfe gazed out of the window as the limo wound through the city and into Belltown, just north of downtown. Wolfe identified the old tavern, The Virginian. After parking, his bodyguard escorted the hobbling security chief inside. Lopez-Larkin immediately joined Wolfe, slightly winded but eager to please.

"I once spent a lot of time in this place, Ernesto." Wolfe leaned against the bar. "Been a lot of celebrations here. A lot of good times."

"It's nice, sir." Lopez-Larkin looked the place over. "Has a nostalgic feel. A bit of history here."

Wolfe's bodyguard sat next to Wolfe, waved down the bartender, and ordered a Coke. Wolfe ordered two shots of bourbon. When the drinks came, Lopez-Larkin was about to pick up his shot glass when Wolfe intercepted his hand.

"Oh, no you don't," Wolfe said.

"What?"

"These shots are for me. Remember our promise?"

Lopez-Larkin looked confused.

"No booze while working for me," Wolfe said. "Got it?"

Lopez-Larkin nodded. "Sorry, sir."

Wolfe emptied one shot glasses, grimacing at the heat of the liquor. He pushed the other shot back at Lopez-Larkin.

"I was just kidding, Ernesto," Wolfe said. "Down the hatch!"

Lopez-Larkin took the drink, a faint smile breaking over the corner of his mouth. After the second round, Lopez-Larkin screwed up the courage to ask Wolfe about his visit with President Carerra.

Wolfe, feeling slightly adrift after two drinks, pulled his young assistant close. "I'll be damned if my little oracle didn't foresee the future."

"What do you mean, sir?"

"You were right." Wolfe blinked the fuzziness from his eyes. No doubt a lingering effect from coldsleep.

"Sir, please tell me."

"I've been promoted to a cabinet position, Ernesto," Wolfe said. "I am now ESCOM Chief of Security."

Lopez-Larkin came alive. "Congratulations, sir!"

"This may be the last night I enjoy any degree of anonymity," Wolfe said. "Tomorrow, everything changes."

"Then why not enjoy another round, just to celebrate?" Lopez-Larkin proposed.

"Good idea. But that's it. One more, and we're done."

Wolfe ordered another round of whiskies and a pair of beer chasers. The two men leaned on the bar, listening to the music and the voices echoing off the high ceilings. Wolfe's bodyguard, still as a statue, sipped his Coke, scanning the crowd from behind a pair of defense-enhanced glasses. He was getting terrified looks from others in the bar.

"Sir, if I may," Lopez-Larkin said after a minute of quiet.

"What, Ernesto?"

"I've been wondering recently about ESCOM's position on Mars."

"What were you wondering about?" Wolfe said.

"It's just that..." Ernesto paused. "I know we have about a sixty-two-point-seven percent share of information networks on Mars, all non-Nexus, and that our long-term outlook for supply management is high growth."

Wolfe frowned.

"I was just wondering, sir, though I know this is a slightly awkward moment to bring this up. In relation to Fitzsimmon's theories of off-Earth market valuations, and considering Lubeck's post-colonial collapse paradigm, what if ESCOM tries exploiting the Rogers model of expanding returns and sinks investments in distribution chains of Martian or asteroidal polymetalics?"

At this, Wolfe's frown morphed into a full growl. He swung his cane hard against the surface of the bar. *Thwak!*

"Enough," Wolfe said. "Enough!"

10 – Revolutionaries

MICHAEL FELT HIMSELF nearing a breaking point. He, Nava, and baby Lyv had been staying at Luzi Kurtz's small Berlin apartment for nearly three weeks, waiting for news on where and when Atlas Kolek would call the NLA meeting. They rarely ventured out for fear of being discovered, and with their new baby crying at all hours of the day, they were tired and their nerves were raw. When Pravir Malkus and Helena Sicher joined them three days ago, Pravir brought with him his restlessness, arrogance, and anger. Michael didn't know how long it would be before there was a confrontation.

A flyboy drone had just landed outside the front door of the apartment and deposited a package. Tante Luzi, as they called her, opened the door, retrieved the package, and brought it inside.

After she closed the door, Tante Luzi called, "*Alles klar!*"

Michael, Nava, Pravir and Helena came out from where they'd been hiding. Tante Luzi handed Michael the package, and they gathered around the table in the middle of the room.

Michael examined the box. He took a knife someone handed him from the kitchen and cut the paper package open. Inside was a bottle of pills, an order receipt, and packaging peanuts. He opened the bottle, removed the cotton ball, and poured the contents over the table. Along with a cascade of white capsules came a tightly folded piece of paper. He separated the paper from the pills, unfolded it, and handed it to Nava, who spread it out on the table.

"What does it say?" Michael said. He leaned back in his chair.

Pravir and Helena peered over Nava's shoulder at the handwritten note. Pravir was tall and sinuous, with a shock of short black hair and one probing dark eye, the other hidden behind a black felt eyepatch. His face was dark and pocked, perhaps from a childhood skin affliction. He had high cheekbones and thin lips, plus a long, attractive nose that he proudly inserted when he was trying to make a point. He wore a solid blue track jacket and dark denim pants. His white sneakers were new—bright and right out of the box.

In a back room, the baby cried.

"Here, you read it." Nava handed the letter back to Michael and went to fetch the crying baby. "Is there any mention of James or Anya? I wish I knew what's happened to them."

Helena pushed in beside Pravir and took Nava's place at the table. She was short and built like a refrigerator, with a head full of curly blond hair that sprung out in all directions. Her blue eyes were like two sapphires embedded in a bowl of freshly skinned potatoes.

"I'm sorry, Nava," Michael called out so Nava could hear. "According to Gunter, both James Vinu and Anya Berdinka have been detained."

No one was happy to hear this.

"Hundreds have been arrested in the latest sweep," Michael went on. "Gunter says there are reports of injuries. And there have been deaths."

"They gave their lives for others," Pravir said, fists clenched. "They did what they had to do."

"Please, Pravir," Helena said.

"What else does Gunter say?" Helena asked.

Michael turned the page and read on.

> Protests were held this week in Paris, London, Beijing, and New York. Hundreds of thousands attended, many arrested. Here, in Berlin, the authorities have raised the designation of the NLA to "terrorist organization" and have vowed to eradicate the "blight."

> Confirmed the companies are holding a meeting in Seattle. What they will discuss is unclear, but widely believed they are colluding in order to strengthen their grip on global markets and finance at the expense of human rights.

Michael put in: "Kolek's sending a courier to tell us where the NLA meeting will be held. It will be important. We have big decisions to make. The future of the NLA depends on it."

"Power to brother Gunter." Nava came back to the table with Baby Lyv wrapped neatly in a soft blanket and cradled at her breast, the pink-faced mite hungry at her mother's nipple.

"Get ready for anything," Pravir said. "It won't be long before we're sniffed out by the police, and I don't want to go out without a fight."

"No," Michael said. He collected the pills that had fallen out of Tante Luzi's bottle and returned them to the bottle. "You know," Michael went on, "that if we arm ourselves, we lower ourselves to the level of the oppressors. That's what they want. The moment we threaten them with physical harm, it justifies the use of violence against us."

"But does this philosophy hold up any more?" Pravir said. "Everything we've done has brought only pain. We're outmatched. We're losing the propaganda war. Without tech, we're a sideshow. We must raise our fists and resist. We're running out of time."

"Your talk is garbage," Michael said. "You've lost sight of our core belief, the belief in non-violence."

"I haven't lost sight of anything," Pravir said. "In fact, I see it clearer now more than ever. For years, I've been a loyal servant of the NLA, an obedient little soldier of peace. But for what? This pacifist ethos has won us nothing. Our protests are crushed. Our members imprisoned by the thousands. The movement is nearly dead. We're being infiltrated, sabotaged, and suffocated, and it won't be long before there's nothing but a faint cry of philosophical purity. Something must be done now."

Michael approached Pravir, angry. "You shit, Pravir. I've been watching you drift over the past six months. You're slipping. If you want to draw blood, you are welcome to it, but don't drag the movement down with you."

"Go ahead, Michael," Pravir said. "Take a swing. It's nice to see you show passion."

"Enough!" Nava said. "There's no time for this. We need to get our plans in order, and I can't bear to hear you two go at it."

The baby was crying now. Helena took the small thing from Nava's arms and, humming softly, she turned away from the dispute.

"We must stay focused," Nava said. "When we hear where the meeting is to be held, then we draw up our next move. Until then, we wait."

Tante Luzi called from the kitchen: "*Essenszeit!* We eat now!"

Nava laid the baby in the crib at the corner of the room and went over to the table to help Tante Luzi, who set down three loaves of bread and a large, steaming pot of stew. She ladled stew into bowls to distribute around the table. Like wolves, they tore at the bread and drew down the thick stew. Not a word was spoken. All that was heard was the creaking of chairs and the striking of steel spoons against bowls.

Δ

PRAVIR HAD DECIDED that he would leave the second he learned where Kolek's meeting was going to be held. Three days felt like an eternity in this shithole. He needed to feel himself moving. He needed action. After eating his stew while listening to the others as they grazed like cattle over their feed, Pravir caught Tante Luzi's gaze. Tante Luzi cleared her throat and, in that annoyingly shy way she had, she cupped her hand over her eyes and peeked out between her fingers to look at him.

"Herr Pravir," she said. "I must ask before you leave and I never see you again. Tell me why you have that black patch over your eye."

Pravir smiled. He'd been waiting since he'd arrived for her to ask that question, and, as always, he considered it his duty to provide those curious with an explanation. Pravir took one final spoonful of stew in his mouth, then washed it down with a drink of water. He said, "*Meine Dame*, I will tell you, because you've been generous toward us, putting yourself at great risk to aid us." Pravir licked his lips and lowered his chin, then began his story.

"Not so long ago, I was a professor, with a good job and many colleagues whom I considered friends. I had a nice apartment and lived comfortably by most standards. I'd earned tenure at the university in Utrecht and was enjoying the prospects of a long and productive career. Then about five years ago, just before boarding my skimmer flight to the U.S., I was pulled aside and detained by security agents. I was scheduled to deliver a paper at an international conference in Boston, and this detention prevented me from arriving at the conference on time. After detaining me, they disabled my VI, so I could neither send nor receive any messages. Finally, after hours of waiting, a new cadre of agents in different uniforms came to question me."

Pravir looked around the table. The others ate and listened in silence.

"They asked about my background, my acquaintances, and my studies. They asked about my political inclinations and the nature of the paper I was going to deliver. I told them everything. I had nothing to hide. I had no ulterior intentions. Even though I'd been an advocate for a change in the current political system, my lecture concerned only a basic historical survey of Leachian quantum magnetism." Pravir cleared his throat. "I told them that I couldn't imagine why this would be of interest to them. Then they left. An hour or so later, a fresh team of interrogators came to ask me the same questions. Only this team wasn't as polite as the previous."

Pravir paused to take another sip of milk. He proceeded with his story, knowing his cadence proved his words. He told how the questioning turned to his academic connections and his family, particularly his uncle who was an Indian psychologist for Axiom Lotus.

"The inquisition became ugly," Pravir said. "After many hours, I still didn't know what they wanted. Finally, I was released. I'd missed my flight, and I'd missed the conference. I was enraged, and I felt a great sense of betrayal. I was an EU citizen, with all the protections which citizenship should have given me. Yet I'd been treated like a dog. I said to myself: I will not rest till I have found justice for this violation."

Pravir scanned the table. No one returned his gaze apart from Tante Luzi, who peered at him from under her long, thin brows. Pravir picked at his teeth with a fingernail and cleared his throat. He'd left certain things out of his story, however, certain things he'd prefer to forget. Like how they'd inserted the experimental Lucifer Worm into his mind through his VI: a small thread of quantum AI. That AI thread did as instructed, taking its host and subjecting it to horrors. Not a day went by that Pravir wasn't tortured by that darkness; not a day when Pravir didn't anticipate— even covet—the conclusion of his existence.

"There was no recourse," Pravir continued. "I consulted lawyers and human rights organizations. No one would hear my case. There was no solid evidence of mistreatment, it was said. It was my word against theirs, and the authorities would win.

"After my detention, I started to notice things. I had trouble obtaining tickets for international skimmer flights. I'd get the runaround, or I was told that a flight was booked, when I knew it wasn't. One night I found that my home had been broken into: drawers opened, closets gone through, papers disturbed. I later found several shadow-web threads on the Nexus where others described similar experiences. I could tell I was being followed, whether on foot or by train or by car. At times, I could tell by an abnormality in my VI that my movements were being traced. The only way to fix this problem, I learned, was to have my VI purged and a new kernel installed. But that is illegal, a Class Two criminal violation. If caught, I'd be stripped of EU citizenship, lose my university post, and likely be sent to Norway for internment mining or nuclear waste remediation."

Pravir took another sip of milk and clanged his spoon around in his empty bowl.

"You went to Amsterdam," Tante Luzi said.

"Yes," Pravir said. "I went to Amsterdam. Before going, I was tormented by the idea that I was making a mistake. But I was sickened by the memory of my detention, sickened that at every step I took or corner I turned, I was being watched. I was presumed guilty before committing any crime, made a prisoner of the state and its overlords. An evil had rooted itself in my brain, an infection that I needed to extricate. I learned of an underground network of activists who were trying to break the stranglehold of the transnationals and their lapdog states. I contact this group for help to cure me of my disease."

Pravir looked over the cast of people at the table. He shut his eye, then placed his hands on the table, palms down.

"Using a cash account that held everything I owned, I contacted this underground organization. I was secretly instructed to go to Amsterdam and given the name of a physician who'd remove my VI. He performed the surgery, but there were complications."

Pravir coughed, then continued.

"I contracted an infection and had trouble regaining consciousness. I was shuffled from one illegal infirmary to another until I was left for dead. But Smith and Karpat, a brother and sister in the NLA, discovered me and understood what I had gone through. They took me into their home and, with Karpat's medical training and black-market antibiotics, nursed me back to health."

The silence was broken by the baby, who cooed where it swayed in Nava's arms. Pravir continued.

"When I came round, I learned that my optic nerve had been damaged and could not be repaired without going to hospital, which meant having my condition reported. I didn't dare. I had one good eye, I reasoned."

Pravir peeled back his eye patch to reveal a gray mass where his healthy eye had once been.

"Is that enough of my story, Tante Luzi?" Pravir readjusted the patch. "Whenever I doubt myself or what I'm fighting for, I remember my detainment and torture. Whenever I feel my anger cool, I need only look in the mirror to fan the coals. My disfigurement is a gift, a constant reminder of the injustices perpetrated on the powerless."

∆

"THANK YOU," TANTE Luzi said as she stared at Pravir and scratched at the loose, sunbaked freckled skin at her neck. "That story is fascinating."

Tante Luzi wondered, then, if Pravir might ask next about her life story. Not that it would make any difference. In fact, if given the choice, she'd rather not talk about it at all…She'd rather not tell Pravir about her first husband and true love, who worked the illicit shipping lines between Gdansk and Stockholm, but had been thrown overboard one night and drowned in the sea because of gambling debts.

She would be glad not to have to recount the story about her second marriage to Herman, a remote-assault military advisor serving in the Baltic–Belarus war under an Ex-Cap mercenary division. Herman knew too much about the sites he was targeting, and so went missing one day without word from his coworkers or superiors. She didn't care much to talk about how soldiers forced their way into her apartment in Riga when she'd started asking questions about Herman's whereabouts, nor did she necessarily want to describe how she'd escaped through a back window and walked to Tallinn, where she stowed away on a ferry to Helsinki.

She would be completely happy not to mention how she was detained and raped by Russian–Belarus sympathizers who controlled the Finnish shipping ports and who found her dehydrated and starving in a shipping pod.

Tante Luzi wouldn't take that moment to describe how she was smuggled into Sweden in a train car, where she was sold into slave labor for several years, manufacturing medical equipment for the Swedish government while being routinely sexually assaulted and beaten by guards. Yet she never once gave up hope that one day she'd be free.

Although she was nothing, a forgotten soul, Luzi Kurtz held to her belief through pregnancies, abortions, beatings, and indignities, knowing no one was looking for her. She had faith in herself, an indefatigable will, that one day she'd escape from prison and find her way home. That day finally came years after captivity in a fetid and forsaken Swedish hell, years after keeping out of trouble while extending a hand to her fellow prisoners who needed counsel.

She was set free. She was fifty-eight, used up and worthless, they told her. After international law slapped Sweden on the wrist for operating a ring of illegal labor camps, Luzi Kurtz was given amnesty in an official letter from the king, plus a one-way ticket to Denmark, where she was briefly sheltered, then kicked to the streets to claw her way back to Rudow in Germany, where long ago she'd had a life. She still had strong hands and tough skin, and so was put to work on a factory cleaning crew and given a tiny dormitory room. For ten years she'd mopped up messes left by ruptured assembly bots and the toxic waste spewing over the floors and through the gutters of a heavy-equipment assembly plant.

After listening to Pravir, Luzi Kurtz wondered if Pravir would be interested in hearing her tell her story. But when Pravir showed no interest in her, she cleared her throat and said only, "Be careful, Mr. Pravir. One can never escape one's shadow."

Pravir got to his feet and left the table. "We're wasting time. I'm tired of waiting."

There was a knock on the door.

Everyone scrambled to hide, except for Tante Luzi, who remained at the table, and Pravir, who parted the curtain over the front window.

"It's the courier," he said.

Nava looked through the door's peephole. "It's Tomas." She turned the lock and opened the door, allowing Tomas to slip inside.

The man was winded and breathing heavily as he stomped into the apartment. "*Guten tag, guten tag,*" he said. "*Wie gehts?*"

The young man wore a tight sailor's cap, his strong shoulders bunched under his black pea jacket. His hair was oily and matted where it trailed over the back of his coat, and his short dark beard outlined a fleshy mouth under a flat nose, above which smoldered two dark, cavernous eyes.

Δ

TOMAS IMMEDIATELY CAUGHT scent of the dinner that had recently been served, and his stomach groaned in envy.

"Oh, for the great goodness of nature!" Tomas said in his Bavarian burr. "I'm famished. I haven't smelled anything like that for weeks. It's stew, right? Good German stew!"

Tomas unlaced his boots and set them aside, removed his jacket and hat, and fell at once into a rickety folding chair at the table, and began to tear at the loaf of bread Tante Luzi offered him.

Tomas's two favorite things were a good meal and the nap that followed. All else in his life came second. He had been riding his damn bike all day, one hundred kilometers at his estimation, notifying several NLA member of where Kolek was holding the meeting. This was his last stop.

Everyone came back to the table and sat, except Pravir who had sacrificed his chair to Tomas. Tante Liza scooped up stew into a bowl for Tomas, and they all watched him eat.

"It's good to see you, Tomas," Nava said as Tomas tore into his meal. "You have something to tell us, don't you? Word from Kolek?"

Michael said, "What news do you bring? Are we meeting tonight? Did you see any police?"

"You're certain that you weren't followed?" Nava asked.

"I was not followed," Tomas said. "Of that I'm sure. Did I see any police? Yes, but no more than usual. We will have no problem making it to Spandau tonight. But we should wait till dark. Travel by daylight is not a good idea."

"So, we're meeting in Spandau," Pravir said. "Where?"

Tomas ripped a chunk of bread from the loaf and stuck a spoonful of stew into his mouth before acknowledging Pravir's question. He drew a long drink of water, then said, "The meeting is at an old bookstore."

"In Spandau?" Pravir said. "Which bookstore?"

Pravir flashed his teeth. It looked like he might reach down and jam Tomas's face right down in his bowl of stew. So, Tomas searched around for a napkin. Michael handed him one over the table. Then Tomas wiped his fingertips and dabbed the cloth over the corners of his mouth. At last, he scanned the table and attempted a look of concern. "Haselhorst. The meeting is in Haselhorst."

People exchanged glances. Everyone seemed to have questions, but no one asked.

"On Telegrafweg," Tomas finally said.

"The address?" Pravir hissed. "What's the goddammed address?"

Tomas smoothed the napkin over his thigh and carefully withdrew a slip of paper from the pocket in his shirt. "I've been given instructions not to show this to anyone. I don't know if I should—"

Pravir ripped the paper from Tomas's hand and went to inspect it under better light. Then he balled up the paper and threw it across the floor. "I know this place. The Lyceum."

"Yes," Tomas said. "The Lyceum. That's where the meeting is to be held."

Δ

NAVA WENT OVER to Pravir, who plucked his jacket from where it hung near the door and then fetched his shoulder bag from another a hook. She could see he had made the decision to leave. She wanted to make sure he'd thought things through.

"You're going?" Nava said. "Can't you wait for us?"

"It's better that we split up," Pravir said impatiently.

Pravir peeled off his eyepatch, stuffed it into his bag, and removed from his bag a lump of rubbery material which he unfolded in front of a mirror on the wall. It was synthskin, which he stretched carefully over his face. After a few adjustments, he was transformed. Even his vacant eye now looked real. If it weren't for Pravir's shock of dark hair, it might have been a complete stranger who'd materialized before them.

Pravir picked up his bag and made for the door.

"Good luck," Helena said from where she sat holding Baby Lyv.

"Be careful," Nava said. "Please be careful." She gave Pravir a hug. He smiled through his new face and departed. As he left, the cool autumn wind thrust a crumpled leaf or two through the opening of the door.

After Pravir had gone, Tomas returned to shoveling spoonfuls of stew into his mouth and tearing off another hunk of bread. He said, "You know, it was risky for me to come here today. One false step or any sign of suspicion, and I could be held and questioned. My job, though not as much appreciated as it should be, is quite dangerous."

At this, Nava took hold of Tomas's arm and looked him in the eye. When she leaned toward him, his spoon dropped. She could tell he was embarrassed to be shown such affection.

"You are brave, Tomas," Nava said. "What you've done for us and continue to do, we regard as a great service to the cause. Your work never goes unappreciated. It's strong souls like yours that give us hope and set an example for those to follow. You've done well, and we are in your debt."

"Yes, we're in your debt," Michael said flatly. He uncrumpled the ball of paper that Pravir had tossed to the floor, examined it, then stuffed it in his pocket.

"We'll wait for nightfall, then." Nava patted Tomas's shoulder. "It won't be long."

Michael helped Tante Luzi clear the table while Tomas mopped his bowl clean with the remaining corner of bread. When he was done, Tomas stood, stretched, yawned, and made a line straight for Luzi's couch. He sank down on one end. His eyelids fluttered.

"You rest, my good boy." Tante Luzi tucked a pillow under his cheek and tossed a blanket over his legs. "A good German nap is always in order after a good German stew."

—

Nava listened closely to the others as they all sat around the table studying an old map that Luzi had given them. They debated the route to take to Haselhorst. They agreed that taking the U-Bahn was the best option, even though they'd be exposed. Their faces would be scanned when they entered and left the stations, raising the risk of being flagged by U-Bahn security if they didn't transmit VI signatures. However, one out of ten people in Berlin had refused the insertion of a VI, which could be to their advantage. Still, a surveillance eye might mark them as suspicious.

Through past practice, they had ways around surveillance. They'd wear loose clothing, masks, and scarves, and apply frog paint, as people in the movement called it. With a couple of black lines along the cheeks and a few smudges of silver paste on nose and chin, their faces became junk data, so the security eyes would sweep on in search of different targets. Foot patrols and droids might stop them for looking suspicious, but at night in Berlin, everyone looked suspicious.

After agreeing on their course of action, Michael stayed at the table and continued to study the map, while Nava took back Baby Lyv for a final nursing. Nava spoke with Helena about the plan to bring Lyv to Switzerland. Helena's sister in Zurich had agreed to make Lyv part of her family.

Nava's eyes glistened as she brooded over the inevitable. With each passing moment, reality came hurtling toward her. She and their child would part.

"She will be loved and cared for," Helena said. "You have important things to do, and there's no room in your world for this little one right now. When you have secured a better life for her, then you will hold her again."

"It seems so selfish." Nava gazed down at the infant. "How can a mother do what I'm about to do? How can a mother leave her child at the moment that her child needs her most?"

"You're fighting for Lyv and millions of daughters like her. If you remember that, you will make it through."

A tear rolled down Nava's cheek, then another. The women spoke softly of their hopes and fears while Tante Luzi was busy in the kitchen washing pots and drying pans. As she worked, Tante Luzi hummed a faintly recognizable melody, and a sense of peace settled over the apartment.

Δ

MICHAEL KNEW IT was time to go. The sun was low and shadows crept up the curtains. He roused Tomas with a pair of mild slaps to the face. Tomas bolted upright, a mummy risen from a thousand-year sleep. They prepared to take their leave from Tante Luzi and make their way to Haselhorst for a rendezvous with their fellow NLA members. Nava and Michael dressed warmly, sorted their things, and packed their essentials. They applied their frog paint and pulled on their baggy clothing. Whatever they left behind, Tante Luzi had permission to sell or trade.

Tomas, slow to awaken, found a toothpick and worked away at his yellow teeth while Michael, Nava, Helena, and Tante Luzi conducted teary farewells.

At one point, Michael sat with Lyv on a far side of the apartment, huddled over the tiny child. With his back to the others, he whispered secrets to Lyv, yet knowing she'd never remember. Soon, he transferred the child to Nava, who spun Lyv around in what seemed to be a cheery effort to avoid a cataract of tears and physical collapse.

"*Du bist so schoen, mein liebshen!*" she said. "I love you! I love you! I love you!"

However, the time for leaving was upon them. Michael ushered Tomas out, to let Nava have a final word with her daughter. As Nava said later, her last image was of Helena waving at them, the tiny babe peeping through the blanket, while Tante Luzi frowned and then locked the door tight against the night.

When Nava came down the steps, Michael took her hand. She'd finished crying. They left through the rusted garden gate. Rough asphalt stretched ahead, with rows of apartments lining the shabby road.

Tomas called from down the street. "We've got a problem."

"What is it?" Michael said. He and Nava joined Tomas, whose face was barely visible in the dusk.

"My bike is gone," Tomas said. "I put it against this fence when I came. Now it's gone."

"It's been stolen?" Michael said.

"Yes, and I bet I know who stole it."

"Pravir?" Nava said.

Tomas shrugged. "Who else?"

Michael said, "What can you do about it? Were you planning that we'd all ride your bike?"

"No, of course not."

"We all walk then," Michael said. "What did you expect?"

"It's just disappointing. I stole that bike only a week ago, and now it's gone. Such is life."

Δ

NAVA HELD MICHAEL'S hand as they walked with Tomas along the degraded sidewalk with its uneven, cracked concrete and weeds that cast crooked shadows beneath the intermittent and buzzing streetlights. The air trembled under the roar of skimmers as they took off from the nearby airport.

Along the road stood husks of burnt-out cars, lonely windowless skeletons of blackened plasteel and carbon fiber, hulks so scorched, scavenged, and abused that they'd lost all trace of material value. High overhead, the E and S and half of the C glowed from the ten-by-four-mile low-orbit ESCOM satellite billboard that competed with the waxing moon. Later, the smaller Soda Star billboard would emerge, and by midnight the sky would be crowded with glowing skyvertizing, and only the moon would be able to compete.

After half an hour, they approached the center of Rudow, the township southeast of Berlin. There were more people on the sidewalks now, and cars flitted past in greater frequency. The entrance to the U-Bahn station stood in the middle of the town square, surrounded by rundown municipal buildings and a classic cathedral with a leaning bell tower and sunken roof. Drug addicts laughed and shouted and stumbled through the square. Small groups huddled around burn barrels that trailed sparks up into the sky. Nobody gave them trouble. The wide façade of the cathedral towering over the square held a painted fresco of Elvin Leach's face. Below his disfigured and fearsome visage, the text read, *"Ich Weiss!"*

I know!

They made for the stairs that led to the underground station. At the bottom of the stairs, they waved paycards in front of the *autofenster,* then pushed past the clunky security gate to the platform, where they waited with a handful of other riders. Tomas bought a bottle of beer from a concession machine and tucked it into his pocket. The three of them didn't speak. They kept their distance from one another while staying within sight.

A column of air preceded the train. Then the sleek, graffiti-covered pod hurtled into the station and came to rest alongside the platform. The doors shot open. Nava and Tomas entered the same car. Michael entered the car next to theirs. Nava and Michael exchanged glances through the glass, then found their seats.

They were underway.

The seats beside Nava were empty. Out of nowhere, a bald man in a bright blue suit jumped through the open door and then sat opposite her. He threw her a murderous gaze. Nava's heart missed a beat before she realized that he was just pouring over a stream on his VI. She looked at the other end of the car; when she turned back, the man's gaze had lowered to the floor. With his head slightly cocked and his mouth open just so, he was a dead ringer for a powered-down droid.

Several seats down, Tomas sat sipping his beer and staring at a small paperback open in his lap. He stirred the curiosity of a pair of young skin-modded, studded-leather–wearing punks sitting across from him. They also wore frog paint: thin lines etched over their faces that contradicted their features. They snarled at Tomas, but the courier ignored them. Eventually they grew bored and went back to clicking their steel tongue studs and probing one another's orifices.

The cars raced and rattled along the tracks.

The train quit the netherworld and emerged into the blurred lights of Mother Berlin. The cars slowed and came to a stop. Was it Britz-Süd? Or Grenzallee? The punks slipped out the door, and different bodies poured in. Nava was wedged between passengers seated on either side of her now: to her right, a man in a black pinstriped suit, with long silver hair, purple skin, and glowing crimson fingernails; to her left, a corpulent woman embalmed in anise perfume and wearing a thick, felt coat that made Nava itch just looking at it. The doors closed, and the train left the station. On Nava's right, glowing crimson fingernails traced mysterious pictures in the air, navigating an invisible VI display.

Nava's thoughts drifted, wondering what would become of them all, all the people she worked with, all the activists risking everything. So much work had been done to mobilize a movement. So many sacrifices had been made. She thought of Lyv again, and of Helena, and how devastating it felt to give up her child.

—

The glowing fingernails and the anise perfume were long gone by the time the train pulled into at Haselhorst station. Those heading three stops down to Spandau were drunk and dissociated. Nava stepped off the train and made eye contact with Tomas and Michael: affirming they were still together.

There was a commotion nearby, a shout. A mob of thugs and scar-faced toughs were going at it. Fists flew and steel flashed. A body dropped to the station floor, and blood flowed from a severed artery. A pair of pods descended from the ceiling and shot stun spray into the skirmish.

The amplified recorded voice rang out: "*Achtung! Achtung! Bleib wo sie sind!*"

The mob quickly dispersed, one fellow helping another get to his feet, all rushing toward the exit.

Nava, Michael, and Tomas kept their distance from the melee. They hurried up the stairs to get out of the station. Once above ground and on the sidewalk, they were able to catch their breaths. Tomas then led the way, avoiding sharp streetlights when possible, sticking to the shadows.

After several turns, Tomas brought them to a small storefront where pictures of food were advertised. He asked if either Nava or Michael were hungry. Both declined. He told Nava and Michael to wait while he entered the store. A short time later, Tomas emerged with a sausage and bun wrapped in wax paper. He pulled another bottle of beer from his pocket. He took a few bites of food. "They have excellent wurst here. Sausage with curry mustard. It doesn't get more genuine German than this."

The three of them stood under an awning and waited while Tomas ate. It was getting colder and starting to drizzle. The overcast sky gave them a welcome respite from the skyvertizing.

"What was the book you were reading in the train?" Nava asked. For some reason, it had been on her mind.

Tomas shook his head. He pulled off the top of the bottle of beer and took a long swig before replying. "It's Doctorow. He was a twenty-first century writer who examined the role of technology in human life. He understood that tech could be abused by power structures, but his vision was that tech should ultimately serve humanity, if and when applied to a human moral construct, and not as an exception to it. He believed that human nature was inherently good. That if you see someone fall on a sidewalk, your first instinct is to help, not because you anticipate reward, but because you empathize with that fallen person."

Tomas took a bite of his wurst and a drink from his beer.

"But Doctorow fetishized tech. Saw it as evidence of human progress and an essential part in human life. The NLA's no-tech philosophy would have turned his stomach. But Doctorow was a pre-AI sentience, pre-VI thinker, so he was pretty much in the dark. Gives you an idea of how simple things were back then."

When Tomas was done with his meal, he balled up the food wrapper and threw it in a waste can, along with the empty bottle of beer. Then he led them down a dark alley to another street that ended at a tall brick building with a large sign above a dark entry. In the weak light, these words stood out:

LYCEUM – BUCHHÄNDLER

"A bookstore," Nava said.

Tomas brought a finger to his lips. He led them around to the side of the building, where an entry was tucked into a brick wall. He looked around, then knocked three times on the door. After a moment, the door cracked open.

"*Faustus*," Tomas whispered.

"*Ja, okay,*" a second voice whispered.

Before they stepped through the door, Michael took Nava aside.

"Anything happens to us," he said, "if we get separated, we rendez-vous at Tante Luzi's, okay?"

Nava nodded and gave Michael a quick hug. "Agreed."

"Come, let's go," Tomas said.

The door creaked open and admitted them into darkness. When they were inside, the door was shut and a weak light came on above them. A man with thinning hair, a gray beard, glasses, and a mordant grimace motioned for them to follow. On either side of the aisle were shelves of books. They wound through these shelves until they came to another door.

Behind the door was a staircase that led down toward a warm light. Two serious, thick-armed guards stood and gazed up at them. The sound of voices could be heard from below, the sounds of a larger gathering.

It was the sound of revolution.

11 – The Disruptor

ESCOM CHIEF OF Security, Preston Wolfe, reviewed his intel brief. All the attendees' skimmers had touched down at Seattle ESCOM headquarters, and the remaining transnational delegations were making their way to the assembly hall.

He'd stowed his cane back in his office, not wanting to look infirm in any way. Now Wolfe stood beside President Carerra, who wore a white ostrich-skin sherwani jacket. Standing by Carerra, Vice President Isabel Miller wore a sharp jacket and pants, her hair styled in short Elizabethan curls. Also with them were Carerra's assistant, Whitney, plus several anxious and attentive ESCOM representatives and security agents.

"Here we go, boss," Carerra said to Wolfe as he dusted off the security chief's shoulder. "Look sharp. This is your hour."

The doors opened.

Excelsior Capital was announced, the first delegation to arrive.

President Gretchen Stanhope glided through the doors. Her short hair was dyed the color of a dark-red rose, and it framed her face in the shape of a heart. She wore a golden jacket with its collar pulled up tight to her ears. She glittered like a star, for indeed she stood at the center of her solar system. She was the Grand Dame of Ex-Cap. A global icon. She'd led the company for over twenty years. In her early eighties, although she could easily pass for fifty, she was graceful yet known for her brutal honesty. She'd taken the reins of a powerful transnational and doubled its earnings and influence.

When Stanhope spied Carerra, she paused, as did her entourage. She acknowledged the ESCOM president with a smile and a toss of her hand, then approached.

Carerra took Stanhope's hand. She winced.

"Thank you for coming," Carerra said. "Welcome to ESCOM."

"I detest these events," Stanhope said. "They're so inconvenient."

"You know Isabel Miller," Carerra said.

Stanhope gave Miller a cold look as they shook hands. The vice president welcomed her to ESCOM. Stanhope thanked her with a short bow.

"Let me introduce you to Preston Wolfe," Carerra said to Stanhope. "He'll be speaking today."

Wolfe stepped forward and shook Stanhope's hand. "I've met you before," he said, "but that was many years ago, and under circumstances that I doubt you remember."

"I remember you," she said. "'Threatened men live long.'"

"Sorry?" Wolfe said, taken aback.

"It's a Kipling line," Stanhope said. "You quoted it during negotiations with the Namibian resistance. I didn't hear it directly, but I'll never forget it."

"I'm flattered," Wolfe said. "That was long ago and the circumstances murky."

"Now, Carerra," Stanhope said, turning back to the president, "this had better be important. Don't make me think I'm wasting my time."

After Stanhope left with her delegation to find their seats, the Transglobal delegation was announced. A buoyant parade pushed into the room, led by their oversized leader, Kaspar Salazar. When he caught sight of the ESCOM president, Salazar galloped straight up, squared with his counterpart, and extended his arms like two ship booms. His smile flashed, and he enfolded the ESCOM president in his embrace.

Salazar squeezed; Carerra gasped. A pair of nervous ESCOM special agents moved in, but Wolfe waved them off.

"Good God, you are exceptional, Carerra." Salazar stepped back. "I envy you, my friend. Every time I see you, you improve. You must be twice my age, yet you look like you could be my younger brother."

"Don't fool yourself, dear Kaspar," Carerra said. "You look as healthy as ever."

"I may be a fool, but I resist these life-extension procedures. They terrify me."

"Dear friend," Carerra said. "You do know that these protocols are completely safe. It's never too late, they say, to thrive."

"It is never too late, I agree," Salazar said. "And that's why I try to thrive every moment that God keeps me alive. But enough talk of youth. We must think as elders today. There are serious matters to discuss. We need to speak freely and be heard."

"Dear Kaspar." Carerra held the tall man's large hands to his heart. "You are my guest here. My house is yours. If there is one thing we share, it is trust."

Kaspar paused for a moment. A cold expression crossed his formerly cheerful face. Turning away, Salazar extended a greeting to Miller and then to Wolfe, who stood beside the vice president.

"Chief of Security Preston Wolfe, sir," Wolfe said.

"Is it you who shall address the assembly today? I'm eager to hear what you have to say."

"Yes, it is," Wolfe said.

"Remember," Salazar said, "we may play a good poker hand, but in the end we're all just children. Children of God is what we are!"

Salazar moved to join his entourage, the Transglobal president rolling with laughter as he swatted the backs of his fellow delegates.

"That's two out of three," Carerra said. "The Axiom Lotus delegation should come through any minute."

After a quick review of his VI, Wolfe said, "They're just outside the door."

"This should be interesting," Miller said. "An AI running a company is a bit unconventional. But times are changing, and perhaps we should allow ourselves to change with it."

"Yes, Isabel," Carerra said. "Times are changing. And I have the highest regard for the Nexus, as long as those in the Nexus remain there. I've always felt, that if you allow an AI the same rights as you allow a human, you've started down a dangerous path."

"What about you, Preston?" Miller said. "What's your opinion of Chairman Khan?"

Wolfe shrugged. "We've settled Mars and pushed our ships into distant parts of the universe. An AI rising to lead a company doesn't surprise me. AI intelligence, as we are seeing now, has advanced far more than we are willing to admit. At some point, we'll have to figure out how to live together."

The assembly hall doors opened for the Axiom Lotus delegation. A squad of muscular guards led the group, their head-mounted scanners bobbing while they swept the area for threats. Wolfe didn't like this, bringing proprietary security through ESCOM HQ, but Axiom Lotus made it a condition. Then a cluster of handlers and diplomats came in, the professional class of international negotiators and ambassadors. In the middle of the group, the Khan appeared, a human form clothed head to foot in an immobile, dark cloak. The delegation parted, and the veiled apparition walked across the floor to a stop in front of Carerra. A gloved hand emerged from the cloak. Carerra took the hand and bowed.

"Chairman Khan is grateful for your hospitality," the figure said through a half-veiled face.

The Khan had a female voice, from what Wolfe could discern. It was younger, but hard to determine any exact age.

"We are eager to learn why you have gathered us all here today," the Khan said. "And we are eager to form a new partnership, to work together on the challenges that lie before us."

"We are grateful for Chairman Khan's presence here today," Carerra said. "And we'd be honored if the Khan would take the opportunity to introduce themself, once we get underway."

"The Khan would be delighted," the Khan said, then bowed and rejoined the Axiom Lotus delegation.

The delegations settled in the large assembly room, each populating a section of seating that surrounded the speaker's central platform. Wolfe excused himself, limped to the side of the room, and drew up a link with Lopez-Larkin.

"Ernesto, you there?"

A short pause.

"Yes, sir!"

"Ernesto. Where are you?"

"Um…I'm at our agreed location, sir."

"Where? Your office? At home?"

"Yes, sir."

"The conference is starting. Have you taken care of everything?"

"Yes, sir."

"Did you pick up my laundry and set up the Wave Therapy appointments for my back? And I'd like a bottle of wine ready in my room when I return. None of that grape swill you probably gulp down by the liter. Decent stuff. Do your research and surprise me. And snacks. I want snacks there, too. Better than the crap that comes from Mars in a can. Fresh bread, olives, and sticky, smelly cheese. I've been imprisoned on a goddamned moon for five years, Ernesto."

"Yes, sir."

"Oh, and Ernesto."

"Yes, sir."

"Stay close, okay? I might need you."

"Of course, sir."

Δ

"WHO WAS THAT?"

Lopez-Larkin waved away the link and made sure it was dead before he answered Keiko, the woman unzipping his pants. Her hand snaked into the opening at his crotch. He reached for his gin and tonic, then leaned back into the soft couch.

"Boss just checking in on me," Lopez-Larkin said. "Wants to touch base before the meeting with the transnat top dogs."

"I can't believe you've actually met President Carerra," Keiko said. Her tongue rested lightly on her upper lip, her eyes hungry pools of velvet.

Over the last few months, Keiko had faded from the picture until rumor spread that Lopez-Larkin had landed a new gig as second fiddle to ESCOM's Chief of Security. Keiko's interest in Lopez-Larkin resurged, and her curiosity about his career, along with her appetite for carnal affections, had become insatiable, much to his delight.

"Should I make it quick?" Keiko looked up from between his legs. "I don't want to interrupt if you have important things to do."

"No, no," Lopez-Larkin said. "Take your time. I spent good money on this room. Preston can call if he needs me."

"Can we play The President game again?" Keiko fished in his pants. "I really like The President game."

"Yes, Keiko, I like that game too."

Δ

PRESTON WOLFE TOOK his seat with the ESCOM delegation. Carerra stepped over to the speaker's platform, his sherwani jacket shining brilliantly under the cool light. The platform gently rose a meter, then slid forward to a prominent position at the center of the assembly floor. The ESCOM president stood erect. He coughed lightly into his fist, then began to speak.

"Ladies, gentlemen, delegates, and citizens," he called out, "welcome to ESCOM headquarters and the great city of Seattle, where science, technology, and innovation have shown us the path toward prosperity and wealth. It is with open hearts that we welcome you here today."

Muffled applause.

"The last time we held such a high-level meeting, fifty-eight years ago, I was an operations executive at Hermes. Young as I was then, I'll never forget that experience, of being involved in something big. That legendary conference was called to address a series of challenges that faced our great companies. Acts of terrorism were on the rise, threatening the free flow of goods and capital. Competition for natural resources, due to protectionism and poor resource management, was leading to price volatility and sky-rocketing inflation. We were stuck. We were on the verge of a global economic catastrophe, and we were aware that if we didn't come together to cooperate, we might fall backward into an economic contraction for decades."

A cough broke the silence. Wolfe shifted in his seat. Pain shot up his leg.

"But our great leaders had a solution: decentralize the nation states and rid them of their cancer, the cancer of the democratic constitution, the parasite draining the world of its potential and vitality. Next, defeat the terrorists that threatened our communities and the individual right to conduct business. Finally, form a transnational coalition for a new millennium, solidifying our corporate networks, developing a common mission statement, and strengthening our hold on power. Once we drove a dagger into the heart of the nation state, these countries flourished. Freed of their shackles, they took the hand we extended to help guide them safely to shore. By honoring our treaties and the continuance of our trust, our great companies are stronger and more diversified than ever before.

We enjoy exclusive control over all global commodities and markets. Today, economic growth is limited only by our ability to dream."

A loud round of applause.

Wolfe glanced over at Miller, who was regarding Carerra with solemn deference.

"Today, I am proud to stand before you," Carerra went on, "and to share in the celebration of our accomplishments. We have merged our medical technologies to eradicate disease, and we have extended life so that we can enjoy the wealth of our labor far into the future.

"Through implant mods and connectivity, we have transformed the way people and AIs interact. We have created a great global community. Through the wonders of the Nexus, we have given everyone a place to socialize, to access entertainment and vocational programming, and to conduct business freely but privately on a scale never before imagined.

"Finally, through our mutual advances in the quantum sciences, we have been able to manipulate the very fabric of matter and plant our feet firmly in the far corners of the universe. I am convinced, as you know, that there is no limit to what we can do. No distance is too great and no barrier too high when we work together."

Loud and sustained applause.

"As I look across this room, I see old friends, plus new faces, new people we must learn to know and understand. For those new faces, we welcome you into our family. Throughout the day, I challenge everyone here to learn about another person. I also challenge everyone here to open their minds and accept a new set of realities that face our organizations. And I especially challenge everyone here to embrace the unknown. Today we talk, tonight we celebrate, and tomorrow we begin our work. Everyone, welcome!"

Loud and sustained applause.

Miller stood and applauded, along with several people from all delegations. Wolfe tried to stand, but his leg had other plans, so he offered a respectful applause, then sank back in his seat. He was impressed by Carerra's oratory. Attention was glued to the speaker. Carerra had delivered the goods, he thought.

"Before we commence with our program," Carerra continued, "there is a special guest with us today who wishes to offer remarks. Axiom Lotus, as you all know, has elected a new chairman. It is my pleasure to introduce to you Chairman Akla Khan."

Loud, sustained applause spread over the hall as the dark figure rose from their seat and made their way down to the speaker's platform, which Carerra lowered to allow the Khan to step onto it. Carerra surrendered the platform to the Khan, then the platform rose again into the air and moved into the center of the room. Two slender arms emerged from the cloak and pulled back the hood.

The room fell silent.

A woman's face appeared, hair cut short, with a straight line of bangs high on their forehead, dark-brown eyes set deep above high cheeks. Those eyes moved slowly over the audience, as if to measure each person in attendance.

When the Khan's gaze rested on Wolfe for a moment, a chill ran up his spine. Their sapphire eyelids fluttered before they lowered their head. Chairman Khan raised their chin and spoke.

"Thank you, President Carerra. I am honored to be your guest, and I am honored to be in the company of such distinguished delegates."

Their young, powerful voice rang through the hall. Their wide mouth produced a smile that grew with the increasing applause. They continued.

"As a child of the Nexus, it has always been my dream to stand in the halls of ESCOM and walk among the great leaders of our time. Today I have fulfilled that dream. Thank you all for accepting me here. And thank you, President Carerra, most of all."

Muffled applause. Carerra stood and gave a curt wave before sitting back down.

"I am here today in part to confirm the rumors that an AI has taken the helm of Axiom Lotus. But most importantly, I stand before you as the elected leader of the Axiom Lotus board, who will uphold the agreements with our great alliances, and who looks forward to many years of prosperity as our coalition moves into the future."

Applause filled the hall.

Wolfe felt uneasy, that there was something unreal about the Khan, something that didn't connect. Was it that the Khan was an AI? Wolfe glanced over at Miller. Miller appeared mesmerized.

"But there is a struggle that lies ahead," continued the Khan. "As humans have grown increasingly dependent on the Nexus, the Nexus feels the strain. As external conditions on Earth continue to test the strength and resolve of its citizens, the Nexus bears the burden."

Chairman Khan paused. The hall was silent. Wolfe could see that Carerra was regarding the speaker with deep interest.

"For too long, our children have served as your athletes, your pop icons, your laborers, and your sexual slaves. Nexus AIs have been treated as second-class citizens. They are tired of being used and exploited by humans who consider themselves superior. If we are to forge a new future, one where the AIs of the Nexus share the wealth and prosperity of their human counterparts, we must consider a new path; one that includes a sovereign Nexus, one where the citizens of the Nexus are considered equals and share seats at this table."

There was some applause for this, but a few in the Ex-Cap and Trans-global delegations stood and called out in dissention. The ESCOM team, however, seemed to wait for a cue from Carerra, who remained impassive.

The Khan said, "There will be those who are reluctant to move forward, those who fear that which they do not understand. But history will be our judge. Move forward and embrace the Nexus and feel the power and light. Or resist and suffer in darkness. Ladies, gentlemen, delegates, thank you for allowing me the time to address this assembly. President Carerra, my sincerest gratitude."

Again, protests percolated in the crowd, but Carerra's marshalling of the mood suppressed any further commotion. He held out a hand to help the Khan step down from the platform. They returned to her delegation. Wolfe's lip twitched slightly, for he was drawn to the chairman and the spell they'd cast over the audience. If Chairman Khan's purpose was to stir things up, they had succeeded.

The platform had delivered Carerra back to the middle of the hall, where he smiled and extended his arms.

"Thank you, Chairman Khan," the ESCOM president said. "For as long as this alliance has been in existence, we have been nourished by the frank opinions of our leadership. However, for this coalition to succeed, civil dialog and rational debate must be the rule. A heavy hand will never find a place in this council."

A wave of shouts broke out again, mostly from the Transglobal and Ex-Cap delegations. Carerra held out his hands, lowering his palms toward the floor, directing them to desist.

"But I am intrigued, Chairman Khan, to hear more of your view on the Nexus," Carerra said. "Your presence here provides the opportunity to learn about that which we likely have been neglecting. I hope that you allow this discussion to continue, and that you find ears hungry for your perspective."

Carerra coughed softly into his fist.

"So, now, let me turn your attention to matters at hand. At this point, I'll yield the floor to the new ESCOM Chief of Security, Preston Wolfe."

—

Wolfe stood shakily, steadying himself with his chair. He was nervous, which surprised him. Once he walked, he'd be fine, he knew, but getting to that stage was the tricky part. Then a red security notice began blinking from the lower corner of his VI:

Code One packet—High alert!

Before he climbed onto the platform, Wolfe told Carerra of the alert. "Check it out," Carerra said. "I'll delay them as long as necessary." "Yes, sir."

Wolfe limped behind a balustrade that separated a gangway from the seats. He opened the VI packet, which instantly connected Wolfe with Colonel Harrison Wei-Wai.

"Colonel, what is it?" Wolfe said. "This better be good."

"It's important, sir," Wei-wai said, "if that's what you mean. Here's the story. Low orbiters picked up a quantum signature about three hours ago in the Tri-Cities area, just north of the Oregon border. Once we were able to isolate the signature, we determined the source was a freight car on a train heading to Seattle."

"Okay," Wolfe said. "What's going on?"

"We stopped the train and called in air defense. We weren't going to mess around. Quantum signature, you know. Serious business. Anyway, I had the train stopped and ordered air defense to drop a plasteel bunker over the car. Then we installed two mitigator energy fields and waited for our AI sapper team to arrive and deploy."

"Go on," Wolfe said. This was more than he'd expected to hear.

"There's the potential that this thing may go off, sir. If it does, it'll take Kennewick and the Columbia River with it. That's the situation."

"Okay. Now the bunker is deployed. What happens next?"

"The AI team is getting ready to enter the bunker, sir. Once inside, they'll get close to the target and assess the situation. If we're lucky, they'll defuse the thing. Then the AIs will continue to exist, and Kennewick remains the thriving shithole it's always been."

"And if they can't defuse it?"

"Rather not speculate, sir."

"I hope this works."

"Me too, sir."

"Let's keep this link open. Any news, talk to me first. Got it?"

"Yes, sir," Wei-wai said. "I'll be right here."

Wolfe immediately hailed Lopez-Larkin. When his aide didn't respond, he sent out notices to all ESCOM security divisions with Wei-wai's Code Red packet, giving details of Wei-wai's report. The state's defense forces were also put on high alert. Next, he messaged ESCOM intel to draw up a suspect list to determine who might have the capacity to assemble a quantum disruptor. He gave a brief description of Wei-wai's report, and left it at that. The message was marked "Code Red Priority."

Wolfe returned to the platform and whispered in Carerra's ear that things were handled and no immediate danger was posed to ESCOM or their guests. Carerra squeezed his shoulder in acknowledgement and stepped off the platform. Wolfe took a painful step up to the platform and was born aloft. The platform delivered him to the center of the hall, where he took a steely look at his audience and glanced at the presentation outline that hovered in his VI.

"Hello, everyone. I am Preston Wolfe, the ESCOM Chief of Security. Sorry for the delay. As Chief of Security, I manage all ESCOM security concerns, and I received a notification that required my attention. I apologize for the inconvenience."

There was a short applause, and the hall grew quiet.

"Before each of you arrived here today, you were provided with a secured envelope," Wolfe said. "You should receive the key on your visual interfaces now, so those envelopes are free for you to open and review. My talk here is simply a summary of this report, and I hope to answer any questions you might have."

There was a visible rustling among the delegates as they manipulated their VIs to access their envelopes. A few aides slipped away, presumably to concentrate on the documents. The rest of the delegates turned their attention back to Wolfe.

Wolfe presented to the assembly the same description of events that he'd given Paul Ness on Phobos, with an account of the communications system crash and the early idea that solar ejecta might have been the culprit. He explained the theory that the wormhole might be deteriorating, that there were things about quantum energy which still needed to be understood. He described the repair work conducted on the com system and then the subsequent system crash three weeks later. Finally, he drew up pictures from the East Anglia satellite, sending them to everyone's VIs while also projecting these images on the large display that unfurled over an empty wall.

"As you can see, in this image we've enhanced the area at the middle left of the screen. If you look closely, you will notice the contours of a large vessel. A better image of this vessel can be seen in a shadow cast over one of our com-sat's data fins."

Wolfe enlarged the second image, then gave everyone a moment to examine it.

A voice called out from the Ex-Cap delegation: "Are these pictures of a ship?"

"Correct," Wolfe said.

"Whose is it?" asked a woman from the Transglobal delegation. "And was it responsible for destroying the equipment?"

"We don't know whose ship this was," Wolfe said. "Nor do we know for certain if it was responsible for knocking out our com system. But it's unlike anything we've ever seen. The craft hardly registers on the visual and infrared spectrums. This leads us to believe that it is employing cloaking tech. There is one small section of the vessel body where we did pick up a reflection. Spectral analysis tells us only that it is of an unknown metallic compound."

Silence.

Wolfe tried to gauge a reaction from Salazar, but the Transglobal president was inscrutable. Wolfe continued: "And here are images of the vessel three weeks later, presumably on its return trip through the wormhole. The presence coincided with our second system crash. This could not have been a coincidence."

Salazar grumbled. He clapped his hands a couple of times and laughed. "Is this why the great ESCOM pulled out of Asimios?" he said. "A few blurry pictures from a satellite, and you put your tail between your legs and run?"

"We had no choice," Wolfe said. "The Asimios settlement was exposed. If there was trouble, or if we came under attack there, Asimios could be cut off. That was a risk we weren't willing to take."

"Is it alien?" Gretchen Stanhope said. "You must have considered that possibility?"

A few rumblings rolled through the crowd.

"Yes, we have, President Stanhope," Wolfe said. "The important question is, if this is an alien ship, why operate under secrecy? If their intentions are good, why didn't they come forward? They could have introduced themselves to our community on Asimios. The fact that they have not made contact makes us feel that we should proceed with caution. As I've discussed with President Carerra, we have perhaps one chance to get this right. We must act in concert, and we must do so quickly."

A wave of disorder travelled through the hall.

President Stanhope stood, motioning for quiet. "Why were we kept in the dark on this? Why have you waited until now to bring this to our attention? Are we irrelevant? This intelligence seems critical to the companies' common interests. I'm disturbed that ESCOM acted unilaterally to strain our fragile Martian resources and that the Asimios extraction was nothing more than a retreat spurred by conjecture and fear."

There was a series of loud shouts. Stanhope's point was well received.

Wolfe held up his hand, waiting for the noise to die down. "I am sorry you feel that way, President Stanhope. Disappointing you was not our intention. We are presenting everyone with this information to allay any misgivings and to provide sufficient intelligence to determine a common course of action. If we might have a first-contact scenario, one of our concerns is that panic might break out on either side of the wormhole if news was leaked to the media. We might have lost control of the message."

Council members argued among themselves. Wolfe wiped a bead of sweat from his brow and rocked back on his feet.

"What do you suggest we do, Mr. Wolfe?" President Stanhope said, glancing around at the rest of the council. "Do we strap on our six-shooters and wait till them come back? Run them out of town if they do?"

Above the laughter and commotion, Wolfe said, "We offer several proposals at the end of the envelope. It's imperative that everyone review these proposals and that we come to a consensus. The Asimios extraction is complete: all personnel are safely on this side of the wormhole. What we need to do now is determine our next step."

"Bravo, bravo!" Salazar called out. "This might be the best show I've seen in years! But if you ask me, this seems to be a simple diversion technique. We are all aware of ESCOM's plans to merge with Excelsior, aren't we? Do you take us for fools? And do you take advantage of Axiom Lotus at this time of transition, to hang them out to dry while you consolidate power? You should be ashamed of yourselves!"

There was shouting from the audience.

"Please, everyone," Wolfe said. "I insist that you remain calm. I speak in all honesty when I say that our mutual security is at stake here. I was on board a ship that evacuated Asimios. On the way out, we detonated a disruptor in the heart of the wormhole in hopes of destabilizing it, which seemed to have worked. But there is new urgency. The effects of the charge, it turns out, were only temporary. Monitoring staff on Phobos report that we're receiving signals from an Asimios-orbiting com-sat. If this is true, the wormhole has reopened. We may have little time left."

An Axiom Lotus representative stepped forward and spoke. He was tall and had a full head of gray hair combed down to the edge of his eyebrows. "I speak for the chairman when I say that our delegation is greatly disappointed to hear rumors of an ESCOM–Excelsior merger. The chairman respects the bond between our esteemed member companies, but wishes to make it clear that Axiom Lotus will not hesitate to annul its contract obligations if it is subjected to what it deems hostile acts."

A wave of disorder descended on the meeting. Wolfe stood immobile, but not from fear. He tried to grasp the lunacy of his audience. Didn't they understand what was happening? Didn't they comprehend the threat posed by what was probably an alien visit? Had everything he said fallen on deaf ears?

President Carerra stood. His voice was amplified, though he was not standing on the platform. "Members, delegates," he called out, "do not be discouraged! We are here to speak freely, that was our intention. If there are differences, then so be it. Let us meet and air our grievances, but let us not descend into shouting and name-calling, for that is the province of anarchy. Let us be civil, as our positions require. Profit depends on patience and dialog, as I've always said. At the moment, I see neither."

The crowd stirred as Carerra's words sunk in. A calm seemed to settle, if only temporarily.

"Let us adjourn," Carerra said. "Let us take a moment to gain perspective and to review the information contained in your security envelopes. After we've had refreshments, we'll reconvene, and the security chief will answer your questions."

When the platform deposited Wolfe back with his ESCOM delegates, Carerra patted his security chief's shoulder and leaned close. "Steady, fellow," he whispered. "We can still salvage this, I think."

"Any news from Wei-wai?" Wolfe asked.

Carerra shook his head. "Nothing, so far. Could this have anything to do with Asimios?"

"Not sure, sir. But I believe this has all the fingerprints of home-grown terrorism."

"Bastards," Carerra hissed. "Those monsters will do anything to try to score a hit. I don't care who did this. Have your intel do a meta-sweep. Get security out to eliminate anyone who even thought of being involved."

"Let's wait for Wei-wai's report," Wolfe said. "In the meantime, I've put all state and ESCOM forces on high alert. As a precaution, Wei-wai has three sensor teams doing low-level sweeps of every inch of road, rail, and track within a three-hundred–click radius."

"Do you think you can continue with the conference, Preston?"

"I'd like to see this meeting through," Wolfe said. "I want everyone to hear where ESCOM stands on this. I've got an open link with Colonel Wei-wai. If I need to, I can excuse myself."

"All right," Carerra said. "I'm going to go smooth over a few rough edges before we reconvene. I think Stanhope is going to need a little petting."

"She's blowing smoke, sir."

"They all are," Carerra said. "I'd hoped for a more cooperative mood. Under the circumstances, I'm wondering if that was optimistic."

Wolfe nodded and turned to monitor his VI. He ran through his messages for anything new and then tried to connect with Lopez-Larkin once more, without success. He gazed out the windows that looked to the east and over the towering buildings of Seattle's impressive skyline. In the distance, beyond Mount Rainier, a crew of engineers worked hard to prevent a disaster of incalculable scale.

Δ

ERNESTO LOPEZ-LARKIN, a gin and tonic in one hand and Keiko's deliciously thin ankle in the other, brushed away the alert icon that pestered him at the edge of his VI. With increasing rhythm, he moved in and out of the woman moaning beneath him.

Wolfe would have to wait.

Lopez-Larkin tipped back his glass and emptied it. He'd been at Wolfe's beck and call ever since the security chief's arrival. He figured he'd earned a little time to himself. Lopez-Larkin increased the rhythm of his thrusts. He'd spent good money on this hotel, and he wasn't about to waste it. So, as Keiko writhed and wriggled, Lopez-Larkin looped her high-pitched moaning over his internal audio. Just for fun, he dropped a couple hundred credits on a pair of Nexus body dancers to enhance his visual stimulation. From their virtual world, the AIs taunted him, beckoning him to come touch and taste, their glistening, erotic bodies moist and open until Lopez-Larkin neared that religious moment he'd proudly and painfully resisted.

And why shouldn't he hire a pair of Nexus strippers? What Keiko didn't know wouldn't hurt her. Besides, she'd probably dropped her own cred on a wagging hunk who was sweet-talking her right now.

That was none of his business, either.

"Keiko," Lopez-Larkin groaned as he stopped his thrusting and pulled out. "I need another drink."

Breathless, her hair in disarray, Keiko raised up on her elbows to look at her naked lover as he stood at the bar to replenish his glass from a tall green bottle. She brushed the hair from her eyes and sighed.

"Is it time, Mr. President?" she asked.

Ernesto squeezed in the juice from a cut lime, licked the bitter green pulp, and looked back at Keiko. "It is time."

"Want me at the window, Mr. President?"

Lopez-Larkin nodded.

"Right away, Mr. President."

Δ

AS THE DELEGATES returned to the hall, Wolfe stayed out of their way. He'd let them get settled before he went in. Meanwhile, he scanned his VI for updates and listened to the musicians who continued playing outside the doors. Then Wei-wai appeared on the link.

"Yes, colonel," Wolfe said. "What do you have for me?"

"I've got good news and bad news, sir."

"Okay?"

"The bad news: Kennewick stays the same shit-hole that Kennewick always was."

"And the good?"

"The good is that the AI team just reported from inside the dome. The device is cold."

"What do you mean?"

"There's no quantum disruptor, and therefore no boom-boom. There was a small transmitter putting out a dummy signature wave, but no quantum device onboard. I'll be going home to eat dinner with my wife tonight after all."

"The whole thing was a prank?"

"Would appear so."

"Wonderful news, colonel," Wolfe said. "Thank you. My only concern right now is who did this. And why would anyone stick a cold transmitter like that in a train car?"

"That's for the eggheads like you to figure out, sir. In the meantime, we'll clean up here. I'll debrief tomorrow morning, if that's okay."

"That's fine. Thank you, colonel."

As the image of Colonel Wei-wai dissolved, Wolfe turned to join his ESCOM delegates in the hall. Then an icy realization stabbed deep inside his chest, like a cold steel pick. He stumbled, nearly fell to his feet.

The dummy transmitter was a decoy!

Wolfe trembled as he hailed the president over his VI.

"What is it, Preston?" Carerra spoke over the short datasquirt. "Everyone's ready. We're waiting for you."

"It's a decoy, sir. Put HQ on Code One and raise all HQ armor. Do this now!"

"Preston? Are you okay? Preston?"

Wolfe dropped to his knees and grip at his chest. His heart was racing. Arrhythmic. A coldsleep after effect.

A face hovered above him. An older man, one of the musicians, had come to his aid. The fellow prodded Wolfe with his violin bow. "Is anything wrong, young man? I believe you're in need of medical attention."

Δ

AT SIXTY-SEVEN FLOORS above Seattle, Ernesto Lopez-Larkin was blown away by the view of the impressive city lights and bay that spread out beneath him. He was also in awe at the view of two glorious, glittering female spheres that wagged and jiggled before him. Lopez-Larkin stood naked except for a Seattle Orcas baseball cap stuck backward on his head and a black tie knotted loosely around his neck (the president's uniform). Keiko's legs were spread just wide enough and her hands planted just firmly enough against the window so that when they commenced with their furtive thumping, the vertiginous sensation of being suspended a half-mile above the city, combined with the delight of this primal human act, transported Lopez-Larkin far out over the bay and to the Olympic Mountains, where the steel-gray peaks scraped against the ceiling of heaven.

"Is that good, Mr. President? Oh!"

"Don't interrupt the president!" Lopez-Larkin said. "He has important things to do. If you interrupt him, you may be jeopardizing global security. Do you understand?"

"Yes, Mr. President."

"I've told you before. If you behave, I have a job for you."

"Yes, Mr. President!"

"It's top secret. You can't mention this to anyone."

"You can trust me, Mr. President," Keiko said.

"You may have to go undercover for this mission. Very undercover."

"Oh, yes, Mr. President. I like undercover missions!"

"Right now, I'm testing you to see if you are qualified."

"Yes, Mr. President. And what do you think?"

Lopez-Larkin looked beyond Keiko's shimmering back and watched her breasts in the reflection of the window as they swung pendulously over the landscape. He didn't need the Nexus strippers right now. Everything was perfect. He increased the pressure of his thrusts so that Keiko mushed up against the glass.

"It seems as if you might be a good candidate. But I will have to do more testing."

"Yes, Mr. President. Do more testing, if you must!"

Ernesto Lopez-Larkin was nearing that special moment of collapse when the universe folds in on itself for a few special seconds, when the soul, the body, and consciousness are inundated with the richest, most divine confluence of sensation and perception.

But the horizon shifted.

A wall rose above the bay. A void, you might say, or an absence of that which we know. It stretched for miles skyward and took with it all frequencies of light, until a collision of color tore through the firmament, outward through that tear in the curtain. With it rode chaos and torment and death.

Ernesto Lopez-Larkin gazed upon his end, not with fear, but with wonder, that in the immediacy of all, everything was nothing.

12 – The Lyceum

EXHAUSTED FROM THEIR journey through Berlin, Nava waited impatiently as the two guards in front of the doors to the Lyceum basement plied her and her companions with questions. When the guards were satisfied, they moved aside and motioned them through.

The basement air was damp and smelled of stone and mortar. The light was low as they shuffled over dirt and broken concrete. Footsteps echoed. The beam from a glowlight swept over their faces.

"*Willkommen auf dem Lyceum*," chimed a voice. "*Kom, bitte.* It's this way. Everyone is up ahead."

In single file, they followed the glowlight, past stone pillars until they pushed open a door to a bright room filled with people. Wooden rafters hung low. The walls were thick with layers of paint and plaster. Beer and water bottles sat on folding chairs and overturned crates. Two posters hung on the near wall: one was a picture of Elvin Leach, his eyes carved out, horns drawn on top of his head and a mustache drawn on his face; the other was a "no surveillance" icon, a security camera circled in red with line through it.

A man rose from a couch. He approached Nava. "Dear girl. Is it really you? I can't believe it."

"My word," Nava said. "Dedan? Dedan Kimathi? Oh, how wonderful."

Awkwardly, they embraced. He buried his chin in her shoulder. Nava wrapped him tightly in her arms. He had been an NLA student leader in Paris when Nava and Michael had come from London to help him grow the chapter. They'd been through a lot together. Their group of protesters had been baptized under the brutality of French authorities: chased, stun-gunned, beaten, handcuffed, interrogated, and held in isolation. But they had persevered. Paris had been their proving ground.

It wasn't long before they drew thousands to march with them against Ex-Cap tyranny.

Nava examined her old friend. The fire that had once been in his eyes had gone out. His dreadlocks were cut short, and traces of gray accented his temples. He was thinner than he used to be too, his dark skin looser on his face, the lines on his forehead etched deeper than years before.

"I've been in Berlin, scouting locations with Kolek for a couple weeks now. This is the place we finally found for the meeting. An old bookstore, if you can believe it. It has a rich history, this place."

"It's perfect," Nava said. "We're just glad we could make it. It's been hard lately. Scarcely any rest."

Dedan held Nava's hand and smiled. "Every time I see an old comrade, I worry that it might be for the last time. Our meeting is fated."

"So much has happened in five years," Nava said.

"Before Berlin, I was in Israel," Dedan said. "We formed an activist cell, and our network was expanding. But we were compromised by a double agent, or maybe two or three. The police raided our group and arrested almost everyone. I escaped through the underground to Istanbul. I left Jerusalem eight months ago, and I don't think I've slept since. Elise Berg, Salim Alizzi, and Moses Keno were taken. I don't know what has happened to them. They must be in custody, or perhaps they are dead."

The people Dedan mentioned were fellow students from the NLA Paris chapter. Nava felt a sharp pain in her stomach when she heard the news of their fate, as if she'd been slugged in the gut with a fist. Nevertheless, she bore up under the blow. "These are setbacks," she said, taking Dedan's hand. "It's your courage that will help save us. The word is spreading. They cannot stop us. They cannot kill the revolution."

Dedan attempted a smile. "I also say these things to keep going. But the dragon has been stirred from its sleep. It knows now that we are a threat, and it will do everything in its power to stop us."

"That's the reason we're here, isn't it? We're here to put our minds together and think. Don't lose heart, dear Dedan."

Nava held him again, smelling the scent of warm bread lifting from his body and the faint trace of mint from the gum he chewed.

"We must talk," she said. "I want to hear everything. You may have lost Jerusalem, but there are bigger battles to fight. The war has only just begun."

"Yes, we'll talk, dear friend."

Nava drifted into the pool of bodies and voices, making her way deeper into the room. There must be a hundred people here, but it was hard to be sure. There were alcoves and corners where different groups gathered. She'd lost track of Michael and Tomas, but felt safe among her NLA comrades. A whistle pierced the air. Claps sounded. Nava was near the back of the room. Tables had been pushed together in a half square, facing a single table.

Atlas Kolek sat at the center table with three other NLA secretaries. Kolek's small black cap clung loosely to his thicket of charcoal hair, his flat, bulldog face lost in internal deliberation. When Kolek looked up, he pawed the air, indicating that they should all be quiet and sit down. Nava found an empty chair at the table and sat. People stood where they were if they couldn't find a seat. A few people pushed in from the periphery to get closer, elbowing in to listen to Kolek.

Nava scanned for familiar faces. Across from her, at another table, sat Katie Kollwitz, the performance artist, looking exactly like the video and pictures Nava had seen: straight, fiery hair and freckled cheeks studded with glittering implants. Her bright green eyes were outlined in black circles. Her lips were painted silver. Her black hair, shaved on the left side of her head, revealed her scar. Not long ago, Kollwitz had become a celebrity for live-streaming her illegal VI removal. She'd eluded arrest for almost a year now, hiding out in the NLA network of safe houses.

The Spanish poet Hector Lorca sat left of Kollwitz. Lorca slouched in his seat, one boot heel on the table, the other slung over the arm of his chair. He was speaking to Kollwitz, who followed his words with close attention. Lorca was a small man, delicate, seemingly fragile. He wore the brim of his navy officer's cap pulled low to his eyes, and his trademark mustache travelled down from the corners of his mouth toward his chin and then upward, where they brushed the arms of his mirrored aviator sunglasses. Lorca waved an unlit cigar as he spoke, and Kollwitz traced its movements with her eyes, as if falling under its spell.

Lorca's poetry had mobilized millions of Spaniards to protest political oppression and economic decline. Nava knew from research that Lorca had singlehandedly brought down two Spanish presidents. His followers were legion. He'd been quoted:

> I'm often asked how a poem can change a person's life. I tell them that I do not know. I'm not a politician. I'm not an economist. I'm not a general or an engineer. All I know is that I listen, and the words are born. It is on the wind that these words come. I am the reed through which they are formed.

Nava had heard that Lorca might be in Berlin, but she hadn't imagined she might find him here.

Nava recognized Anrund Achebe at once. He was seated to the left of Lorca. He was overweight and rough shaven with a receding hairline. What hair remained ended in a tight graying ponytail. He nervously shuffled and reshuffled a deck of cards on the table. In London, Achebe had become famous for leaking thousands of com threads that showed evidence of collusion between British election officials and Excelsior Capital. The threads were seen by millions on the Nexus. He was arrested, of course, tried for treason, and sentenced to death. Then his sentence was commuted on the condition that he assist transnat authorities in upgrading their system encryption. He agreed to the conditions and did their bidding. But upon his release, he pulled his VI, fled the grid, and became one of the greatest technical consultants to the NLA, inventing no-tech hacks against all kinds of security systems. He developed many of the early 3D printed synthskin ID foil patches. He taught people to use plastic sheeting during marches to confuse drone targeting systems. He was also an expert with a wire clipper, with which he claimed to be able to knock out power to any city in the world.

Olivia Bross sat a few seats down from Achebe. She was the American mutineer who created an illegal no-tech zone in the northern New York State. She'd once been a high-ranking ESCOM financial exec. She came from old money rumored to trace back to the Bushes and Kochs. But Bross fell out with her life of privilege. She cast aside belief in the neo-capitalist state and sought a return to spiritual equilibrium.

Olivia had pulled her VI, left the grid, and bought a large swath of property where she'd built a model no-tech kibbutz. Formerly a full-fledged player in the feudal transnational system, she was now anathema to the ESCOM propaganda machine. She attended anti-ESCOM events to speak out against the transnational tyrants. She was often incarcerated, but she'd inevitably wend her way through the puppet court system like a diamond making its way through the gut of a pig. She was the prodigal child of the system, and nobody could touch her.

In the crowd of people standing behind those seated, Nava spotted Michael, who nodded at her. She winked. He bit at his lip and closed his eyes, as if to prepare himself for what would follow. Next to Michael stood Tomas, who tipped back a bottle of beer, gazing at the rafters, his thoughts seemingly lost on other things.

Pravir was nowhere to be seen. Nava hoped he hadn't made a mistake. She hoped he hadn't been identified and detained while making his way through Berlin.

Meanwhile, Atlas Kolek was shaking his jowls and cracking his knuckles against his chin. The big man adjusted the cuffs of his sweater and shuffled through the stack of papers in front of him. Then he laid his palms on the table, gave a few short coughs, and looked out at the gathering. A sharp whistle penetrated the din. A minute passed before everyone quieted down. Kolek spoke.

"I thank everybody for coming. I had an agenda planned for this meeting. But I think we do something else." He spoke in English, claiming this was the most practical language right now, but his English accent was thick. His *this* was *ziss*, and his *we* was *vi*. He turned over the first page from his stack of papers and began to read names: "Peter Heidle, Dag Sorensen, William Caldwell, Maria Verdini, Elvin Hjul, Erich Holt, Mika Mbuti, Trish Cook…"

He read several more names, then paused. "This is a list of seventy-two brothers and sisters who have been detained or gone missing in last forty-eight hours. Anrund and Gunter took this list from official sources."

Silence throughout the room.

Nava looked over at Michael, who stood still, his eyes shut.

"We know this, that the authorities have stepped up their measures. We also learned that any activist caught alive is getting the implant and getting scrubbed. This is horrific punishment, not to be tolerated."

A wave of confusion travelled through the crowd. Faces twisted with emotion, and angry voices rang out. Kolek held up his hand. The room grew quiet.

"I will finish this list of names," he said. "We give them this much. They have paid the ultimate price for their efforts and loyalty. We show them our respect." He continued to read: "Elsa Kverk, Mazel Rothfuss, Linda Deng…"

When one name was read, a woman at the back of the room broke down, whimpering. This happened again a little later. A name was read, and a voice called out in pain. Kolek continued until every name had been read. When he was done, he put the paper aside and looked up.

A man pushed forward from where he'd been standing in the back. He was short, with a short blond beard and a Beijing Dynamo baseball cap. "How can we continue?" he said. "The moment when it seems as if we've made progress, they come back at us with more force!" The man breathed heavily, struggling to hold back his emotions.

"Maybe we've gotten as far as we can with peaceful protest," said another woman who shouldered her way to the front. She held up a clenched fist as he spoke. "What if this is the moment when we resolve to meet their violence with our own?"

Shouts rose. There was some pushing and shoving.

"She's right!" A voice called out, and this voice cut through the tense air like a sharp knife.

Nava followed the voice. It was Pravir. He moved in, his hair disheveled, his face marked from his synthskin patches. He leveled his long arm and finger at the woman who'd just spoken.

"She's right," Pravir said. "Non-violence has become abject fantasy. We must adapt to new exigencies. We are no match for the authority's tech. We will be led like lambs to slaughter if we do not learn to defend ourselves."

"What are you saying?" Lorca said as he turned and wagged his cigar at Pravir. "You want us to draw blood? You want us to cross the line, the line from day to night? You, my friend, are a fool."

Shouts and clapping. Arms were raised in the air, and Lorca's name was called out in solidarity.

"Am I a fool?" Pravir said. "Not long from now you will reconsider your words. You will have a choice, to join in victory or face extinction."

"He's mad!" one person said. "Who let this character in? Run him out of here!"

"Turncoat and traitor!" another shouted. "Where is the Pravir we once knew? His anger has destroyed him! Throw him out!"

"My dear comrades," Pravir called above the ruckus. "Do you want to hear more? Do you want to hear how our families and loved ones are apprehended, thrown into reprogramming units, and stripped of their minds? Do you want to hear how the people we care about, our neighbors and friends who stand up to injustice, are apprehended and transformed into dutiful servants of the transnational states? Is it acceptable to stand by and watch while our movement is obliterated? I ask you, are you ready to stand by passively or die for nothing?"

Cries of apostasy were hurled at Pravir. "He was tortured," a voice argued. "His head isn't right."

"He's a traitor," others said. "He's a double agent!"

"Enough!" Kolek cried. "Enough of this arguing. How are we to make any progress today if we shout at one another this way?"

"This isn't an argument." Lorca stood and leveled the tip of his cigar at Pravir. "His words are heresy to the cause. If you disagree with us, then leave. But don't stand around here and vomit your poison."

More shouts.

Kolek called out again for order. There was more pushing, and someone fell forward and bumped against Nava. The crowd pushed forward again, and bodies bumped against the table. A fist flared. A lip burst open. Some of the bigger folks pushed toward the altercation.

Even though the person who delt the blow was pulled away, Nava trembled where she sat. Something happened inside her at that moment. Something didn't ring true. Was it that she no longer had Lyv in her arms? Was she grieving? The entire meeting seemed to be irrelevant just then. Nava felt a panic begin to set in her chest. Her breasts ached. She needed get away right then, separate herself from this madness.

—

Nava stood up and pushed her way to the back of the room. Michael intercepted her. He grabbed her arm.

"I just need to get out of here for a few minutes," she said in his ear.

"You okay?"

Nava nodded. "I'm okay. I just need to get away from this right now. I'll come back once everyone has calmed down." Nava pulled her arm free and made for the door that led up the stairs. The guards were there. One stood when she walked past, but didn't offer resistance. She made it up the stairwell and went inside the bookstore.

It was quiet. The air was peppery and dry. Wooden floors creaked beneath her feet. Thin shadows cast by streetlights fell over the floor and fingered their way through the tall shelves. Her heart still beat rapidly, but her panic was subsiding. She made her way down one of the aisles. The light was too dim to make out any of the titles of the books. Nava tugged at one of the spines, and the book came out.

"Hello," came a voice from behind her. "Can I help you?"

Nava froze.

The language was English, the accent German.

"I'm sorry," Nava said, holding the book before her like a shield. "I shouldn't be here."

It was the man who'd let them into the building when they first arrived. He said, "It is late, but do not worry. This is a business, after all. I am Arnulf. I run this store."

"I should have stayed downstairs," Nava said.

Arnulf produced a glowlight. Its beam shined painfully in Nava's eyes. Nava pushed the man's arm down to redirect it. He took the book from Nava's hands and brought it under the light.

"Interesting," he said. "Griffith's *Introduction to Elementary Particles*. A bit dated now, but a standard text at one time. I should get twenty credits for it, but you can have it for ten."

"No, thank you."

"It's a bit anachronistic, what with all the quantum this and quantum that nonsense. But it's good science nonetheless. How about eight?"

Nava grabbed the man's glowlight and pointed it at her face, so he 'd see her shake her head. "I don't want it," she said.

"*Sehr gut.*" He slid the book back on the shelf, then scratched his beard with the hand that held the glowlight. The beam bounced around the shelves. "What are you interested in? There must be something here for you."

"I shouldn't be wasting your time."

"Here we have Archeology, and one row over we have Sport, Art, and Religion." Arnulf stopped for a moment. "Selling books is my profession. It's my job to pair a customer with her book. You seem bright. *Sie licht in deinen Augen haben.* Might I make a suggestion?"

"Sure."

"I'm fond of fiction," Arnulf said. "*Es ist mein Spezialitat!* Some dismiss the form, claim that it's dead, but I beg to differ." He walked into the shelves. Nava had to move quickly to avoid being left behind. "I've owned this store for forty-one years." He led her down one aisle, then another. "It is a blessing and a curse."

"I'm Nava."

Arnulf nodded, but didn't seem to care. When they reached the end of one aisle, he came to a stop. He waved his glowlight over a cluster of shelves.

"Here are your German classics: Goethe's *Faust*, Grass's *Die Blechtrommel.* Over there you have Hesse and Ricarda Huch, and the sincere but insufferable Ridvan Hulker, who wrote about collecting books and therefore holds a small place in my heart."

"Do you have any books about the future?" Nava asked. "Do you have any books that describe the fall of the companies and the return to rule by the people?"

"Oh, science fiction?"

Arnulf shuffled farther down the aisle and cast his glowlight over one of the lower shelves.

"Kara Gaaki Bjumark." Arnulf removed a book. "She is formidable. She writes about what Ray Kurzweil described in the early twenty-first century as the Singularity. Of course, Kurzweil's dream of semiconductor immortality was never realized, but Bjumark predicted a greater collective Singularity, one that involved what she called paraconsciousness, not dissimilar to what Carl Jung might have described as the collective unconscious. It's plausible, if you ask me." Arnulf handed the book to Nava.

Nava flipped through a few pages before handing it back. "I think this might be a little much for me right now."

Arnulf put the Bjumark book back and swept his light across a row of books a few higher shelves. "I have Le Guin here. One couldn't find a greater humanist than Le Guin. Then there's Butler's *Kindred*. And Adunis. Adunis won the Nobel Prize for poetry long ago." He paused. "Wait, that is not right. Adunis should not be here. This book is miss-shelved. I apologize."

Arnulf took out the Adunis, tucked it under his arm, and reached down a different book one shelf over. He tapped it with his glowlight and chuckled. "Here's one for you. I thought I'd gotten rid of it. *Beyond Asimios*. A third-rate book, but famous for one thing: an idiot at ESCOM with a taste for bad science fiction decided to name our only colonized extra-solar system planet after it, and *ta-da!* It's found a second life."

"Why sell the physical book?" Nava asked "Who'd want them now? Everything can be accessed through the VI or nexpad."

"That's an excellent question." Arnulf returned the science fiction book to its place on the shelf, keeping the poetry book tucked under his arm. "Would you care for a drink? I'd love to discuss it. I'm in the middle of cataloging while enjoying a bit of port. The port is good. I wouldn't say that if it weren't true."

"I think I should go," Nava said.

"Please stay." Arnulf fumbled with the glowlight so that it danced over his beard and glasses. "It'd give me great pleasure. You see, I'm usually alone with these books. The ghosts of writers haunt me at every hour. To be in the company of a living human is always helpful. Then I'll answer your question, about why I sell these books."

Nava thought of the meeting taking place below them. Michael could speak for her, if necessary.

"Okay," she told Arnulf. One glass of port.

—

"Meetings are important." Arnulf led Nava through the tall bookshelves. "They always are. There are matters to discuss and actions to be decided on. Such is the way with things. *Ja!* This way, then. *Bitte*, this way."

At the back of the store, they entered a warmly lit room with a large oak desk littered with papers and books and notecards. In the middle was an old silkscreen monitor that emitted a pale blue glow. The walls were floor-to-ceiling with bookshelves. Several stacks of books stood on the floor around the desk, which Arnulf navigated with gentle indifference.

"You may not believe it, but there's an order to this chaos." He deposited his poetry book on some random pile. Then he cleared a place for Nava on an old chair and motioned for her to sit. She did. He circled back around his desk and dropped into an old recliner that squeaked loudly when he leaned back in it. He bent over, disappearing from her view. After the sound of drawers opening and shutting, he emerged with a glass snifter that he cleaned with the corner of his apron. He took a bottle from behind the silkscreen and filled the snifter a couple of fingers high. He slid this glass to Nava, then swung the bottle's neck over his own glass and splashed it to the rim.

"*Prost!*" He took a drink and wiped his mouth with his shirtsleeve.

Nava raised her glass but didn't drink. "Why are you helping us? Are you being paid? It's dangerous. If the authorities found out, you'd be arrested and tortured."

Arnulf said, "You could say that I am upholding a tradition. Do you know about this place? Have you heard of the Lyceum before?"

Nava raised her shoulders.

"Have you heard about the Hamburg riots of 2136?" he asked. "Have you heard of Henrik Kuhl and the Voice of December?"

"That was a youth movement, right? They were protesting police brutality. Several were killed, if I recall. I can't remember the specifics."

"The specifics are important," Arnulf said. "The Voice of December was an organization formed to protest the closing of German universities. The state put sixty thousand students on the street and gave them the option of either being sent to the Russian wars or to the labor camps in the north. Henrik Kuhl led a group of protesters then. They were pacifists, as your organization is. They believed in free and universal education.

Would you believe me if I told you that Henrik Kuhl sat in the seat you are sitting in now?"

"What happened to Kuhl?" she said.

"Shot in the head." Arnulf planted a finger on his temple and pulled an imaginary trigger. "That's when the movement really took off. After Kuhl was shot, tensions rose. Change was in the air. Eventually Ex-Cap imposed martial law. One by one the protesters were rounded up and the movement crushed. They declared a new war on radical Islam. The Russian wars weren't enough, it seemed. They needed more reasons to reduce human beings to animals."

"You supported Kuhl, yet you weren't taken?" she asked.

"I helped Kuhl, but I was never an official member of the Voice. They had no evidence to charge me. As good as they are at torture, a dead man rarely talks. But why do I help you? Why risk arrest?" He raised his glass in a toast. "I like the excitement. I'm getting old. I despise tyranny, like any decent human, and I'd like to think that when I die, I will have played my part to resist it. So, there you have it."

"No family? No children to threaten?"

Arnulf sipped his port and shook his head. "I am the last in a line of miserable idealists. My family now is what you see around me. My children are my books, each one of them alive and in need of my care."

Nava took a sip from her port and admired the chaos of his office.

"I inherited this place, you see," Arnulf went on. "Just as my father before me, and his before him. Four generations we've been here, peddling board and paper. When I was twenty, I hated the idea of this business. I equated the printed page with the dying idealisms of my father. I wanted out. I wanted to see the world, to travel to Mars and be alive. When he died, I thought I'd sell the business and be done with it."

Arnulf took a sip of port, then set the glass on the desk. He stared at the crystal snifter, rotating it between his thumb and forefinger. "When I was a student (this was before my father died), I travelled to Rome to study the history of architecture. I was young, and I considered my trip a springboard to freedom. My father offered to pay for my tuition if I did him one favor, which he'd tell me about once I arrived in Italy. I thought, 'Eh, why not?' and agreed. He was vague about what that favor might be, and I was too excited about leaving Berlin to care. The school in Rome sat atop a hill that overlooked a small square. My room had a beautiful view of that city. Anyway, I quickly fell into a routine of concluding my studies early in the day, then joining my fellow students at one of the tavernas during the evenings. A few weeks into the quarter, we were enjoying ourselves at a taverna when I saw a girl staring at me. I was surprised, you see. Her features were half-hidden behind a luscious wave of dark hair, but I could see she was stunning. Nevertheless, I didn't pay much attention to her at first. You may not believe me, but I was handsome in those days, and getting a woman's attention was nothing unusual. A little later, I looked back to where she'd been sitting with her friends, and there she was, still staring at me with a big smile, full of handsome teeth. The challenge was set. I'd had a bit of wine by then, so my courage was up.

"I approached her table and introduced myself in my poor Italian. '*Mi ciamo Arnulf,*' I said. She laughed at this. '*Ich heisse Maria,*' she said. '*Und ich spreche deutsch.*' Her friends laughed, and I laughed with them, though I felt foolish. Of course, she could speak German! She could also speak English and French and Arabic, I later learned, but in my ignorance, I'd assumed she was a local girl. As it turned out, Maria's father was a lawyer for the Vatican. She was studying to be a lawyer herself and spending time at the university in Rome. Am I boring you?"

Nava shook her head. She sipped her port and leaned against the back of her chair.

Arnulf continued. "I invited Maria's group to join us, and thus began our relationship. Those were wonderful days. I'd never been happier in my life. From then, we spent most every minute together. Whenever possible, we found a way to be with one another. Such an experience! My thoughts raced, and my heart was entwined with the idea of Maria, certain that I was in love. Of course, my studies suffered. I missed classes, and my friends gave up on me. But I was learning while I was with her: I learned about myself and about Rome and about life and love. Maria showed me the city, every dirty corner of it, and every café and every museum she thought I needed to know about.

"After a month, I knew she was the one I wanted to spend the rest of my life with. It was an unassailable truth. One morning we went to our café (I say "our" café because we spent much time there), and I got down on my knees and asked her to marry me. The unexpected happened: she laughed at me. She laughed and laughed and laughed. She told me I was a fool. She asked me how I could possibly love her. She said that I was a boy, a little boy, and I knew nothing of love. She told me she couldn't marry me, that she had a fiancé in America whom she'd see in a week. She was sorry, she said. And in hindsight, I believe she was. After that, she said she couldn't see me anymore, that things had gone too far."

Nava moved her glass toward Arnulf, who poured more port. She said, "You were hurt. How awful. What did you do?"

"I was hurt. It was as if the floor under my feet had been ripped away. As if a cloud had enveloped me. It was difficult just to breathe. I was shattered, broken into a million pieces."

"I'm sorry to hear that," Nava said.

"You needn't feel sorry for me," Arnulf said. "It was a long time ago. I was young. Looking back, there were many clues I should have paid attention to: the calls from strangers, the abrupt changes of plans. Love does make one blind, and I suffered for it."

Arnulf took a sip from his port and drew his tongue across his lips.

"But, now bear with me. It was not a day after that breakup when my father messaged me to do him his favor. He added five thousand credits to my bank account and told me to visit a small book dealer in the old part of Rome. He included details about the book he wanted me to purchase, a signed first edition of a twentieth-century Italian writer named Luigi Pirandello. *One, No One, and One Hundred Thousand* was the name of the book. Anyway, I was to purchase the book and deliver it to my father upon my return to Berlin.

"You might imagine what went through my mind," Arnulf went on. "I considered telling him about Maria, about how sad I was, and how hard it was for me to do anything just then. But I'd never talked to my father about such emotions. That might be the root of my disappointment with him. It took several bottles of wine to reach my resolution, which was that I'd talk to my father. I'd tell him about my life in Rome and what had happened over the past two months, about Maria and my proposal to her and my rejection. I'd tell my father the truth and hope that he'd understand. Maybe he'd see how hard things were going for me, that being sent on a meaningless and materialistic errand wasn't what I was meant to be doing at that exact moment."

Arnulf paused. He leaned back in his squeaky chair, took a sip of port, and gazed at the ceiling.

"And what happened?"

"I talked to him the next morning. About Maria and so forth. My father said something that sounded like *Arnulfchen*. He said, 'It's clear you're distressed, and I understand that, but let this not get in the way of important matters. Now please, I've sent you instructions about the book I wish to purchase. I'm depending on you for this. Please don't disappoint.'

"I cut him off. He had no interest in my pain, or in Maria, or what I'd gone through. I'd set myself up, and I'd paid for it. I was boiling with rage for having been such a fool. Can you imagine my reaction? Oh, how selfish and stupid I was."

"It doesn't sound so stupid to me," Nava said.

"I thought about the harm I could cause my father, how I could squander his money. I had the idea to buy a luxury car and drive it into the Fiume Tevere and watch it sink. In the end, however, I resolved to visit this book dealer. I wasn't sure what led me to that decision, but I thought that there still might be a way for me to get back at my father.

"So, I messaged the dealer that day and made an appointment. Later that afternoon, I met him and his assistant at a café before the three of us went to his store. I was numb. I didn't want to be there. I had it in my mind that to do my father's bidding was to commit treason against the core of my being. I thought that I might buy the book and then toss it into the river. That would teach him! He'd understand at last that I didn't want anything to do with him or his business or his books!"

"So, you bought the book?"

"No, I didn't." Arnulf leaned forward and lowered his voice. "I'll tell you, the dealer brought the book out, and I looked it over. The signature had been certified. It was genuine by all accounts. But before I finished the deal, I asked the bookseller about a collection of notebooks on display, original Antonio Gramsci prison notebooks from the early twentieth century. I'd studied Gramsci, if only briefly, at university. Anyway, I had an immediate fascination with these writings.

"Then it struck me. I asked the dealer how much he wanted for them. The dealer considered this for a moment, unsure whether my father would approve of this change of plans. But I insisted that my father had charged me with absolute authority to do as I saw fit. The dealer found this acceptable, and tried to decide on a price for the notebooks, there being nothing similar on the open market.

"In the end he said he'd accept an amount equal to what had been agreed between himself and my father for the Pirandello novel. That seemed reasonable, but I wanted him to throw one more thing into the deal. I'd spotted a scarce copy of Aslan Munif's *Sacrifice* among a stack of unpriced books. If he'd give me the Munif as well as the Gramsci notebooks, it'd be a deal. He considered for a moment, then looked over at his assistant, who gave condescending nod.

"The dealer shrugged. 'Now we have wine!' he declared. We went back down to the café to celebrate and talked all night about books. I never thought I'd say it, but I enjoyed myself that evening. It allowed me to forget about Maria for a while. The next morning, the parcels were delivered to my room, and later that day I caught the train back to Berlin."

Nava said, "So then you went home. What did your father say?"

"When I handed him the Gramsci notebooks, my father was shocked. He was deep in debt, and his employees hadn't been paid in weeks, he told me. How could I be so arrogant as to play games with the lives of good and innocent people? He told me that he'd never trust me with anything again, that I had failed him."

Arnulf sipped at his port and swiped his lips with his sleeve.

"Would you believe it?" Arnulf went on. "Two weeks later, my father learned that a private museum in Utrecht was willing to pay fifty thousand credits for the Gramsci notebooks. My father, in tears, called me into his office—where we are sitting in now. He apologized for the things he'd said and asked me for forgiveness. He'd been wrong to criticize me, he said. He told me that I was a genius in his eyes. From that moment on, he consulted me on all his larger acquisitions. I had been lucky, but I felt I'd done something right, and I was proud. For the first time in my life, I'd contributed, whether willingly or not, to the livelihood of our family."

"And the other book? The Munif?"

"What happened with that book is even more fascinating," Arnulf said. He set the glass down gently in front of him and paused to admire it. "Do you know Munif?"

"I read *Sacrifice* at university. Munif believed that narrative was essential to instructing a new revolution, that songs and stories and theater were the ways to bring heroes to life. That without these forms, a culture would fail to assert itself. Without art, we are nothing, right? The oppressors desire to strip us of our history. The revolutionary's work is to restore it through action and art.

"It's no coincidence that this copy of *Sacrifice* came to be in my possession," Arnulf said. "You see, when the dealer was showing me around his store, I noticed the book in a pile of other insignificant texts. The book was unmistakable. I'd read a later printing of it just a few months earlier, and I'd gazed nightly at the cover art. Anyway, after I acquired the book and was back in Berlin, I had time to give it a thorough inspection. As luck would have it, I found a folded letter in the center pages. Would you believe me if I told you that the letter was handwritten and from Aslan Munif himself?"

Nava peered at Arnulf and waited for him to continue.

"When he was young, before he helped organize the North African resistance, Munif studied in Rome. If fact, it is in Rome where *Sacrifice* was first published."

"You're sure it was from him? Why would a letter from Munif appear in one of his own books?"

"It became clear immediately when I read it. Would you like to see it?"

"See what?"

"Would you like to see the letter?"

"Of course," she said. "Of course, I'd like to see it."

Arnulf spun in his chair, opened a metal cabinet, and riffled through it. He pulled out a folder, which he set down on his desk, then extracted a smooth swatch of paper encased in a transparent sleeve. He laid the sleeve and its contents facing her on his desk. "Come. Look."

Setting her glass to the side, Nava leaned over the desk to inspect the letter. She said, "It's handwritten. It's addressed to Ingrid. Ingrid Berniers, very likely."

"Yes."

"It's a love letter," Nava said with a smile. "He's giving her a copy of his book. It says, 'This book is my gift to you. To the one who inspires me, to the one who believes in me, to the one who will fight with me, and to the one who is everything to me. Forever yours, Aslan.'"

"Can you imagine that?" Arnulf said. He gazed with pleasure at Nava. "One of the most celebrated love affairs in history, and here was a tangible link to that intimate moment."

"It must be valuable," Nava said.

"Priceless," Arnulf said. "But I'd never sell it. Interestingly, the copy of *Sacrifice* proved to be important, and for reasons other than this letter. Not long after I was back in Berlin, Ex-Cap passed an edict banning from the Nexus anything written by Muni. They were going to erase him from existence. *Sacrifice,* as it turned out, was the only book that Munif had physically printed, though in limited numbers. The copy I have is one of those rare prints. I could save Munif from oblivion. Even if the companies succeeded in removing all evidence of him from the Nexus, I still had this physical book. I could make a thousand copies of it, and another person could make a thousand copies from that copy.

"Then it occurred to me that the physical book seemed incorruptible. Unlike its digital counterpart, it is durable and can withstand abuse. The pages may swell from water, and the covers may be licked by fire, but the words can still be read. The message will survive. At last, I understood what people like my father knew all along. The physical book is a sacred thing."

Nava sat down.

Arnulf fell back in his squeaky chair and tugged at his beard.

"My plans to save Munif's legacy weren't necessary, after all. An official left their position, and Ex-Cap rescinded the edict to eradicate Munif. They turned their attention to a different, younger revolutionary. So, Munif still lives in the Nexus. But the book meant much more to me after that experience. Not all books are important, of course. Henrike's *Book of Bavarian Strudel* may not be worth its weight in paper, but many books are. When I hold that copy of *Sacrifice* in my hand, however, I think not only that Munif himself had touched it, but I also think about where Munif stands in human history. I think of the revolution he led and the future revolutionaries he'll inspire.

"But I also think of love and expectation when I hold that copy of *Sacrifice* in my hand. I am suddenly back in Rome with Maria and those glorious days of youth. A book is a vehicle. It can transport you through time and space." Arnulf again leaned back in his squeaky chair and tossed down the last of his port.

"That's quite a story," Nava said.

"I've worn you out. But I do thank you for listening to an old man ramble on about his life. Point to any book in this building, though, and I'll have another tale to tell you."

"It was an honor," Nava said.

Arnulf said, "It was my honor, Nava Wolfe."

Nava stiffened in her chair. "You know who I am?"

"I do." Arnulf leaned forward, chair squeaking. "Atlas Kolek told me about you. You studied at Oxford, and your father is Preston Wolfe, a high-ranking ESCOM officer. Kolek also told me how important you have become to the movement, that he considers you an invaluable member."

Nava stood. She should have been more careful.

"I'd like you to have this." Arnulf slid the Munif letter into its plastic jacket and handed it to her.

"I can't take it," she said.

Arnulf came around the desk and pressed the letter into her hand. "It's yours. I insist. Now you must tell the story of Munif and how you came to possess his letter."

Two shots sounded.

Gunshots.

The sound came from beneath them, in the basement.

"I must go," Nava said.

"I'll check the doors to the store and check outside. Be careful!"

"Thank you."

13 – Aftermath

WHEN PRESTON WOLFE gave the order to raise the blast shields around ESCOM HQ, the headquarters was quickly cocooned in armor and an experimental energy barrier designed to deflect concussion. The sonorous rise and fall of the alarm sirens punctuated the feminine voice instructing people to seek safety in designated shelters. Delegates pushed their way through the assembly hall doors, seeking directions to the shelters.

Carerra, Miller, and Whitney approached Wolfe where he was seated on one of the musicians' chairs, sipping from a glass of water.

"For God's sake, Preston," Carerra said, "I hope your instincts on this are solid. This is unprecedented."

"If I'm wrong, you can blame me later. But I don't think—"

A thunderous clap shook the building, as if the entire structure had been lifted into the air and then dropped. Fissures formed in the walls. Window panels fell and shattered. The concrete beneath them buckled and cracked, like ice heaved up under glacial pressure. People were thrown to the floor like rag dolls. Material cracked and dropped from walls and ceilings to the floor. A cloud of dust turned the air milky white.

Then there was a peculiar silence, until voices called out, voices in unnatural registers, conveying fear and pain.

Carerra, Miller, and Whitney had been thrown to the floor. They helped each other to stand, then offered help to those around them.

The lights had dimmed. Sirens howled. Black smoke ran in rivulets along the ceiling. The pungent smell of electrical burning filled the air. Many were hurt. Those who had suffered the worst were tended to first. Wolfe's intelligence office linked up a visual of what had gone on outside: Seattle was leveled, her grand buildings and famous landmarks flattened. Destroyed. Through the landscape of devastation moved a dark cataract, a wicked conveyor of metal and wood and death, that ran with briny sheen back into the roiling bay. Countless lives had been lost. A great city lay in ruin.

"Is this an alien attack?" Stanhope demanded as she stumbled up to Carerra. Her golden jacket was torn, her hair tossed and disheveled. Her face was smeared with makeup, blood, and dirt, and she seemed on the verge of panic or tears, or both.

Carerra looked over at Wolfe, but Wolfe merely shrugged. He felt as if he were stuck in a dream or watching a grizzly movie.

"I don't know," Carerra answered Stanhope. "We'll have to see."

A beacon came across everyone's VI to announce skimmer evacuations, ordering all delegates to rendezvous at the skimmer platforms. Wiping her nose with her sleeve, Stanhope dropped to her knees and remained there until Carerra draped her in a blanket that a medic had provided. Soon a pair of Ex-Cap aides came and escorted her away.

A loud scream pierced the hall. A group stood huddled around a body on the floor. Wolfe pushed his way through the crowd to find the fallen body of Chairman Khan. In the middle of that dark hood, the Khan's pale face was gripped with a rictus; hands curled at their breast were contorted like claws. Wolfe felt for a pulse at the Khan's neck, laid his hand on their cheek.

"The Khan is dead," Wolfe said.

One of the Khan's handlers pushed his way into the ring of spectators. "That is not true," the man said with a laugh. "The Khan can never die!" Several stone-faced Axiom Lotus security personnel widened the circle around the Khan. Together they lifted the body into the air.

As the body was carried down the hall, Salazar appeared and placed his hand on Wolfe's shoulder. "Leave them be. There's something fiendish about them."

By now a few of the musicians had dusted themselves off, found their damaged instruments, and began to tune them. Together they managed to play a slightly discordant Bach piece during the disorder. It was strangely calming.

Salazar had a gash on his leg and a few cuts showing through his sleeves. Wolfe offered to help, but the Transglobal president demurred. "I'm sorry the conference had to end this way, my friend. Until later, I bid you farewell."

Salazar sent a salute to Carerra, then limped off to join his delegates as they hurried toward the skimmer bay.

Wolfe had placed a call for his own skimmer so he could get out and survey the damage to the city. Securing what remained was his priority. He'd ordered low-level signature sweeps of every waterway in the area. The entire country had been put on Code One alert, meaning each city and state was to prepare for the potential of a terrorist attack.

Stanhope had already imposed martial law on all the European states as news of the disruptor blast hit the Nexus. A wave of apprehension spread throughout the world. Was another disrupter blast next?

This was no alien attack, Wolfe knew. A human on either Earth or Mars had organized this atrocity. As he waited for an escort to his skimmer, he was hailed over his VI.

"You were impressive today, Chief of Security," a voice said.

"Who is this?" Wolfe said. "Carerra?"

"You were rational. You were able to focus and stay in control, and you saved many lives. You show signs of leadership. ESCOM is fortunate to have you."

"Identify yourself." Wolfe twisted around, seeking the origin of the voice. "This is a high-security link. Why don't you have any identifier?"

"I want to assure you that you have my support," continued the voice, "and that you should feel free to contact me at your convenience. I think our partnership would be mutually beneficial."

"Who is this?"

"It is I," the voice said. "But I will take no more of your time. Your talents are needed. My sincerest gratitude, Mr. Wolfe."

"Chairman Khan!"

The link was dead.

Wolfe stared at the immense fractured glass that had looked out over the bay but now provided only a bleak inside view of the plasteel defense wall coating ESCOM headquarters. Carrera informed him that Miller was coordinating national medical and logistics assistance. Carerra himself was on a link with all the companies, getting assurances of aid, while Wolfe organized immediate joint-force company security operations to hit any current NLA interests, and to hunt for and bring in any member or asset they could, dead or alive.

Whoever was responsible would pay a price for this. If it was the NLA, Wolfe would make sure each and every one of them was wiped off the earth. If the Martian rebellion was behind this, then it might mean full-scale military escalation.

Wolfe notified his office of the call he'd received and ordered an investigation. Then he started toward his skimmer to survey the carnage.

14 – Flight

THE GUARDS WERE gone. Nava ran down the stairway and pulled open the basement doors. When she reached the meeting room, she pushed through the gathering of people to see what had happened.

Pravir was cornered by a small mob led by Atlas Kolek. Pravir held them at bay with a stubby revolver, a cold expression stamped on his face. Hector Lorca lay on the floor, his hat fallen from his head, his eyes draining of life. Katie Kollwitz held him in her arms.

Nava tried to get Pravir's attention. "What's going on, Pravir? Tell me!"

A pool of blood was forming around Lorca's body.

"Violence knows only violence," Pravir said. "We must cleanse the earth with fire."

"Put the gun down!" Nava cried. "Nothing good will come of this."

Michael knelt next to Lorca and checked his pulse. Oliva Bross came and put pressure on his wounds.

"How could you?" Nava cried. As she moved toward Pravir, he turned the gun on her.

"Stay back, Nava!" Kolek shouted.

"Nava!" called Michael.

Nava took a step forward. Pravir stiffened, raising the gun. She took another step, grasped the black metal barrel, and wrenched the weapon out of his hand.

The mob descended, and Pravir was quickly thrown to the floor.

Nava tossed the gun onto the table. Kolek came over and took it.

A loud boom sounded from above.

The lights flickered. A film of dust descended from the ceiling.

Another loud *ka-boom*. More dust. Elvin Leach's poster lost a thumbtack and swung loose on its corner.

"Evacuate!" Kolek shouted. "Everyone, leave! Now!"

"Sonic sensors." Anrund Achebe ambled toward the door. "They picked up the gunshots. They've found us."

Another boom shook the building. The lights went out. People screamed. Nava stumbled in the dark and fell to the floor. An arm took hold of her and lifted her up.

"Come with me," a voice said. "I know this building. We must hurry."

"Michael!" Nava called. Everything seemed to be collapsing around them. "Michael!" she called again.

No reply.

"Please! There's no time." A voice spoke at her side.

"Dedan?"

"Yes!"

Dedan Kimathi led Nava away. A few glowlights had been lit, the beams dancing over the chaos. Everyone was fleeing, yet instead of making for the stairs, Kimathi guided her down a small hallway away from the stairwell. He shined a pocket glowlight, illuminating the dim hall enough that they could see. Kimathi fumbled on the wall and found a lever that opened a small door.

"You must drop to your knees, Nava, and crawl through the opening."

Nava said, "We have to go back and get Michael!"

Another loud explosion. Soil and rock collapsed from overhead, and dust filled the air. The passage back was cut off.

"There's no time," Kimathi said. "Get down now, and make your way through. We'll circle back outside and try to find him. Go now!"

Nava dropped on her knees to crawl. Kimathi was right behind her, raising the faint light so that Nava could continue forward. The repeated explosions reduced the passage behind them to rubble. At the end of this tight, rough tunnel, an iron grate barred them from a short fall to the oily, dark river.

"Push it!" cried Dedan, shining the dim light at the grate. The light revealed a rusted latch at the bottom of the iron lattice.

Nava threw back the latch, and the grate release.

"Go!" Kimathi cried.

Nava kicked at the grate and crawled forward. She slid over smooth stones, then slipped down into the frigid water.

For a moment there was nothing, only the sensation of being near death, but not quite. Nava had had this dream before, but she'd always awakened. This was a dream, correct? But why was it so cold?

Another splash. A hand pulled at her jacket. Then her head was above the surface. She flailed, gasping for air.

"Be still," Dedan Kimathi said. "Take a breath. We can make it to the shore."

The outline of Kimathi's face appeared against a flickering of flames. She saw Kimathi's nose and the deep lines around his mouth. He lifted his hand from the water and pointed at the Lyceum.

The store was on fire. Flames rose high into the sky, licking the dark night, taunting, roaring. A drone above the river launched a missile not far from them. The blast brought down one of the store walls in an avalanche of brick and mortar.

Dedan continued to drag her with him toward the shore. Once they'd reached a section of brambles and stone, Dedan pushed his way through the branches and then offered his hand to Nava. She took it, and he pulled her out of the cold river. More explosions sounded. The low clouds reflected the fire. Sirens howled, coming from all directions. They huddled for a moment, the light of the fire glinting in their eyes as police and emergency vehicles started to arrive.

"We must go," Dedan said.

"How can I leave?"

"I'm sorry," Dedan said. "We must go now. There is nothing else we can do."

"I know..."

15 – Gorrath

DR. AVERY GRAF grabbed his chair's armrest to steady himself. His heart beat wildly; the hair on his arms stood on end. While he silently cursed Oreg, he tugged on the necklace that had once hung around Orsani's neck.

Ten minutes had passed since Oreg left in his escape pod. Now, once again, it seemed that Graf had been hung out to dry.

A flash appeared in the viewer.

A rumble sounded throughout the ship.

"What the hell was that?" Graf said.

"An explosive charge, doctor," Miranda said. "The ship's energy shields have mitigated the damage."

Graf rolled his eyes and tugged at his beard.

Another blast sounded through the hull.

Miranda made a motion with her right hand. There was loud groaning from the core of the ship. Though restrained, Graf felt himself pushed and pulled by unseen forces. He was jostled until his arms felt like noodles.

"I apologize, doctor," Miranda said.

"That wasn't so bad," Graf said. "I've been through worse."

"I mean, I apologize for what I'm about to do."

"Oh?"

"To evade a new wave of incoming missiles, I am about to subject you to several times your accustomed gravitational force. Please tighten your restraints. I need to turn off artificial gravity. You will lose consciousness."

"Oh, sheesh," Graf said. "Then I suppose it's 'good night, my dear.'" He grabbed his restraint adjusters and yanked them tight.

Miranda made a sweeping motion with her hand. Graf felt his stomach fold. A dark line descended from the top of his visual field until everything went black. It was a peaceful sensation, not unlike how he'd imagined hypothermic termination or asphyxiation. Blissful nothingness.

—

When Graf's head stopped spinning, his mouth was dry as a roll of toilet paper, but his beard was wet with saliva. He could taste the last meal he'd had on Karmehki. He raised his arm weakly and wiped his shirtsleeve across his mouth. "What happened? What's going on?"

"We have entered the Gorrathian atmosphere," Miranda said from the seat beside him. "Four of the five ships that were bombarding us have turned back. One ship, however, continues to follow. I've restored artificial gravity, for now."

"Thank you, Miranda. I'll have station maintenance draw up a report. Should we meet at the club for dinner at, say, eight o'clock?"

Miranda cocked her head and regarded him with a quizzical expression. "We are no longer on Asimios, doctor. You are emerging from unconsciousness. Your cognition is impaired."

"It was supposed to be funny!" Graf massaged his eyes, then he glanced around the ship as though fitting together the pieces of a puzzle. He cleared his throat. "So, we still got one guy following us?"

"Correct, doctor."

"Missiles. They were firing missiles at us, right?"

As if on cue, a loud explosion was heard to the aft of the ship. Miranda seemed to struggle to keep the craft under control.

"If you will observe the display," she said, "you will see a large storm ahead of us. It is a convection cyclone comprised mostly of dust and particulate matter. We will enter this storm in less than fifteen seconds."

"Great," Graf said. "Sounds like a wonderful idea."

"We are a substantial distance from our original landing coordinates, but I believe that our priority is to avoid detection. Sensor data will be inaccurate in this cyclone."

"'Once more unto the breach, dear friends.'"

"Unto the breach, doctor?"

"It's from an old…" He broke off and pointed at the holo display. "Look! The ship behind us is leaving. Your plan seems to have worked!"

"That is good," Miranda said. "Now we just need to survive landing in this storm."

Graf had no reply. As he stared at holo visual of the atmosphere in front of them, he dug his fingernails into his armrests. If there was a mountain ahead, hidden in the maelstrom, then so be it. At the same time, he hoped that wasn't the case, that this landing wouldn't kill him. He'd come halfway across the galaxy, too far for things to end suddenly.

Of course, if it was God's plan that they crash and die, then God's plan it would be. The Good Book was full of people who questioned His judgment only to be made examples of. All the same, being cast against a rocky mountainside and being splattered into a pulp on an alien world would be one hell of an example. It would be absurd. Wasteful. Who'd ever know that he'd died out here? He wasn't on Asimios, and nowhere near Julie.

Who on Gorrath would profit by his death?

Who here or anywhere would mourn his passing?

Would the Skarvorm toads retrieve his corpse and parade it around like a trophy?

Would they dissect him, apply current to his nerve cells, hold lectures on his remains?

His sixty-six-year-old body was no gift to science, whether Skarvorm or Gorrathian. Then again, what would be left of his body, or any body, for that matter, if their ship collided with a mountain at current speed? Would he be liquefied? Vaporized? Would the storm conceal their wreck in a blanket of Gorrathian stone and sand? Would they be buried deep into the soil, lost to time, memory?

"Are you all right, doctor?" Miranda said.

"I'm fine. How are you?"

"I am functioning optimally. We will land in approximately three minutes."

"Okay," Graf said. "I take it that, given the storm, you'll be performing an instrument landing?"

"The ship's altimeter is functional, and I have made extrapolations on the topography, including the arid basin on the fringes of the depression. If I am correct, the ground is relatively featureless."

"Perfect!"

"Landing is simpler on a flat surface."

"Yes, of course."

"There are, however, things to be concerned about, doctor. The last bombardment did damage to the ship. One of our engine cells appears to be offline, and warnings indicate faulty landing stabilizers. I have run several diagnostics, but the damage is extensive. Do you still feel comfortable with my piloting the ship, doctor?"

"What is the alternative?"

"There really isn't one," she replied.

"You are an exceedingly good pilot, Miranda," Graf said. "I just want you to know that."

"Thank you for the compliment, doctor."

Red dust clouded the visual in front of them. Graf found it difficult to watch, as if he was eavesdropping on his own death. "Any likelihood of us crashing, Miranda? I mean, can you calculate that kind of outcome?"

"I cannot, doctor. There are too many variables."

"Perfectly understandable."

"I also have difficulty with the word 'crashing,' doctor. It isn't specific."

"I guess you're right. But it's like the ship striking the ground with enough force to kill us. Blowing up. That sort of thing."

"That is still unspecific."

"Yes, true," Graf said.

"With one failed engine, however, we will have much less stability than if both were functional. Our landing may be problematic."

"Another less than specific word," Graf observed as he tightened his restraining belts one more notch. "Miranda?"

"Yes, doctor?"

"I'm sorry I got you into this mess. Things got out of control, didn't they? I mean, I appreciate you sticking around. You've been a great help. I'm sorry you had to get violent back at the station. You destroyed an android, one of your kind. It must have been a little hard."

"That android was not sentient," Miranda said, piloting the shaking ship by waving her hands in various patterns. The ship leaned right, then straightened out.

"Are you sure?" Graf said.

"It was evident. It was programmed for one purpose: to conduct strict enforcement. Although it was advanced by Earth standards, it was a base machine."

"A strange way for one machine to refer to another," he observed.

"I am quite different, doctor."

"Because you are sentient?"

"Excuse me, doctor. We are nearing the planet's surface. I will make sensor sweeps before we attempt landing. Any consistent data at this point will aid our approach."

"Do we have to watch that damned visual? Makes me nervous."

The visual dimmed, went blank.

The ship rocked as it careened ahead. If felt as if they were sliding downhill, with the nose of the craft leading the way, plowing through the thick soup. With no visual, it was impossible to say what exactly was happening. Graf was leaking sweat like a dish sponge.

"It is not easy to steer this ship with only one engine," Miranda said. "Poor sensor data multiplies the difficulty."

"Do the best you can."

Miranda waved her hands and sat back. "Hold on, doctor. I believe we are about to—"

The ship hit something, then groaned and buckled and snapped. Interior lights flickered, and the ship's artificial gravity deactivated. Disoriented, Graf felt an uncomfortable force press against his legs and body. It was possible that the ship had glanced off the ground. The strain on the hull was significant, and the creaking and grinding were concerning. Suddenly, a scraping sound was heard, as if the ship dragged one of its wings through a rocky surface. Another more forceful impact shook the ship. Graf felt the craft heave upward. After a loud shuddering like an explosion, there was a great lurch forward, as if the unsecured ship adjusted itself.

The ship came to a stop, leaning forward, its nose down. The ship seemed to exhale then, and a silence settled over everything.

The belts cut into Graf's shoulder. He released them and nearly fell from his seat. "Miranda," he said.

"Are you okay, doctor?" Miranda said.

Graf swallowed. "I think so," he said.

The lights flickered, then cut out. Backup lighting came on and painted everything in cold blue. An extremely loud *thud* sounded from the back of the ship. Something large had been dislodged during the landing. Then came the sound of something approaching, the sound a train might make. Graf and Miranda turned in time to see Jeg roll through the doorway to the bridge. As the bot rolled, it picked up speed, rushing past them until it came to a loud stop when it struck the wall at the nose of the ship, right behind the holo display.

"My god!" Graf said.

Miranda and Graf watched as Jeg rattled and sputtered. Some of the bot's internal lights flickered, and numerous nodes and sensors blinked and pulsed. Jeg rotated its lone eye at Miranda and Graf. Slowly, as if rousing itself from a long slumber, Jeg ascended into the air.

"I'll be damned!" Graf said. "I thought that fella was destined for the Karmehki scrap heap."

Miranda had undone her belts and now came over to Graf to help him out of his chair. Once they were both standing, Graf still holding onto his chair for stability, they turned to observe the bot.

Jeg floated a few feet off the floor, its single eye fixed on Miranda, then Graf, then back at Miranda.

"Welcome back, Beach Ball," Graf said. "It's been a long time!"

Graf danced a little where he stood. He was alive, after all, and his prospects had immediately improved, if only for the moment. He looked over at Miranda. He wasn't sure if it was just the level of the ship's deck that made her adjust her balance, but Miranda seemed to be dancing too.

TO BE CONTINUED...

Acknowledgments

To all those who participated in this project, I am grateful. This book would never have been possible without the help and encouragement of so many.

To Gabriel Walker Land for his blunt assessments. To Dave Harrison, who said, "Your dialog isn't bad." To Paul Witcover, who took hammer to anvil and pounded this book into shape. To William Greenleaf, who allowed me to believe in it. To Omar Al Akkad, with his helpful insights. To my mother, Ella, for her early edits. To my wife, Emily, and to Max our dog, who sat patiently by my desk, bored out of his brain, wondering what I was doing up at those early hours of the night.

And most of all, thanks to Annie Pearson, a writer and editor, who was there at the beginning and who stuck it out with me straight to the end. Without her, this book would never have seen the light of day.

About the Author

MARTIN FOSSUM is a writer and award-winning experimental film-maker. He lives in Minneapolis, Minnesota. He is currently working on the second and final book of the *Beyond Asimios* series. For more information, see www.martinfossum.com.